THE
JANUS RUN

DOUGLAS
SKELTON

CONTRABAND ✇

Contraband is an imprint of Saraband

Published by Saraband
Digital World Centre, 1 Lowry Plaza,
The Quays, Salford,
M50 3UB

and

Suite 202, 98 Woodlands Road,
Glasgow, G3 6HB, Scotland
www.saraband.net

ISBN: 9781912235254
ebook:9781912235261

*All characters appearing in this novel are fictitious.
Any resemblance to real persons, living or dead,
is purely coincidental.*

Printed and bound in Great Britain by Clays Ltd, Elcograf S.p.A.

1 3 5 7 9 10 8 6 4 2

MIX
Paper from
responsible sources
FSC® C018072

Dagda awakens

Everything happened at such dizzying speed that he didn't have time to process the events. Not consciously.

First one guy had burst in, weapon at the ready. Now there were more.

He didn't know who the hell they were, didn't really care. All he knew was they were spraying bullets around his apartment.

The advertising executive part of his brain ducked for cover. But the other part of his brain—the secret part, the part that had lain dormant for ten years, the part that was Dagda—sprang to life. It surprised him, it delighted him.

It scared him.

In all those years he hadn't held anything more dangerous than a cell phone, but the weight of the gun in his hand was both familiar and comforting. He snatched it up without thinking. Or, rather, Dagda did. He ignored the bullets as they buzzed around him. Bullets were old friends. Bullets. Blood. Killing. All the things that he thought were behind him. The things that were Dagda.

He rolled and took aim at the closest gunman. It all seemed so natural. He fired. It all seemed so easy. Aim the gun, fire the gun, take a life.

And that was when he knew for certain that Dagda was back.

Dead certain.

1

One week earlier...

The room was spinning.

That wasn't good.

He closed his eyes, lay still for a few moments, but the world continued to lurch alarmingly. Christ, what the hell was going on? He hadn't had a drink for... he risked a look at his wristwatch... well, okay, only five hours, but he hadn't had *so* much that he was still drunk.

Had he?

He shifted, hoping the carny operating the carousel that was his apartment would head for a coffee break pretty soon, and felt the weight of another body beside him. His eyes grated in their sockets as he turned his head, taking it nice and slow, and saw the dark-haired woman in a deep sleep. Something like that didn't happen every day so he smiled, but even that simple contraction of his facial muscles made his flesh protest, so he stopped.

Easing himself into a sitting position so as not to disturb her and then standing up was quite a feat, and he was proud of himself. Now he challenged himself to remain upright without upchucking, because the room sure was whirling. Naked, he focused on the woman, in part to distract himself from the spinning but also because she was something to look at, with dark hair, dark eyes, smooth olive skin and a smile that just the memory of made him go weak at the knees. Gina Scolari. Even her name was beautiful, although admittedly he had a soft-spot for Italian women. Gina was US born and bred, but her mother was Sicilian. There had been a woman in Milan he'd almost married once. Almost. He'd lost her. It was messy. But that was long ago and far away, and he

2

didn't like to think of the man he had been back then.

That made him think of Sophia. His ex. His former spouse. His no longer significant other.

It seemed strange to think of her in that way, even though he'd longed to do it for four years. He hadn't always felt like that, of course. He'd loved her—at least thought he had, although he'd never actually said the words—but that had turned sour. Maybe she was to blame, maybe he was at fault, for he knew he wasn't as emotionally available as he should have been. He'd tried but somehow couldn't quite make the necessary connection, and that should have told him something. Gina was different, Gina who was lying naked in his bed for the first time. He felt differently about her, knew this was the real thing.

And yet, even with her, the words still would not come, as if there was a roadblock between his brain and his tongue. He wanted to say them, but he couldn't.

Now, as he stared at himself in the bathroom mirror, he tried to find the face of the cocky young student who could make women fall into bed with him with such ease that his pals wanted to bottle whatever it was he had and sell it. He was callous back then. Find 'em, fuck 'em, forget 'em, had been his motto. He was, it was true, a bit of a bastard. Cold, self-seeking, hard. That was then, though, this was now. He had changed, he knew it. The Sophia years were over, time to turn the page, start a new chapter. Yet another new chapter.

He stared at his face, tried to see the man he had been. The years had been kind, but still, he had aged. The hair not quite so golden, the irises not quite so blue, the chin and jawline not quite as square and sharp. It was a face that had seen things, done things that an all-American boy shouldn't see, let alone do, and his eyes reflected the disappointments and sadness that life so often brings. He thought of Gina and something warm spread through his chest.

This doesn't happen to you, Cole, not now. You don't feel like this.

But it had and he did. He stared at himself in the mirror.

Why don't you tell her then?

3

No, he decided, keep it simple for now, don't complicate it with something invented by the romance novelists of yesteryear and propagated by the boys in Tin Pan Alley. Whatever there was between Gina and him would be there whether he said the words out loud or not. He winked at himself, gave his face a wash, and padded back into his bedroom. It was cold in the apartment, so he checked the thermostat, saw that the heating hadn't come on, flicked the switch, then moved back to the bed.

She was still lying in the same position, on her back, eyes closed, mouth slightly open. Still gorgeous, though. He was more awake now and the room had stopped sliding around. He was lucky; he seldom suffered from hangovers. Whenever he got hammered, which was increasingly seldom now, he always woke up hungry. In his military days his pals often complained of a lack of appetite following a night of alcohol abuse, but he was up and looking for the eggs and bacon. As if on cue his stomach grumbled, so he jumped onto the bed and said, "Hey, Gina…"

She didn't stir, so he gave her a little shove through the sheet that covered her modesty. "Sleepyhead," he said, "how do you feel about some breakfast? I've got the fixings in the icebox. I'll even make it, how about that?"

She didn't move. He frowned, reached out for her shoulder. "Babe?" he said, his fingers touching her bare flesh.

He drew back as if he'd been stung.

Her flesh was ice cold.

He threw himself from the bed, landing on his feet, backed away a couple of paces. She was too cold. This wasn't because the heating hadn't come up. He moved to the window, pulled back the drapes to let the gray light in, not caring if anyone across the street saw his nakedness. He moved closer to the bed, leaned over, studied her. Her flesh was pale, he could see that now, her lips slightly blue. His hand trembled as he reached out, not wishing to touch that flesh again but knowing he had to be sure. He pressed them into her neck, searching for, hoping for, a pulse. But there was nothing.

2

When Logan Fitch walked into a room, everyone knew he was a powerful man. It wasn't just his build, although for a man of almost 70 he was very imposing and kept himself trim. It wasn't only because he was still a handsome man, with his iron gray, perfectly coiffed hair, his chiseled jaw, his brown eyes clear and sharp. It was something about the way he carried himself, the set of the broad shoulders, the confidence in those eyes, the assurance in the timbre of his voice. And, of course, because he was worth something upwards of $1 billion. You can buy a lot of power with that kind of money.

His desk was also a commanding statement. It was wide, matte black, its surface devoid of clutter, pride of place given to a framed photograph of his wife, Esther, and their three children. After 50 years he still loved his wife, even though his appetites had led to many brief affairs over the years. He justified it, if only to himself, by reasoning that there are certain things you cannot expect a wife to do. His children were grown up now. His two daughters both married with children of their own, their husbands successful men, powerful men, but not as successful nor as powerful as he. His son, however, was a disappointment. Fitch had hoped he would follow him into business, but he eschewed the pursuit of profit to follow an artistic career. He was in San Francisco, living with his male lover and fashioning himself as a new Jackson Pollock, producing large-scale abstract pieces that sold very well. The fact that it was Logan Fitch himself who paid handsomely for his chaotic daubs was a closely guarded secret. He was disappointed with the path the boy had chosen, but he was still his son.

Behind him a glass wall looked over the city towards the

Hudson and New Jersey. It was a view he loved of a city he called his own, but today he paid it no heed. He sat at that wide, black, tidy desk and waited. He knew a call would come in on the cell phone that lay before him. Once received, that phone would be destroyed, for it existed only for this single call.

He was not feeling particularly confident as he waited, although had anyone walked into his office at the pinnacle of the 30-floor office block owned by Enconomy they would not have noticed it. On the surface he was calm, composed, completely in control. He did not shift in his leather chair, he did not fidget, he did not drum his fingers or jiggle his knee. He was Logan Fitch, and he was a Master of the Universe. But underneath he could feel an array of bugs buzzing in his stomach. He knew they would not still until he received the call to tell him that the job had been carried out satisfactorily.

The phone vibrated.

He did not snatch at it, even though his fingers were desperate to do so. He let it rumble on the desktop for a few moments before he picked it up and said in the perfectly modulated voice that had brokered deals, ruined lives and made presidents, "Fitch."

"It is done." He recognized the deep, slightly accented tone of the man he knew only as Mr Jinks. They said he was a French Canadian, they said he was Russian, they said he was a Cajun. They said a lot of things, but Fitch suspected none of them were true. What it boiled down to is that he didn't much care. All he cared about was getting the job done. And Mr Jinks was very good at getting the job done. He had known of the man by reputation because he had worked extensively for the parent company but had never dealt with him personally. It had been his own head of security, Miles Jefferson, who had arranged everything, and normally it would be he who reported in, but Mr Jinks insisted on dealing with the principal himself. It was one of his rules.

"Untraceable?" Fitch knew his question was redundant as soon as he posed it. Untraceable was Mr Jink's trademark. And Logan Fitch despised clutter.

"Not to us," was the reply. "Her boyfriend has some interesting times ahead, though."

Fitch felt the bugs fluttering again. "She wasn't alone?"

"She went home with him."

"To his apartment?"

"Yes."

Fitch thought about this. "I thought your people had ascertained that never happened? What changed?"

"Mr Fitch, need I remind you this was a rush job?" A hardness had crept into his tone. "I have not been able to learn everything about Coleman Lang. You wanted the woman silenced and that is what I have done. I have done it in such a way that suspicion will fall on her boyfriend, should the authorities discover that her death was not natural. I think, given the time I had, we are as fireproof as we can be."

Fitch was mollified, but only slightly. It was true he had given Mr Jinks only a few weeks to find out what he knew about Gina Scolari and her life. But she had to be dealt with and dealt with speedily. However, the presence of her boyfriend was alarming. Mr Jinks had discovered that she had never visited his apartment, and he had never stayed overnight at hers. What had changed the previous night? Coleman Lang was beginning to sound suspiciously like clutter.

He asked, "And what of the loose ends?"

"They will be tied off when the time comes."

"And if this Coleman Lang becomes a loose end?"

"Then he will also be tied off. But that will require a separate business arrangement…"

3

Lieutenant Rosie Santoro chewed hard on her nicotine gum as she looked down on the body and told herself that it was such a waste. Young woman, was a looker, kept herself in shape, but she still ended up dead in some guy's bed. Santoro hadn't taken off those holiday pounds from Christmas 2000. And all the Christmases in between. Hell, her husband hadn't come anywhere near her for more than a peck on the cheek for ten years and had a gut on him like someone had stuffed a pillow under his shirt, so what the hell did she have to stay trim for? She loved her man, always would, but she believed beauty was transient and those who pursued it became just a little bit desperate and, yeah, creepy looking. She abhorred the botox and the nips and the tucks, even hair dye—her auburn hair, once long and straight but now cropped close, had long since turned gray and she was happy to leave it like that. This DOA had been a distance away from losing her looks and her shape, though. She'd never lose them now. This face, this figure, was the face and figure that people would remember. Santoro's jaw worked harder at the gum. It was becoming increasingly harder to be a smoker in this city now, so she'd decided to try to give it up. It wasn't easy as she'd been a 40-a-day gal since she was 18, and that wasn't yesterday.

Detective Second-Grade Tom Ralston straightened from where he'd been kneeling beside the bed, a woman's purse in his hands. He poked through it, came up with a wallet, fished out a driver's license.

"Gina Scolari," he said across the bed. She was grateful he didn't come any closer because she'd caught his breath earlier and someone somewhere had been a mite too heavy-handed with the garlic.

8

There was no call for that amount of seasoning unless there'd been an outbreak of vampirism in the city.

"Address in Brooklyn Heights." Ralston held the photograph on the laminated card up to compare it with the DOA. "That's her, sure enough."

"Anything in there suggests a medical condition? Pills? Card? Anything?"

He rifled around again, pulled out a slip of paper. "Yeah, note here from her doctor that says, 'Do not have sex with me—danger of death.'" He grinned like he was the successor to Robin Williams. Santoro gave him her best deadpan, kept chewing, and turned away. Black humor was necessary on the job, but it had to be humor. Ralston missed the mark every time.

He pulled another ID from the bag, held it up to study it. "She's a lawyer. Works for Harper, Schreiber and Kinberg."

"Heard of them?"

He shook his head. "Some bunch of shysters uptown, I'll bet, screwin' profits from hard-workin' stiffs. Goddamn shit-suckin' lawyers."

Rosie turned away, concealing a smile. It was a cop's natural state to dislike lawyers, but Ralston turned it into an art form. He'd been skewered a couple of times on the witness stand, and he'd never got over it. It was his own damn fault, Rosie thought, it was part of a cop's duty to be prepared and he just hadn't been ready. The collars had been solid as far as she knew, but with Ralston there was a fine line between righteous and bogus. She'd pulled him up more than a few times over sloppy police work.

She looked around the studio apartment, taking in the polished hardwood floors, the tasteful modern art on the pastel-colored walls, the living area that comprised of a twin-seater couch and a matching armchair, both of modern design, a wall-mounted plasma TV. An old-fashioned coat stand dominated the corner by the big windows that stretched up to the lowered ceiling and looked out beyond the black metal fire escape to the SoHo street below. A solid wood bookcase carried paperbacks and hardbacks, mostly US history. A low coffee table in front of the couch was devoid of the kind of mess you'd expect. No magazines, no dirty coffee cups, not even a remote. She'd not studied the kitchen, but she knew it would be as clean and tidy as the rest of the apartment. She moved to the built-in closet, slid the doors open to reveal an array of suits, all blue or gray, a pile of crisply laundered shirts, white or blue, a separate pile of brand new ones still in their clear wrapping in a drawer. A shelf along the top carried pairs of shoes, some sneakers, a pair of hiking boots, all expensive. Other drawers revealed t-shirts, sweatshirts, jeans, underwear, socks.

"Hey, Ralston?" she said, staring at them. "When you put your socks in a drawer, do you fold them?"

His brow furrowed. "My socks?"

"Yeah. You fold them when you put them away?"

"Hell, no. They're lucky if they're paired. Who the hell folds socks?"

"This guy. His boxers, too. And they look like they're pressed."

Ralston moved to her side to study the drawers, and she recoiled slightly as his breath reached out to none-too-gently tweak her nose. "Jeez—color-coordinated, too," he said. "Black socks together, brown socks together, sports socks, dress socks."

"I don't know who he is," said Rosie, looking around the apartment again, "but I should hire him to do my cleaning. What you think a set-up like this would set you back?"

Ralston looked around, at the walls, at the ceiling, as if someone had painted the dollar amount there. "Building like this? 24-hour door service? Three/four grand per, easy."

"And this guy Lang, he does what?"

"Advertising, I hear. Some big exec down on Madison Ave, no less."

"And what would he clear doing that?"

Ralston grinned. "A shit load more'n you and me, LT."

She nodded, thinking about her brownstone apartment over in

Prospect Heights. "We're in the wrong business."

He gave her a solemn nod in agreement. "Been sayin' that for years, LT. We shoulda gone into TV, become advisors like that Gold Shield from the Bronx did with *NYPD Blue*."

She wrinkled up her nose. "Nah, we're too pretty for TV, they'd never accept us. Where is the guy, anyway?"

"Lang? I had a unit take him to the House, figured you'd wanna talk to him there. We don't need him hangin' round here."

She nodded, still impressed by the studio's neatness. Her own apartment was always a muddle, even now when she didn't have the two kids to blame. They were both off to college, but she and her husband still managed to live in what often resembled a bomb site.

"He got OCD, you think?" she asked.

"Huh?"

She jerked her head around her. "Obsessive-compulsive. Place is like a new pin. Looks like it just been cleaned."

Ralston looked around, saw it as if the first time. "Oh, yeah. Maybe he's a clean freak."

"I was thinking maybe ex-service."

Ralston looked around again, shrugged dismissively. "Could be."

She stifled a sigh. That was why he never got any higher than Detective Second—no curiosity. She was nosy as hell, got that from her mother and her grandmother, two of the nosiest women in the old neighborhood. There wasn't a curtain in their apartment that wasn't worn through from being twitched.

"This place got CCTV?"

"Camera down in the foyer, nowhere else."

"Get downstairs, talk to the doorman who was on duty last night, what's his name again?"

"De Blasio, Oscar de Blasio. But he's finished for the day, LT, gone home."

"Get his address, go see him. And get the tape from the camera."

"Probably digital now."

"Yeah, whatever, just get it. And send a unit over to the dead woman's address—where you say it was?"

"Brooklyn Heights."

"Yeah, get them to check if she had a medical condition. Trace her relatives, get someone down to that law firm, talk to her co-workers."

"Jeez, what for? Chances are she just had some sort of seizure, blew something out. Looks to me they was bumpin' uglies and maybe it all got too athletic. I saw the guy, and he looks pretty fit. Could be it all proved too much for her."

She tossed the gum around inside her mouth even though there was no flavor left. She was hardly aware she was doing it.

"It's a suspicious death, Detective, and you know what cops do when we hear the word 'suspicious'?" She waited for a response but all he did was stare back at her, the woman's purse still in his hands. She sighed. "We investigate, that's what we do. So until the autopsy comes back and we get a tox screen I'm not taking any chances. Canvass the building, see if anyone heard or saw anything."

He wrinkled up his nose. "Come on, LT, we got enough on our plate without adding to it, jeez!"

Santoro ignored him and walked across the apartment to the open front door. She studied the lock. She expected a piece of shit that wouldn't keep a baby out if he really wanted to get in. With a doorman on duty round the clock, guys like Lang usually didn't need good locks. But this was a top-notch number, and she'd lay odds it hadn't come with the door. She inspected the keyhole on the hallway side of the door. There were a couple of scratches but nothing that couldn't have been left naturally. If someone had picked that mother, they knew their business. She heard the elevator open along the hallway, and she turned to see the Medical Examiner's team heading towards her hefting the black body bag.

The first guy recognized her and said, "She ready to go?"

"All yours," she said, stepping back to let them pass. She watched as they laid the body bag beside the bed and, with casual efficiency, hoisted the DOA into it. Rosie wondering how many times a day these guys had to handle a corpse. She wondered if they thought about it at night. She wondered if some of the things they saw haunted them. Probably not. They'd be like cops in that way. After a few years you get used to the blood and the death and the sheer tragedy of it all. Ralston was right, though—they did have enough to be working on and didn't need another dead body to add to the list. But she couldn't shake off this feeling that something about this didn't smell right. And it wasn't just Ralston's garlic breath.

Ralston watched her from the other side of the room with his patented "What the hell's she doing now?" look. He was a lazy cop; how he ever got his gold shield was beyond her, and he never looked past the obvious. She wondered whose ass he puckered up against to get this far, then felt instantly guilty. She was a Latina whose own progress from uniform to lieutenant had been dismissed by department dinosaurs as the result of kissing more than asses. Even so, she felt something itching in her gut, and it told her there was something hinkey about this set-up. The fact that a seemingly healthy young woman just up and died unsettled her. Hell, the guy's neatness made her skin crawl.

"Detective Ralston," she barked, "you not got a guy to speak to?"

He looked like he was about to argue the point, but she gave him the look that tamed two rebellious teens, so he simply nodded. He didn't say a word as he left the apartment, but she could tell by the stiffness in his shoulders that he was pissed.

She didn't plan on losing any sleep over that.

4

Cole Lang sat alone in a bare little room on the upper floor of the station house. He was still dressed in the baggy sweatshirt, gray sweatpants and sneakers he'd pulled on after he'd called the cops. The coat he'd snagged from the stand after that detective had instructed two uniforms to take him to the Precinct House was draped over the uncomfortable wooden chair. A wall to his left was marked by a long mirror. He assumed it wasn't there for anyone in the room to check their hair. It would be one of those two-way glass set-ups: the people on the other side could see him, but he couldn't see them. He'd seen enough cop shows to know that. He wondered if it was used now or if it had been rendered obsolete by video technology. He presumed that if cops wanted to observe an interview, they could watch the feed on a monitor.

He'd recovered from the shock. At least, he thought he had. Every now and then he shivered, but it was cold in this room. He pulled his coat free and draped it over his shoulders. It was better, but a slight tremor still rippled through his frame from time to time.

Gina was dead.

He couldn't come to terms with it.

She was in her early 30s and she was dead.

He shook his head, partly because he was having trouble processing this and partly to try to dislodge the image of her lying on his bed. He had seen death before, but seeing Gina like that, remembering her as young and vital and laughing...

Pull it together, Lang, he told himself. *Breathe, relax, breathe...*

The door opened and a slightly overweight woman with short gray hair stepped in. She was chewing something and her face, smooth and still youthful looking despite the gray hair, was grim. Lang put her at somewhere around 50. but he could be wrong, maybe she was older. Or younger. Hell, what did it matter?

"Hi, Mr Lang, I'm Lieutenant Rosita Santoro. You okay?"

He heard a faint trace of the *barrio* in her voice in the way she rolled the "r's" in her name and spat out the "t's". He nodded, pulled the coat tighter around his shoulders.

"It musta been a shock, finding your girlfriend like that. She *was* your girlfriend, right?"

He nodded again.

"Okay, so just gotta ask you a few questions, then you can go. You got someone comin' to get you?"

Another nod.

"Cos, I could arrange a unit to take you anyplace you like, when we're done…"

"I'm fine. I called a friend, he'll come get me." He'd contacted Reuben as soon as he arrived in the Precinct House. He called him as a friend, not his lawyer, because he didn't think a divorce lawyer would have had much exposure to cops and sudden death.

"Good," said Rosie, "I won't be long, this is just routine. So, how long you know the deceased?"

"About a year." He thought about this, then said, "Exactly a year."

"Did she have any kind of medical condition you know about?"

"No."

"Was she taking any sort of medication…?"

"No."

"…or did she say she was feeling unwell?"

"No, she's not been sick since I knew her."

"And how was she last night?"

Laughing, he saw her laughing.

He asked, "In what way?"

"I mean, she wasn't complaining of a headache or any pain? Anything like that?"

15

"No."

"She was fine?"

They'd been in in the Kon Tiki lounge, one of those theme bars uptown he thought had gone out of style in the 90s—the staff dressed in south sea costumes, the drinks on the bar in front of them piled high with fruit to disguise the kick of the alcohol. Gina's eyes dancing as she smiled at him.

The memory hit him like a boot in the guts.

He said, "She was drunk, we both were, but apart from that she was as healthy as ever."

"And you woke up this morning, found her dead?"

He closed his eyes, opened them again as the sight of her on his bed burned itself on his eyelids. He nodded.

"How drunk were you, Mr Lang?"

He frowned. "What? Like on a scale of one to ten?"

"No, I mean, were you a little tipsy? Falling down drunk? Did you pass out? What?"

In the cab to his apartment, they were kissing, Gina's thigh across his groin as if she was about to straddle him, the driver's eyes in the rear view disinterested, like he'd seen this before. Cole had mentally shrugged, not caring whether the guy was interested or not, all that mattered in that moment were Gina's lips on his, the feel of her body against him, her scent more intoxicating than the Waikiki Slammers in the bar.

He said, "I was pretty drunk. I remember it all, though. We were celebrating."

"Celebrating what?"

"My divorce being final. I guess we both passed out eventually."

"Eventually?"

"Yes, eventually."

"But you had relations before you passed out?"

In his bed, Gina perched above him, her head back, her hips thrusting downward.

"Yes, we had relations."

16

"And before you passed out she didn't say she was unwell?"

"No, I told you. She was fine. She was fine when we were in the bar, she was fine when we were back in my apartment, she was fine when we 'had relations', she was fine when I fell asleep. The only time she wasn't fine was this morning when I woke up and I expected to find her lying beside me alive and well but she wasn't. She wasn't fine then."

He knew his voice was beginning to harden, but he couldn't help it. He didn't want to be in this bare little room with no heating. He didn't want to think about Gina lying cold and alone in some mortuary. He was aware of Santoro watching him closely while he vented, and when she spoke again, her tone was patient. "Take it easy, Mr Lang. I gotta ask these things. You understand? Now, did you and Ms Scolari have any kind of argument?"

He didn't buy it. Something in her tone, in the way she stared at him, set bells clamoring, bells he thought had stilled years before. He had to put aside his feelings of loss and pay attention. He sat back in his chair, stared at her, one hand resting on the scarred wooden table, his fingers making lazy circles. "I need a lawyer in here, Lieutenant?"

"You think you need a lawyer, Mr Lang?"

"I think there's more to your questions than just routine."

She sat back too, chewed her gum, stared at him, obviously weighing him up. Then she leaned forward again and said, "I'll tell you, Mr Lang, there's something about this that makes my gut itch, you know? A young, healthy woman dies suddenly in your apartment, in your bed. No sign of a struggle, no sign of forced entry, no history of a medical condition, far as we know. Now, it could all be kosher, and we'll know once the autopsy's done, but until then my policy is to treat the death as suspicious. So, I'll ask you again, did you and Ms Scolari have an argument?"

"No."

"You sure?"

"I think I'd remember, Lieutenant Santoro, was it?"

17

She inclined her head, yes. "Was she having trouble with anyone that you know of?"

Gina in her apartment, two months before, stretched out on the couch with one of her beloved puzzle books, her head on his lap as he read a magazine. He became aware that she was staring into space, lost in thought. He called her on it, but she gave him her smile—that smile—and told him she was only daydreaming, nothing more.

He said, "No."

"At work?"

There had been times when he saw her eyes cloud, as if something dark had taken root in her mind. Again he'd ask, but that smile would come again and she'd say it was nothing.

He said, "Nothing out of the usual, far as I know."

"The usual?"

"Work stuff. You know…"

Just work stuff, that's what she'd said. He accepted it.

Santoro chewed. "Any problems in her family?"

He paused, then said, "I wouldn't know." He felt shame color the words, but there was no point in lying. Santoro would find out soon enough if she didn't already know. "I've never met her family."

Santoro raised an eyebrow, her jaws stopped working. "Really? You been going out a year—exactly a year—and you've not met her folks?"

"It was complicated."

"Complicated how?"

He sighed. "Does this matter?"

"Maybe. Why don't you humor me?"

He got up, tucked the coat around his shoulders, moved to the mirrored wall, stared at his own reflection. "You not got any heat in this place?"

"It's an old building, sometimes it's sluggish. Why was it complicated, Mr Lang?"

He looked at himself for a moment, came to a decision, turned back. "I was going through a messy divorce. My wife—well, my ex-wife—and her brother were making things awkward. I didn't want to draw Gina or her mother into it if I could help it. So we played things careful. Also, Gina didn't want her mother to know she was dating a married man. She said she'd find it difficult enough to accept the fact I was divorced, let alone simply separated."

"Her mother's old-fashioned, huh?"

"It seems so. She's Sicilian, came over here when she was a teenager."

Santoro seemed to understand what he was saying. "Yeah, my mother was the same. Came up here from Mexico, still clung to a lot of the old ways. I couldn't date till I was 18." She smiled. "At least as far as she was concerned." He knew she was trying to bond with him, trying to relax him, get him to say something he shouldn't. Silently, he wished her luck. He hadn't said anything he shouldn't for over 20 years. "You think your wife was having you followed?"

It had occurred to him. Sophia was possessive, he learned that soon after they were married. He couldn't as much as look at another woman without the anger flaring in her eyes. His own aloofness didn't help. Sure, there had been heat in the early days, but her jealous rages soon turned the thermostat down. Then there was her brother, Silvio—medicine man to the hypochondriac wealthy in Connecticut, keeping them well supplied with tranquilizers and Viagra. On their wedding night, Silvio had taken him aside and warned him that if Lang ever hurt Sophia, he'd make it his business to ruin his life. They were tight, that brother and sister. He'd come to know them as the Psycho Twins. Lang knew they would be looking for anything to use against him, anything they could that would hurt him. That was why he'd never taken Gina back to his apartment until last night in case they'd paid off any of the doormen.

Lang said, "I wouldn't put it past them."

"Your wife want your money, that it?"

He gave her a grim little smile. "No, my wife is wealthy in her own right, she doesn't want or need my money. For her and her family, her brother in particular, this was just about power. They didn't like me breaking away from them and so made it as difficult as possible. I believe they'd've turned on Gina somehow, made life hard for her, just because she was going out with me. So we kept our relationship discreet. The divorce was made final yesterday, so last night we celebrated."

Rosie nodded. "What's your wife's name?"

"Ex-wife," he corrected. "Sophia Manucci."

"Not Lang?"

"She didn't take my name, always retained her own."

"That bother you?"

"Didn't make a difference to me. It was her I wanted, she could call herself Shitbag for all I cared." And he *had* wanted her, back then. That changed, of course, when he saw her true colors. Whatever he'd felt for her died, which was why he'd been unwilling to accept the feelings he had for Gina, why he'd never told her he loved her. He feared it might die. He wished he had told her now. He wished the last words he'd said to her were words of love.

"And you mentioned a brother?"

"Dr Silvio Manucci. He has a practice up there in Westport."

Santoro pursed her lips as if she was impressed, but Lang had the sense she was not so easily awed. "Fancy," she said.

"They're a very fancy family."

"How'd they make their money?"

"Real estate, thanks to their great-grandfather buying land when it was cheap. I think they own most of New England and a hefty chunk of Manhattan."

Santoro's head tilted. "They related to Senator Manucci?"

"Their father."

The Senator, that's what Sophia called him. Not father or dad or the old man. The Senator. Wealthy, powerful and vindictive, he was as deeply embedded in Capitol Hill as the foundations to the Senate Building. He'd never hidden his dislike of Lang and his disapproval of the marriage.

Santoro was impressed. "So that means Supreme Court Justice Manucci..."

"...was their grandfather."

She whistled. "And you wanted to divorce yourself from that?"

He stared at her, his gaze hard and cold. "Money isn't everything, Lieutenant."

"No, but it makes up for a lot. Okay, so you never met Ms Scolari's mother or family?"

He shook his head. "Her mother lives in Queens, far as I know."

"And her father?"

"Dead. She didn't talk much about him. I got the impression there was little love lost—her mother had remarried."

"And her work? She talk much about that?"

"No, but I think she was very good at what she did. She'd been promoted, I know that. Junior partner, something like that. That was the day we met."

He'd forced himself to go out that night. He and Sophia had been living apart for three years, which should've been long enough even though New York didn't have a "no fault" rule, but she'd thrown every delaying tactic imaginable. He needed a respite, so he went out. Hit a bar, was drinking alone when he caught the eye of one of Gina's more forward friends. She struck up a conversation, next thing he knew he was sitting with them at their table.

Santoro asked, "What kind of law she practice?"

"Corporate. Had some big clients."

"For instance?"

"For instance, I don't know. She never mentioned names. She was careful about confidentiality. And, to be honest, I didn't care. It was enough that she told me she handled some big names. I was proud of her for that."

"You're in advertising, right? Need lotsa contacts to make that game work, right?"

"Right," he said, giving her a sideways look, guessing immediately what she was inferring. "But before you say it, I didn't see her as a way to further my own business." He saw from her expression that she didn't believe him, so he expanded. "The kind of outfits she handled don't advertise, Lieutenant, because they don't need to. They're into all sorts of things. We're talking big conglomerates, multinationals. Their subsidiaries will use agencies like mine but not at the level Gina represented."

She nodded, but he knew she was unconvinced. "Okay." She stared at the grimy window high up on one wall. He had the impression she did this a lot during interviews. She asked, "Were you in the service, Mr Lang?"

"Why do you ask?"

"You got the look. You're what, maybe late 30s?"

"Forty."

"Right, but you carry yourself well. And your apartment, I haven't seen anything so spick and span outside of a construction site show home."

"I could have a good cleaning service."

She inclined her head, conceding that. "That you could. But you fold your socks, Mr Lang. Only guys I've ever met who fold their socks so neatly are all ex-military. So, I ask you again, were you in the service?"

"What does this have to do with Gina's death?"

"As I said, humor me."

He breathed out through his nose, fighting his irritation, growing weary of humoring her. "I was in the Marines, satisfied?"

A thin smile when she was proved correct. This was a woman who liked to be right. "*Semper Fi.*"

"Damn straight," he said automatically. His old gunnery sergeant used to say it: you can take the boy out of the Corps, but you can't take the Corps out of the boy.

"You see action?"

He shrugged. "If you call filing paperwork at Quantico 'action.'"

"No tours in Iraq or Afghanistan?"

He nodded. "I was in Iraq for a time, based in headquarters."

"Filing paperwork."

"Yes, filing paperwork. I was a hell of a filer. The Corps can spot real talent a mile off."

"Couldn't've been fun, though. You musta had buddies who saw action over there but never came back. I got a guy on my squad, was with the infantry in Iraq. He don't talk about it much. Plays it down, you know? Says he saw more trouble in the commissary when the french fries were cold than he did out in the streets. I didn't buy it."

Her tone was pointed, and Lang knew she didn't believe him about his military service, either. He didn't care what she believed. "Lieutenant, I'm not here to tell you war stories, okay? Even if I had any to tell. My girlfriend was found dead this morning, in my bed. She was young and she shouldn't be dead. I had buddies who were also young and some of them are dead, too. So, tell me, what does that prove?"

She was about to answer when voices filtered through from the hallway before the door burst open and Reuben King pushed his way past a harassed looking detective. He stormed into the room, his face set in a tough guy scowl.

"I'm sorry, LT," said the detective, "this is Mr Lang's counsel…"

"Damn right," said Reuben in a tone Lang had never heard before. "You questioning my client, Lieutenant?"

"We're talking, is all," said Rosie, obviously not fazed in the slightest by the lawyer's tone.

Reuben pointed at the mirror behind Lang. "There better not be anyone behind there, and you sure as hell better not be recording this little talk because, so help me, I'll stir up a shitstorm of such biblical proportions there'll be cults stripping off and climbing mountains."

The Lieutenant stifled a smile. "As I said, counselor, we're just talking."

Reuben stood in the center of the room, confident he had the floor. "They been making any wild accusations, Mr Lang?"

Lang stared at the detective for a moment, then said, "Like Lieutenant Santoro said, we're just talking."

Reuben nodded, satisfied. "Then we're out of here. You have any more little chats in mind, Lieutenant, you contact my office." He laid a card on the table in front of her. She looked at it but didn't pick it up. Reuben held out an arm, gestured towards the door. "Let's go, Mr Lang."

Lang walked out without another glance at Santoro, who was watching Reuben with laughter dancing in her eyes. Before the lawyer could follow his client, she said, "Counselor?" He turned, waited for her to say something more. She waited a beat, then said, "Cults taking their clothes off up mountains?"

Reuben smiled slightly. "Too much, you think?"

Rosie inclined her head towards the card before her. "A little bit, yeah. I guess you don't do much of this, being a divorce attorney."

Reuben opened his mouth, closed it again, smiled. "I've always wanted to do that, burst into a precinct, demand they free my client. Not enough divorces wind up in a police station, you ask me."

"If it's any consolation, counselor, you did really well."

"You think?"

"Keep it up, you'll soon be ready for the majors. Before you know it, you'll be getting scumbags out of jail all over the state."

Reuben finally caught her mocking tone. He narrowed his eyes like he'd seen actors do on TV court dramas and said, "In the meantime, Lieutenant, remember what I said. If you have anything further for my client, you give me a call. Number's on the card there."

He left the room before Santoro could hit him with any further sarcasm.

5

The man called Austin Lomax didn't like pizza, yet he owned a pizza joint.

Go figure.

That was his standard response when anyone asked why he spent his working life dishing up foods that he found inedible. Occasionally he shook his head, shrugged and said, "What you gonna do about it?" Which was not the sort of thing you'd expect an Austin Lomax to say. But he was from New York and, as far as his customers knew, all New Yorkers spoke like that. Sure, they thought much of his vocabulary was merely an image, a role he played, and they were largely right. He did play it up because he knew they liked it. The pizzeria boasted a good location, right on Main Street of Butte Crags, Nebraska, and given it was the only fast food establishment in the small town, he did a roaring trade. The kids loved to come in, share a 12-inch thin crust and hang out; the cowboys—or whatever the hell they were—liked to set a spell and let their saddle cool; the older crowd appreciated the constant soundtrack of crooners on the speakers.

Austin Lomax hated it all.

He played his part, though. He was always the perfect host, welcoming customers whenever he was out front, which was as often as possible because he also disliked being in the hot kitchen. He had a smile, a handshake for the men, a chaste hug for the women if he knew them well enough, and after ten years of living and working in this shit hole of a town, that amounted to a lot of handshakes and hugs in any given week. He'd become a firm fixture in the town's life, but he never felt really settled. He had nothing against the place he'd called home for those years, but he still referred to it as Butt Crack, always to himself, though, for the townsfolk were fiercely proud of their little community. And little it was. It used to be a one-horse town, but the horse got bored and wandered off in search of excitement.

The local sheriff was a young snotnose, full of enthusiasm, but the most he ever had to do was write up a few parking tickets to supplement the town's budget and occasionally break up a fight when the farm hands tussled with the cowboys, for the farmer and the cowman can't always be friends, go screw yourselves Rodgers and Hammerstein. There was no real crime to speak of, and Lomax missed New York's constant rumble of traffic, the sound of the sirens in the night, steam hissing from manhole covers and the constant reminder that life raged all around you. Here, come sundown, it was so quiet you thought the whole world had died. And it was frigging dark, too. Some nights he'd stand in his own yard and look at the array of stars above, for growing up in the city he'd never known there were so many of the goddamn things. Those nights he'd stare at the wonders of the universe, sip his bourbon and rocks, and long for a bit of light pollution. Just a little bit, a chink, a sliver, something to prove that mankind was alive and well and saying up yours, nature.

The thing of it was, not only did Austin Lomax not talk like an Austin Lomax, he didn't look like an Austin Lomax, a fact that had been remarked upon many times in Butte Crag. An Austin Lomax was a country club kind of guy, fair-skinned and blue-eyed, who would blackball a fella because he had a hook nose. This Austin Lomax was not a tall man, but he gave off the impression of being more than capable of looking after himself should those farmers or cowhands ever turn ugly in his joint. He was dark-skinned, of average height, muscular enough but no Big Arnie, and his hair, thick, with a natural kink and always kept unfashionably long. He was very vain when it came to his hair, and he kept it dark with regular applications of dye, which he bought surreptitiously from the drug store. The druggist himself was as bald as a goddamn eagle, but he knew the need to keep his customers' little secrets.

There was a scar running the length of Lomax's left cheek, which was the cause of much debate in Butte Crag. He told people that it was caused in an automobile accident when he was a teenager, but no one really bought that. The simple fact was, no one wanted to know the truth. The local pizzeria owner was a man of mystery, and that was the way the citizens of Butte Crag liked it. In a town where most people knew exactly when their neighbor was going to break wind, a little mystery was something to be savored.

No, this Austin Lomax looked more like an Anthony Falcone, which was his real name, but he'd left that back east along with his old life. He tried not to think too much about that old life because looking back wasn't something he did often. As a child he'd taken the story of Lot's wife to heart, and he was in no rush to be turned into a condiment. Or dog food, which would be more to the point given that certain individuals back there would be glad to know their old buddy was alive and well, if you could call living in Butt Crack living.

It had been a busy morning. He'd driven to Ogallala to pick up some supplies, taking a detour over some rough terrain because he loved to feel his pickup truck bouncing around. It was one of the few pleasures in his life, and he took off into the wilderness as often as he could. He may have missed the cut and thrust of the streets, but he also appreciated the silence of the open range and the mountains. In small doses, naturally. Out there he could blast away with his Glock 18, just to keep his hand in. It wasn't a new gun, but he liked it. He liked the way he could switch from semi-automatic to fully automatic at the flip of a toggle, although the stream of rounds that flooded out took some getting used to. Back in the streets he'd fired guns, sure he had, but nothing like this. The first time he let loose on fully automatic, the weapon had bucked and bounced in his hand like it was trying to make a break for it, but he'd learned to lean forward, put his weight behind it, and eventually got the hang of the thing. It could discharge ten rounds in a second or two, so he'd bought some 33 round mags, most of which were still unused. Still, he was a firm believer that ten bullets a second isn't much better than one if you know what you're doing. And he knew what he was doing, which was why he was still around while other guys his age were dead or in the joint, which was worse than being dead, you ask him. He didn't think he'd ever need the weapon, despite being in the wild west, but hell, you never knew. He liked it, he'd bought it across the state line, in Cheyenne, and no one knew he had it, not the folks back in Butt Crack, not the US Marshals who kept an eye on him from time to time. So, whenever he could, he drove out to the Sand Hill country, found an isolated spot and blasted away at tin cans and bottles, just like a gunfighter in the cowboy movies he loved.

Once back in town, he had the lunchtime stampede to deal with, although it wasn't so much a stampede as a leisurely walk to milking. Still, his chef was off with a serious case of crotch itch—he'd been paying attention to the wife of a long-distance trucker until the husband came home and took a torque wrench to his legs. No one reported the incident to the sheriff, it being a matter of honor, but it left Austin short of a cook, meaning he had to rustle up the thin and crispies himself. After two hours of sprinkling cheese, smearing tomato and chopping ham, he wished the guy had kept it in his pants.

It was about 2.30pm when he completed the final order, and he had an hour or so to himself before he'd have to start preparing for the evening crowd, although "crowd" was also overstating it somewhat. He turned the crooners the customers expected off and selected a mix of hits from the 80s and 90s. He poured himself a coffee—he prided himself on his coffee, one of two things the Colombians did right, the other being the production, marketing and ongoing supply of cocaine. They could also kill a man in a variety of ways, but that no longer bothered Austin, even though there were a couple of those greasers who would gleefully cut his heart out with a rusty spoon if they got their hands on him. That was all in the past, though. Ancient history. And he didn't look back.

He sat at his counter, sipped his coffee, smiled in a satisfied manner—for he'd learned to appreciate the simple things in life—and swiped the screen of his tablet to reveal the online version of the *New York Post*. He read it every day without fail. It was his way of keeping in touch now that he couldn't speak to anyone back home.

He found the entry in the Metro section. He hadn't been looking for it, he'd just been idly clicking through when he saw her face. He hadn't seen that face in over ten years, but he knew her. The headline was "Lawyer found dead in SoHo loft", and part of him hoped she was a pal of the dead lawyer, or was representing someone accused in connection with the death, but deep down he knew.

The details were sparse, just that Gina Scolari, a lawyer with Harper, Schreiber and Kinberg, had been found dead in a Soho apartment the day before. Sources close to the police department said there were no suspicious circumstances, but investigations were continuing into why a previously healthy 32-year-old woman would die suddenly. Lang had been questioned as a matter of routine but released. Joshua Kinberg, her employer, said that Ms Scolari's death had come as a tremendous shock to the firm and their thoughts were with her family and friends. Ms Scolari's mother, Angelina Ferraro, was not available for comment. A family friend asked that she be granted some privacy in this most difficult time.

He laid the tablet down, tears filling his eyes. Gina, his little Gina. Dead. She'd been 22 when he saw her last, and just 15 when he split from her mother and she had stopped using his name, reverting to her own. He couldn't blame her, for he hadn't been much of a husband. He'd managed to see Gina just before he was whisked away by Witness Security, tried to tell her that he still loved her, but she gave him the cold shoulder. He remembered that red-haired US Marshal, McDonough, telling him that he couldn't see, speak, or in any way communicate with his family. It would be dangerous for him, dangerous for them. As a husband he'd been shit, as a father he'd been next to useless most of the time, but he didn't want any harm to befall them so, after that one painful encounter, he'd left them alone. Angelina remarried, some housebuilder, but at least he was Sicilian. Gina, his little Gina even though she'd rejected his name also, went into the law. He was proud of her, but from afar. He still saw that little girl with the bangs that always got in her eyes, running out to meet him on those occasions when he came home at night. He still felt her weight on his lap asking him incessant questions as he read the paper. He could still see the joy in her eyes when she set him little treasure hunts through the house, leaving notes with clues until he found the prize: generally some candy which he gave to her, as she knew he would. He loved those days when he could pretend that his life was normal. He still heard her crying when a boy at school had shown her disrespect. It was some Irish kid, he recalled, and Austin—no, Tony, for he was Tony then—had him taught a lesson. He didn't do it himself, the kid was 12 for Christ's sake, but he paid some teenagers from the same school to show him how to treat a lady. The little Mick lost a couple of teeth, but he got the message, for the next day he apologized to Gina in front of the whole school, got right up there on the stage in the auditorium during morning prayers and said he'd been wrong to call her a dirty wop whore.

He stared at the picture, wondering where they got it. She was smiling, her dark eyes, so like her mother's, filled with life. With promise. She was beautiful, just like her mom. She was young. She shouldn't be dead. Not yet.

And so he sat there, alone in a pizzeria, a cup of coffee going cold at his hand, staring at a picture on a tablet while Billy Joel sang about an Uptown Girl on the MP3 player.

6

Lang stood in the center of his apartment, not knowing what to do, what to touch. It was an unfamiliar experience for him as all his life he'd known what to do in any given situation. It was his gift. It had served him well in college, it had served him well in the Marines, it had served him well in the years before and after he joined the firm. But now it had deserted him. It was as if someone had drawn all the air out of the apartment, and he was flailing around trying to suck in what oxygen he could. It was all internal, of course, he knew all Reuben would see was his stillness as he stared at the unmade bed. The bed in which she died. Gina.

Reuben cleared his throat. "Maybe you should stay with me another night, Cole."

Lang shook his head. For two nights he'd stayed at Reuben's townhouse near Prospect Park in Brooklyn, smiled at his pal's wife Charmayne, bounced his kid Kaydin on his knee, made enthusiastic noises when Charmayne served up an indifferent meal, for she was no threat to Julia Child. And later, alone in the spare room, he had wept. They didn't know it, he didn't want them to know it. His mourning was as private as it was deep. But he knew he would only spend those two nights with Reuben and his wife. He'd face this the way he'd faced up to most things: head on. He could handle it. Reuben had pushed at NYPD to allow him to return home, but they had to wait until the results of the autopsy. Nothing untoward had been found, so Reuben argued that with no evidence of a crime there was no need to treat the apartment as a crime scene. Santoro reluctantly agreed, under pressure from the suits at One Police Plaza thanks to Reuben's contacts, but insisted that Lang not move anything from the apartment or even

31

bring in cleaners. He had no intention of doing either.

Reuben said, "You know Lieutenant Santoro suspects homicide, don't you?"

"Yeah, she made that kinda clear."

"What do you think?"

Lang dragged his eyes from the bed with its crumpled sheets and the indentation of Gina's head still in the pillow and fought the burning sensation behind his eyes as he gazed at his friend and said, "She was a healthy woman. She died suddenly. It can happen."

"So you don't suspect anything?"

"Reuben, anything's possible."

Reuben pressed his point, always a lawyer. "But if it is the case?"

Lang's face turned to stone and he looked back at the bed again, remembering the softness of her skin, the coolness of her lips, the sensation of her hands on his body. "Then I'll deal with it…"

7

Austin Lomax also cried for Gina. He also did it alone. He couldn't remember the last time he'd cried, let alone the floods of tears he'd shed since he'd read about Gina's death. Being a Made Man brought with it certain responsibilities, and one of them was that you don't burst into tears like a girl lest your buddies take it for a sign of weakness. On the streets, weakness can be dangerous: weakness can lead to temptation, and temptation can lead to getting your fingers caught in the cookie jar, and getting your fingers caught in the cookie jar can lead to those fingers being cut off. Back when Austin was Tony, he'd not only got his fingers caught in the cookie jar, but he had gone on to do something far worse in the eyes of his old buddies, and that something far worse would've led him to being whacked had he not been spirited away.

He stared at the gold cigarette lighter he'd held in his hand since he read the report. Gina had given it to him when they were still a family for his birthday, he forgot which one. Of course, her mother had actually bought it, but it was Gina who wrapped it and presented it. It was gold and it was heavy, and he loved it. He held it in his hand as he sat in his empty restaurant, the tears oozing from his eyes, his thumb gently stroking the metal, feeling the words etched into the side.

To the best dad in the world, all my love.

Gina had just been a kid. She'd meant it, then. He wiped the moisture from his face with the back of his free hand then raised the lighter and clicked it on. The flame danced as he recalled his little daughter's face lighting up while she'd watched him unwrap it, heard the squeals of delight when he swept her up in his arms and told her he'd keep it with him always. He'd kept that promise.

He fingered a cigarette from the pack on the counter, lit it, sucked in the smoke. He usually stepped outside to smoke, but to hell with it. He was alone, it was his place, and he didn't want anyone to see him like this. He should've given up years ago, but he never could. It was an old habit, but that's what life was, a series of old habits. Some of them die hard and some of them never die. And some lie dormant. And as he sat in the restaurant that he'd called home for ten years, the light dying beyond the windows, he knew he'd need some of those old habits in the coming days.

He acted like nothing was wrong that night and the day after. He met his customers, he served them food, he smiled and laughed and told stories of his life in the East. None of the stories were true, of course, because his customers knew nothing of Tony Falcone. He kept the pretence up one last time because he didn't know who would be reporting back to the US Marshals' office. He suspected that snot-nosed Sheriff kept them up-to-date, and he was in the restaurant that night with his fat little wife and their fat little kids. Austin Lomax had met him like a brother, but Tony Falcone had recoiled from him.

He closed up at midnight, pulled the shades, balanced the register, carried the credit card receipts and the cash to the office. He took a Remington landscape print from the wall, opened the safe underneath. He reached in, took out an empty leather holster, then the Glock wrapped in an oily rag. He unwrapped the weapon, enjoying the feel of it in the palm of his hand. He placed the stack of receipts in the safe, took out two canvas bags, one filled with ammunition and another with bank notes. He sighed, not because he knew his life in Butt Crack was over but because he knew he'd never be able to get on a plane with the weapon. He'd have to drive back to New York. Be better anyway, he decided, too easy to be traced buying a ticket, even with the credit card he kept under a phoney name. The US Marshals knew nothing about that card, it was one of his many secrets, but he didn't want to use it unless he really had to. He had more cash in the bank, but there

34

was no way he'd be able to get to that, he knew the feds would be checking any unusual withdrawals from his account as a matter of course. He wasn't in the pen, but he was still a prisoner—and all because he did the right thing back then. On the other hand, if he hadn't done what he'd done, he'd've ended up lying in the trunk of a car like a spare tire. A flat spare tire.

He'd always been a careful guy, which was why he'd lived so long. He had the credit card for emergencies, and he'd been salting away the cash for years for a rainy day—and now it was cloudy out. He had another bank account, also in a false name, and soon as he could he'd clean that out, give himself even more operating money. From now on he'd be a cash-on-the-nail guy. He had enough to see him through for a while, at least until he'd done what he had to. After that, it didn't matter.

Part of him always knew he'd go back to the city one day. He didn't look back, but a little voice inside him always whispered that his life there wasn't over, that he had unfinished business. He just wished it wasn't this way.

He took off his jacket, wrapped the holster round his shoulders and under his arm, slid the Glock into it, then pulled on an old leather bomber jacket. He looked in the mirror, pulling at the leather until it sat naturally and satisfied himself that only an expert would know he was carrying. He thrust the canvas bags into a small travel bag along with a change of clothes. He'd buy more along the way. He flicked off the lights, opened the door, peered out. His pickup was parked out front, and there were no cars in the small lot beside the restaurant. No vehicles cruised the Main Street, surprise, surprise.

He stepped out, locked up, threw the bags into the passenger seat, then climbed into the truck. He sat for a moment, looking back at the pizzeria frontage. He swallowed once, feeling something like sadness. This had been his home for ten years, and it had been a good one. He had his problems with Butt Crack, but they were of his making, not the town's. It was a good place, and the people were decent, if a little dull. Despite his internal bitching, despite his longing for his old life, he now realized that what it boiled down to was that he'd been almost happy here.

Helluva time to realize that, now that he had to leave.

He'd left Austin Lomax beyond the door of the pizza joint. He didn't think he'd meet him again.

It was Tony Falcone who started up the truck and pulled away. It was Tony Falcone who put that life in Butte Crag out of his mind. It was Tony Falcone who steeled himself for what lay ahead. Austin Lomax couldn't do what needed to be done now. But Tony Falcone could.

8

Rosie Santoro was eating a hamburger when the phone on her desk buzzed.

"Santoro," she said, spraying some fragments of lettuce into the mouthpiece. She was thankful that no one saw and that there didn't seem to be any meat lost. Her cholesterol count would be happy that its numbers were set to grow, because misery loves company.

"Rosie," she heard the slightly nasal voice of Dr Rachel Simons, the assistant ME.

"What's up, Doc?" Rosie laid the bun down on the greaseproof wrapper. No need to lose any more precious calories.

"Ms Gina Scolari, deceased. Got the report here, thought I'd give you a heads up before I drop it in the system."

This was the second autopsy. Rachel's colleague Dr Frank Ross had performed the original examination, but his work was notoriously slapdash, especially as he coasted his way towards retirement. He'd declared the death to be from natural causes, but Rosie hadn't been convinced so she gave Rachel a call. They went way back and, in any case, Rachel had a poor opinion of her colleague's abilities. She had once observed that Ross "couldn't find his ass with both hands and written directions, which is quite something because it's big enough to petition for statehood." So she'd agreed to have a look herself. Ross, she said, wouldn't give a shit. It had taken her two days to get to it because if there was one thing New York didn't lack, it was corpses.

"Appreciate that," said Rosie. "So what's the skinny?"

"Well, sure as shit isn't you or I," said Simons, a smile in her voice. Rosie had known the doctor a long time and they'd both

37

agreed very early on that they were far from sylph-like.

"Hey, I'm cutting back," Rosie said, a defensive tone creeping in.

"You're eating a burger right now, aren't you?" Automatically, Rosie glanced around her office, as if looking for hidden cameras. "And I'll bet you're washing it down with a soda." Rosie's eyes guiltily darted to the can on her left. "And then there's the double helping of fries."

Rosie sighed. "How the hell did you know? You got a spy in my precinct?"

"Hell, no—'cos I've got the same here and I'll be diving in soon as I finish this call. And it's not getting any warmer, so let me get on with this."

Rosie smiled, picked up a pen and said, "Shoot."

"Okay, DOA was a female, aged 32…"

"Jeez, Rachel, I know that. Get to the good part."

"Yes, right. Okay…" Rosie visualized her scanning her notes. "Okay, here we go. She was healthy. She died suddenly."

The doctor stopped and Rosie, her pen still poised, waited for more. When nothing came, she said, "That it? All those years in medical school and cutting people up and that's all you give me? She was healthy and she died suddenly? I know that already."

"Now, now, Rosie, don't get your panties bunched. Have you heard of Sudden Death Syndrome? Vics can be young, maybe up to 35 years of age, show no signs of heart weakness yet die in their sleep?"

"I've read about it, sure."

"Well, that didn't happen here."

"Ross didn't think so, either."

"For once he was right. Wonders will never cease. I found signs of hypoxia in the tissue, which told me this girl asphyxiated in her sleep. Did she suffer from central sleep apnea?"

"I have no idea what that is."

"A respiratory disorder that basically makes the body forget to breathe while sleeping. If she did suffer from that, then it, compounded by the impressive amount of alcohol, could be the cause of death."

"Yeah, that's more or less what Ross said, although he didn't mention this central sleep thing."

"Apnea," said Rachel. "And he does mention it in his notes, but I'll bet you only read the summary. It doesn't often lead to death, but shit, as they say, happens."

Rosie felt deflated. "So you agree with Ross?"

"I didn't say that."

Rosie sat up, knowing the other shoe was about to drop. Rachel liked to spin things out. She should've been a writer. She was, in fact, writing a crime novel based around her experiences as an ME. Rachel didn't read much crime fiction, and Rosie didn't have the heart to tell her about Kathy Reichs and Patricia Cornwell.

"So what are you saying?"

"I didn't find anything."

Rosie felt her heart sink further. She had been certain Rachel would find something. She should've been relieved, after all her squad had enough work to do without an added homicide, but for some reason she felt disappointed. Her gut had deceived her. It had let her down.

But then Rachel spoke again.

"So, I had another look…"

Rosie felt a familiar jolt as her gut told her she hadn't been wrong after all. "And?"

"A-a-and…" Rachel was really playing to the gallery. "I found a small puncture mark, just under the left breast."

"And Ross missed it?"

"Well, if I was being fair, I'd say it was easy to miss and I only found it because I was really, really, REALLY looking, thanks to the famous Santoro gut. But why should I be fair to that lazy, incompetent asshat? Yeah, he missed it."

Rosie said, "So we're talking homicide here?"

"I don't see any other reason for jamming a needle into the

inframammary fold—that's where the breast meets the chest, by the way."

"Yeah, I cracked that code. She wouldn't feel the needle?"

"There were no other signs of trauma, so I'm guessing she was asleep when it was administered. She had enough alcohol in her bloodstream to re-float the Titanic, so I'm guessing she was pretty well out of it. Oh—and she'd had sexual intercourse very recently."

That I knew, Rosie thought. "So what killed her?"

"Well, being the ace medical sleuth that I am, I figured whatever it was wouldn't show up in the routine tox screens, so I had to dig a little deeper, look for substances that are kinda sneaky."

"And you found what?"

"Succinylcholin, or suxamethonium chloride if you'd rather."

"Sux what?"

"Close enough. It is also known as Sux. They used to call it the untraceable murder weapon, but that's a load of balls. The drug itself works fast, but it breaks down very quickly. So you can't test for it directly, but the metabolites—the results of the breakdown—can be found. It's a neuromuscular paralytic which is used as a short-term anaesthetic, usually for intubation purposes. It's also been used as part of the three-drug cocktail in lethal injections to paralyse the muscles before the kill drug takes effect. But it's pretty lethal in its own right, shuts everything down and the victim dies of asphyxia."

Rachel let this sink in before she said, "You expected this, didn't you?"

"Gut feeling."

"Always go with your gut, that's what I say. Speaking of which, mine is telling me my throat's been cut, so if you've not got anything else to ask, I'll get on with the business of eating this lunch. A cow died for me to harden my arteries, the least I can do is eat it while it's hot."

Rachel hung up without a goodbye, leaving Rosie with the receiver still in her hand and her own lunch congealing and forgotten about. Gina Scolari was murdered, that much she'd already sensed—don't ask her why, she always had this sixth sense when it came to homicide. The only person who was with the dead woman was Cole Lang, and he struck her as being wrong somehow—again, don't ask her why. There was no sign of forced entry apart from a couple of scratches around the lock, but that didn't mean anything. The doorman didn't let anyone up to the apartment after Lang had gone up with the DOA. Turned out the surveillance camera was on the fritz, though, so maybe the doorman was lying. The convenience of the busted security system aside, she had no evidence to suggest anyone else had been in that apartment. That left her with Lang. But why would he kill her? What the hell was his motive? And why do it in such a way that only he could be suspected? Unless, of course, he thought he was being so clever he'd never be suspected. Killers thought like that sometimes. Some were even right.

She glanced at the burger, decided she didn't want any more. She could hear her arteries thanking her.

9

Lang sat in his armchair, the lights off, the only illumination in the apartment provided by the street lights through the large windows. He held a tumbler of 20-year-old single malt loosely in one hand, but he'd not even sipped it yet, and was only dimly aware of the classical music wafting delicately around the room from his iPod. Rachmaninov, some piano concerto or other. He didn't know which one, didn't care, all he knew was he liked its lyricism, its full-blooded Russian romanticism.

Earlier, he'd checked the door for signs of covert entry and had spotted the same marks Rosie Santoro had. He'd squinted at them, trying to gauge how fresh they were, but in the end couldn't tell. He'd examined the large windows, and even though he could see they were locked, he still pulled at them, the tactility somehow less than reassuring. He looked through the iron balustrades of the fire escape to the street below. SoHo streets are busy during the day but can be dead at night, and it would've been a simple thing for someone to reach the black metal fire escape and climb up. But once up, how would he have gained access to the apartment? He was satisfied the windows were secure and there were no signs of them being tampered with. If someone had killed Gina, they had to have picked the door lock and left the same way. And that meant it was someone who knew what they were doing.

If someone killed Gina…

His eyes drifted back to the still unmade bed, as they had done many times in the past few days. He hadn't slept in it, couldn't sleep in it. His couch wasn't the most comfortable in the world, but it would do for now. He looked away again, took a hit of whisky, and let the music soothe him.

He needed to tap into skills he thought he'd left far behind. He needed to become the logical, highly trained specialist his instructors had worked so hard to create, cool and calm in a crisis. He had to put aside the ache in his chest and think of the cause of it as a puzzle to be solved. He'd tried and failed in the nights he'd staying with Reuben. He'd tried since he'd returned to the apartment, but the memories were too painful and he gave up.

Now he knew it was time. He had to ignore the pain, ignore the grief. He had to take himself back to see what was not unseen the first time, but unnoticed.

He closed his eyes, thought back to that night, to the bar. He recalled faces, positioning, body language. The memories were fragmentary, for the alcohol he'd consumed had blunted the edge of his senses, but he was glad those months—hell, years—of training back then hadn't been wasted. Gradually, the music faded into the background and his brain sharpened, focused. He hadn't used that part of his memory for years. The ability to see the little things, the details people tend not to notice consciously, especially when impaired by too much alcohol, and then to pull them out of some recess of the mind. He thought it had died, but now he knew it had merely been lying dormant, for he was back in that dimly lit faux island paradise. He could hear the fake lava bubbling in the volcano, he could hear the clink of glasses, even smell the fruit as it was ladled into the various drinks.

And there was Gina—beautiful, wonderful, Gina—smiling at him, laughing with him, both of them rejoicing in the fact that there was no longer any need to worry about being seen together. As he visualized her face, the cold blade that had been lodged in his chest the moment he found her dead drove itself deeper, but this time he forced his mind to power on, to move to the people around them, the ebb and flow of the customers from the bar to tables and booths, carrying drinks, making connections, getting lucky, striking out. The faces came and went, the voices rose and fell, the movement slowed and froze until finally he found himself once again seeing the two men.

The two men watching Gina.

His body tensed as it sat in the armchair in his apartment, but Lang forced his mind to remain at that table. He'd seen them as he left the men's room. He'd thought they were looking at her with a view to picking her up, and he recalled feeling proud of himself as he thought, *eat your heart out, fellas, she's with me*. But now, with the benefit of hindsight, he knew that wasn't the case. There was something not right about them, something he hadn't noticed then. But now he saw.

They were both dressed in sober, dark suits, dark ties, white shirts, but that was nothing. One was tall, sat very erect at the table, thinning fair hair, serious face, rimless glasses. The other man was smaller, stockier, seemingly more relaxed than his buddy. They looked like lawyers, something the city did not have a shortage of. He'd thought then they'd come to the bar straight from the office looking to unwind after a hard day, and that certainly could've been the case.

Except they weren't drinking alcohol.

On the table before them were two bottles of Evian water. Sparkling, sure, but that wouldn't give them the buzz they needed for a pick-up.

And their focus was too intent, too narrow. They weren't checking out the bar. They were zeroed in on Gina. He hadn't thought much of it at the time, but now he was certain.

Then, as Lang had passed their table, the fair-haired one turned his impossibly pale eyes in his direction. In his chair, in his apartment, the concerto building to a climax, Lang frowned. He hadn't been aware of that look then because he was out of practice and drink had fogged his instincts but now, with that part of his brain reawakened, he saw it for what it was. Lang had seen that look many times before. It was the look of a professional. Of a predator.

He flashed forward to when they were leaving and his own glance back at the men. He'd given them a smile, a sign of manly one–upmanship. But now… yes… he saw that single-minded look on their faces. They weren't just watching her leave, they were *watching* her, period. And again, the tall one's gaze flicked to Lang, sizing him up. In his armchair, Lang squeezed his eyelids tightly shut as he tried to dredge up some other detail, something that would confirm his growing suspicions, something that he didn't consciously note that night but nevertheless had lodged there in his subconscious. When it came, he felt nerves tingle from the base of his ears down to his shoulders, his arms and on to his fingertips.

They had stood up.

Just as Gina and he pushed through the doorway to the street, the two men rose to their feet.

He willed his mind to focus on that, to replay what hadn't impacted at the time. His fingers tensed on the glass. He put himself back in the rear of the cab. He could feel Gina's body pressed against him. He could smell her perfume. He looked through the cab window. Saw the door of the bar. Saw it open.

Saw the two men emerge.

Saw them stare at the vehicle.

Saw them gesture to a dark SUV parked across the street.

His eyes snapped open. It had been a fleeting look, just a glance back at the street as he concentrated on the woman he loved, but it was there, in his mind, waiting to be accessed, to be analyzed. It could've been a coincidence. They could've simply been leaving at the same time.

Lang didn't believe in coincidences.

He knew.

He laid the tumbler of whisky on the wooden table beside him, not caring there was no coaster, then moved to the bedroom area. He slid the closet door open, shoved aside his suits and shirts and then crouched. He knew the cops had been poking around, but he was confident they hadn't found his safe, hidden behind a section of false skirting board. He'd fitted it himself shortly after he moved in, and it couldn't be spotted unless you knew what you were looking for. The rental company wouldn't be pleased if they found out, but he didn't give a damn. There were certain items he had to store securely. He gave the wood a tap on all four corners and the section popped away, just as it had been designed to do. He punched the combination into the compact iron safe and the door swung open.

He'd fitted this safe shortly after moving in but hadn't accessed it since because he'd never felt the need. He'd hoped he'd never have to. The contents of the safe were remnants of a past he'd intended to leave behind, a past he'd worked hard to leave behind.

The cell phone was old but functional. It could text but had no camera, no wi-fi, no fancy add-ons. He didn't bother pressing the power button because whatever juice had been left in it when he stored it away would have drained. He reached into the safe again, found a bulky, old-fashioned charger, and connected it to the mains supply.

The number was pre-programmed, so all he had to do was punch a button. He waited while he first heard a series of buzzes and bleeps and then a long, low ringtone. It rang four times before a man's voice said, "Designation, please."

"Janus Alpha, service number 103." The words seemed both familiar and alien to his ear.

The line was silent, but Lang knew he'd not been disconnected. He waited and a moment later the voice said, "Authorization code, please."

Lang's response came quickly, as if he had said it every day for the last ten years. "Lang, Coleman, USMC, ID tag Dagda six alpha."

More buzzing, then, "You're off the grid, Dagda."

"There has been a development. I need to talk to Odin."

"Odin is also off the grid, Dagda."

That was news but not surprising. Odin had been in control of Janus since its inception, but Lang had been out of the service— off the grid—for a decade. There was bound to have been changes at the top. "Who is at Olympus now?"

"Not relevant, Dagda. You're off the grid."

He sighed. He knew this wouldn't be easy, but the call had to be made. If Gina's death was not natural, and if it was connected to his past, then Janus had to know.

"I need to come in," he said. "I need to speak to whoever is at Olympus."

"Not relevant, Dagda. You're off the grid."

Lang could feel his temper beginning to fray. "I know I'm off the grid. But I told you, there has been a development. I may have been compromised, targeted."

More clicks and burrs. "Not relevant, Dagda. You're off the grid."

"Listen to me." Lang's teeth gritted to hold back the flood of curse words he so desperately wanted to fire at the voice. However, he knew that wouldn't do any good. The contact operative wasn't a machine, but he wasn't far off it. "A woman may have been murdered in my apartment. She may have been targeted in order to implicate me. It could be connected to my work with Janus. I need you to pass that up the line to Olympus. I can be contacted at this number. Can you do that? And for Christ's sake, don't tell me it's not relevant and I'm off the grid. If this is connected to Janus then it is relevant, and I may need to get back on the grid."

Silence, punctuated by the whistles and clicks as technology kept the line clear and untraceable. Lang also knew the entire call was being recorded.

Then the voice returned, still emotionless. If the operator had been offended by Lang's tone, or even aware of it, he didn't show it. "Are you using a designated device?"

"Yes. It's old but it works. Do you need the number?"

"Not necessary."

More bleeps, more crackles. Then...

"Stand by, Dagda."

The line went dead. Lang knew the matter would be passed up the line, but whether it would reach Olympus and whoever had taken Odin's place was unknown. All he could do now was wait.

10

Detective Barney Mayo climbed the stairs to his apartment, cursing the building's super for not ensuring the tiny elevator was fully serviced. Goddamn thing was always on the fritz and all because that son-of-a-bitch couldn't do his job. In the morning he'd wake the bastard up, tear him a new one, but for now he was tired and just wanted to get to bed. He was coming off the four-to-midnight shift, another round of junkies, thieves, pimps and drunks—and that was just his buddies on the squad. He smiled to himself as he thought of that. Shit, if he had one of those Twitter things he'd've put that out. But Barney Mayo was too old for such nonsense. He didn't Twitter, or whatever the hell the verb was, and the only Facebook he knew was the ones they used to use to keep track of perps. Anyway, he didn't have a PC, and his cell was so old it barely received calls now, let alone access the internet. He'd have to get himself a fresh one, but he dreaded going into the store because he knew they'd give him the big sell, try to get him to take some flashy space-age thing that did everything but wipe your ass. He couldn't face it, but he knew the day was coming. The battery didn't retain power anymore, and just today he'd tried to call his son in Boston, but the buttons wouldn't press. No matter how much he shoved, pushed, touched, caressed and eventually swore, the number wouldn't dial. His partner told him his keypad was dying. No shit, Sherlock, you go to the academy to learn that?

He'd be glad to get home, get his shoes off, pour himself a belt of booze. After that tour he deserved—no, needed—more than one. Around ten they'd been called to an apartment in a rundown tenement where a guy had gone postal, slit his old lady's throat in front of their ten-year-old-daughter then tried to off himself. He was still alive, last Barney heard, but chances were he wouldn't last the night. Girl was too hysterical to make much sense, but it seemed he'd snapped when her mom wouldn't let him watch the ball game on TV. Jesus, this city, he thought. He'd been with the department for 25 years, never got used to it. Didn't have anything to show for it, either, apart from an ex-wife, a son in Boston, bad feet and a duodenal ulcer that gave him merry hell. He reminded himself he only had a few months to go before he'd finally put in his papers and take up that cushy-tushy security job an old pal was holding for him. Sit on his ass all day, read the paper. It wasn't much of a job, but it would prop up his pension.

He reached his fifth-floor apartment, unlocked the door, clicked on the hallway light. He moved into the living room, didn't bother with the lamp here because the apartment wasn't that big and the hallway light was ample. He stood beside a small coffee table and unloaded his cell and his wallet with his gold shield— the only item of value he owned thanks to the goddamn divorce lawyers; screw them and his ex-wife, the bitch. He immediately regretted thinking that. His wife wasn't bad, she just couldn't take life with him no more, he wasn't no picnic, he knew that. Too long on the job, too long seeing all the shit that people can dish out, too long being on the defensive against opposing counsel, too long listening to people telling him that every cop on the force is on the take. He'd never taken as much as a nickel that wasn't due to him. Sure, he'd accepted drinks on the arm, who hadn't? But he'd never taken a bribe, never been on the pad, never been anyone's guy on the force. And there had been times, oh boy, there had been times when he'd been tempted, but he'd never done it, no, sir. Shit, maybe he should've. Maybe he wouldn't be living in a crummy one-bedroom shithole with a busted elevator, no wife and no goddamn savings.

The voice that came from the armchair beside the window made him jump.

"You need to put a better lock on that door, detective." Mayo's arm jerked towards the Sig 226 in its holster lying on the table top, but the guy clicked on the lamp beside his chair and said, "Take it easy."

Barney squinted in the sudden illumination, felt an initial surge of delight and then deep concern. "Jesus, Tony—what the hell you doing here?"

Tony smiled. "Came to see an old pal."

Barney bustled to the window, peered into the street, pulled the blind. "You crazy? Coming back to the city? What if someone saw you?"

"Relax, no one saw me. Came in under the radar. Country roads all the way from Nebraska." Tony stood and grinned. "You not gonna say hello?"

· Barney returned the smile. "Jesus, Tony..." They hugged, two old friends reunited. They'd grown up together back in the old neighborhood, two street kids who shouldn't've been pals but were. Tony's pop was a soldier for the Marino family, while Barney's wore the NYPD blue, a street cop as straight as they came. Old man Mayo didn't like his boy hanging around with the son of a mob guy, but there was nothing he could do about it. Pals will be pals, and though Tony was five years older, they'd remained like that into adulthood, even when Tony drifted into the rackets and Barney followed in his father's footsteps straight out of the army. There was space between them then, of course, but they still kept in touch, each one not wishing to step on the other's toes. When Tony was in trouble with the Marino family, it was Barney he'd turned to for help. Barney had convinced him to turn state's evidence, put him in touch with the feds and the rest was history.

"Jeez, *paisan*, it's good to see you," said Barney. "Lemme get you a drink, I got some whiskey in the kitchen..."

Tony followed him into the cramped space, watched as he fetched a bottle of Jameson's from under the sink, two glasses from a shelf, poured two hefty belts. Barney handed him one glass, raised his own.

"Best of times, worst of times," he said.

Tony didn't smile but raised his glass in the toast they'd used when kids. They'd read the phrase in a book, he couldn't remember which one. "Best of times, worst of times."

They drank deeply, each sighed as the liquor bit at the back of their throat.

"I heard about Gina," said Barney.

He saw Tony blink. "That's why I'm here."

Barney wasn't surprised, making him wonder if a hidden part of him had expected this reunion. "Helluva thing, Tony. She was a beautiful girl."

Tony stared at the cop. "Was she murdered, Barney?"

"Hell, Tony—I don't know. It happened way over in Manhattan."

Tony waited a beat, his face set in stone. "Barney, I've known you since we were kids. I know that even if cops didn't talk, you hear about this thing and you make it your business to find out about it, because she's the daughter of an old friend from the neighborhood. So I'm asking again, was Gina murdered?"

Barney poured another two belts, took a deep mouthful. Tony didn't touch his as he waited. Barney said, finally, "Word is, probably."

Tony closed his eyes tightly. Barney saw that even though the man had been prepared for the answer, it still brought pain. The girl was his daughter. He'd not seen her in years, but she was still his daughter. That didn't die.

"They know who?"

"They like her boyfriend for it."

Tony's eyes opened. "Boyfriend?"

"Some advertising guy, she'd been seeing him for a while. She was found in his apartment." He didn't mention she'd been found in the guy's bed. Some things you kept from the fathers.

"Why they like him?"

"He was the only one in the apartment apart from Gina. No sign of forced entry."

"How'd he kill her?"

"That's the hazy part. Word is, some kind of lethal injection."

"They taking drugs? My Gina?"

"Tony, buddy, I don't know, that's the truth. All I hear is that it looked like natural causes but turns out not."

"They made an arrest yet?"

Barney shook his head. "Not yet, but they're not far off. The loo over there, Santoro, she's one of those thorough types, likes to get her ducks in a row before she blasts the suckers. Guy isn't a flight risk; I hear he doesn't even know it's being investigated as a homicide."

"What's the guy's name?"

Barney shook his head, guessing what was in his old friend's mind. "Don't do it, Tony…"

"I just asked the guy's name."

"Tony, I know you, I know what's going on in your head. Leave it to the law, Tony."

"She was my daughter, Barney…"

"I know, but…"

"My GIRL, Barney. And she died alone. Before me." Barney saw the naked emotion in the man's eyes. He'd grown up with him, but he'd never seen him like this. Truth was, he didn't think Tony Falcone was capable of such emotion. Barney knew what his old friend was, knew what he'd done back in the day, but he'd never asked questions. As long as he kept his activities to his own kind, Barney didn't have any problem with it. It was a tricky moral line, but it was one he walked with confidence. As long as Tony Falcone only killed other scumbags, then it only saved taxpayer dollars in arresting and prosecuting them, was the way Barney saw it. Far as he knew, Tony had never moved on an honest citizen. Far as he knew…

"That shouldn't happen, Barney, kids dying before their parents. And this guy, whoever he is, he took her from me, took her from her mother. But worse, he took everything she could ever be.

And for that he got to pay. So—what's his name?"

"I don't know, Tony, hand to God."

"But you can find out for me?"

"Tony…"

"Barney, you can find out for me?"

Barney stared into the dark eyes of the boy he'd once run with and for the first time really saw the man that he had become. He didn't know where Tony had been for the past ten years, but he'd not lost any of the power that he'd first sensed back when they were kids. Tony'd been a leader back then. He still was. But those eyes held something else, something Barney didn't wish to dwell on.

"Sure, Tony, I can get it for you. But listen to me when I say don't do anything rash. Leave it to the system."

Tony patted him on the arm. "Sure, Barney, you've done your duty, you're a good cop. But you know I can't leave it to the system. This is something I gotta do, like in those western flicks we used to watch, remember? A man's gotta do, or he isn't a man, you know?"

Barney nodded, knowing there was something greater working here than a childhood love of old movies. Something cultural. Something Sicilian. Barney's Irish blood understood. "Okay, Tony, I'll do it for you, for old times' sakes. But you gotta do something for me. You gotta be careful. You stick your head out, there's guys out there waiting to cut it off, you know? Fat Vinnie is still around, and he hasn't forgot you."

"I can handle Fat Vinnie. Just you get me the guy's name and address. Leave the rest to me."

11

Fat Vinnie Marino wasn't fat, not anymore. Sure, back in the day he'd been a blubber fest, but when his poppa was put away and he assumed control of the family business, he decided it was time to slim down some. So he went on a crash diet, he stopped drinking soda, he checked out the fats and saturated fats in his food, he embarked on an exercise regime that would've made Rocky Balboa poke out the eye of the tiger. He lost the weight over six months. He'd been told that doing it slow meant those pounds stayed off, and now he didn't need to buy his clothes at the extra-large counter.

But they still called him Fat Vinnie, although not to his face. After all, he was the boss of the Marino family, not what it was but you wouldn't want to piss them off. The Italian Mob was down but sure as shit not out. The Colombians and the Irish and the god-damn Russians and Chinese had moved in over the years—Christ, it was like the United Nations on the streets now—and they may have taken over much of what Vinnie and his ancestors had built, but the Italians were hanging in there. Call them what you want, the Mafia, La Cosa Nostra, the Organization, the Syndicate or just the Boys, they were there and they were there to stay. Sure, it had been tough going for a few years, but the feds concentrated more on catching terrorists these days, which was how it should be, far as Vinnie was concerned.

He lived in White Plains in a pink house that pained him to look at, but that was what his wife wanted, and he always gave Violetta what she wanted, not because he loved her so much—which he did—but because she was one of three people in this world of whom he was genuinely terrified. The first was his father, old Guido, currently resident in Attica but whose reach still extended beyond those penitentiary walls to the streets. Violetta's own father had been a *capo regime* in the Bonaventura family, a fierce, dark-haired man with a temper like a cornered cat, which his daughter inherited. She was no beauty, which didn't matter because Vinnie was no John Travolta, but she was fiercely loyal and a good mother to their two kids. She was also pretty energetic in bed, something which Vinnie now fully appreciated having lost the weight. Before she would sit on him like she was riding a whale, but now they were able to experiment more freely with other positions and it had opened up a whole new world of pleasure to him.

The third person Vinnie feared was Nicoletto Bruno, although he'd never let the guy know that. The thing about Bruno was that he didn't look scary. He wasn't a big guy and he looked soft, like he'd had too much of his momma's pasta when he was a kid. Vinnie knew that he wasn't soft, though. He smiled a lot and he joked a lot. And he sang, it seemed like all the time. He'd be sitting there beside you, listening to whatever the hell you were talking about, and suddenly he'd start to sing, sometimes it was loud but more often than not it was quiet, *sotto voce*, as they said in the old country. He didn't have a great voice, but he liked to use it. He had a vast repertoire of songs floating in his head, and sometimes it was so obscure that Vinnie didn't recognize it. The boys started calling him Juke Box, and soon it was shortened to the Juke. Nicky "the Juke" Bruno. As nicknames went, it was pretty unthreatening, but that was the beauty of it. Because Bruno was a dangerous guy. Despite the singing and the joking and the smiling, the guy was so cold he'd give a polar bear frostbite. Vinnie hated having to deal with him, but with the international forces of crime always encroaching on his territory, he needed a guy like him on his side. And if there was one thing Vinnie could say about Nicky "the Juke" Bruno, it was that he was intensely loyal to the Marino family. And while he was singing and joking and smiling, his dark little eyes were always watching, and his tiny little ears were listening.

Vinnie punched in Nicky's cell number, and as usual it was answered with the guy's customary salutation in the heavy Sicilian accent he'd never lost, "Hey, you reached Nicky Bruno. Say what you gotta say."

Vinnie could hear faint traffic noise in the background. He envisioned the guy with the phone to his ear, smiling. And watching. Always watching. Guy gave Vinnie the creeps the way he was always watching.

"Nicky?"

"Hey, Vinnie, what's the happs?"

Vinnie heard the distant squeal of a siren. He didn't know what Nicky was working on—or who—but he wondered if he'd caused that siren to go off. "Where you at?"

"I'm around, Vinnie." The voice was low and rough, like Vin Diesel with a sore throat. "Takin' care of some business." He pronounced it busy-ness, like he'd not been in the goddamn country for years. Not for the first time, Vinnie wondered if it was all a pose, part of the Juke persona.

Vinnie said, "You hear about Gina Falcone?" He knew she'd taken her mother's maiden name, but he used her given name anyway, just to make it clear who he was talking about. Vinnie didn't know if the Juke had heard about the woman's death or not, so he told him anyway. "Found dead in some guy's apartment."

"No kidding?" The words came out so flat Vinnie couldn't tell whether or not Nicky was surprised. He could never read the son of a bitch, even though he'd been around him since he was a kid.

"Was thinking," Vinnie said, "it may bring that *stronz'* Tony out from under his rock. What you think?"

Bruno chuckled. It sounded like someone rattling some gravel in a tin can. "Could be, Vinnie, could be."

"Yeah, that was what I was thinking. I know you got a cop contact over there…"

"I do."

"So, what I thought was, you could tap him, get some details, we could maybe get the bastard once and for all."

There was a pause before Nicky said, "Sure, why not? I'll get right on it."

Then the connection was cut. Nicky was the only person who would dare cut Vinnie off like that, but he didn't let it bother him, mainly because the alternative was to let him it bother him and that could open up a can of worms that might just turn out to be goddamn cobras.

12

As soon as he hung up on Vinnie, Nicky punched in another number on his phone. He stood beside the open loading bay of a disused warehouse, listening to the ring tone as he sang a few bars of a Sicilian folk song his mother used to sing while also aware of the siren in the background. He'd heard the insistent wail of the cop car somewhere out there in the streets of Red Hook—his hearing was so acute he could hear a gnat belch—and had opened the wooden door to ensure it wasn't heading his way. He was confident it wasn't, but if there was one thing that had kept him alive all these years it was never taking anything for granted.

"Ralston," said the familiar voice in his ear, and Nicky turned away from the man in the chair, looked out towards the river again. He could smell the waters of the Upper Bay as it flowed past the foot of the building. It was like something rotten lived under the gray waters. He liked it.

"Hey, my old friend, what's the happs?"

There was a moment's hesitation on the line, then Ralston's voice dropped to a hoarse whisper, "Jesus, you know I can't talk to you when I'm in the station house…"

"Relax, baby, I called you on your personal cell, didn't I? What you take me for, some kind of *buffone*?" He sang two lines of "You Got a Friend in Me", then stopped suddenly and said, "What do you know about Gina Falcone?"

Ralston didn't comment on the use of the dead woman's old name. Nicky didn't think he would. They'd've made the connection by now. "What do you want to know about that for?"

Nicky said, "You think you want to know?"

Even down the line he could hear the cop's brain ticking before he sighed. "Her name's Scolari now, or was, anyway. DOA in an apartment in SoHo, her boyfriend's place. Looked at first like natural causes, but now it's being treated as homicide."

Nicky thought about this. "That's a crying shame, she was a beautiful girl. Suspects?"

"The boyfriend, is all."

"You got him in custody?"

"Not yet. My LT has spoken to the ADA and they both feel we need something more before they can go for an indictment. He doesn't seem to be going nowhere."

"And her father?"

"Not our concern. Her mother's been informed, of course. She's remarried, lives over in Queens with her new husband."

Nicky knew about that, but the former Mrs Falcone was off limits. The word had come directly from old Guido ten years before and that word remained law. He repeated his question, slowly this time. "And her father?"

"We don't know where he is. Feds play that shit close to their vest. But if he reads the papers, he'll know about it."

Nicky thought about this. He knew Tony Falcone, he knew he'd keep up with the news in New York, no matter where he was. It was easily done online.

"You wanna gimme the boyfriend's address?" His voice was, as ever, friendly but it was not a request. Ralston rattled it off in a whisper and Nicky committed it to memory. He didn't trust anything to paper. He heard a groan behind him, and he twisted round to look. Time to finish the conversation.

"Thanks, my friend," he said to Ralston. "There'll be something a little extra for you this month."

He disconnected without another word and turned back to the man tied to a wooden chair, his head drooping to his chest, blood dripping from his hands to pool onto a large square of thick plastic sheeting. This guy was a broker who had made the mistake of thinking he could skim some funds that Nicky had invested.

Nicky had been in the process of showing him the error of his ways when Vinnie had called. Some teeth pulled and a few fingernails wrenched off with pliers had loosened his tongue enough for Nicky to learn that his money was irretrievably lost, which was bad news for the banker. Any hope of getting it back might've lengthened his life, if only slightly. He didn't worry about the man's screams. This wharf wasn't used much now, and the warehouse was empty. There may be some bums somewhere out there, but they wouldn't hear a thing. After all, they never had in the past.

Nicky dropped his phone into the pocket of the long black coat that he had earlier draped carefully over the back of a wooden chair. He glanced at the wooden table standing beside it, an array of battery-operated power tools laid out in a row, then lifted an automatic pistol and a suppressor. Still singing "You Got a Friend in Me", he moved slowly across the floor, screwing the silencer into the muzzle. The banker looked up, and the pain that had filled his eyes earlier was drenched in terror. He mumbled something, but his lack of teeth made it difficult for the words to be coherent. Nicky didn't care what he was saying. Nothing he could say was of any interest now.

The man shook his head from side to side as if that would convey something that might divert Nicky. It didn't. There was never any chance it would. All that had to be said had been said. Nicky didn't waste any more words. He raised the weapon, aimed it, pulled the trigger.

The man's head snapped back, blood splashed first from his forehead and then almost immediately erupted from the back along with bits of bone and brain.

Nicky stared at him as he unscrewed the silencer again, blew down it carefully as he always did, and walked back to the table. The weapon was returned to its place. He regretted the loss of his funds, but money can always be replaced.

Loyalty, though, that was another matter. Loyalty and trust. The banker had breached both when he stole Nicky's money.

So had Tony Falcone. And for that he had to pay.

Nicky "the Juke" Bruno was still singing as he began to untie the corpse from the chair and stretched it out on a plastic sheet. From the table top he selected a sturdy power saw. It and the other tools would help make the corpse more easily disposable. Some of the body parts would be weighed down and dumped in the river that night, along with the overalls he was wearing. Others would be buried in the basement of a derelict property in Brooklyn. They wouldn't be alone.

13

Lang returned to work three days after Gina's death. Katherine Elkans, his boss, thought it was too soon, but he told her he couldn't sit at home and do nothing. The police had spoken to him two more times, going over the same ground. That was what they did. He knew they were suspicious of him, but there was nothing he could do about that. There was no word from Olympus, and that annoyed him. He'd given them years of top grade service, he'd been commended three times for Christ's sake, and now they were leaving him high and dry? On the other hand, given time for reflection, he couldn't bring himself to believe that it had taken ten years for his past to catch up with him. If Gina had been murdered, and he was not certain of that, there could be another culprit, but he couldn't bring himself to believe even that. Were Sophia and Silvio capable of murder?

In his office he stared absently through his window at the Chrysler Building across the rooftops. Zak Ustinov—no relation, he always said, mystifying the increasingly young people who staffed their industry—was talking about campaign ideas for a new computer game the agency was about to pitch for. Zak was a rotund little man with a shaven head and smart suit who thought fast, talked fast and could work fast. His team had put together a TV spot which they planned to screen to the clients the following day, and Katherine had asked Lang to sit in on the meeting. He'd paid little attention to Zak's fast-paced commentary, even less to the slick visuals on the LED. He contributed nothing, no ideas, no critique. He had no interest in the product, had never played a video game. This was yet another first-person shooter to entertain millions of young men and women who had no idea what it was like to aim a weapon let alone experience a firefight. For them, death was always in the abstract, on the other side of a screen. They didn't know what it was to pull a trigger and snuff out a life. They didn't know anything about the sights and smells and the muscles that twitched beyond death as if they had a will to live that the body as a whole had lost. They didn't know about the faces that could loom in the night, dead faces, and the voices that echoed in the shadows, dead voices. He hoped they'd never know.

He knew Katherine had noticed his lack of presence since his return, but she said nothing. She wasn't what you'd call gorgeous, her features were too severe for that, but she knew how to sell what she had—she was in advertising after all. She was tall, she was elegant, and she had a presence that more than one man had noticed over the years, including Zak who was so in awe of her that he would do anything, work on anything for any length of time, just to please her. He was wasting his time as Katherine remained totally faithful to her husband, even though he had passed away.

Lang was aware she was watching him as Zak wound up his presentation. He saw concern in her brown eyes. She thanked Zak, told him it was great work and sent him away like a little puppy with a bone. She rose and closed the door behind him, then leaned against it with her arms folded and stared at Lang. He knew her well and knew this was her *I mean business* pose. Odin had helped place him with the agency, and he'd not only shown a flair for the work, he'd become very fond of Katherine, a feeling he knew was reciprocated. When her husband died five years before, Lang had supported her through it. He'd collected her son from school when the young man's drug habit got him into trouble with the campus police. Lang had sat with him for three nights to keep him from climbing the walls. She didn't know it, but Lang had dealt, in a forceful manner, with a particularly enthusiastic pusher who didn't like to see a steady customer climb off the supply ladder. Katherine was like the sister he'd never had, and he knew she'd spotted his increasing disenchantment with the business but now, with what had happened, he also knew she would have to say something sooner or later.

He helped her out. "I'm sorry," he said, and he meant it. "I'm not much help these days."

She exhaled and relaxed, grateful that he had opened the door, and said, "I think you should take some time off, Cole."

"I'm okay, Katherine."

"No, you're not. You think I don't see that? Take some time off. Take as much as you need. Christ, Cole, you're grieving."

She'd been the only person he'd told about his relationship with Gina. She also knew all about his problems with Sophia and her brother. She had, in fact, urged two years before he finally took the plunge that he should get out of the marriage. She knew him better than most people, even Reuben, who Lang had known since college, and she could see everything. Her next words confirmed exactly how much she had seen.

"And Cole, you need time away from here. You need to reassess your life. You're free of Sophia now. You have no financial responsibilities in that regard. You need time to decide what you want to do with your life. Because, let me tell you, it isn't this."

He started to say something, but she waved a hand. "Come on, Cole, I've seen you around here this past year or two. Your heart's not in this anymore. Ten years ago you were pissing all over the place, keen to make your mark. And you had a knack for it, you know? Now you just go through the motions. Cole, I love you, I owe you, but you've got to decide what you want to do in life, because it's not this. Not anymore. You've lost the killer instinct."

The killer instinct.

If only you knew, he thought.

They talked further, but he didn't argue with her. He knew the time had come for him to make up his mind, and she knew him too well to be taken in by any bullshit he could come up with.

He left the office just before lunch.

Something told him he'd never be back.

* * *

He didn't want to go back to the apartment, so he walked the streets until he found himself in Central Park. Maybe, deep down, that was where he was always heading, he didn't know. Naturally, he found himself standing on Gapstow Bridge. Gina loved this little stone crossing, and he stood facing Fifth Avenue, the Plaza Hotel and, beyond it, the black glass of Trump Tower. Traffic roared, horns beeped and engines coughed fumes into the weak autumn sunlight, but standing there it all seemed to fade away. He leaned on the stone wall, ignored the people crossing the parapet and the tourists snatching photographs and stared down at the murky waters of the Pond below. And he thought of Gina. He thought of her alive and vibrant, not cold and dead. He thought of his life and whether his actions in the past had led to her death. He thought and he remembered and as he stood there, the trees leaning towards the Pond, golden even in the pale light cast by the gray skies, he felt the tears burning at his eyes once more. For the first time in his life he felt helpless. Although he had worked solo for years, had been in situations where he had only himself to rely on, he now felt completely alone.

14

Rosie Santoro rubbed her eyes and decided against another piece of nicotine gum. She was tired, she needed the hit, but she was so goddamn sick of chewing. She longed to place the filter of a Newport between her lips and fire it up. She thought of the grate of the match against the strike pad, the flare of the flame, the crackle as the paper and tobacco take light and then that first glorious inhalation, the one that really punches all the buttons. She sighed, as if mourning the loss of an old friend, and tried to fill the void with a mouthful of cold coffee from a Starbucks container. It didn't hit the spot.

She saw Ralston's face at her door and motioned him in. He had a yellow legal pad in his hand, and he seemed pretty excited. This must be something, she thought.

"We got us a break, LT," he said.

"In what?" Ralston would really have to narrow it down. They had three active homicide investigations, five sexual assaults, a clutch of grand theft autos—and they weren't a game—and a series of purse-snatchings. And then there was the usual round of drunks, punks and skunks.

"The Coleman Lang thing," he said.

Santoro was suddenly interested. "What you got?"

"Patrolmen were searching the area, just as you ordered, and they found a hypo in a dumpster about five blocks away."

"When?"

"This was yesterday."

"And I'm only hearing this now?"

"You were off duty when the word came in. The captain sent it to the lab for analysis."

That explained it. The captain was down at One PP looking for fresh asses to climb up, and so she hadn't crossed his path that day. Still, the inept son-of-a-bitch could've left a message. That's why they invented Post-its. She put her annoyance to one side. "So what's the deal?"

"Results came back in. Traces of…" Ralston referred to his notes. "Succ… Suxi …Shit, LT, whatever the hell it's called, they found it. But that's not the end of it."

Ralston paused. Santoro waited. Finally, she said, "So you gonna stretch this dramatic pause out much longer or am I gonna come round there and beat it out of you?"

He smiled. "They found prints on the hypo. You'll never guess whose."

"Coleman Lang," she said.

"Bingo," he said.

She reached for the phone to call the District Attorney's office. This was even better than a nicotine hit, she thought.

15

Lang knew whose limo was parked outside his building as soon as he saw it. He paid the cab he'd flagged on Fifth, keeping the limo's rear window in his peripheral. No one rolled it down, but he could feel the Senator's eyes on him. He always could. He knew he was in there, watching him, hating him. He wondered if Sophia and Silvio were with him in the plush interior, but as soon as he entered the foyer of his building he knew they weren't.

They were standing at the desk while Carl, the day-shift doorman, blocked their way to the elevator. Carl was an ex–Marine, a former gunnery sergeant who had served in Vietnam and ended his military career training new recruits, and was always ready to trade stories about the Corps. The two of them would swap banter, peppering their conversation with Corps slang. Lang much preferred Carl to the night man, Oscar de Blasio, and he felt a swell of pride when he saw him standing his ground, leaning on his cane, his weathered face set in the fierce expression that no doubt terrified the fresh bloods at Parris Island. He'd had his hip replaced the year before, but he hadn't lost any of his grit.

The Psycho Twins looked mightily pissed, and Lang guessed they'd wanted to go up to the apartment, but Carl was not allowing it. Good for him. Had it been Oscar on duty, Lang had little doubt he'd've found them waiting for him at his door. Lang had long suspected that Oscar had been keeping them apprised of his movements, now he knew. He'd never much liked the guy, something about him was off-putting. He'd been on duty that night, the night Gina died, and Lang really hadn't liked the way the man eyed her up and down like he was measuring her for something. As he and Gina entered the elevator, Lang had wondered if Oscar would call Sophia or her brother right away. Not that it mattered at that stage, for the divorce was final and there was nothing either of them could do about it. But still, he'd wondered.

"You got visitors, Mr Lang," said Carl. "They been waiting."

"This man refused to allow us upstairs," said Sophia, her voice heavy with a mixture of disdain and outrage that had taken years of breeding to perfect. The fact that a mere doorman had held sway over her would really piss her off. The fact that he was black was even worse.

"That's his job," said Lang, nodding his thanks at Carl, who gave him a little smile and limped around the desk to take his seat. Lang stared directly at his former wife, and when he spoke even he could hear the exhaustion in his voice. Whatever was coming he really wasn't in the mood. "What do you want, Sophia?"

Silvio stepped towards Lang with his familiar smile, the one that always seemed more like a sneer. He hadn't fared well in his scoop of the Manucci gene pool. He was small and bald and running to fat. His lips were fleshy and his eyes were slitty, and if it wasn't for the aquiline nose he shared with his father, Lang might've thought that he had been adopted. Close they may have been, but looking at them you'd never think he and Sophia were siblings. She was her usual elegant self. Her dark hair was expertly coiffed, her clothes expensively designed, her skin carefully smoothed. She was beautiful and she was composed, but Lang knew how quickly all that could turn to ugliness.

"We hear you've got yourself into trouble, Coleman," he said.

"And you came to see if you could help, right?"

Silvio's smile/sneer expanded. "The way the Senator hears it, you'll need help. Not that we'd be offering."

Lang looked over his shoulder at the limo outside, just to let both twins know that he was aware the Senator was sitting in the back. "I'm not in any trouble."

Sophia couldn't contain herself any longer. "The Senator says I was lucky to get rid of you when I did, otherwise I might've ended up dead like that little whore."

Lang felt anger flare, but he fought to suppress it. He asked again, "What do you want, Sophia?"

She pointed to a small box on the desk in front of Carl. "I wanted to return that to you."

Sophia stepped back to let Lang open the box and peer inside. He found a small, china teddy bear holding a heart. He'd bought it for her very soon after they met. "That was a gift," he said.

"I want nothing in my life that reminds me of you," she said. "Especially now that I know what kind of man you are. The Senator warned me years ago, but I didn't listen. He told me you were no good. He told me you were filth. He told me I was wasted on you. Now I know how right he was."

Lang closed the box again, knowing that she could easily have thrown the bear in the trash or mailed it back to him, but she had delivered it in person. She wanted another chance to wound him.

Silvio sneered. "You could've given it to your girlfriend, if she was still around."

Lang's head snapped towards him and the sneer froze, then slid from Silvio's face. His mouth opened as if he was about to speak again, but he thought better of it.

"Silvio," said Lang, his voice stretched tight as he held his anger in check, "you once warned me that you'd ruin me if I hurt your sister. I don't expect you to understand that hurting her was never my intention…"

"You didn't hurt me!" Sophia said. "You disappoint me, you disgust me, but don't ever think that anything you could ever do or say would hurt me because…"

Lang cut her off, still looking at Silvio. "But if I find out that you had anything to do with what happened to Gina? Believe me, you will know the meaning of hurt."

Silvio felt the heat from Lang's eyes and, even though the words were spoken softly, he knew they were written in stone. He squared his shoulders and raised his head in a bid to appear unconcerned.

"Is that a threat?"

"Look on it as a promise," said Lang, then he turned to Carl and nodded to the box. "Carl, police that, will you?" Carl plucked the box from the desk and made a show of dropping it in a trash can underneath. Lang and Sophia stared at each other, a cold flame kindling in her eyes. Lang gave her a wave of the hand, as if dismissing her. "Tell the Senator I said hello."

Carl had moved to the doors and opened them. "I reckon you folks will be leaving now."

Sophia's dark eyes burned into Lang. "I wish we executed murderers in New York," she said. "I'd love to see you fry on the electric chair."

He let that hang between them for a beat, then said, "Nice to see you, too. Always a delight."

She made an exasperated *tut*, whirled and swept out of the open door. Her brother gave Lang that smiley sneer and followed. Carl closed the door behind them.

"Mr Cole," he said as he walked back to his desk, "I hope I'm not out of line when I say you are better off without them?"

"You're not out of line. The marriage was a real goat rope."

The only time Lang ever used Marine jargon was with Carl. In this case, he was saying his time with Sophia was messy.

Carl grinned. "I hear that. And her brother is a hot-shit, you don't mind me saying."

Hot-shit. A guy who was too arrogant for his own good. Yes, that summed up Silvio.

Lang turned to the elevator. "Take her easy, Carl."

"Any way I can," said Carl.

The glimpse Lang had of the old man returning to his desk as the elevator doors slid shut was the last time he'd see him.

16

The call came at 6.30pm. Lang had just about given up on ever receiving word back from Olympus, but the old cell burst into life as he was preparing a salad. He'd not had much of an appetite since Gina died, his encounter with the Manuccis earlier hadn't helped his digestion, but he forced himself to throw something together. He'd carried the cell around with him since he'd made the initial call, and it sat on the work surface as he tossed the salad. He snatched it up, flipped it open.

"Janus Alpha, service number 103."

Crackles and bleeping, then, "Authorization code, please."

"Lang, Coleman, USMC, ID tag Dagda six alpha."

"Stand by, Dagda."

Lang couldn't tell if it was the same operator as before, they all sounded alike. He waited, listening to the electronics working to ensure the line remained secure. He knew what would be happening. The control operator would be patching the call through to another location, to wherever Odin's successor was based. That could be anywhere—a government office, an army barracks, a company boardroom. That was the secret of Janus, all the operatives were rooted firmly in the "real" world. Each one of them had two faces—the one they showed in their everyday lives and the one they wore as an operative. The roster was filled with tradesmen, doctors, dentists, phone company employees, computer specialists. Anyone who had abilities that Janus could use. Lang hadn't lied when he said he was a file clerk with the Marines. But he had other skills which had been utilized by Janus across the globe.

"Dagda, this is Asa."

The woman's voice was strong, rich and cultured. It was a good voice, one that inspired trust. The codename Asa would be from mythology, but Lang couldn't place it. Every Janus operative—and their opponents—were given names of mythological figures. His codename, Dagda, came from Irish folklore and was the ancient god of life and death. Given some of the jobs he had been assigned while with Janus, that wasn't far from the truth.

"Good to hear from you, Asa. How long have you been in Olympus?"

"Since Odin retired five years ago."

Odin had been the man who had originally devised the Janus teams and who had recruited Lang in its early days, although he'd never actually met him. They had communicated through intermediaries and on secure lines such as this, but never face-to-face. That was another one of Janus's strengths, no operative or asset knowingly met another unless Olympus deemed it necessary. In the main, they worked solo, under the radar, for the more people who knew of an operation, the more chance there was of it being blown. Occasionally, for complex operations, they would be teamed with one or more Janus operatives, but they knew each other only through their codenames. Lang had no idea how the upper echelons of the organization worked, only that it was an ultra-secret black bag operation whose structure was known only by a few—the President of the United States, the White House Chief of Staff, the head of the Joint Armed Services Committee and by Odin, or in this case, Asa. Its funding was fudged and hidden by various complex means. No oversight committee was privy to its operations.

"I understand you have yourself a situation," said Asa.

"So you've been briefed?"

"Yes, and I've done some research of my own. I've read your record, Dagda, and I must say I can see nothing in it that would merit a move against you at this late remove. You were efficient, certainly, but the individuals and operations with which you were

73

involved are all off the grid or deactivated."

Deactivated. Black ops speech for dead. Lang had deactivated many of them himself.

"Gina was a healthy young woman…"

"I know that, Dagda, and I sympathize. But I can't see what Janus can do to help. You are off the grid by your own choosing."

"I did my bit."

"Yes, you did, and I was very impressed by your proficiency. Odin spoke very highly of you in his notes. And three commendations, that's something of a record. You served your country well, Dagda, but in the end, it was your decision to go off grid."

Lang hadn't thought about that period of his life much—apart from the nightmares, of course, in which the faces and voices of the dead lived on. Even they had tailed off in recent years, the passage of time an unguent that eased a troubled conscience. He had been enthusiastic in the beginning, suffused in patriotic fervor, or perhaps the arrogance of youth. He'd joined the US Marines, became one of the few and the proud, and was tapped almost as soon as his Marine training had completed, for Odin had spotters in all walks of life to search for likely Janus assets. Lang had been a crack shot and had discovered an aptitude for self-defence which had surprised even him. Those skills, coupled with the facts that he had few family ties and had been a grade A student who had sailed through college exams as if he'd had access to the answers, made him an ideal candidate. Odin had sent a recruiter, one of his minions, and later spoke to Lang himself over a secure line. Work for Janus, he'd said, and serve your country in ways the Corps couldn't. Lang had agreed, and he was taken away for further training in skills the average jarhead would never need, then returned to his unit. The only outwards sign of anything unusual about his rotations was that he was transferred more often than other men, sometimes to hot spots, sometimes to locations nowhere near an enemy line, where he was immediately seconded to headquarters. Only Lang and Janus knew the real reason for him being in that part of the world. And, eventually, his targets.

He served for seven years before he burned out. The stress of maintaining a double persona—one face the affable filing clerk with a ready smile, the other the professional operative who sought out enemies of his country across the globe—took its toll. He recognized the signs himself: the questioning of orders, the slight hesitation before taking the kill, the increase in drinking. Knowing it was only a matter of time before he'd make a terminal error, he finally told Odin he was through. Odin took it very well, accepted Lang's own judgment, and ended the association. He was officially off the grid.

"Asa, if you've looked into this, then you'll know that the police do not believe this to be a natural death."

"I do know that."

"And you'll also know that they think I had something to do with it."

"I do. I also know that a Lieutenant Santoro has requested sight of your service record."

"So? She'd only see the official record." His real record, even if she gained access, would not just be sealed, it would be practically non-existent. Some trail would exist, for even in the world of covert activities there was paperwork, but that would be buried so deep it would never be found.

Asa said, "My understanding is that it is lost."

"Lost as in the Pentagon don't want her to see it?"

"No, lost as in it's been misplaced somewhere."

"Surely it's all digital now."

"Yes, but your digital record has been somehow deleted, too. It happens, Dagda. Yours isn't the only record they've lost over there. It's what your colleagues in the Marines would call a clusterfuck, am I correct?"

Lang couldn't help but smile. To hear the profanity used by such cultured tones struck him as funny.

Asa went on, "Usually they can restore it, but in your case the hard copy file has also been misplaced. They'll find it, I'm certain."

Asa sounded very casual about this, but inside Lang's mind alarm bells were ringing. Gina was murdered, he was sure of that, and then his service record goes missing. Shit happens, certainly, but was this a coincidence? Of course, it could be that the record had been missing for some time and it had only come to light because of Gina's death. Or had Asa, whoever she was, pulled strings to ensure that there was no possibility of anything being traced back to Janus?

To Lang, that was the most likely explanation.

"So, what are you saying, Asa? You're leaving me out in the cold?"

"Dagda, I wish there was something we could do, but as you know, Janus cannot interfere with civil authorities, especially as you are no longer part of the fold. I can, however, offer you one piece of advice."

"What's that?"

"Run. Run now. Because they're coming for you…"

And that was when the door was kicked open.

17

The man was small and dark, and the Glock 18 in his hand made a liar of the flower store delivery jacket he wore. Lang recognized a professional when he saw one. The gun barrel didn't waver, the man holding it in his right hand, the other steadying his aim, but he didn't move any further into the room. Lang froze, knowing that whatever he did the man would keep the weapon on him but not get too close. He forced his body to relax, to stay fluid, knowing that if this guy meant to kill him he'd've fired as soon as he entered.

Lang jerked his head towards the splintered doorway. "You ever heard of knocking?"

"Knock-knock," said the man.

"Who the hell are you?"

"Are you Coleman Lang?" Lang didn't see any mileage in denying it, so he nodded. The man said, "My name's Tony Falcone. Gina was my daughter."

That was a surprise. Gina had told him her father was dead. He remained silent as Falcone eased further into the apartment, his eyes swiveling as he took in the studio apartment, but always keeping Lang in sight.

"They tell me this is where she died."

Lang remained silent, wondering why the hell Gina had lied about her father.

"They tell me you're the man who killed her," said Falcone.

"I didn't."

"She died in your apartment, you was the only one there. She didn't die from no natural causes, she was as healthy as a god-damn ox. But she's dead."

"Not by my hand."

"Cops think different. Cops are on their way now to pick you up. I decided to get here first."

"Mr Falcone, why would I want to kill your daughter? I…" he still couldn't say he loved her. "She meant something to me. She meant a lot to me."

"So you say. But they found a puncture wound, like it was left by a syringe. Someone pumped some shit into her and that's what killed her. And you was the only one here."

Lang took the news in. Puncture wound. Syringe. Covert. This *had* to be connected to Janus.

Falcone had moved slightly closer but was still far enough away that rushing him was not an option. He was being careful. Don't get too close and you cut down the chance of leaving any trace of yourself on your victim. Lang could see a faint resemblance between this man and Gina now, maybe around the eyes. They were sharp, just like hers. And they had the same dark hair, although Falcone's was swept back in an old-fashioned style. Lang guessed it was dyed. Falcone said, "She never told you about me? About what I've done?"

"She said you were dead."

A flash of pain flitted across his face but then his features hardened again, and he said, "Well, maybe to her I was. But she was my girl. And someone took her from me. And someone has to pay."

He raised the gun and Lang knew this man was about to kill him. He could see the rage and the grief in his eyes. For him this was a matter of honor and it had to be settled by him, not the cops and the courts. Gina had said he was dead, there had to be a reason for that. He was prepared to kill, and Lang sensed he'd done it before. Lang knew the sort of man he was facing, and he'd finish the job he set out to do, no matter what he said. But he had to try, if even just to play for time.

"Mr Falcone, think about this. If I killed Gina, why would I do it like that? And in my own apartment? It doesn't make any sense."

"Cops think you believed it would be dismissed as natural. Almost worked, too, but for some detective smelling a rat."

"So what's my motive? Why did I want her dead?"

Falcone thought about this. "I don't know. I don't care. Maybe you're working for the Marinos." Something flickered in Lang's mind. The Marinos, he'd said. Did he mean the crime family? Did Falcone have something to do with the mob? He filed that away as Falcone raised the weapon slightly and said, "But here's the thing—motives are for lawyers and crime shows. I don't give a shit about motive."

"Yes, you do. Now, I don't know what happened between you and Gina, but I can see you love her. You want to kill me, there's nothing I can do about that..." Not unless Falcone came a little closer, but he knew that wasn't going to happen. His only hope was if he could keep talking and edge forward, then he might have a chance of taking that Glock away. Let's see how tough he is without a weapon. "But you want to get the right man, and hand on my heart, Mr Falcone, it's not me. The cops are wrong, I didn't kill Gina. She meant the world to me, I wouldn't harm a hair on her head."

Another couple of feet and he could rush him. Just another couple of feet.

He kept talking. "And if you're right and the cops are coming, then how's it going to look, you standing over my body with a gun in your hand? You going to honor Gina by killing an innocent man and then going to prison? That your plan?"

Falcone was listening, although Lang couldn't tell if he was getting through to him. He continued to close the gap between them.

"Someone killed Gina. I'm grieving, too, believe me. And I've got a couple of ideas who, but I can't do anything about them if I'm dead, or if I'm in police custody. Let me go, Mr Falcone, I guarantee I'll find out who did this..."

Lang was within striking range and was about to move when Falcone started to laugh and stepped back.

"What, you take me for, some kind of *buffone,* eh? You talk and you talk and you think you can pull one over? See, what you did here, all this talking has you got closer, tells me that you're capable of anything, *capisce?* Most guys would've been begging for their life about now, you know? But not you, you're cool, hell, you ain't even sweating. So I think maybe the cops are right about you. I think maybe you did kill my Gina and thought you could get away with it. And don't worry about me being here when the cops arrive, I'll be long gone."

"Kill me and you'll never know who really murdered Gina. Or why."

Falcone smiled, raised the Glock slightly. "That's something I'll just have to live with."

But the first bullet didn't come from his gun.

18

Lang's first thought was that they were cops, but there was no warning, no identification. Two bundled through the door at once, firing wildly, the bullets heading in the general direction of Falcone but not even coming close to threatening him. A third man in their wake couldn't get anything like a clear shot because his buddies were in the way.

Lang hit the deck and rolled, not away from them but towards them. He'd assessed instantly they weren't interested in him, but he wanted to get closer. He glanced back, saw Falcone was as cool as an open refrigerator as he dropped to one knee, took careful aim and fired. The gunman nearest him made a coughing noise and pitched forward, his weapon clattering on the wooden floor.

Falcone swung his gun towards the second man, but the third one was taking careful aim. Lang threw himself forward, palmed the dropped weapon—a Beretta 92FS—as he pulled himself to one knee, bringing the gun up, grasped his wrist with his free hand and fired once. He didn't hesitate. He didn't stop to think. It felt natural and easy and the thing to do. The third man hadn't even loosed a shot and never would, for Lang's slug blew away part of his chest.

He watched him fall, fighting the nausea that bubbled from his stomach.

He didn't want this back in his life.

Falcone dropped the remaining gunman with ease and then ducked behind the couch, ejecting his empty magazine and slamming in another. He peered over the back of the sofa, his eyes flicking once towards Lang and then to the open door.

The silence that followed the burst of gunplay was deep. Lang waited, the gun in his hand leveled on the door but his body was trembling. He had killed that man through pure instinct and was stunned at how normal it had felt. As if Dagda had never been away. He didn't look at the body of the man he had just killed, though. He could feel the bile burning at his throat, but something told him he couldn't afford to come apart. He focused on the open doorway for both he and Falcone sensed the same thing. There was someone else out there.

And then they heard it. Someone was singing. The melody was worn down by the rocks in the voice, but Lang could still make out "I'm Gonna Live Till I Die". He looked back at Falcone, saw the deep lines etched in his face and knew he'd recognized whoever was out there. And he didn't like it.

The singing stopped and the heavily accented voice that drifted in from the hallway was casual and even friendly. "Hey, Tony, long time, eh? I guess you ain't lost your touch."

Falcone's eyes narrowed and his tone was guarded. "That you, Nicky?"

"Yeah. Vinnie says hello."

Lang heard Falcone curse under his breath as he looked around the apartment for an exit. Whoever this guy was, he had made Falcone forget about him for now.

"Where you been, Tony? We been lookin' everywhere for you."

"I been around."

"Yeah? Good to have you back. We knew you'd make a play for this guy, sooner or later."

The singing started again, and Falcone's thoughtful gaze found Lang, who couldn't discern what was going through the man's mind. For his part, he was trying to figure what the hell was going on.

The singing stopped again. "You shouldn'ta come back, Tony," said the voice.

"Did you kill my Gina, Nicky?"

A laugh, but there wasn't much humor in it. "We got unfinished business, Tony. You, me, Vinnie."

"If you were behind it, Nicky, you know I'll kill you."

The man laughed again. "Sure, Tony, sure…"

The sound of sirens floated towards them from the street below. The shots would've alerted someone, but Lang knew the law had arrived far too quickly. They had already been on their way when they received the call about shots fired. Asa had said they were coming. Asa had said he should run, and it was good advice. He had to get away from the apartment, hit the streets, put some distance between him and the cops. He couldn't get to the bottom of this if he was locked away in The Tombs or on Riker's Island.

"We need to get out of here," he hissed to Falcone as he stood up. "Forget about your pal out there—he's gone."

Falcone looked unconvinced and edged towards the door. He eased it open further, peered out, looked up and down the hallway, then turned back to Lang. "How the hell you know that?"

"I know," Lang replied. He knew Nicky, whoever the hell he was, wouldn't hang around with the law so close. He knew how men like him thought, but he had no intention of explaining it to Falcone. There was no time. He looked around for the Janus cell phone, saw it still sitting on the low table behind Falcone, moved towards it. The man snapped his gun arm in his direction. Lang did the same. They faced each other over the couch, neither weapon wavering.

Dagda was taking over.

"You fired that thing like a pro," said Falcone, his chin jutting towards the Beretta pointed at the center of his forehead.

"You're no first-timer yourself," said Lang, his voice hoarse. He wanted to spit out the foul taste in his mouth, but it wouldn't do any good.

The sirens grew louder, and he knew it wouldn't be long before he heard tires squealing to a halt in the street below. "So, what we going to do, Mr Falcone? Stand here like extras in a Tarantino movie until the NYPD charge in and arrest us? We've got three bodies here, and it'll be kinda difficult to explain."

Falcone's jaw worked as he considered the situation, then grudgingly lowered his Glock. "So how we get outta here?"

Lang dropped his arm but kept the Beretta in his hand as he gestured to the windows. "We'll take the fire escape." He thanked God for the SoHo residents who had insisted that the old-fashioned iron staircases be retained. "We move fast, we'll get to the street before the place is crawling with NYPD."

Falcone must've agreed, for he moved to the window. Lang, though, crossed the room to the closet, slid it open.

"We ain't got time for you to pack a bag," said Falcone, but he ignored him and punched open his safe again. Reaching in, he hauled out a fat leather wallet containing his rainy-day cash. Then he swiftly moved to Falcone's side, without looking at the man he'd killed, and grabbed a thick woollen seaman's jacket from the coat stand by the window, then unlocked the frame and slid it upwards. He stepped over onto the fire escape outside, feeling the cold night air bite. He took a deep, cleansing breath, and it made him feel better, if only slightly. He peered over the balustrade to the street below, saw no one waiting, thrust the gun into the pocket of the jacket, then began to descend. He didn't look back to see if Falcone was following. He knew he would be.

Lang swung down the lower section of the fire escape and reached the street below just as the first marked unit screeched up to the front door of his building. He stepped back into the shadow of a small tree to wait until Falcone joined him, watching two uniformed officers dart into the building. He thought of the doorman. Somehow Falcone had bluffed his way upstairs by pretending to make a delivery, but how did the gunmen get by? Carl would still be on duty, and Lang hoped he was okay but feared the worse.

Falcone finally hit the street and let the hinged section of the fire escape swing back into place.

Lang asked, "You got a car?"

Falcone nodded. "I got a pickup, parked up in West Houston."

"Okay, we'll need to take the long way round." Lang whirled away from where more blue and whites had arrived and were clogging the narrow street. He turned his back against the revolving riot of flashing lights, thrust his hands deep in the pockets of his coat, hunched his shoulders and walked in the opposite direction. He didn't walk fast—he fought the urge to run, for he knew a running man would attract attention.

"You saved my bacon up there," Falcone said as he fell into step beside him, the words stiff and grudging.

"You're welcome."

"Means I owe you."

"I did it for Gina, not for you."

Falcone stopped, grabbed Lang's arm, pulled him to a halt, too. Lang shot a look back at the front of his building, saw an unmarked vehicle pull up and Santoro climb out. He wanted to press on, but Falcone had a point to make. "Maybe you're innocent, maybe you're not. For now, you get the benefit of the doubt. But I find out you killed my Gina? I'll take you out. Understand?"

Lang saw Santoro stop before she entered the building and stare at the crowd that was beginning to gather. It was dark but the street lighting was good, and he feared she might spot them, but they were a fair distance away and standing in the shade of scaffolding around a building under renovation. The detective turned again, spoke to a uniform who was in conversation with a young man. The young man was obviously trying to get into Lang's building, but the cop had prevented him. Santoro said a few words, shook her head then turned and vanished through the entranceway. Lang realized he'd been holding his breath, and he let it out slowly. The young man moved away from the cops and stared up at the apartments. Lang had the feeling he was seeking out a specific window. Was it his? A squad car passed by, and Lang saw the cop in the passenger seat studying him. It was early yet, but his photograph would be circulated just as soon as it was confirmed he wasn't among the dead. In any case, they wouldn't be looking for two men. Still, they had to get away from here and they had to do it fast.

"Mr Falcone, we can debate my guilt or innocence more later," Lang said. "Right now, we've got to move…"

19

They walked swiftly. Lang could hear the sound of car doors slamming but resisted the impulse to turn again. Turning was a bad idea. Keep walking, not too fast, not too slow. Light flooded from the closed storefronts, a few people came out of an upmarket bar and stared at the commotion. None of them paid any attention to the two men as they crossed the intersection with the much wider Broome Street.

He felt exposed here, as if they had emerged from a canyon onto a prairie. An itch irritated his skin between his shoulder blades as he imagined eyes drilling into him. They had to get off the street, somewhere the police cars couldn't follow. They could outrun a cop on foot, but they couldn't outrun a vehicle. He grabbed Falcone's sleeve, tugged him into an opening between the buildings, wedged between a store selling fancy ladies shoes and a design studio. He pushed the black metal gate open; he knew it would be unlocked, it was never secure. It was something he checked now and again because some part of him—Dagda—never knew when such knowledge would come in use.

The opening led to a communal backyard for the apartment blocks surrounding it, currently under renovation. From there he knew there was another alley at the far side they could take. He didn't think they'd've seen them enter, and they hadn't mobilized the aerial surveillance yet, which was a blessing. They had to get under cover somewhere to give them breathing space while he worked out how they could get to Falcone's pickup, because without wheels it would only be a matter of time before they were caught. The cops had no way of knowing yet he was with Falcone, so wouldn't know about the truck. Sooner or later surveillance cameras would pick him up, but there was nothing he could do about that.

He could hear Falcone's labored breathing as they pounded along the narrow alleyway. Lang had kept himself trim, but Falcone had obviously not read the chapter of the fugitive's manual that dictated physical fitness. He stopped when they reached the backyard, and Falcone doubled over, trying to catch his breath. Lang scanned the area, saw no one. He hadn't expected to. He saw piles of earth and deep holes waiting for something to be planted or built. Concrete slabs were piled at various intervals, wooden stakes neatly stacked awaiting to be plunged into the dirt. A small concrete mixer stood nearby. He looked at Falcone, who was still gasping.

"You okay?" he asked.

Falcone waved him away. "Don't worry about me."

His pickup was four blocks away, not too far, but dodging NYPD would make it seem longer.

"Okay," said Lang, "we can do it, but we'll have to take a circuitous route, just to make sure we don't hit any cops. You manage it?"

Falcone straightened. His breathing was better now. "I told you, don't worry about me."

Lang nodded. "Right, we'll head down here and…"

"POLICE! On the ground! NOW!"

The voice carried some authority but was young and thin and reedy. Lang looked back and saw what he would've assumed was a teenager if he hadn't been wearing an NYPD uniform. He was standing at the edge of the backyard, his service weapon drawn and aimed in their direction, although even from that distance Lang could see the barrel trembling. He wondered if the young cop had ever held his weapon on a real person before. Then he wondered how he'd managed to pursue them along the narrow alley without being heard. Where the hell was Dagda when he needed him?

Lang backed a few steps further into the backyard.

"Don't move!" The young man was so nervous there was a danger he would discharge his weapon accidentally. Lang held his arms out from his sides while Falcone edged behind him, his hand snaking under his delivery man's tunic towards the butt of his Glock. Lang shook his head, but Falcone ignored him and gripped the weapon.

"Officer, let us explain," Lang began but the young cop shifted his feet, firming up his stance and steadied his aim. He had guts, this kid.

"You can do that later. Right now I need you to get down on the ground, hands on your head, fingers laced and..."

The young cop suddenly stiffened and his arms fell away, the gun dropping. He seemed suspended for a moment, like a marionette, but then someone cut the strings to let him twist, his knees folding, his hat slipping away to reveal a sticky mess oozing from the back of his head. Lang threw himself to one side, Falcone dodging the other way, his weapon already drawn. For a moment Lang wondered if Gina's father had shot the cop, but he'd heard no report, and Falcone's weapon wasn't silenced. Then something puffed into the earth about a foot away from him, and he knew they weren't alone. He rolled, the trick being to keep moving and hope the darkness here would conceal him, while Falcone did the same, taking refuge behind a pile of slabs. Lang reached the concrete mixer just as another bullet pinged into the metal.

"You see him?" he hissed to Falcone.

Falcone shook his head. "He must be in the shadows up there, just at the mouth of the alley."

"You think it's your pal from outside my apartment?"

"Yeah. He must've waited for us to come down, the son of a bitch."

Lang peered over the top of the bucket, eyes trying to pierce the darkness, but he couldn't see anyone moving. The guy—Nicky, Falcone had called him—wouldn't have taken them out in the street, there were too many cops. Their running into this backyard was a godsend to him. The cop's body still jerked slightly, and Lang felt a twinge of sadness. The kid was just doing his job, probably thought he'd get a commendation. He must've seen them enter the alley and came after them. Why he was alone in the first place he couldn't even guess. Unless Falcone's pal Nicky had already killed his partner, which was possible. Probable even. The question is, had the kid or his partner, if he had one, called their location in? He didn't want to wait to find out. Another shot pinging off the bucket reminded him that it didn't provide much protection.

He whistled softly to Falcone to catch his attention. He pointed first to where they thought Nicky was hiding, then back at Falcone, made a gun out of his forefinger and hand, jerked his thumb like a hammer falling and pointed at the shadows again. He hoped Falcone would understand. He saw the man thinking about the sign language, then nod. Lang slipped the Beretta from his pocket, saw it was the gloss coat model which held 17 nine mm rounds, and slid the magazine free. He had ten bullets left. Not enough to wage a war but enough for this job, he hoped. He slammed the magazine back in place, clicked off the safety, held the weapon two-handed in front of his body and positioned himself into a crouch so he could straighten fast. He took a deep breath, tried to ignore the fluttering in his stomach, then gave Falcone a brief nod. Falcone closed his eyes—Cole wondered if he was praying—before he raised himself up slightly and loosed four rounds into the shadows. The returning fire came immediately, and a series of bullets ricocheted off the slabs, forcing Falcone to duck down again. However, Lang had seen what he needed. Nicky's weapon was silenced, but that didn't disguise the very slight muzzle flare in the darkness. As soon as Falcone was back out of sight, he straightened, swung his arms over the bucket, resting them on the rim to steady his aim further, and fired four bullets in swift succession in a pattern around the area of the flash. Then he ducked for cover again, back against the solid metal, his breath sharp and ragged. He waited, but there was no answering fire.

Falcone peeped round his pile of masonry, straining to see something in the darkness. "You get him?" he whispered.

Lang shrugged and waited. There was only one way to know for certain, he thought. He raised himself to a crouch again, readied the Beretta to fire if he had to, and slowly stood up, expecting a series of bullets to rip through his flesh at any second. He was fully erect before he began to breathe a little easier.

Falcone carefully got to his feet, his gun still aimed towards the mouth of the alley, then took a step towards it.

"Leave him," said Lang.

Falcone said over his shoulder, "Bastard might still be alive."

"Mr Falcone, if we don't get back to your truck and get out of this neighborhood within the next hour, we're dead meat."

Falcone didn't stop. "We don't finish him off, he'll keep coming, believe me. This guy's like goddamn herpes."

Lang sighed and moved warily after the older man, ready to snap the Beretta into play if he had to. Falcone reached the deep shadowed area, reached in his pocket and flicked a lighter to life. He moved the flickering flame back and forth, searching for a body, but there was nothing there. Lang stopped by the dead cop, knelt beside him. He was on his back, eyes wide open in surprise or pain or both. Lang gently cupped his hand over the lids, drew them shut. The guy couldn't've been more than 25 and didn't deserve to be lying dead in the middle of a construction site. He was too young for this. Then Lang recalled he'd been even younger when he was plucked by Janus from the Marines, and that by his 25th year he'd already killed seven people, two of them women.

And now he was killing again.

He looked over to Falcone, who was walking down the alleyway with his lighter still showing the way, then glanced back at the dead cop. He saw the gold band on the young man's left hand. Somewhere his wife was getting on with her life, oblivious to the fact that her man was dead. Lang wondered if there were kids, too, and felt sadness crush his chest. The cop shouldn't have spotted them ducking into the alley. He shouldn't have followed them. He shouldn't be dead. This was how Lang had felt towards the end of his time with Janus. He'd begun to see his targets as people and not merely operations. He'd begun to wonder about their personal life, whether they had family, kids, pets. It was a dangerous state of mind for an operative.

And then he remembered a voice from years before, Odin's voice, when he told him he wanted out.

You can run from what you are, but you can't escape it.

Odin had understood why he needed to leave Janus, but he also knew Dagda would forever be a part of him. Lang hadn't believed it at the time. Now he knew better.

Falcone came back, his lighter back in his pocket now. "Son-of-a-bitch is gone, left his gun behind, though."

"You left it where it was?"

"No, I brought it back with me, just so I'd get my fingerprints all over it and I'd have it in my possession if the cops catch me. What you think? This ain't my first rodeo." He made a disparaging noise and then went on. "There's a blood trail leading down to the street, so you winged him. I'd like to think the creep crawled away to die alone like a mangy dog, but I know him. He's got more lives than that guy with the ice hockey mask." He looked past Lang to the young cop's body. "His cruiser's out in the street, his partner's lying beside it. Guess Nicky got to him, too."

Lang sighed. Two dead cops. And they would be laid at his door, he knew it. Jesus, could this night get any worse?

And then he heard the clatter of the helicopter and over the top of the surrounding buildings saw the stab of a spotlight heading their way.

20

Santoro stood in the doorway of Lang's apartment and took in the carnage. She found it all hard to comprehend. In fact, the whole sorry state of affairs was difficult for her to grasp. First a young woman was murdered in a most bizarre way. Shooting, knifings, stranglings, beatings—hell, she'd even had one case where the vic had been purposely thrown into a hole where he'd been eaten by rats. Sure, the intent hadn't been homicide, but you put a source of fresh meat in with some starving rodents and you're sure as shit going to get a buffet.

But the woman was offed with some goddamn drug she couldn't even pronounce—jeez, it was like something out of *Murder, She Wrote*. She expected Angela Lansbury to walk in, solve the whole damn thing in time for the final commercial. They had the syringe with traces of the drug found a few blocks away, Coleman Lang's prints on it. That was careless. Sure, it had given her a solid reason to haul him in, but it was sloppy. And Coleman Lang didn't strike her as sloppy. Now there were three dead men in the suspect's apartment, an elderly doorman with his brains all over the nice white walls downstairs, the suspect himself in the wind, and to cap it all she'd just heard two blues had been shot to death near an alleyway with initial reports suggesting there had been an exchange of fire between persons unknown. Now the Deputy Commissioner himself was on his way from One Police Plaza to see exactly what she and her squad were doing to trace and secure this dangerous felon, Coleman Lang. That's the way the Commissioner's aide put it: trace and secure. Dangerous felon. One day she'd meet one of those guys who didn't talk like a departmental memo.

She popped some gum in her mouth and began chewing with extreme prejudice.

Ralston straightened from where he'd been kneeling beside one of the vics and joined her in the doorway. "I know this guy, LT. Sean Whelan, did a bit for armed robbery ten/fifteen years ago. Just got out last year. Been working as hired muscle."

"Who for?"

"Whoever will pay him."

She chewed some more. "What about the other two?"

He looked at the two drivers' licenses, both encased in plastic baggies. "This Leo Semple I never run across, but he has the look of a hired gun. Guiseppe Torro I heard of. The Bull, they call him. Marino family hanger-on."

Ralston had done a stint with Manhattan South's Narcotics Squad and been seconded to the Organized Crime Control Bureau for a while. He knew a lot of the faces in the Italian and Irish mobs, knowledge that had come in handy a few times since.

Wise guys, Santoro thought. Now we got wise guys in the mix. Her teeth worked furiously at her gum as she tried to see the whole jigsaw, but it was too mixed up and anyway, she didn't have all the pieces. Gina Scolari, she knew, was the daughter of Tony Falcone, but he'd been out of the picture for a decade or more. She didn't see Coleman Lang, a Madison Avenue smoothie, having much to do with the mob, but you never knew. And where the hell was his army record?

It was a mystery, and she hated mysteries. Screw you, *Murder, She Wrote*.

She heard voices in the hallway and poked her head out to see who it was. A veteran sergeant, name of Malone, was at the end of the hallway preventing a tall black guy with the face and body of a former football player and a good-looking red-haired woman from moving any further towards the crime scene. The big guy was dressed impeccably in a dark blue suit and crisp white shirt with a blue tie Kojak would've sold his lollipops for, but the woman was more casual in a thick sheepskin, blue jeans and brown boots. They weren't reporters and they weren't from headquarters, so she decided to find out what was going on. As she drew closer to them, she saw the big man wave a badge and right away she knew they were some kind of feds. She felt her stomach lurch at the thought, because federal involvement always meant trouble. Or at least, additional paperwork. And if there was one thing she hated more than a mystery, it was additional paperwork.

She stepped past a CSU pulling prints from the wrapping of a large bouquet of flowers that lay against the wall beside the door to Lang's apartment. Just another goddamn mystery. Of course, if this was TV, the CSU would solve the whole thing, even interview witnesses. Rosie hated TV cop shows. They made her feel so goddamn inadequate.

The red-haired woman hadn't said a word while her partner argued with Sergeant Malone, but it was she who became aware of Santoro's approach first. "You in charge here?" she asked, and Santoro detected some kind of accent from where folks shook rattlesnakes out of their boots and rode livestock for fun.

"Lieutenant Rosita Santoro," she said. "And you are?"

The guy pushed past Malone, who took exception to being shouldered out of the way like some rookie. He looked as if he was about to make an issue of it, but Santoro shook her head. Malone was also a big guy, he'd played ball at college and had as much respect for the feds as she did but, even though she might've enjoyed seeing him going toe-to-toe with Mr Suit here, it was a crime scene and they had more important things to do.

"Henry Burke, Lieutenant," he said, flashing his ID like it was an invitation to a party. "United States Marshal Service." He jerked a thumb at the redhead, and Santoro saw her bristle slightly. "This is TP McDonough, my partner."

"I'm here in a purely advisory capacity," said McDonough, prompting a pointed look from Burke. Right away, Santoro liked her.

Burke turned back to her. "We called at your precinct and they told us you were down here."

Santoro made a mental note to have a meaningful discussion with someone back at the house, "What can I do for you? I got a multiple homicide here and…"

"That's why we're here, Lieutenant. Our assignment may have a direct relation to your case."

Her stomach flipped again at the thought of paperwork she imagined was already piling on her desk just because she was speaking to them. "In what way?"

"Tony Falcone."

"What about Tony Falcone?"

"We think he might be back in the city. We think that whatever went on in that apartment was his handiwork."

Santoro chewed for a moment, her gaze flitting from Burke to McDonough. "So you lost Falcone from wherever it was you stashed him all those years ago?"

Burke said, "He wasn't in a maximum security prison, Lieutenant."

"Yeah? Maybe he should've been. Falcone's a stone killer. You ask me, he should've been put away and not living in the lap of luxury on the taxpayer's dime."

Burke sighed. "Lieutenant, I'm not here to debate the rights and wrongs of the Witness Security Program with you. But Falcone wasn't living in the lap of luxury and he made his own living, clear? And we're here to get him before he can cause any further mayhem. Now, we can do it on our own, but given the circumstances, I feel it would better if we worked together on this. Now, how does that sound?"

Santoro realized that whatever nicotine hit she'd had from the gum had been chewed out, so she unfolded a paper tissue from her pocket, held it to her lips and removed the remains from her mouth. Burke waited, his face impassive.

McDonough said, "You giving up smoking?"

"Yeah. I figure it's only a matter of time before they make it a felony to even think about firing one up."

"I gave up five years ago, it was hell. Tried everything, finally had to go cold turkey. I was like a bear with a burnt ass and PMS for two months. You tried the patches?"

"Yeah," said Santoro, thumbing another piece of gum from a blister pack, "but they stuck to my teeth."

Burke grew impatient, obviously not one for small talk. "Lieutenant, what do you say? We working together or what?"

"I'll tell you what, that's a decision above my pay grade. The Deputy Commissioner's on his way now, why don't we wait till he gets here and you and him can have a nice little chat about it. In the meantime, I'll get on with my job, which is finding Coleman Lang."

"Lieutenant…"

His constant use of her rank was beginning to piss her off. "Deputy Marshal Burke, let me tell you what I know here. I got one dead woman, and her boyfriend is my only suspect. I got enough bodies in this building to fill a goddamn morgue and another two—police officers, I might add—down the block. I got my guy in the wind. Now you come along and tell me that some wise guy from back in the day is in town and on a killing spree. You got evidence of that? You got an eye-witness who places him at this scene? You even got anything concrete that he's back in my city? You show me that, I'll play ball. Or you wait till my boss gets here and convince him to order me to cooperate. In the meantime, I need you to go back downstairs and out to the street, because this whole area is a crime scene and I wouldn't want you to get any blood on that fancy suit."

Santoro knew she had taken the wrong approach, she knew they'd get the authority to insert themselves in her investigation, but she didn't give a damn. Burke had pissed her off. Feds always pissed her off. Hard lines etched in Burke's face as he listened to Santoro's speech, of which, despite knowing she was wrong, she was inordinately proud. McDonough obviously enjoyed it, for her green eyes sparkled. Santoro had suspected her crack about being there in an advisory capacity meant there was little love lost between her and her partner, now she knew for certain.

She jerked her head towards the uniformed sergeant and said, "Mike, please show them the way to the street."

Burke was about the take the matter further, but Malone stepped in front of him and said, "The elevator's that way, sir. And please mind the step when making egress from the building. Wouldn't want you falling on your ass."

Her back to them as she returned to the apartment, Santoro grinned. Egress, she thought. Malone's been reading again.

She'd just reached the door to the apartment again when Ralston came rushing out, a cell phone in his hand. "We got 'em, LT," he said. "Units in pursuit…"

21

Lang couldn't be certain what any eye witnesses in the surrounding buildings had seen in the back lot. They'd certainly have heard the gunshots, but he was fairly sure it was too dark for anyone to make them out clearly. Nevertheless, he didn't want to take any chances. With the helicopter buzzing around and other units on their way, he knew they'd be bottled in pretty damn quick, so he decided it would be best if they stole a car.

They left the lot quickly, sticking to the shadows, pausing whenever the helicopter hovered overhead, keeping track of the searchlight as it swung up and down the buildings and roamed across the ground like some luminous creature. They stayed off the main streets, avoided pedestrians when they could, walked casually when they couldn't to avoid creating suspicion. They ducked along alleys, through yards, over walls and fences. Tony, though, was not in the first flush of youth, and Lang became aware the man was flagging. Also, it was only a matter of time before they attracted some unwanted attention—all the skulking around dark corners was not exactly the act of men with nothing to hide.

When he posed his idea to Tony, as they hid in the doorway of a bakery to avoid a patrol car zooming by, the man looked dubious.

"Been a while since I boosted a car," he said. "They got security now, immobilizers, alarms, all kinds of shit."

Lang was way ahead of him. He'd spotted an old model Ford across the street. It didn't look as if it had moved in a while, and he hoped it was still operational. When the cruiser was long gone and the chopper was far enough away, although they could still hear it, they sprinted across the road where they lingered while they checked no one was around. SoHo streets can be very quiet at night—they were dead this night, which was lucky for them. Either the TV schedules were unmissable or word had spread and a lot of people had gathered outside his building, for this was real-life drama. When he was fairly certain it was as safe as it could be, he pulled out his pocketknife and selected the screwdriver blade. He twisted it in the lock a few times, felt it give and pulled open the door. Falcone watched the ease and speed with which the door was forced and said, "You done this before?"

Lang shrugged. He wasn't about to share anything with the man just yet. He slid into the driver's seat while Falcone ran round the hood and into the passenger seat. The car was spotless—it may've been old, but it was well cared for. He felt guilt stab at him over what he was about to do, but he was desperate. He made a promise to himself that when all this was over, he'd find the owner and make reparations for the damage. He used the butt of the Beretta to batter open the casing around the ignition lock, hauled out the tumbler, checked the wires were all intact, then thrust the point of the screwdriver in the lock. He twisted it a few times, heard the ignition switch turn, and the car coughed into life.

Falcone gave him an appraising look. "You know, first I saw you, first I heard about you, I think, this guy's a powder puff."

Lang jerked the gear lever, pulled away from the curb. "No, you thought I was the man who killed your daughter."

"Yeah, that too. But now? I see the way you dropped that guy in the apartment, the way you handled Nicky, now you're boosting automobiles like a goddamn street punk. I wonder just what the hell are you?"

"I'm complicated." He left it at that. "Tell me about this guy Nicky."

Falcone snorted. "Always gave me the creeps, that guy. They call him the Juke, on account of the singing, you know?"

"Why does he want you dead?"

Falcone fell silent, and Lang thought for a moment he was going to clam up, then realized the man was gathering his thoughts. "I was one of the boys, you know? Until about ten years ago."

"One of the boys? As in the Mob?"

"Yeah, call it what you want, but I was in it. But it all changed, you know? Used to be we were kings of the city, masters of the goddamn universe. Used to be. But then the Colombians came in and the Russians and the Chinese and Koreans and the South Americans and soon we were all chasing the same dollar. But the feds made us their priority—us. We were goddamn Americans, and they made us public enemies number one while all these other guys, these immigrants, came in here and took over our streets and our businesses."

Lang figured Falcone wasn't big on the welcoming of poor, huddled masses section of the USA's public relations. "So you got out?"

"In a manner of speaking, yeah. I was working with the Marino family, you heard of them?" Lang nodded. Organized crime had not been something with which Janus had concerned itself, but he did read newspapers. "Made a good living, too, but then it all turned to shit when Fat Vinnie took the reins from his pop. Old Guido had been a steady hand, but Vinnie, he was a piece of work, you know? He had guys whacked just for calling him Fat Vinnie. And he *was* fat, believe me, had a gut on him that had its own weather system, you know what I'm sayin'? Guido was still in the picture, but he'd taken a step back, was lettin' his kid run the show. But then, a few years back, Vinnie heard I was making a few bucks on the side sellin' some porno DVDs made by a guy I knew over in Jersey. This wasn't no sick shit, you understand, this was just straight up jerk-off material, no kids or nothing like that. Anyway, I wasn't giving Vinnie his cut, and he took exception to this and ordered that I be whacked. I mean, just for taking a coupla bucks on the side, this nutjob wants me dead?"

He fell silent for a moment as he thought about this injustice and shook his head slightly. Lang drove carefully through the streets, keeping his eye out for the cops and for anyone following. He didn't like Falcone's buddy Nicky being out there somewhere, wounded or not.

"So, I hear about it and I give Guido a call." Falcone was talking again. "I spill that I've been a bad boy, kept some bills from him but hey, it wasn't a big enough deal for his boy to punch my ticket over. Now Guido, he's semi-retired like I said, tending to his goddamn tomato plants up there in White Plains like he's Vito Corleone, but he tells me that it's not about the money, it's about respect. Respect, Jesus! Let me tell you somethin', Guido Marino still has the first dollar he ever made. He didn't give a damn about respect, he just wanted the green. So right there I know he's given the nod to the whack order, and him and his no good, blubber-gut of a kid are in this together. So, I hang up and go to the feds, blow the whistle on the whole thing."

"You turned state's evidence?"

"You bet your ass I ratted the bastards out! They think I'm just gonna sit there and wait for the goddamn Juke to put one behind my ear? I was separated from Gina's mom by that time. Gina was at law school, she didn't need me no more."

"She told me you were dead."

Falcone was silent once more, and when he spoke his voice was low and soft. "Yeah, well, I guess to her I was. I did my thing in court, blew the Marino operations wide open, old Guido and his brother and a coupla the top guys were put away on RICO beefs, Vinnie skated free somehow, goddamn lawyers."

"Gina was a lawyer and a damn good one."

"Yeah, but there's lawyers and there's the pieces of shit who push and probe until they find some technicality that lets a nut job like Fat Vinnie Marino back out on the streets."

"So you were put into Witness Protection?"

"Yeah, a shithole of a town out west. They set me up in a pizza joint, so I spend my days serving food to cowpokes and farm hands."

Lang said, "Tell me more about Nicky the Juke."

"Ain't much to tell. He's Vinnie's attack dog. He might seem like an okay guy, but believe me, he got no respect for human life, none at all. I've killed people, don't get me wrong, I'm a bad guy, but the Juke? He's a piece of work. And I'll tell you this—he won't give up. You might've hurt him tonight, you might've hurt him bad, but he'll get himself patched up and he'll come after us again. You can make book on that."

"Come after you again, you mean."

Falcone's face tightened in a grim little smile. "I wasn't the one who shot him."

Lang sighed. He thought he'd left violent death in his past, but here it was back again, unbidden, unwanted. It hadn't been part of him for ten years, not consciously. He thought he was a different man. He'd been growing increasingly disenchanted with his new career, certainly, but he would've stuck at it for Gina. He'd never have admitted it at the time, but he'd harbored hopes of a future with her, of building another new life, of buying a house, over in Westchester maybe, New Rochelle, Scarsdale, somewhere like that. He'd even begun to check out the real estate ads, telling himself he was just browsing but knowing deep down it was more than that. He was looking to really, finally, properly settle down. With Gina. But the hopes and dreams of Cole Lang lay cold and dead on a morgue slab while Dagda breathed again.

"These mob guys," he said. "How bad do they want you dead?"

"I'd say so bad they can taste it."

"Would they have had Gina killed to draw you out? I'm guessing they'd've known that was the one thing that'd make you come running."

"Yeah, sure, Nicky the Juke, even Fat Vinnie, woulda done that easy, but for one thing—old Guido. He's a greedy piece of shit, but he's kinda old fashioned and would never involve family. Even though me and Gina's mom weren't together, even though Gina didn't call herself Falcone no more, they were still family, and you don't touch family in Guido's eyes. Now, maybe when the old man is gone, yeah, cos Fat Vinnie don't have no morals, no honor. But not till then."

"Maybe the old man's losing his grip. He's in jail."

Falcone snorted. "Jail don't stop him from running things."

"I thought Vinnie ran the business."

"Yeah, but Guido runs Fat Vinnie. Nah, the old man would never sanction a hit on my daughter."

"But the Juke could be working independently..."

"You don't understand, Nicky is the Marinos' guy. Apart from a coupla businesses they let him run, he don't work independent. It's one of his few whatchamacallits, saving graces, this loyalty he has to the Marinos. Sure, he don't think much of Vinnie, never has done, but Guido says he's the boss, so he's the boss. And if Guido says you don't touch family, you sure as shit do not touch family. That's it. It's like Moses came down off the mountain and decreed it. That's the law."

Lang wasn't so sure and decided that next time he and Nicky the Juke crossed paths, he'd make sure they had a conversation.

"Anyway," said Falcone, settling back in his seat, "I've not crossed you off my list of suspects. Don't forget that. And it's a short list."

"I loved your daughter, Mr Falcone."

There, he'd said it. He was surprised he'd said it, and he instantly regretted never having said it to Gina.

Falcone glanced at him. "So you say, but I saw the way you handled that gun back there, and that makes me wonder about you."

Lang had nothing to say to that. Falcone had told him about his past, and he knew some sort of code required he do the same, but he couldn't bring himself to do so. It was more than just his training holding him back. He had killed a man in the apartment without a second thought. Had he managed a kill shot with Nicky, he wouldn't've have shed a tear. There was a part of him that was roaring back to life, and he didn't want to face it by talking about Janus. He knew Falcone was waiting, and when he didn't respond the man sighed, slumped down and stared through the window.

They drove the rest of the way in silence. Falcone had told him he'd parked the pickup on West Houston, and they found it still there, sitting in a restricted parking zone. He'd been lucky it hadn't been towed or hog-tied with a Denver Boot. Lang dumped the stolen car at the corner—he didn't think a parking violation would contribute much to any jail term he could expect—and they walked slowly towards the truck. They could still hear the helicopter whirring in the night sky, and cars slid by on the street. No traffic at all would've been preferable, but this was the city that never slept. He wished it would go for a little nap.

Falcone unlocked the truck, climbed into the driver's seat while Lang walked round and got in the other side. Falcone had taken the Glock from his pocket and laid it on the seat beside him. He peeled off his delivery man's tunic and pulled a sheepskin jacket out from behind the seats.

Lang watched him, then asked, "What did you do to Carl?"

Falcone thrust his arms into the thick sleeves of the jacket. "Carl who?"

"The doorman at my building. How'd you get past him?"

"I waited till he went for a leak, slipped past him. Doormen got needs, you know? What, you think they sit at that desk for 12 hours without moving? Had this pansy-assed jacket and some flowers as a back-up, in case the guy was superhuman or somethin', but I stole it for nothin'."

Seeing no evasion in Falcone's eyes, he accepted his word. He doubted, though, if Nicky the Juke would've been so considerate and felt sadness wash over him again. He looked around him, took in the empty fast food bags, soda cans and plastic water bottles kicking around the floor. He guessed Falcone had spent some time in the truck, no doubt driving from the shithole he'd talked about out west. He was too smart to risk traveling by air or rail.

Falcone keyed the ignition but didn't pull out. "So where to?"

Lang paused. He'd only thought as far as getting to the truck, which annoyed him because he should've had a game plan all mapped out. But he hadn't. He'd been out of the game too long. His instincts were still sound, he'd learned that already, but the ability to plan out the moves ahead like pieces of a chessboard had not yet reawakened.

The priority was get out of SoHo, find somewhere to hole up. There was every possibility that they had been picked up on street cameras and alerts issued, so they had to move and move fast. They'd also have to ditch the pickup soon, but for now it was useful.

His first thought was Reuben, but the only cell he'd picked up was the dedicated Janus line, and he didn't want to use that in case it was being monitored. Asa had told him to run just before Falcone arrived, but he didn't think that was the reason for the warning. She had known the police were on their way to arrest him and was perhaps even cooperating with them somehow. If Janus was monitoring the line, he didn't want them to know where he was going. Janus might also have a tap on Reuben's line, but he'd have to risk that.

"You got a phone?" he asked.

Falcone handed over a cheap phone which had obviously been bought in a supermarket. "It's okay, it's a burner," he said.

Lang punched in Reuben's number, listened to it ring a few times before he heard his friend's sleepy voice say, "Hello?"

"Reuben, it's Cole."

"Cole?" Reuben still sounded half asleep. "Jesus—you know what… I mean, Christ… sorry, fell asleep in my chair here." He was waking up fast. "What's up? You okay? Is it the police again?"

"I don't have time to explain, but I need help. Can we meet up?"

"Sure, come round…"

"No, I don't want to come to your apartment—and believe me, you don't want me there either. No, let's meet somewhere…"

"What, now?"

Lang thought about this. If Reuben left now it would seem suspicious. The chances were the police would assume he'd contact his lawyer, but it was too soon for them to have surveillance running on him, and, in any case, to do that to a respected member of the New York Bar Association was risky. Whoever killed Gina would also know about their connection, and they may already be watching him. If Janus was keeping tabs on Lang, then they could very easily be watching Reuben—and even listening to this call. Shit, maybe he shouldn't have called.

"No, it'll keep till tomorrow," he said. "Remember the dislocated finger?"

There was a pause as Reuben tried to decipher Lang's question. Then he remembered. "Sure…"

Two years before, they had been throwing a frisbee at Battery Park, near where the Liberty Island ferry docked. Reuben slipped, landed badly, threw his middle finger seriously out of whack—it was bent at a right angle from his hand. He bitched about it for months afterwards.

"Meet us there tomorrow," said Lang. "10am."

"Us? Who's the 'us'?"

Lang glanced at Falcone, decided against trying to explain. "Never mind that now. Tomorrow, Reuben. And watch your back."

Reuben knew better than to pursue it. He was smart enough to join whatever dots he could see, and he now knew that Lang was ducking the law. "Okay, I'll be the one looking furtive. Cole, I've got to say this as an officer of the court—whatever has happened, come in, let me sort it all out through proper channels."

Lang shook his head, even though Reuben couldn't see it. "No. I'm being set up here for some reason, and there may be cops involved."

"What? You think NYPD is part of some conspiracy?"

"No, not the whole department but certainly one, maybe two. And they may think they're doing the right thing. There's more to this than we think, Reuben, I know it." He glanced in the wing mirror, saw a police cruiser had pulled in behind them. He hung up without saying anything further and handed the cell back, cursing himself and Falcone for momentarily letting their guard down. He saw Falcone's hand edge towards the weapon he'd laid on the seat between them so he laid his own hand gently on the man's arm and whispered, "No shooting."

One of the uniformed cops knuckled the driver's window while his partner stood a few feet away on the sidewalk, his hand on the butt of his weapon. The cop's voice came through the glass. "Sir? Would you mind opening your window?"

Falcone made a show of rolling the window down with one hand, while with the other he levered the truck into "Drive". "Can I help you, officer?"

The cop took a step back. He was wary, Lang sensed, and understandably for there had been a multiple homicide a few blocks away and news of the two downed officers was bound to be out by now. "You know you're parked in a restricted zone?"

Falcone did his best to look innocent and almost succeeded. "I'm very sorry, officer, I just pulled over to take a phone call." He held up the cell phone still nestling in his hand. "It's dangerous to drive and talk on the phone."

The cop obviously wasn't buying it. His eyes flicked from Falcone to Lang, and something clicked. It had been almost an hour since they'd fled the building, more than enough time for NYPD to circulate his picture. It was just a brief flash of recognition, a widening of the eyes, a tightening of the muscles, but Lang knew.

"Drive!" he yelled, and Falcone responded immediately. The pickup lurched forward just as the cop drew his weapon, screamed at them to stop, then let off a round, which went wild. His partner moved, too, pulled his gun and fired. His aim was better, and bullets thudded into the rear of the truck as it veered into the street, swung round a Toyota that seemed to be dawdling, and careered west. He looked in the side mirror and saw the cops leap into their cruiser and follow them.

"Shit!" he said.

Falcone glanced in the rearview and muttered, "*V'fancul*". Lang didn't know what it meant, but he could make a guess.

"Can you lose them?"

107

Falcone said nothing but spun the wheel sharply right and sped towards the next intersection where he swung left.

Lang said, "You know this is a one-way street?"

Falcone ignored him again, just as he ignored the screech of tires and the angry blare of a horn as an oncoming car swerved to avoid him. Another two cars spun out of his way as he roared ahead as if he was playing chicken, the police car hard on his tail. They could see more red lights flashing and coming their way.

"*V'fancul*," Falcone said again, and Lang knew for certain it wasn't something you'd say in church. Figures were silhouetted in squares of light in the apartment blocks overlooking the roadway. Ordinary people who lived ordinary lives for whom the roar of the engines, the whoop of the police siren and the sound of gunfire was merely an extension of what they saw on TV. Once the sounds died, they'd return to the pretend world of the box and perhaps in the morning they'd check the news or social media to see what the fuss was all about. Lang wasn't a part of their world, not now. Maybe he never had been.

Falcone twisted the wheel sharply to the left and bounced into a narrow alleyway, the buildings on either side less than six inches from the panels of the truck and tearing off both wing mirrors. Lang tried to remain calm as he said, "You know where this goes?" Falcone gave him a look that told him to shut the hell up, so he did. He craned over his shoulder, looked through the glass panel behind them, saw the police car had followed them into the alley, its blues and twos flashing, its siren wailing. They would've called it in, and it wouldn't be long before other units joined the pursuit. He was about to ask Falcone what the plan was when the truck came to a sudden halt.

"Out, now! Leave the door open." Falcone had already grabbed his Glock and his travel bag and was throwing himself from the truck. Lang squeezed out and realized what Falcone had done. He'd found a point where the alley walls veered away, allowing them to open the doors enough to get out. As he followed Falcone down the lane, he heard the cruiser's tires crunch on the hard ground and the cops swearing as they tried to open their doors but hit solid wall on either side. Lang looked back, saw a weapon being clumsily aimed out and over the barely open door. There was a half-hearted call for them to stop—they were suspected in the murder of brother officers, after all—and then the crack of gunfire. The bullet whined over Lang's head, so he ducked to present as small a target as possible and zig-zagged. Falcone, just a couple of feet ahead, glanced back, saw what he was doing and did the same.

They could hear more sirens now and they had no idea what they would meet when they burst out the other side of the alley, but there was nowhere else to go. They emerged onto West Houston again, turned right and ran towards a playground at the intersection with Sixth. They climbed the wire fence, dropped down into the darkness beyond and found a space among some bushes to catch their breath.

A cruiser zoomed past, its lights bouncing off the walls behind them and they hunched down, watched it pass.

Lang said, "Gimme the phone again."

Falcone handed it over, and Lang prised open the back, took out the SIM card and snapped it in two. Then he laid the phone on the ground and smashed it with the heel of his boot. Falcone watched this without a word. If he mourned the loss of the cheap burner, he didn't show it.

"So what now?" Falcone asked.

Lang was stumped. They'd lost the truck sooner than he'd planned. If they proceeded on foot they'd be picked up. They were still only a few blocks away from the source of their problem, the bodies in his apartment. They were being hunted by the cops and by the Mafia. Falcone was on the run from federal authorities. For all he knew, Janus could be helping them all.

"We need to find some wheels, and we need to find somewhere to lie low until morning," he said. "Somewhere safe. Any ideas?"

Falcone thought about it. "Maybe…"

22

The two uniforms shifted restlessly as they recounted how Lang and his accomplice had evaded them. They were ashamed that they'd allowed the cop killer to escape—and that they had found themselves wedged in their car during the pursuit. They'd had to reverse back down the alley in order to get out, scraping both sides of the vehicle on the way. Santoro gave them a stern look, but she didn't mean it. She'd been told about Lang's missing military record and that meant covert shit to her. Whatever Lang had been back in the day, he sure as hell wasn't a mere filing clerk. If he was some kind of super spy, then he'd be trained in evasion techniques, although this particular manoeuvre seemed to rely more on luck than skill. She and Ralston took another look at the truck, still sitting where it had been left in the alley, the engine running, the doors open, and then headed back their unmarked car.

"What you think, LT?" Ralston asked.

"I think Lang's buddied up," she said.

"Yeah, but who with?"

She didn't answer as she popped a chunk of gum from the pack and began chewing. She already had a suspicion that when the autopsies were completed on the bodies from Lang's apartment, they'd find two different sets of ballistics. She also suspected that the feds were correct—for some reason Tony Falcone had teamed up with Lang. That bothered her. The hypo bothered her. Lang's mystery past bothered her. This whole case was a gigantic pain in the ass. That pain intensified when she reached the street and saw the two feds. The guy, Burke, was standing on the sidewalk, eagerly awaiting her return. The woman, McDonough, was leaning on the hood of their car, her palms resting on the metal, her legs crossed at the ankles. She looked as if she didn't care whether she was there or not. Being in a purely advisory capacity was obviously free of stress.

Burke moved towards them when they emerged from the dark alleyway. "I hear it's been confirmed there's another man involved," he said.

Rosie wondered who had been blabbing, then put it from her mind. It didn't matter, if she was right she'd have to bring the Marshals into her investigation. Pain in the ass that it was.

"Let me guess," said Burke, unable to keep a triumphant tone from his voice, "average height, thick dark hair, dark complexion, New York accent, a scar running from below his left eye to his jawline?"

She felt her teeth grind. She didn't mean to, it just happened. "Sounds about right."

He darted a meaningful look at McDonough, who still hadn't moved from the hood of the car, then said, "Tony Falcone. Our guy."

Santoro couldn't keep the edge from her voice. Burke was pissing her off again. "Yeah, well, when we catch him, he'll be *our* guy. He's a suspect in a multiple homicide, including the deaths of two NYPD officers."

"He was your guy back in Houston Street..." He pronounced it *Hyuston,* and instantly both Santoro and McDonough corrected his pronunciation.

"Howston."

Burke frowned. "It's spelled Houston."

"Yeah, but it's pronounced Howston," said Santoro.

He still looked puzzled, but McDonough shrugged. "It's New York," she said, as if that was all the explanation that was needed.

Burke dismissed it as irrelevant. "No matter. The thing is, your people had them and let them go..."

"They didn't let them go, they evaded capture."

Burke looked as if he was about to argue but then thought

better of it. "Fair enough," he said, "but let us assist you. We have knowledge of Falcone that could be helpful."

"What kind of knowledge?"

Burke looked back at McDonough again. Santoro moved closer to her. "Is that your advisory capacity? You know Falcone?"

McDonough pushed herself from the car. "I was on the WitSec detail when he was giving evidence against his old pals. I had to learn a lot about him."

"He's on the run. You any ideas where he'll go?"

McDonough gave her a smile that Santoro would bet her pension had the other US Marshals panting. "A couple..."

23

They stole another old model car, managed to reach Queens without incident, although some flashing lights did cause a few moments of concern. Falcone told Lang that Barney was an old friend, and he'd help them. They ditched the vehicle five blocks from the man's apartment building, completed the rest on foot. The elevator was out, and they climbed the stairs to the cop's door. Lang was reasonably fit, but the strain of the past few hours was beginning to register. He needed a place to rest, grab some shut-eye. He could only guess how Falcone felt, but to the man's credit he didn't complain, although he seemed to be hauling himself up every step.

They reached the door, and Falcone was about to knock when it opened and the business end of a Sig 226 was thrust towards them. Lang took an involuntary step back as the door opened wider to reveal a squat, balding man in a Dodgers t-shirt and sweatpants. He put a finger to his lips and motioned them inside, checked the landing as they passed to ensure no one had paid any undue attention to his late-night callers, then closed and locked the door.

"I heard you coming up those stairs like a steam train, Tony," said the man.

Falcone looked ashamed, as if age was something he could avoid. He pointed at the gun. "We need the hardware, Barney?"

Barney looked at the weapon and shrugged. "You shouldn't've come back here. The department hears about me helping you, I'm finished…"

Lang frowned. The department? He should've realized when he saw the Sig. "Your buddy's a cop?"

Falcone waved the comment away with his hand. "This cop's a

buddy, is what you need to know."

Barney licked his lips, swallowed, then let the gun drop. "Tony, this old neighborhood thing will only get you so far." His eyes rested on Lang. "You Lang?"

"Yes."

"They like you for killing Gina."

"I didn't do it."

"Yeah, so you say."

"Look at it this way," Lang jerked his thumb at Falcone beside him, "if he was certain I'd killed her, would I be here?"

Barney took this on board, gave Falcone a questioning look. Falcone shrugged. "Hey, it's a long story. Now, how about you make us some coffee and I'll tell you all about it."

The cop in Barney obviously wanted to turn them in, but the buddy was beginning to waver. Finally, he sighed, ran a hand over his bald pate and said, "Jeez, Tony, you're gonna cost me my pension."

"We'll be gone by first light, Barney, you have my word. Your bosses won't even know we been here."

24

Vinnie watched the doc patch Nicky up. He knew the man had taken bullets before, but this one must really hurt, not because the wound was bad, but because he'd had that rat Falcone almost under his gun. Vinnie shared his disappointment. Ten years he'd wanted to get the son-of-a-bitch, ten years of wondering where the feds had stashed him, now he was back on his home turf and he'd slipped through his fingers. Or rather, Nicky's fingers. That had never happened before, far as Vinnie could remember. Nicky the Juke had always been his father's most lethal weapon, but he'd slipped up this time. Vinnie didn't know who that other guy was, Cole Lang, but Nicky said it was him who'd plugged him and for that he'd pay, for if there was one thing Nicoletto Bruno did, it was repay his debts. Vinnie understood that, even though he had been born and raised in New York. It was a Sicilian thing.

Nicoletto Bruno had been brought over from the old country in the late 1970s when the old bosses—Carlo Gambino, Stefano Maggadino, Vinnie's own father—had seen the power of the five families begin to wane and needed new blood to counter the dilution of the ranks. There had been too many turncoats, starting with that rat Joe Valachi, may he burn in the fires of hell, and too many of the younger members who didn't want to involve themselves no more with the old money-making rackets like loan sharking, extortion, running numbers or hijacking trucks. They wanted to push dope and snort dope and rub shoulders with Hollywood producers and snort some more dope and get themselves a book deal so they could go to fancy parties and snort even more dope. The mob was in deep in the narcotics trade, but they didn't want their guys cutting into the profits by taking free samples. Vinnie grew up with those guys, and he despised them, for his pop had instilled in him the old ways. The old guys realized they had to take a step back in time, to maintain the traditional markets, the ones that had made the five families great, while also making sure they had more than a piece of the drugs action because, hey—a dollar's a dollar. However, they knew many of the young home-grown recruits were too far gone to be trusted. So they reached out to their relatives and associates in Sicily, and hundreds of native-born men were smuggled into the USA through Canada and Mexico. They called them "Zips", Vinnie didn't know why, but they always did their bosses' bidding, no questions asked, for that was the old way and the five families needed such men.

Nicoletto Bruno was only a teenager, but he swiftly proved himself to be just what the old Dons needed. He was obedient and lacked conscience, which meant he was efficient in his brutality. He also had one advantage over many of the other Zips—he had no record in Sicily. He'd never been arrested, never been through the system. He was as clean as you could get, and being an illegal in the States meant there was no birth certificate, no social security number, no fingerprints. So if he managed to keep himself out of the hands of the law, the Marino family had themselves a ghost to do their bidding. And that's exactly what he did.

Come the early 90s, old man Marino decided that it was time Nicky became a US citizen, so paperwork slipped through greased palms—God Bless America—and hey presto, Nicky the Juke was legal. But US citizen or not, he still did whatever the Marino family needed him to do. And he'd never failed them.

Until now.

As he watched the doctor work, Vinnie wondered if the Juke was losing his touch. It could happen. After all, he wasn't a young man no more. And if he had lost it, what was Vinnie going to do about it? If it ever got out that Nicky was not the man he once was, then the *bastarde* who were nibbling away at the Marino family's businesses would think it was open season.

Vinnie had also heard disquieting rumors that Nicky had his own scams going on the side. The irony of the situation was not lost on him. This whole mess began when Falcone was caught padding his bank account without paying the family their interest, now here was the man hunting him supposedly doing the same. Vinnie had long thought Nicky the Juke was past his sell-by date, and maybe it was time to take him out of circulation. However, he'd let him play this hand out.

The doc had finished patching Nicky up. He'd lost some blood, he said, and would need to take it easy for a few days. Vinnie smiled—yeah, like that would happen with Falcone out there. He'd used this doc before, he was a resident in a hospital in Brooklyn and would keep his mouth shut. Vinnie paid him well to patch up any of the boys who got hurt, and he knew that if he spoke out of turn there'd be repercussions. The doc had a young wife and a kid, and if he wanted them to stay healthy he'd make sure he was on call 24/7, take the generous compensation on offer, and keep his mouth shut about what he saw or heard. Money was a great reward, but fear meant security.

Vinnie waited until the doctor had left before he said, "So, what went wrong, Nicky?"

There was no expression on Nicky's face, no pain, no shame, no rage. "I screwed up. I didn't factor in this Coleman Lang."

Vinnie pursed his lips. "You sure he was the one who shot you?"

"Yeah. And I lost my favourite gun."

"You think maybe he just got lucky?"

Nicky shook his head. "No. The *finocch*' knew what he was doing." *Finocch*'—calling a guy a queer was the biggest insult Nicky could make. He hated homosexuals, and whenever he had to deal with one professionally he tended to become more creative.

"So, we got Falcone out there, and he's in tow with some guy who knows his way around a piece."

Nicky nodded at Vinnie's summation of the facts.

"So what you gonna do about it, Nicky?"

The Juke stared at him again, his face still blank. Shit, Vinnie didn't recall him ever not smiling. And he'd stopped singing. That could only be a bad sign for Falcone and that other guy.

"I'm gonna find that *bastardo* Tony Falcone and his *finocch'* pal," Nicky said, like he was talking about buying groceries, "and I'm gonna make 'em wish they was never born, that's what I'm gonna do about it." He pushed himself off the table on which he'd been lying while the doctor had been working. "And Vinnie—this time I take off the gloves. There are no rules from this moment on."

The muscles of his face had not moved, but there was something in Nicky's eyes that Vinnie had never seen before. There was a fire burning deep in there that came from hell itself. Vinnie swallowed. He wasn't a religious man—sure, he went to Mass, but that was for show—but even so, he resisted the urge to cross himself and ward off the *diavolo*. He didn't know what Nicky meant by no rules, but he was certain of one thing—he didn't want to know.

25

Lang squirmed in the armchair, trying to find a comfortable position so he could to grab a couple more hours of sleep. Falcone was stretched on the couch, snoring softly. Barney was in his own bed, which was only fair. There was no heat in the apartment, and Lang could feel the chill seeping through the blanket the cop had grudgingly given him. Fit as he was, he could feel his muscles grumble, he presumed thanks to a mixture of the night's exertions and tension. He could only imagine how Falcone felt, but he seemed to be resting well enough.

He'd slept fitfully. Every time he closed his eyes he saw Gina's face, her beautiful face, and then it would morph into the lifeless face he'd found in his bed. And when he slept he heard her voice and her laugh. He woke with a start, and he thought he still heard her whispering his name from somewhere in the darkness of the apartment. He listened to the sounds in the street below and the apartment around him, but he didn't hear her voice again. It was an old building, and it creaked and groaned like a senior citizen. At one point he thought he heard soft footfalls on the stairway, so he got up, crept to the front door and peered through the spyhole, but the corridor was empty. He stood there for a full ten minutes anyway, his ears straining to pick up any sound, controlling his breathing so he could hear everything. But there was nothing.

He returned to the armchair, tried to make himself comfortable and considered recapturing sleep but knew it was useless. He sat there in the semi-gloom of street lights bleeding through the drapes and thought about how his life had changed.

A week ago he'd been just another white-collar worker in the streets of New York, bored certainly, but safe and secure. He'd been in love with a beautiful woman with whom he'd planned to share the rest of his life. Now all that was gone. It only took an instant—a hypo and some kind of toxic substance. Gina was gone, his future was gone, his safe, secure, boring life was gone. He wished he had that boredom now.

He'd known things would change once the divorce was final, but he hadn't expected this. He thought they would begin to look up once he had the Psycho Twins off his back. He, Falcone and Barney the cop had talked for two hours, and Lang had told them about his stormy marriage and for the first time wondered aloud if they were behind Gina's death. He told them that sooner or later he had to go to Westport to confront them. Falcone still didn't buy it completely, but he went along with it. Barney was harder to read. He was a cop, and Lang knew how his mind worked—his colleagues in Manhattan were satisfied there was sufficient evidence to have him arrested, that should've been good enough for him. However, the fact that his old buddy Tony hadn't put one behind his ear seemed to go a long way.

He thought about Sophia and her brother. Were they crazy enough to do this? Had they somehow found out about him and Gina and did this to destroy his future happiness? Were they really capable of homicide?

He'd seen madness in Sophia's eyes many times, generally when she was screaming at him because he'd smiled at another woman. He recalled the lengths she would go to find out where he was, what he was doing. She would analyze every word he ever said and throw them back at him months later. He recalled her brother Silvio's cold, dark expression one night when he'd had one of his little chats with him, warning him that if he ever hurt his sister he'd not rest until he'd hurt him. "We're Italian, Cole," Silvio had said, "and our passions run high, our blood runs hot. When we are struck, we strike back, maybe not right away but we never forget the blow, for it still stings. And if you hurt Sophia, you hurt me. And I don't forget, Cole, I never forget..."

It all sounded a bit operatic, and Silvio was prone to making grandiose statements, but was there some element of truth there?

It would've been simple for them to bribe the doorman to tell them when he brought a woman back to the apartment. Oscar would be up for it, not Carl, of that Lang was certain. Sophia had been to the apartment two or three times, maybe she'd somehow made a copy of his key. No, that was too furtive for her, she'd never pull it off. Silvio would've bought some kind of passkey maybe or hired someone to pick the lock, creep in and kill Gina. He'd not do it himself, he was too clever, and there would be a number of middlemen along the way, but was Silvio really capable of organizing it? He had the medical knowledge to come up with the method, certainly, but would he really murder just to hurt his sister's ex-husband? Were they really that psycho?

The more he thought about it, the less convinced he was. Lang had met many men and women who would not hesitate to kill, or have someone else kill on their behalf. At the time, he thought Silvio's words were just the posturing of a man puffed up with his own self-importance. Deep down, he still thought that.

So, if not the Psycho Twins, then who? Falcone's former associates, in order to draw him back to the city? Could it be something from Lang's own past? Janus didn't seem to think so.

Or was there something in Gina's own life that she hadn't shared with him? Her moods had been changeable of late. She turned pensive for no reason. Was there something he didn't know?

Lang knew the next step. He'd meet with Reuben in the morning as planned, ask him to obtain Oscar the doorman's address—he'd not mentioned the lawyer to Barney, there was a limit to how far he trusted him—then he'd head up to Westport.

The sound of a footfall at the front door snatched him from his thoughts. He'd missed whoever it was climbing the stairs, and he mentally berated himself for allowing his old instincts to blunt, but as soon as he heard the steps halt at the door, he darted from the chair and gave Falcone a shake, shushing him as he started to grumble. Falcone understood immediately and began to rise as Lang opened the bedroom door. Barney was already up and tightening the belt of his robe, but he had the haggard look of a man who hadn't slept.

The knock at the door was loud and it was forceful. It was a cop's knock.

Lang and Falcone quickly gathered their coats and Barney waved them into the bedroom. Lang swiftly took in his new surroundings. The small double bed was a mess, there was an old dresser and an even older wardrobe. A chair in the corner was piled with discarded clothes. Drapes were pulled across a window that looked down onto the street. Barney left Lang and Falcone standing together in the dark room, heads pressed to the wooden panels of the closed door. Falcone slid his Glock from the holster but held it at his side. Lang gave the weapon a pointed stare then shook his head. Falcone shrugged but didn't holster the weapon.

They heard Barney open the front door and say, "What the hell's going on here? You know what time it is?"

Then came a voice Lang recognized, Santoro. "This is important, detective. Can we come in?"

Lang assumed Santoro had flashed her badge because the next thing he heard was the rustle of clothing and footsteps clumping on the wooden floors as they moved down the short hallway into the living room. He couldn't tell how many there were out there, but Santoro had said "we", so at least one other person was with her.

"You over from Manhattan, Lieutenant?"

"Yeah."

"You're a long way from home. So, what's so important that you can't just call me or wait till morning?" Barney sounded pissed off, which he probably was.

"Anthony Falcone, detective." A man's voice, deep, commanding. "What about him?"

"When was the last time you heard from him?"

A pause. "Who's asking?"

"Detective," Santoro again, "these are US Deputy Federal Marshals Burke and McDonough..." Three of them, thought Lang. Must be getting pretty crowded in there. "Your old pal Tony has dropped below the radar. They need to find him."

"And you think I know where he is?"

"You were the one who brought him to us ten years ago," said another woman's voice, a Texan drawl to it. Beside him, he felt Falcone tense.

There was another silence, and Lang had a vision of Barney sizing the speaker up. "McDonough, yeah, I remember you from back then. You were on the security detail." Now he understood why Falcone had stiffened. When Barney spoke again, there was a grin in his voice. "So Tony gave you all the slip, eh?"

"Not my watch," said McDonough, her voice tight, like dried out buckskin. "I'm here purely in an advisory capacity."

"So—I'll ask again," the man's voice. Burke. "When was the last time you saw him?"

"Ten years ago, down at the courthouse, when he put old man Marino and his gumbah pals away. After that, you guys had him stashed someplace, and not even New York's finest knew where."

"With good reason," said Burke, "NYPD being so mob-friendly and all."

"Not all of us," said Barney, and Lang heard an edge in his voice so straight it could slice bread. "In fact, not many of us. And sure as shit not now."

A throat cleared, and Lang presumed it was Santoro because her voice came next. "Relax, detective. No one's accusing anyone of anything. You know the drill here—we've got to follow up on leads. So all we got is the people Falcone knew back then, and over the past few hours we've called on a few. You're just next on the list, is all. We need you to help us if you can, detective. Falcone's daughter was murdered a few days ago, maybe you heard?"

"I heard."

"And he's been seen back here in the city. He's on the run again along with the guy I like for her murder."

Barney laughed. "Tony Falcone's in the wind with the guy who murdered his daughter, that what you saying?" He laughed again. "Then your guy's dead, that's for damn sure."

"We're not so certain," Burke again. "We think they're working together."

"Bullshit!"

"Looks like they killed three guys in an apartment in SoHo, then two cops in an alleyway."

Things went quiet again, and Lang could feel Barney's surprise. "Two cops?"

"Yeah, two young guys, gunned down in the line. So, we need to find this pair, and we need to find them before anyone else dies."

Falcone stepped away from the door, spread his legs, raised his weapon and trained it straight at the wood. Lang knew what he was thinking. Two dead cops was a game changer. Barney would turn them in. He was an honest cop, a good cop, and the old pals act didn't cover killing brother officers. Lang looked around the bedroom, eyes falling on the window. It was the only way out, but they were five floors up and it was a long way to fall if there was no fire escape. The way Falcone was thinking—blast their way out— was suicide. Two cops and two US Marshals were not the three goons in his apartment.

But then Barney was speaking again. "Can't help you, I've not seen or heard from Tony in all that time. I doubt he'll look me up when he's in town, either."

"You were old friends," said McDonough.

"That was then, this is now. We were kids, we didn't know any better back then. Now I do, even if he don't. He came to me ten years ago to do the right thing, from what you're saying he isn't doing no right thing this time round, so he won't come to me."

Another silence as they weighed up his words. Barney sounded pretty confident, but Lang hoped he'd got the body language right—no shifting around, no looking away, no nervous little smiles. He'd been a cop for God knows how long, and he should know how to lie, but sometimes it's the little things that trip you up.

Then McDonough said, quietly, "You alone in the apartment, detective?"

"No," said Barney, "you're here."

"Uh-huh," Burke's voice got a little louder, and Lang knew he'd moved closer to the bedroom door. "What's through here?"

Lang jumped back to stand beside Falcone.

"The bedroom," said Barney.

"Mind if I take a look?"

The door handle squeaked slightly as it began to turn, but it was as loud as a gunshot. He produced his own weapon but remained unwilling to engage in a firefight. They'd never get out of the window in time, they'd be sitting ducks as they tried to get over the sill. Their only hope was if they got the drop on the cops and the feds, but he knew that was unlikely. This didn't look good at all.

"Go ahead," said Barney.

The door opened a touch.

Then Barney's voice again, "Just show me the warrant first."

The door stopped. Lang imagined a hand still resting on the handle on the other side.

"Detective…" Santoro's voice carried a warning.

"No, Lieutenant, you guys come here, wake me up, ask me about a guy I've not seen for ten years, then this one wants to search my home? Well, I got rights, you know? And unless you got a warrant, I don't want no snot-nose fed poking through my gear. I'm sorry, but you don't like it, you take it up with my boss and we'll sort it all out in his office with my union rep."

Light knifed between the open door and the jamb. Lang held his breath as he stared at it, expecting it to widen. He had the feeling Falcone had done the same. They waited. The seconds stretched. Lang amended his stance, raised the Beretta without thinking. That troubled him. Instinct had kicked in. He kept it leveled, hoping to only send whoever came through that door ducking for cover, to wound at worst. He didn't want to kill anybody. Not again. His gaze flicked to Falcone, tried to divine what he was thinking, but he already knew. Falcone would drop whoever came through that door without a thought.

Then Santoro's weary voice said, "Okay, detective, there's no need for that. You are perfectly correct, you have your rights as a New York Police Department officer and a citizen. All we ask is that if Falcone gets in touch, or if you hear anything in relation to him, that you get in contact with me. That fair enough?"

"Fair enough, Lieutenant."

Burke must've let go of the door handle for they saw it twist back into place.

But without him holding it, the door began to swing open on its own.

Lang and Falcone edged further to their right to remain in the shadows because they didn't know how far the door would move of its own volition. The sliver of light grew, began to illuminate more of the bedroom. He heard Santoro and the others still talking, but the words didn't register. The door continued to swing inwards, slowly, but it still moved. They had run out of darkness, it was not a large bedroom, and the light began to rest on Falcone's left shoulder. All it would take was for Santoro or one of the feds to glance into the room and the jig was up. He reached out with his left hand and gently stopped the door from opening further. The Beretta was still poised in his right. He eased the pent-up breath from his lungs, willed his body to relax.

Finally, he heard Santoro and the others move away from the living room and back down the hallway. Lang kept his eyes on the open door and didn't pay any attention to what was said as they left. His pounding heart echoed in his ears, and he jumped when the door was thrown fully open and Barney was framed in the light from the living room.

"They know you're here," he whispered.

Falcone asked, "How can they know that?"

"I don't know, but they do. That McDonough, she'd wandered round the room while they were talking, then she kept looking at the bedroom door all the time. That Burke character saw her and took the initiative. He seemed like the kind of guy that'd catch someone else's hunch and play it."

Lang looked past Barney into the living room, trying to see what McDonough might've spotted. He saw it almost immediately. "The coffee cups," he said. Barney craned over his shoulder, Falcone leaned over to get a look. There were three cups on the small table. "Why'd you need three cups if you're on your own?"

"Shit," said Barney, his face creasing with dismay over missing something so obvious. "You gotta get out of here. My guess is the feds'll stick around while Santoro goes for that warrant."

Lang was already pulling his coat on. "Is there a back way?"

"Yeah, but if they're any good they'll split up, one out front, one out back. You'll have to go over the roof, get to the next building, or better still a couple after that. But you'll have to move fast because if I was them I'd be calling for back-up right about now."

"What if we can't find an open door on another roof?" asked Falcone.

Barney shrugged. "Keep going till you find one. Or get far enough away that you can bust one in. I don't know. All I know is, you stay here, you're as good as banged up on Rikers. The key to the door up there is on a hook beside it, you can't miss it."

"You're not coming?"

Barney shook his head. "You need to mess me up some, then tie me to that chair." Lang understood immediately, but Falcone looked surprised, so Barney laid it out for him. "They suspect you were here, I need to make it look like I lied to them under duress. I'll tell them you threatened to kill everyone in the room if I didn't do as you say. You put my lights out, leave me tied up, they may not believe a goddamn word, but they won't be able to prove nothing. You'll find some twine in the kitchen drawer that should do the trick."

Lang saw the sense, even though it would demonize them even further in the eyes of the law. But Barney had helped them, and now they needed to help him.

Falcone hesitated. "Barney, those cops…"

Barney shook his head. "That was the clincher, Tony. Up till then my mind was open about all this, but you wouldn't shoot a cop, that I'm certain of."

Falcone's face tightened, and Lang wondered if Barney's confidence was misplaced. Back in the bedroom he'd sensed that whoever had come through that door first was dead meat, no matter who it was.

Barney exhaled heavily again. "Okay, you don't got much time. Get it done."

Lang could tell Falcone couldn't do it, so he slammed Barney across the side of the head with the length of his gun. The cop rocked back on his heels then fell flat on his ass. He wasn't knocked senseless, but somewhere a referee was counting to ten. Falcone gave Lang a long look, then helped him haul the limp Barney onto the wooden chair and moved wordlessly into the kitchen. The cop's head lolled onto his chest, and when he tried to raise it, an ugly red welt was forming from his cheek to his temple, but the skin was unbroken. Falcone returned with the twine, and they bound him to the chair, not too tight that it would impede his circulation but tight enough that he couldn't break free without help.

They made sure they hadn't left anything behind, and as they made for the door they heard Barney's voice. The words were slurred, but he was coherent. "Tony, guess these are the worst of times, huh?"

Falcone stopped, looked back, stared at his pal. "Barney, past few years? I can't tell the difference." He lingered in the doorway, looking back at his old friend. "You look after yourself."

"I'll be okay," said Barney, almost sounding convincing. "It's you who needs to be careful."

"I'm always careful," said Falcone, "how the hell you think I've lived this long?"

"I always put it down to you being a stubborn son-of-a-bitch," said Barney, a lop-sided smile on his face. Lang watched the two men stare at each other, Barney with that off-kilter grin and the faraway look and Falcone, his features taut but his eyes fluid. For a fleeting second he thought Falcone was going to cross the room again and give the old cop a hug. But he didn't. Instead he gave him a curt nod, wheeled and left the apartment.

Barney gave Lang a lop-sided stare. "Hit me again, kid." Lang hesitated. "Gotta make it look real, put my lights out."

He did as he was told. Barney's head snapped to one side, then drooped onto his chest. Lang checked his neck, felt a strong pulse, then gave the knots a final tug. He glanced around the room once more and followed Falcone through the door.

26

It was still dark, but Lang could see the faint glimmer of the new day to the east and the blinking lights of planes heading in and out of La Guardia to the north. The street lights cast oblique shadows across the flat roof. He moved to the edge and peered carefully over it to the street below. He couldn't see anyone watching the building but he knew they'd be there—Barney was right, front and back would be the smart play here. He pulled away and walked to the point where the building gave way to the adjoining one. He stepped over the small boundary wall and continued across the next roof. He tried the door, but it was locked.

"We're too close," said Falcone. Lang nodded, he knew that but thought he'd try anyway. He didn't know what was ahead, and he needed to know if there was a possible escape route back here.

They moved on, walking quietly, until they reached the end of the second building. And there they hit a problem—there was a gap of about four feet between the roof they were on and the next. And the one they wanted to reach was slightly higher. On the plus side, Lang could see the door to the building was ajar. But they had to get to it first. He looked down into the darkness of what was a narrow alleyway and said, "We'll have to jump across."

Falcone looked at the gap, then down, and said, "You kidding me?"

"You got a better idea?"

Falcone thought about this, looked around, shook his head. "I ain't no pole vaulter, is all."

"Just as well, 'cos we don't have a pole," said Lang then took about ten paces back to give him a run up. He threw himself off the building and slammed hard into the wall opposite, wrapping his arms round the edge of the roof. He hauled himself up, toes scraping against the brickwork, and then lay flat on the rooftop, his chest heaving with the effort.

"Jesus—could you have made more noise?" Falcone hissed as he leaned over to look down.

"Let's see you do better," retorted Lang. He knew he'd made some noise, but he hadn't thought it was that loud.

Falcone looked doubtful. "I don't know—it looks like quite a leap."

"It's just a narrow gap, you'll do it easy."

Falcone moved to the street side of the building first and checked to see if Lang had attracted attention with his scrambling. Lang knew he was putting off the inevitable. After seemingly satisfying himself that no one had heard, Falcone walked back to the middle of the roof, obviously feeling he needed a really long run, and prepared himself. He took some time to prepare himself.

Lang waved him on. Falcone nodded but didn't move. He waved again, his chopping motion a bit more emphatic. Falcone, who had been shuffling his feet in readiness, stopped and jutted both arms out to say "Give me a break, here." Then he crouched like a runner waiting for the starter pistol, took a deep breath and suddenly he was moving, legs pistoning, feet slamming against the tarpaper roof, heading for the gap. Then he was in mid-air and Lang suddenly realized that despite the lead up, Falcone hadn't achieved the necessary velocity and was going to fall short, his hands were flailing ahead of him, grasping for the top of the wall, but he was going to miss and drop straight into the dark alley.

Lang reached out, caught Falcone's hands in a firm grip, feeling the pull of gravity jerk at his shoulders as he strained to haul him up to safety, Falcone's feet also scratching at the wall and making far more noise than they should. They both lay on the roof staring up at the sky. Where there had been blackness before, Lang could now make out some definition as the sun, just beginning its rise over to the east, caught the underside of the cloud cover. He heard Falcone's labored breathing beside him.

He said, "You call that jumping?"

Falcone took a deep breath. "You call that narrow?"

Lang smiled, stood, dusted some dirt from his pants then held a hand out to Falcone, who looked at it for a moment then allowed the younger man to help pull him to his feet. He nodded his thanks and brushed grit from his clothes.

"That's twice I've saved your life," said Lang, keeping his voice low. He'd seen the way Falcone had looked at him in Barney's bedroom when the cops were talking about Gina and it was clear he still harbored doubts over his innocence, so Lang felt it best to have another debt locked in.

Falcone stopped beating at the back of his trousers and looked back. "How you figure?"

Lang jerked his head to the alleyway below. "You were heading for the big drop."

"No way."

"Yes way. I hadn't caught you, you'd be splattered all over that alley right about now."

Falcone studied the space between the buildings once more, then he shook his head. "Nah, I was good for that."

"Yeah?" Lang smiled. "Only if you sprouted wings and flew the final two feet."

A smile flickered at the corners of Falcone's mouth. "Bullshit, I'd've made it."

Lang laughed softly. "You keep telling yourself that, old man. It'll make you feel better."

The unlocked door was tempting, but Lang felt they had to put more real estate between them and the feds waiting back at Barney's building. However, when they walked to the far edge they found that this apartment block was a stand-alone property, with another alleyway separating it from the next. The two men stood on the parapet, looking down into the darkness below. Neither of them spoke. Finally, Falcone shook his head. "I say we take the door."

"We're only a couple of buildings away."

"Yeah, but the door here is open and we don't know what we'll find up ahead."

"And you know you can't make the leap."

"No, I just think we got a bird in the hand here and there's no use beating around the undergrowth, is all."

"And you know you can't make it."

Falcone sighed. "Look, we can stand up here flappin' our gums until the sun comes up, or we can get down off this rooftop and get away while it's still dark." He started to walk back to the doorway. "Me? I'm taking the stairs."

Lang's smile broadened as he caught up with Falcone. "Admit it, you owe me twice over."

"Screw you, Lang," said Falcone as he pulled the door open and entered the building, then he stopped and placed his hand on the frame, his arm blocking Lang's access. "Listen, you had your little joke here, you caught me, okay—thanks for that. But what's happening here isn't happening, you hear me? We ain't bonding, you and me. We still got unfinished business."

Lang saw the intensity in the man's eyes but, even though he was ten years out of practice, he'd been in too many dangerous situations to let it worry him. He had been trying to bond in some way, but he saw it hadn't taken. Screw it, he thought, time to lay it out for this guy. "We're in this together, Mr Falcone, whether you like it or not. I'll tell you this one time more and then never again—I didn't kill Gina. I would never harm a hair on her head. But someone did. And I intend to find out who. Now, you can help me, or you can put a bullet in my eye right now, but I've got a job to do and I'm not going to worry about you, understand? You're a distraction I don't need. So, what'll it be? You give me the benefit of the doubt and back me up, or you finish it right here, right now."

Falcone stared at him, and Lang wondered if he was considering putting a bullet in his eye, but then he turned without saying anything further and walked down the steps into the building. Lang let his breath ease from his lungs and followed.

27

They crept down the stairs as quietly as they could, both acutely aware that the hallways, as in Barney's building, were like echo chambers. The last thing they wanted was someone to poke their nose through a door to see who was skulking around and then raise a ruckus when they spotted two strangers. However, they reached the ground floor without incident, and Falcone headed for the front, but Lang caught his arm. Falcone, still slightly steamed after their conversation on the roof, whirled but Lang raised a finger to his lips and pointed to the rear of the building. It was too well lit in the street, and he still felt they weren't far enough away, but Falcone had been right, they could've scrambled across those rooftops for hours looking for another open door. And, all joshing aside, he knew Falcone really didn't have it in him to leap across another gap. The back of the building, though, should be darker, he reasoned, and hopefully easier for them to get away without being seen.

He pushed open the back door and stepped out, his head darting from side to side to ensure no one was there. It was a large common area shared with the buildings on either side and with those opposite. He moved across the paving stones that cut through some scrubby grass, heading for the blocks on the other side. They'd parked their stolen car a few blocks away, and they had to get back to it before daybreak for they were sitting ducks on foot, but as before, they'd have to take a circuitous route. They also would have to change vehicles again real soon. He didn't know how long it would take Santoro to obtain a warrant, wasn't even sure that was happening, but he didn't want to take the chance of the neighborhood being flooded with cops.

"My God, could you two have been more predictable?"

He recognized the woman's voice immediately, even though he'd only heard it for the first time in Barney's apartment. It was low and throaty, and the Texan drawl was unmistakeable. She was standing in the alleyway, deep in the shadows of the next building so he could only barely make out her outline. He looked around for her partner, but she was alone. Beside him, Falcone already had his Glock in his fist.

"Tony, you best come in with me," said the US Marshal as she stepped into the dim light thrown in from the street. Falcone leaned forward, straining to focus on her.

"I know you," he said. "You was on my security detail."

"That's right. You trusted me then, Tony. Trust me now when I say you can't run. This isn't back in the day, and you're no kid."

Falcone said, "What's your name again, honey?"

If being called "honey" offended her, she didn't show it. "McDonough."

Lang knew Falcone remembered her. He was playing for time, giving them the chance to think of a way out of this situation. "Right, no first name, just initials, right? TC?"

"TP," she corrected.

"Yeah, TP. Well, listen, honey—thank you for the invitation, and there's nothing I'd like better than to go with a fine-looking redhead like you but I'm not ready right now. This guy and me, we got some work to do."

McDonough looked at Lang, and he realized she didn't have a weapon in her hand. "He's wanted for the murder of your daughter, Tony."

"I know that."

"He killed her, Tony."

Falcone gave Lang a sideways look and smiled a little. "Allegedly."

"Two cops are dead, also."

"Not our doing."

"Why should I believe you?"

"I don't have no control over what you believe or don't believe. But here's the thing, I don't see no gun in your hand. But I got one." He held up his Glock for her to see. "My young friend here is also packing, but he's too polite to aim it at a lady." He raised his gun in her direction. "Me? I'm not so delicate. So unless you've got some kind of SWAT team around here, I don't think we'll be coming along with you tonight. If you'll excuse me, we got places to be."

She didn't make a move as they edged around her, Falcone's gun centerd unwaveringly in the center of her body mass, Lang keeping his eyes and ears open for her partner. They backed along the lane, and she watched them all the way.

"We'll get you, Tony," she shouted. "You can't run forever. This ends one of two ways—either both of you in cuffs or both of you dead in the street. Far as NYPD is concerned, you're cop killers and they'll shoot first and think about asking questions later. Come with me, you'll at least be alive."

Falcone was still backing away. "Honey," he said, "the cops are the least of our worries..."

28

Nicky waited until there was only the woman and her husband in the house. It had been a long wait, for they were Italian and they took grief very seriously. His Sicilian blood understood this, but his head was wired differently. He didn't have time to waste on grief, he caused it.

It was a nice little house, neat, tidy. Her husband had a small construction business which was doing well, and it was reflected in his home. Their friends looked prosperous, too. Some of them showed their prosperity around the gut, which disgusted Nicky who was repulsed by any kind of excess fat. He'd never warmed to Vinnie until he'd lost the blubber, if warmed was the correct word. He knew what guys like Falcone thought, but it wasn't true. Vinnie was old man Marino's kid, and Nicky was loyal to his Don, but back then the very thought of being in the same room with that tub of lard made him feel sick. Now Vinnie was Don and he'd slimmed down it was different. Now Nicky's allegiance was to him. Up to a point.

He let himself in via the back door and moved silently through the house. He'd watched them turn off all the lamps downstairs, and then a light went on in the front bedroom. He'd never been in the house before, she'd been deemed off limits by the Don, but he'd been in places just like it. Tract housing, they used to call it, all the little boxes the same as the one next door. Uniformity, something else Nicky despised.

He eased up the stairs, the silenced Glock 43 in his good hand. That *bastardo* Lang may have put one in his right shoulder, but he could shoot just as well with his left. The new weapon was smaller than he was used to, but it would do for this business. He paused at the top of the stairs just long enough to get his bearings and listen. The door to the bedroom was to the right, light seeping under the door. He pulled a ski mask from his pocket, hauled it over his head, feeling his wound tighten with the movement. He'd make that son-of-a-bitch Lang pay for that.

Then he kicked in the door.

He'd learned long ago, as a boy in Sicily, that the best way to make an entrance is to make it big. He could've simply opened the door and stepped in, but this way was better, for it carried with it a greater element of surprise. But more than that, a guy with a gun, his face masked, suddenly bursting in, scared the hell out of people. The woman didn't scream, but the guy recovered first and lunged from the bed. Nicky didn't know what the goddamn idiot was thinking, but he put a bullet into the wall just where his head had been a moment earlier. He could've just as easy put it right in his skull, but he just needed the guy to see sense. For now. The woman was shocked, but she stared back at him with dark eyes filled with both contempt and defiance.

"What d'you want here, *stugots*?" Her voice was level, her tone derisory, and by calling him a dick she showed she had no fear. She was a piece of work, this woman, but then she'd been married to Falcone for years and would have to be.

"Your husband," said Nicky.

"This is my husband," she said, holding a hand out to the man at her side, then pulling him back towards her.

"You know who I'm talking about, *signora* Falcone."

"That's not my name now and I haven't seen that *stronz'* in years." Piece of shit. Yes, thought Nicky, that's exactly what he is.

"He's back in town."

That surprised her, for her dark eyes widened. She recovered quickly and dismissed the thought. "He'll not come anywhere near me. He knows he's dead to me."

Nicky knew that to be true, but that was not why he was here. "Who would he contact?"

"How the hell should I know?"

"You *know* him."

She waved a hand, as if the thought was ludicrous. "I never knew that *giamoke,* that loser, not really. He was a *sciupafemmine,* I knew that, screwed around like a tom cat in heat, that I knew. But no one ever really knows Tony Falcone, so you're wasting your time here, *stugots,* go away, leave, this is a house of grief."

Nicky stared at her, trying to gauge if she was telling the truth. He had always been taken with her when he'd seen her at family events, and she remained a handsome woman, her hair still dark, her eyes still fiery, her body still shapely. She had looked after herself. He had always thought her too good for a *stronz'* like Falcone. But he couldn't believe she didn't know something about her husband. No, she *had* to know something. She just needed to be reminded. He smiled, started to sing "Love and Marriage".

He put a bullet into her new husband's leg.

She screamed at him, "*Animale!*" She threw herself across her husband, who had not made a sound right away, but now the shock and the pain kicked in and he cried out. It was a strangled sound, for he was ready to pass out. His wife pressed at the wound, blood streaming through her fingers.

"It's nothing," said Nicky, his voice calm, "a flesh wound, no more."

She looked over her shoulder, saw him raise the Glock once again. "The next one won't be," he said. "So, if not you, who would Tony go to in New York?"

"*Bastardo!*" she said, and then she spat at him. She hadn't a hope of the spittle reaching him, but she wanted to show him how little she feared him. He liked that in a woman.

Singing another stanza of the Sinatra song, he adjusted his stance to level his aim, the muzzle aimed right at the man's head. He'd passed out now—what was he, some sort of *mezzofinnoch'*? A half man? Nicky had seen worse flea bites. "*Signora,* I'm waiting," he said.

She swallowed, but if looks were bullets he'd be a slice of Swiss cheese right about now. Oh, yes—she was a piece of work. Finally, though, she saw that he meant business and said, "Barney Mayo, he's an old pal, a cop. He'd go to him."

He nodded, of course. The cop Falcone knew from his childhood. He lowered the weapon. "*Grazie, signora,*" he said.

She spat on the floor between them again. "*Vaffancul', stronzo!*"

Underneath his mask, he smiled. Even when a gun was on her, even when her husband had a hole in him, she was still defiant. As he left, he wondered what she'd be like in bed.

29

The sky was uniformly gray, the waters of the Upper New York Bay where both the Hudson and East rivers met were just as drab. Across the water the silhouette of Lady Liberty stood out against the dull sky, her raised torch still welcoming the tired and poor huddled masses, even if the country no longer did. Ellis Island sat to the right while way over to the left Lang could see the piers of Brooklyn, Governors Island and, further away, the thin spires of the Verrazano Bridge to Staten Island. Another island. Sometimes he forgot he actually lived on an island. Shit, New York was practically an archipelago.

Thanksgiving was only a week away, and the weather was turning wintry. It was too early for snow, but there was a chill in the air that threatened icy rain later. Despite the cold, the tourists were already thronging Battery Park, queuing up for the ferries to Liberty and Ellis islands, cameras at the ready. Time was, street traders preyed on them like wolves on caribou, offering them baseball caps with I ❤ NY printed on them, or the symbols of the Yankees or Dodgers, and garments bearing various acronyms like a sweatshop alphabet soup, whether it be NYPD, FDNY or FBI. The wolfpack had thinned over the years and now Lang could see only one brave soul working the line. Lang had made his purchase earlier in the day.

He sauntered along the pathway beside the old fort dressed in a dark hoodie bearing the acronym FDNY in bright yellow above the insignia of the Fire Department on the front and a Yankees baseball cap on his head. He would've liked the day to have been brighter so he could wear the shades he'd bought, but with the sky overcast he thought he'd stand out too much, so he'd settled on a cheap pair of reading glasses he'd also found on a stand in the drug store. They blurred his vision slightly, but it's amazing what the addition—or removal—of spectacles can do to a face. He had an inexpensive camera slung round his neck, he'd bulked his body up with two sweatshirts and a scarf. And his fair hair was darker now, thanks to some cheap dye applied in the men's room at Grand Central. He hadn't shaved since the previous morning, so he sported bristles like a male model on the catwalk. He tried to alter his gait—not too much because a limp would get him noticed, and that was the last thing he wanted. He stooped slightly, but kept his head up, for being furtive would draw attention. It was all very simple, very easily put together and, he knew, very effective. You didn't need intricate disguises or specially moulded rubber face masks. Glasses, hair dye and bulking up works just as well. He didn't know if Reuben was being surveilled, but he wasn't taking any chances.

The cash to facilitate his rudimentary makeover came from the leather wallet he'd pulled out of his safe the night before. Falcone had watched him count it—around twenty grand in fives, tens and twenties—and asked, "You always keep that kind of bundle in your apartment?"

Lang paused, one hand holding a wad of uncounted notes. "I was saving up for something special."

Falcone looked at the banknotes. "Yeah? Like what?"

Lang sighed. He didn't really want to talk about it, but he had to say something. "I was going to take Gina on the vacation of a lifetime, Europe, Asia, maybe."

Falcone didn't respond, and he carried on counting. What he'd said about the vacation was the truth, although he'd started saving the money long before he met Gina, salting the bills away in the leather pouch, some gut feeling telling him it would be prudent to have an instantly accessible getaway stash. Since he left Janus, some of those old instincts had gathered dust—he'd learned that in the past few hours with the mistakes he'd made, rookie errors.

He'd muddled through with Falcone's help, but if he was to survive what was coming, he had to sharpen his focus, allow Dagda to take over again. He didn't relish the notion, but he knew it was necessary. However, whatever had motivated him to create this special fund had been right on the money, as it were.

Falcone then showed Lang his own fund. Between them they had just under forty grand in cash and a fake credit card account if they really needed it. It would be handy in the coming days, weeks or months, depending how long they remained at large. Or alive.

Falcone didn't understand why Lang needed to talk to his lawyer, had tried to talk him out of it, arguing that Reuben, being an officer of the court, would only try to convince him to turn himself in. Lang knew this to be true, but he needed Reuben's help to find Oscar de Blasio, the doorman.

He spotted his old friend looking out of place among the casually dressed tourists in his expensive three-piece suit and dark cashmere coat. He was standing just in front of a stall pushing snacks, one hand in his coat pocket, the other holding an untouched hot dog. He didn't recognize Lang as he walked past, which was good. Lang stepped behind him, kept his back to him and studied the goods on offer.

He leaned back slightly and said, "Don't turn round, Reuben."

Reuben's voice was startled, "Jesus, Cole! How the hell did you creep up on me?"

"I've walked past you three times. I look a bit different. Chew on your hot dog, don't be coy about it, get your jaws working. It should cover the fact you're talking for a while."

Reuben's mouth was slightly muffled by the food when he spoke. "I wasn't followed, Cole."

"You can't be sure."

"I took the subway, I doubled back on myself, I changed cab three times, I even hopped a bus."

"How'd you know to do all that?"

"I've read a shit load of Robert Ludlum."

Lang fought the urge to smile. "You still can't be sure. The hot dog was a good touch, though."

"I was hungry. Although it tastes like shit." Despite that, he took another bite. "The cops called me, asking about you, had you been in contact?"

"What did you say?"

"I told them I had you holed up in my spare room, what the hell do you think I said? I headed them off at the pass. They bought it. They're not tailing me, I'm certain."

"Reuben, it's not just cops after me, it's the feds." He felt, rather than saw, his old friend begin to turn, so he snapped, "Don't turn around!"

The lawyer froze, but Lang knew he was shocked. "The feds? What the hell are they involved for?"

"Long story, Reuben, and we don't have much time. When you leave here, check the third trash can between here and the fort. You'll find a Big Mac bag on the top. Inside there's a burner phone. There's also a 30-day SIM card which is activated and good to go. You'll find a number taped to the underside of the phone. Use that to reach me. Use it only in an emergency, otherwise I'll call you. If I have to change my phone for any reason, I'll text you the new number. And when I tell you to destroy the burner, you take it apart like a surgeon and smash everything."

"Cole…" began Reuben, and Lang sensed him turning.

"Don't look at me! Keep chewing!"

"Jesus, Cole…" There was a pause as Reuben took another bite and chewed it to a sufficient size to let him speak. "I'll bill you for the Pepto-Bismol after this."

Lang lowered his head to hide a smile. "The doorman of my building is named Oscar de Blasio, he lives somewhere in Brownsville. I need an address, and I need it fast."

"Okay, I can do that—what the hell is going on, Cole?"

"The less you know, the better. Anyone finds out you're helping me it'll be the end of your legal career, you know that?"

There was a silence from Reuben then as the true significance of what he was doing sank in. Then he said, "Ah, hell—I always wanted to be a beach bum, anyway. But I have to say again, wouldn't you be best to hand yourself in?"

"No. I don't know if this whole thing was intended as a set-up from the get-go, but the way it's worked out I'm in the frame. Cops won't listen, courts won't listen. I've got to get to the bottom of this myself and in my own way."

There was another silence as Reuben considered his next question. "I have to ask this, Cole—did you kill anyone last night?"

Lang thought about the thug he'd dropped in his apartment. He was dead, he knew that. He hadn't taken the time to take careful aim. And it's easier to kill than wound. All the same, he didn't want to do it again. He didn't want to become that guy once more. He swallowed hard. "Once again, best you don't know, gives you deniability." He knew he was confirming it anyway, but at least it gave Reuben wiggle room if he needed it. "But I did not kill those cops."

Reuben breathed out heavily. "Jesus, Cole, you're in so much shit it's going to take a mini-sub to get you out."

Then, as if to underline the point, Lang heard Falcone's voice in his ear. Their rudimentary disguises weren't the only thing on his shopping list that morning. A visit to a spy tech store gave them a set of two-way radios with Bluetooth earpieces. The receiver was clipped to Lang's belt under his layers of clothing.

"Two men, dark suits, don't like the look of them, just walked past me and heading your way," said Falcone, and Lang's eyes darted around him. He couldn't see anyone converging yet, but Falcone was watching from beside Castle Clinton with a pair of small but high-powered field glasses, also bought from the spy tech outlet—ain't capitalism a gift? Anyone looking at him would see a guy wearing a Big Apple baseball cap and a black New York Mafia hooded top—Lang loved the irony—seemingly taking a close look at Lady Liberty. In reality, he was watching the rendezvous point and the trash can, to ensure no one paid it undue attention. He'd instructed Falcone to say as little as possible should there be any trouble and to switch the radio off immediately to avoid detection. Lang may have been paranoid, but they really were out to get him.

"I'll be in touch, Reuben," he said, and wheeled away from the stall, walking purposefully towards the crowds waiting for their ride to Liberty Island. A glance over his shoulder revealed the two men, and he didn't like the look of them either. They wore dark suits, just like the two in the bar the night Gina died. Lang didn't take the time to study them carefully, but they were not the same men. He spotted the same thing that Falcone had: the way they carried themselves spoke of the military, their watchful eyes revealed them to be hunters. He ducked into the press of bodies and pushed his way through, ignoring the complaints from tourists who thought he was cutting the line. He slipped the spectacles from his nose and tossed them to the side. He ditched the baseball cap. As he moved he hauled off the dark hoodie, unveiling a Yankees sweatshirt, and dropped it at his feet. People gave him curious glances, but no one said anything. If the hunters had spotted him talking to Reuben, they would be searching for a man with a baseball cap, glasses and an FDNY hoodie. That man was gone. It was a basic evasion technique and it would work with cops, but something told him these guys weren't cops and they weren't feds. He stopped moving and risked a look through the bobbing heads and saw they had come to a halt and were scanning the crowd. There was a precision to their movements, their alert eyes taking in every face, every feature, every movement. Reuben had vanished, and he hoped they had no further interest in him. They were professionals, and that could be deadly for anyone connected to him.

He wondered who the hell they were.

The line for the ferry was beginning to shuffle forward as the passengers boarded, but he couldn't move with it, for he had no desire to end up being trapped on a boat bound for Liberty Island. He couldn't remain still in the crowd, either, for he would stand out like a rock in swirling waters. He had to risk moving.

He straightened and adopted a confident bearing as he emerged from the line, his back to the men as he walked. The burly street vendor stepped into his path and shoved a sweatshirt in his face. He was Asian, but his accent was pure Brooklyn. "Hey, dude, wanna buy a Lady Liberty memento?"

Lang stopped, fingered one of the sweatshirts, which were of remarkably good quality, "How much?"

He wasn't interested in making a purchase, but he used the man's body as cover while he checked out the men in the suits. One was big and muscular, the other slightly older, smaller, but also packed with muscle. They were still studying the milling tourists. Then the larger of the two moved into the crowd, pushing people out of the way, their angry words falling on deaf ears. The man stooped then, straightened again, the discarded FDNY hoodie in his hand. His partner understood and immediately scanned the perimeter. Lang was still ostensibly haggling with the street trader, but when their eyes locked and the man's back stiffened, he knew he'd waited too long. There was nothing else to do now but run.

He sprinted across the grass, skirting the circular castle and dodging the slim trees, heading for Battery Place and West Street. He didn't need to look back to know the men were in pursuit, for he heard more complaining shouts as they shoved tourists and traders alike out of their way. Lang felt the weight of the Beretta under his remaining layers, but he didn't want to start waving it around as he knew that would only result in them doing the same. He didn't know who the hell they were, but they were most certainly armed, and he didn't want to run the risk of innocent people being wounded or killed. He had to draw them away from the crowd, lead them to the grassy area, which was more or less deserted, reach the streets on the other side and lose them there. It wasn't much of a plan, but it was all he had.

When he did look back, he saw the smaller man was fitter than the other, for he ran with a powerful step, good and steady, legs pumping, arms working. The other guy was all power but no pace, and his partner easily raced ahead of him on Lang's trail. He was the initial danger, and Lang estimated that he'd intercept him before he could get out of the park.

Something had to be done.

Lang slowed, made it look as if he was flagging—which he was, but not that much—and then just when the first man was almost on him, suddenly spun. His pursuer was moving too fast to halt in time and Lang careered right into him, slammed both hands into his chest, feeling something rigid and immoveable under there, and knocked him backwards off his feet. The man landed hard, the wind exploding from his lungs. He was down but not out, and he reached under his jacket for his weapon. Lang had expected that, and he rammed his foot hard onto the man's wrist, pinning it to his chest. He ground his heel down and the man groaned, tried to get up. Lang pulled his foot away, wheeled, and lashed out with his other, connected with his cheek bone. The man's head snapped to one side, and although still conscious, Lang knew it would hold him for now.

He stooped and picked up the man's weapon—a 9mm Heckler and Koch P30S—then felt something wing past him and bury itself in the dirt with a puff of dust. Lang dodged to one side, rolled, and brought himself up on one knee, instinctively bringing the HK level. The second hunter had halted and was aiming his silenced automatic for another shot. Lang didn't want to fire, the risk of collateral damage from a wild bullet was still too great, so he threw himself to the ground again just as the man fired. Lang felt a sudden rush of agony as the bullet seared across his arm. He didn't know how badly he was hit, but he kept tumbling, had to keep moving. Another bullet slammed into the ground about an inch from his head, and by this time the first man was pulling himself to his feet and, although still groggy, Lang could tell he was going to come after him, and that was not a good thing.

He pulled himself erect, loosed off a quick shot to let the big guy know he'd had enough but kept the muzzle low so that the bullet slammed into the ground at his feet. He still didn't want to shoot anyone. Not again. The HK he'd taken wasn't silenced so the sound of the shot cracked through the chilly air, sending birds flapping from the trees. There were screams as civilians nearby dropped to the ground or ducked for cover. The first man was on his feet now, a small gun in his hand—Lang should've known he'd have a back-up piece—and was walking forward, holding it in both hands so Lang had no choice but to switch his aim: he had to put him down. He felt his body still and the world slowed down as he aimed. The HK bucked, and the man came to a sudden halt as two slugs thudded into his chest, then he swayed and slumped to his knees. Lang had placed his slugs carefully. He'd felt the unyielding bulk of the Kevlar vest when he'd pushed the guy to the ground and knew the worst he'd done was knock the air out of him, maybe even crack a couple of ribs. Another couple of shots whined past his head, and Lang shifted his position in order to deal with the second man who was running towards him in his lumbering way whilst shooting, which was never a good idea. There was genuine rage on his face. Even bad guys have buddies. Whoever these guys were.

Lang hesitated. He didn't know if this man was also wearing a vest, didn't want to assume that he was, so he lowered the barrel, sighted on his legs. Bringing a moving target down with a non-lethal shot looks easy in the movies, but it's less so in real life, and Lang took careful aim. He only had time for one shot, and it had to count.

Another shot rang out from behind and something tugged at the man's thigh and then flowered red, and he stumbled and fell, his gun flying from his hand. Lang didn't wait any further. He leapt to his feet and ran again, seeing Falcone beckoning to him and, behind him, the stolen car parked illegally on Battery Place, both the driver's and passenger's doors wide open.

Lang said nothing as he threw himself into the passenger seat, keeping his eye on the two men as Falcone dropped into the driver's seat and gunned the motor. They could hear sirens now, and people were still screaming. The man Lang had shot was beginning to pull himself to his feet, but his buddy writhed on the ground, holding his wounded leg.

"Did you know they were wearing vests?" Lang asked as Falcone floored the vehicle past the Robert F Wagner Memorial Park onto Battery Place as it curved into Manhattan.

"Hell, no. I was going for a body shot. I missed."

Lang sighed, then winced as his left arm burned. Falcone shot him a look but said nothing as he expertly weaved through traffic, turning left and right onto what streets he could, keeping his speed as steady as possible, his eye constantly darting to the rearview, until he turned onto Liberty Street and then left onto West Street. They were passing the 9/11 Memorial before he said, "So who the hell are those guys? They weren't cops, and they weren't Nicky's guys."

Lang was gingerly feeling the wound. It didn't feel too bad now, the bullet must've grazed his flesh, but he knew there was a deep welt and he could feel blood trickling down his arm. It would keep, but he'd have to tend it as soon as he could.

"Lang? You hear me? Who the hell are those guys?"

Lang twisted to look through the rear window until he was satisfied no one was in pursuit, although the car would've been spotted, if only by CCTV cameras, so he knew they'd need to ditch it.

"Beats the hell out of me," he said.

* * *

Logan Fitch let the special line ring six times before he answered it. He knew who the caller was, and he didn't want him to know how eager he was to receive the call.

"Logan Fitch," he said, his voice calm, modulated.

"You wish to talk to me?" Mr Jinks didn't sound irritated, curious or excited. Mr Jinks never sounded irritated, curious or excited.

"Mr Lang is proving to be troublesome."

"I understand."

"He is not in police custody, and he is on the loose."

"There was always that possibility."

"It must be dealt with."

"Already in hand."

"You will tie off the loose ends?"

"As I said, already in hand."

Fitch paused before he said the next words. "This is becoming something of a farrago, Mr Jinks."

There was silence on the line for a moment. "The best laid plans can go awry, Mr Fitch. And as I said before, this was not anywhere near the best laid plan. It was made in haste, and that carries pitfalls. It will be dealt with. The loose ends will be dealt with. Mr Lang will be dealt with."

The connection was cut, leaving Fitch still holding the phone to his ear. He would destroy it later but for now he simply laid it on the desk top and stared out at the city.

30

Rosie Santoro couldn't remember the last time she'd been this tired. Giving birth to her second child had been a long, tough delivery during which she'd screamed for more drugs, but the exhaustion she'd felt after that came a close second to how she felt now. Before they'd hit Barney Mayo's apartment, McDonough had led them to everyone she could think of whom Falcone might've called on for help. Santoro had tapped the duty judge for the warrant—he'd taken a bit of convincing, given the subject was a serving police officer, but he'd finally agreed. Of course, Lang and Falcone were in the wind by then. McDonough had told them about her encounter, and Burke was far from pleased that she'd let them slip through her fingers. However, she'd been unarmed. What was up with that? Santoro looked across her desk at the red-haired US Marshal who was dozing in a wooden chair, her head slumped to her chest, her breathing slow and regular. She was young, she was beautiful, but she had no staying power, and that pleased Santoro.

For herself, every movement was in slow motion, and she knew she would have to go home soon, get some rest. The Captain had ordered her to stand down, the Deputy Commissioner, who was now personally supervising the case from the comfort of his office at One PP, had told her to stand down, her own inner voice had screamed at her to stand down, but she'd ignored them all. She didn't much care about three wise guys who'd been dropped in Lang's apartment, they were scumbags, but the elderly door-man and the two young cops had died on her watch and she felt responsible. If only she could keep her eyes open.

Burke was still awake, although he looked as rough as Santoro felt. He stood in the corner of the office, talking low on his cell, presumably bringing a superior up to speed.

Santoro took a mouthful of cold coffee from the Starbucks container in front of her and stretched in her chair, arms above her head, feeling her muscles pull and—truth be told—complain. She'd been on duty for almost 24 hours straight, and they weren't happy about it.

The phone rang, and McDonough looked up. Her eyes were bright and alert, and Santoro wondered if she'd been asleep at all. Maybe she'd been wrong about her staying power. Damnit.

Santoro picked up the handset, said her name, wishing her voice didn't sound like she'd been gargling with sandpaper.

"Got a call for you, Lieutenant." It was the precinct operator. "Says it's Coleman Lang."

Santoro sat up straight, all weariness suddenly gone. "Can we track him?"

"Doing it now."

She glanced at McDonough, who was leaning towards her over the desk. Her head bobbed a question, *Who is it?* "Okay, put him through," she said, then hit the speaker button, put the receiver back in its cradle. "Mr Lang, nice of you to call."

Burke heard the name, cut his own call short, stepped closer, and stared at the phone as he listened.

"I don't know if you're tracing this, but I'll be long gone before any units arrive, Lieutenant," said Lang. "I just wanted you to know that I'm innocent."

Yeah, sure, thought Santoro. "Come in, we'll talk," she said.

"I know you don't believe me," said Lang, as if Santoro hadn't spoken. "But it's the truth."

"You can't run forever, Mr Lang. It's a big city, but we'll get you, sooner or later, you have to know that."

There was a slight pause. "I'm sorry about your officers. I didn't kill them."

"That remains to be seen."

153

"You found a weapon at the scene, right?"

"You must've left it there. Careless, Mr Lang. I'll add littering to the list of charges."

They heard a sigh from the speaker. "Have you heard of some-one called Nicky Bruno—they call him the Juke?"

McDonough must've recognized the name for she leaned for-ward. Burke frowned and stepped closer.

"His name's come up a few times, works for the Marino family," said Santoro. "We've never been able to pin anything on him."

Burke leaned forward into the speaker. "Did Falcone tell you about him?"

"Who is this speaking?"

"Deputy US Marshal Henry Burke. We almost met last night. Did Falcone tell you about this individual?"

"He's the one who killed your officers, Lieutenant, trying to get to Falcone." Lang had obviously decided to ignore Burke. Santoro liked that.

She digested his words. It fitted together, certainly, because the dead men in Lang's apartment were known to be mobbed up or wannabes. The average wise guy didn't kill cops unless it couldn't be helped. However, Nicky Bruno was not an average wise guy. NYPD and the FBI had been itching to make something stick on him for years, but his Teflon coating made John Gotti's look like a knock-off.

"But there's someone else in the game," said Lang. "You heard of the shooting this morning at Battery Park?"

Santoro had heard something about it but had paid little heed, her plate being pretty damn full, but she still mentally slapped her-self for not putting it together. "Don't tell me—you and Falcone?"

"They came after us. I didn't want anyone to be hurt, you have to believe that."

"So who were they?"

"I have no idea, but you can speak to the men, find out. One was wounded in the leg, and he'd require medical attention."

"Okay, I could do that, and I will, but here's the thing, Lang—you've got to come in, let me clear this mess right up."

A small laugh. "Time's up, Lieutenant."

"Lang—listen to me, if you really are innocent you got nothing to worry about..."

Lang laughed again. "That's the way cops think all over the world, the innocent got nothing to fear from the law. But that's not true, is it? How many innocent people have been put away, maybe executed? No, Lieutenant, I'll keep one step ahead of you as long as I can."

Santoro sensed he was about to hang up, but she blurted out, "Lang—has this anything to do with something in your past?"

Silence again, then, "What about my past?"

"We tried to access your military record. The Pentagon says it's lost."

"Lieutenant, I was a US Marine but I pushed paper for most of my tours. There's nothing there."

"But your record has vanished. I find that kinda curious."

"Lieutenant, don't read too much into that. Sometimes a lost record is just a lost record."

And then he was gone. Santoro, McDonough and Burke stared at the speaker as if it was the answer to their prayers. Then Burke said, "You believe him about this Juke guy?"

Santoro shrugged. She didn't like Burke much and wasn't inclined to share her thoughts. She picked up the phone, punched a number. "Ralston, get me as much as you can on a shooting incident at Battery Park this morning." She hung up before he could question why, then punched another number. "What you got?"

The operator said, "Number's registered to a burner, Loo. We're trying to contact the carrier now, see if it's got GPS."

She hung up again without saying anything further. They'd get nothing, she knew that. Even if they managed to pin down a location, the most they'd find was what was left of the discarded phone. Lang knew what he was doing.

"Are you buying all this?" Burke stared at her, his eyebrows knitted.

"I'm not buying anything, I'm doing what any good cop would do, I'm back checking."

He leaned on the desktop. "Lieutenant, you've got a suspected murderer and known mob killer working together. You've got six dead already and all probably by their hand. I don't know what this incident this morning is about, but has it occurred to you that Lang could be snowing you?"

"Yes, Deputy US Marshal Burke, it has occurred to me that all this could be a load of shit, but you'll forgive me if I check it out, will you?"

"And in the meantime my guy is still out there, back to his old ways! You've already lost two men—how many more have to die?"

The reminder of her dead officers pissed Santoro off. She stood up, leaned across the desk to jut her face into Burke's. It wasn't easy because he was a good foot and half taller, but she gave it her best. "Just what the hell do you want me to do? We've got officers across the five boroughs on this. We're following up every single lead, but there are damn few. Now we have Nicky the Juke involved…"

"So Lang said…"

"Yes, so he said, but right now that's all I've got. Add to that we have some shooting incident at a tourist spot. We got Mr Coleman Lang himself, who may or may not have murdered his girlfriend—your guy's daughter—and who may or may not have some sort of special forces background. And then we got your guy, apparently teaming up with him. So, you tell me, Mr Fancy Pants Hotshot, what the hell else do we do?"

Burke's jaw clenched as he continued to stare down at her, but Santoro didn't flinch. She'd come up through the ranks of NYPD, she'd faced gangbangers and pushers and city councilmen. She'd encountered aggression on the streets and in the squad room. She'd worked her way out of the bag and into plainclothes. She was a Latina and a mother, and she was not about to take any shit from a glory-hunting west coast narcissist today, thank you very much.

"You got nothing to say?" Burke had broken away from her stare and was looking at McDonough, who shrugged.

"I'm here in a purely advisory capacity," she said.

"Yeah, and what the hell good is that? You let them get away last night…"

"I'm unarmed, remember? What was I going to stop them with? Sex appeal?"

Santoro smiled. She'd lay odds that McDonough's sex appeal would be enough to stop most men. She heard something rasp at the back of Burke's throat. She didn't hide her smile, and that seemed to annoy him even further.

"And as for the NYPD, you're not covering yourselves with glory here, are you?" he said. "One of your own, aiding and abetting a wanted fugitive?"

"Detective Mayo may well have assisted them, but then again, his story may also be true. They may have held him at gunpoint, forced him to fob us off by threatening to turn his apartment into a slaughterhouse. Fact is, we don't know, but the guy has a record so clean and white it made my eyes hurt, so guess what—until evidence is presented to the contrary, I'm going to give him the benefit of the doubt."

Burke looked as if he was going to argue the point, but then he suddenly turned, stomped towards the door, jerked it open and left the room. It would've been a dramatic exit had he not almost collided with Ralston heading in. There was a pantomime moment of each man trying to get past the other but still ending up in his way before Burke in exasperation dodged to the side and stormed off across the squad room. Santoro shook her head and sat back down again. She leaned back in her chair, aware again of just how tired she was, and noticed McDonough looking at her with a smile on her face.

"What?" she said. "You got something to say, too?"

"Hell, no," said McDonough, standing up, "but if you were a

guy, I'd want to have your babies…"

Santoro smiled, then remembered Ralston was standing in the open doorway. "What you got?" she asked.

"The shooting at Battery Park," he said. "Witnesses said two individuals chased another individual, they exchanged shots, the first two were dropped and the other one got away in a car, driven by a fourth individual."

"Gang-related?"

He shook his head. "Wits say they were all too old. The two in pursuit were well-dressed, like bankers or some such."

"Where they at? I need to talk to them."

Ralston shook his head. "That's the thing. The two guys that were dropped? By the time the first units responded they were gone. Seems they were picked up by another three men who carted them off to an SUV. They were dressed like bankers, too, according to eye witnesses."

Santoro and McDonough exchanged glances, both thinking the same thing.

What the hell is going on here?

31

Oscar de Blasio had lived in Brownsville all his life. With a black mother but a white father, it hadn't been easy. Other kids picked on him, called him half and half, or Oreo—black on the outside, white inside—even halfro and domino. His father had died when he was ten, which hadn't made life any easier, but Oscar came through it, largely thanks to his mother, Celestine, a strong-willed Alabama woman who as a child had seen the Klan march and heard stories of activists being shot at, beaten and even murdered. She'd been Celestine Rivers when she met his father, Gil de Blasio, when she came to New York in the mid-1970s. He was her foreman at the shoe factory where she'd found work, and her smooth black skin, trim figure and ready laugh made him forget that she was of a different color. His family turned their back on him when they married. They had no interest in guessing who was coming to dinner. The turmoil of the 1960s told the world that the times were a-changin', but for some they hadn't changed one bit. But Gil de Blasio hadn't cared and neither did his new wife, for they had each other, which to them was all that mattered.

Oscar was ten when his father died, and Gil's passing hit his mother hard. Her usual good humor deserted her, and she withdrew into herself, but only for a while. She bounced back and faced the world, just like she'd always done. It wasn't easy bringing up a boy on her own, but she managed it, didn't spoil him, tried to instil in her son a respect for others, even those who called him names. She kept the apartment like a new pin, held her head high as she walked the streets, even when the gangbangers taunted her. Oscar kept his distance from the young men, he didn't have the nature to run with them, his well-padded frame and meek demeanor not being conducive to life with a street gang. They still threw a few insults his way, but they recognized he was no threat and generally left him alone.

His mother never once thought of leaving Brownsville. This was where she'd settled with her husband, this was where they'd had their son, this was where they'd lived and loved. As the neighborhood turned ever more violent, Oscar would broach the subject of moving elsewhere, but she dismissed him every time with a wave of her hand and said, "Never run, never will. You know that's the neighborhood motto and I live by it. Anyway, they good folks here, mostly. We their people, they ours. Those kids out there in the street? We ain't no annoyance to them. They got each other to think on, they too busy to pay no 'ttention to us."

Oscar was 40 when she passed away. She died where she'd lived, in her own bed in her own apartment, the framed picture of her husband facing her on the bedside table. She'd looked at it one final time, then caressed it with her fingers just as she always did before turning in. Far as Oscar knew, his father's face was the last thing she saw in life because she was taken in her sleep. He found her next morning. She looked so peaceful, and there was what he thought was a little smile on her lips, like she was happy to be wherever she'd gone.

He remained in the Ville because it was home, be it ever so violent, and because he couldn't afford to go anywhere else. He watched from the safety of his apartment as the gangs stalked the streets and shot each other. He once watched as rivals blasted away with semi-automatics—Jesus H. Christ—and managed to miss everything but an old lady and her little dog. His mother, had she been alive, would've been out there, screaming at them to stop. Then she'd've tended to the old woman. But Celestine de Blasio had been gone two years by then. The woman survived, but her dog died. That little mongrel was all she'd had, her husband was gone, her oldest son taken in Vietnam, her daughter had succumbed to an overdose back in the 80s, and she had no more family. The old woman passed on two months later. A neighbor lady told Oscar that it was like she just gave up. No one was ever arrested for the shooting.

So Oscar had lived in the Ville all his life, but he hated it. The world had moved on, and he was more or less accepted, but he never felt at home. He'd made the best of it when Celestine was alive, but she'd been gone three years now, and he longed to escape. However, being a doorman didn't pay that kind of scratch. His rent here was reasonable, it couldn't be anything but in this neighborhood, but there was no way he could afford an apartment anywhere else.

That was why, when those guys paid him to look the other way in the SoHo building, he took the money and did what they asked. One of the guys he'd seen before a few times. He'd come in on occasion, asked about Mr Lang, who was he seeing, what was he doing, slipping him a hundred every time. First day he showed up in the building he said he was a private detective doing a background check for a potential employer, but Oscar knew that was horseshit. Mr Lang was doing okay at his advertising agency, and he wasn't about to change. Old Carl, the day man, had got friendly with Mr Lang, and he said things was going good for him, especially now he was almost a divorced man. But even so, Oscar ignored the obvious lie and pocketed the C-note the man had pushed across the desk and proceeded to tell him what he knew. The guy slid him another bill, asked him to find out what else he could, and Oscar agreed. What harm could it do? So he started asking Mr Lang a question here and there, real subtle-like, and when the guy came back he was able to tell him a few more things, nothing major, but the guy seemed happy and another picture of Benjamin Franklin made its way across the desk and into Oscar's pocket.

The guy had the look and feel of a cop, just something about him, but Oscar didn't see the harm in passing what little information he had from time to time. After all, it wasn't that he could tell the guy anything, not really. Oscar once asked the fellow why he was so interested, by that time he knew for sure it wasn't for no job opening, but the guy just gave him a look that said the deal didn't include questions.

That night, the night the woman died, it was different, though. The guy was usually alone, but this time he had someone with him, tall guy, looked like a goddamn pallbearer in his black suit and tie. Oscar used to watch reruns of "The Addams Family" on the tube, and the guy reminded him of Lurch, the butler. The guy never said a word, just stood in the foyer, his pale eyes watching him. Oscar couldn't be sure, but he didn't see the guy blink, not once. Creeped him right out. The first guy slid an envelope across the desk and said they wanted to go up unannounced. Oscar wasn't so sure. The guy had given him a friendly grin, told him they just wanted to surprise Mr Lang, there was nothing to worry about. Lurch didn't smile. Oscar didn't think the guy could smile. Oscar felt his palm itch as he looked at the envelope. He could tell by the thickness that there was more than just a picture of old Ben Franklin in there. A helluva lot more. It might not be enough to get him out of the Ville, but it'd be a start. After all, what harm could it do? If Mr Lang said anything later, he'd say he'd gone to the john and the guys must've sneaked past. The building's CCTV was offline, goddamn Korean shit. No one would know.

But those guys must've killed that woman. That wasn't part of the deal. When the two men came back to the foyer, the first one leaned in real close and told Oscar not to say anything about them. If he did, he said, then the next time they met it wouldn't be an envelope stuffed with cash they'd be giving him. When the guy left, Lurch hung back, staring at Oscar with those colorless unblinking eyes. Didn't say a word, just stared. And Oscar knew that if he breathed a word then Lurch would pay him a call and it wouldn't be nothing social.

He'd bluffed it out with cops when they came to question him, and he pulled it off, but inside he was jelly. Couple of times he almost barfed it up right there in the kitchen. He didn't know how he'd controlled it. But he told himself it was better to lie to the law than face Lurch. It helped that the lead cop, snotty little bastard called Ralston, didn't seem all that interested. Oscar felt he was just going through the motions. So if the cops didn't give much of a shit, why should he? That's what he told himself. But he knew what he'd done was wrong.

He should've told the cops the truth, but he'd taken the money. And Lurch's cold dead eyes had haunted him ever since. He couldn't leave the cash—two grand, Jesus H. Christ!—in his apartment, and there was no way he was leaving it at work. He couldn't deposit it in his bank, for he didn't know if the police would monitor something like that, or if the bank employees would flag it up somehow. A sudden injection of two grand would look suspicious. So he carried it with him, tucked away inside his jacket. He was sure he could feel it burning against his chest as he traveled to and from his home. When Mr Lang passed by the desk, he felt like it would sear its way right through his ribs.

Now all hell had broken loose at the building again. He'd arrived at the building to start his shift the night before and found the street swarming with cops. There were TV vans in the street outside, paparazzi too. The uniforms at the cordon didn't let him through, but when they found out who he was, they sent a detective out to talk to him, a sharp-suited black guy. He told him that someone had riddled old Carl with bullets and that there were more bodies in Mr Lang's apartment. Oscar couldn't tell him anything about it, truthfully this time, but he was told to hang around for a couple of hours in case they needed help in the building.

And all the while the envelope burned like the fires of hell against his chest.

The cops were still there when he left. There'd be no doorman on duty for the rest of the day because Oscar couldn't raise the stand-by guy. Anyway, with all that law swarming around there wasn't no need for a doorman. Old Carl being dead gnawed away at his conscience, though, and he struggled with it, but he didn't tell the cops anything. He couldn't. He'd taken the money, and that made him an accomplice. And then there was Lurch. There was always Lurch.

Now Mr Lang was on the run, and Oscar just knew the cops were itching to finger him for all the killings. It had been real strange in work that night with cops still everywhere. There was an atmosphere you could just about taste. Even the tenants who normally stopped for a chat or exchanged a "How you doin'?" just kept walking. They'd nod, but then they'd avert their eyes. Oscar's guilt told him it was because they knew he'd been involved somehow. He'd never been so glad to get to the end of his shift.

It wasn't cold as he walked from the railway station, but he hunched down into his coat anyway. The temperature didn't need to drop too far before he started to feel the chill. His mother used to say it was the mixture of his hot Italian blood and even hotter Alabama blood. It wasn't raining, though, thank God, although the sky was as dull as a Brit TV show on PBS. His route from work never changed. He'd hop the subway to Fulton Street station where he'd catch the MTA 3 Train to take him all the way to Brownsville. He walked the final few blocks. He'd walked it many times, rain, snow, sun, never had no trouble. This was home, at least until he could figure out a way to parlay what he had into something bigger. His conscience was playing him up, but what's done was done. Him being in jail wouldn't make things better, but if he could use that money to improve his situation somehow, surely that was a positive? But how to do that, was the question. He'd never been a gambler, so he wouldn't play the horses. The market, maybe, guy in the SoHo building was a trader, he may have a tip or two. Oscar didn't know how legal that was, but that was the guy's look-out. If he didn't want to help him, then screw him, he'd find someone else.

He didn't notice the kid at first. He was just another young man, walking the streets, wearing a red baseball cap and a thin red hoodie that zipped up the front but was lying open to show off a New York Knicks shirt. He'd crossed the street just as Oscar turned into it, his mind on his newfound fortune and how to make it grow, his subconscious doing its best to smother the guilt he felt. The guy stopped in front of Oscar, stared at him. Oscar frowned, thinking, *What's his damage?* He recognized him, had seen him in the street running with the guys, tried to dredge up a name but came up short. He thought the kid must be freezing in that skimpy little thing, but it wasn't manly to feel the cold.

Then the kid's hand raised from where it had been dangling at his side, and there was a gun in it. Oscar didn't know what kind nor did he care. All he managed to say was "Hey!" and raise an arm before the kid pulled the trigger and the bullet exploded through his hand to bury itself in his jaw. Oscar stumbled backwards, the agony in his face intense, like it was on fire, and he hit a trash can with the back of his legs, went over, crashed into the sidewalk. The kid stepped closer, aimed the gun at his head. Oscar tried to say something, but his tongue wouldn't work, and then he heard the gunshot and saw the muzzle flash and there was a blinding explosion of light and pain.

And just at that moment he remembered the name Shaymar, the kid's name was Shaymar. And then he remembered nothing at all.

32

Santoro really wanted a drink, but she wasn't so desperate to hit the bottle at lunchtime. She knew so many cops who found solace in liquor that it was practically a cliché, so she settled for three cups of black coffee to back up a burger and fries. McDonough, she was pleased to note, tore into her own double meat and bacon stack like cholesterol was a story to frighten children. Santoro liked her more and more.

Burke had not reappeared, so they decided to head out for something to eat without him. Santoro didn't give a damn, and she sensed McDonough felt the same. Her cop's curiosity got the better of her.

"I'm guessing you weren't christened TP, right?"

"You'd guess right."

"So what does it stand for?"

"My two first names."

Santoro waited, but McDonough wasn't about to volunteer her names. Santoro let it pass. "How'd you get into the marshaling business?"

"My daddy was a Texas Ranger, my brother's a homicide cop in Fort Worth. I joined the military, ending up an MP, so I guess it's in my blood. How about you? How you end up in NYPD?"

"Was always naturally nosey, inherited that from my momma and her momma, who were the nosiest women on the block. Cops always seemed to be in the know, so I joined up."

"You like it?"

"I'm still doing it. You like being a Marshal?"

"I'm still doing it, too."

Santoro popped a fry into her mouth while McDonough bit

off a chunk of beef in a bun. "So what's the deal between you and your partner?"

McDonough chewed, swallowed, then said, "He's not my partner. I'm here in a…"

"Purely advisory capacity, yeah, you said. So what's that all about?"

The Texan laid her burger on her plate, wiped her lips with a paper napkin. "Burke was on the detail supervising Falcone. He lost him. They brought me in because I knew Falcone, and they felt he might respond better to a familiar face. I guess we learned last night that wasn't going to happen."

"They sent you out here without a weapon?"

Something painful crept into McDonough's eyes as they flicked away towards the TV on the diner wall. Santoro saw a news broadcast just beginning. "I had to turn my weapon in." She looked back to fix Santoro's own gaze but said nothing else. Santoro didn't need to hear anything more. McDonough had been forced to use her weapon in the line. She'd put someone down. That person had not got up. She had the feeling McDonough wouldn't be losing much sleep over it, but killing a man should never be easy. Santoro herself had never been in that position, and she hoped she never would, but she knew enough to give McDonough space on the matter.

"I get the impression you and Burke are not the best of pals. You two got a history?"

McDonough smiled. "You don't miss much, do you?"

"I got a gold shield and two kids. It's my job not to miss much."

The US Marshal popped a fry into her mouth. "Burke is ambitious, plays the political game in the service. I don't have any time for that. He's the kind of guy who will always turn your hard work to his advantage."

"He did that to you?"

"Once. We were tracking a fugitive in LA. I found him, Burke took the credit in his report."

Santoro sipped her coffee. She didn't need to know anything more. Burke was an asshole, she'd already worked that out. But this conversation wasn't about him. "And that's all? Work stuff?"

"What else could there be?"

"Oh, I don't know. Something personal maybe?"

McDonough grinned. "Jeez, Santoro—you want my bra size, too?"

"We're working together, the three of us. I need to know what kind of dynamic is in play here. So, there something more between you two?"

McDonough gave a slight shake of her head, and her smile turned into something bashful. "He's a good-looking guy. We were working together in a strange city—and LA is strange, let me tell you. Once the job was done, this was before I found out about his report taking all the credit, one thing led to another."

"And he didn't call you after?"

McDonough looked up again. "No, I didn't call him."

"Because of the report?"

A pause, another fry into her mouth. "Sure. Because of the report."

Santoro got it. Burke was steamed because the woman didn't go back for more. That was the guy's job.

She saw McDonough watching the TV intently and looked up. The screen was filled with two head shots side by side. She couldn't hear what the newscaster was saying, but she could guess. Armed and extremely dangerous. Do not approach. Lang and Falcone.

"God damnit," she said.

* * *

After he'd hit Oscar, Shaymar didn't run. He thrust the 9mm back into the deep pocket of his hoodie and walked back in the direction he'd come. Running just draws attention to you, he knew that. His man Malik told him that when he first put a piece in his

168

hands ahead of some trouble with the 8 Block crew. After you cap someone, unless you got heat, you best walk away like you out for a stroll, Malik had said. Shaymar had looked up to Malik like a brother—shit, they was brothers, when it came right down to it—and he followed his advice to the letter at all times, whether it be how best to pop a cap or to nail a chick. Malik told him about that, too. Should've been Shaymar's old man who taught him, but he didn't pay much attention to his youngest son on account of he ran with the Young Guns. He was an honest man, he wanted his sons to be honest, and he didn't take kindly to Shaymar's buddies. So it fell to Malik to teach him the ways of the world, the real world, man, not the "get a job, do right" world of Shaymar's father.

As he walked away from the body, he heard someone come out from somewhere and call after him, not by name, but he ignored them. They wouldn't speak to the cops, and even if they did, they'd regret it. Malik and his brothers would see to that. Even so, he was unconcerned by the thought of jail time, not that he'd be sent to the pen.

People ran past him in the street, paid him no mind, just wanted to get to where the Oreo had got himself shot. Shaymar's sister would hear about it sooner or later, and she'd give off that little smirk she had when she was proved right and say, *Only a matter of time before some fool done that boy. There be a lot of folks not happy with him, God save his soul, just 'cos he be half white. A shame, too, 'cos he ain't done no one no harm.*

Shaymar had nothing personal against Oscar—hell, didn't even know his name for sure until the day before, only knew him as the Oreo, even though he didn't care much what color he was, inside or out. It was a business thing only. Dude wanted the boy dead, Shaymar made it so. He smiled when he thought that, sounded like that bald white guy on TV. Make it so. That's just what Shaymar had done. Maybe he'd make that his own catchphrase: Shaymar'll make it so. That'd be cool.

He made his way to the alley he'd been told to meet the guy at to give him back the gun, which was all part of the deal. It was an L-shaped alley, and he saw him sitting in a car at the turn, up against a wooden fence, white guy, thin-faced, wispy blond hair. Eyes such a washed-out blue they was almost gray. He unfolded himself out of the car as Shaymar approached. He was tall and skinny. Paint his head red he could be a matchstick, Shaymar smiled to himself.

"You get it done?" The guy's voice was so deep it practically made the ground tremble. Dressed all in a black suit, too. Shaymar's sister had shown him photographs of Malcolm X from back in the day, and he wore suits like that. Except this white boy wasn't about to fight for no black power, no way. This white boy had Aryan Nations coming out of him like a smell. He didn't have the tattoos and shit, but Shaymar had seen pictures of those Nazi dudes over in Germany, and this guy could be one of them. He had that look in his eye, too, like he thought Shaymar was some sort of insect, useful maybe but still something that needed stepped on when the time came. Didn't bother him, long as he paid up. For Shaymar, it was all about the business.

"He lyin' dead in the gutter," said Shaymar. "You got the rest of my money?"

The man made no move to pay the bill. "You have the weapon?"

"A' 'ight, man, got it right here," said Shaymar as he handed him the 9, which was a shame because it was a nice piece. He'd've liked to have kept it, but a deal's a deal. The dude wanted it back, the dude got it back. He was paying for the privilege to call the shots. He watched as the man studied the weapon, removed the clip, checked the load, then slammed the magazine back.

The sound of sirens made Shaymar turn and stare back up the alley. A cruiser sped past, lights flashing, the cops inside not even looking down their way. He knew they were rushing to where he'd left that Oscar dude. Shaymar smiled. That was a job well done, you ask him, well worth the Ben Franklins he was about to be paid. He turned back to face the white guy and just had time to realize that he was staring into the muzzle of a silencer before the bullet pierced his left eye and erupted in a splash of blood and brains from the rear of his skull.

Mr Jinks stood over the body for a moment, watching the boy's nerves twitch their last. He felt nothing as he stared at what had once been a living, breathing human being. He had long ago divested himself of any emotion. Humanity was troublesome in his line of business.

He didn't need to feel for vital signs. He knew the boy was dead. He was well versed in his chosen trade. When the body stilled, he checked no one was watching from the mouth of the alley, then climbed back into the car and reversed out, leaving the body of the 14-year-old hitman behind.

33

Lang didn't know why he'd called Santoro, he just knew it was something he had to do. Falcone had argued against it, believing it was best to have as little contact with the cops as possible, but he had ignored him. He was glad he'd done it, he'd said what he needed to say, but he didn't think it would do much good. Yes, it was a risk, but he knew it would take time for them to track the cell down to an individual mast and then the area it covered, known as "the apron". He would only use that particular device once, he'd assured Falcone, and as soon as the call was complete he took out the SIM card and crushed it under his shoes. Then he slipped the battery off and dropped it into a trash can. The phone body he threw in a separate trash can.

They had put as much distance as they could between them and Battery Park that morning before they stopped at a drug store to find something to treat Lang's wound. He'd been lucky, it really was little more than a graze, and it no longer hurt, but he'd cleaned it up and wrapped a bandage around it all the same. He could feel the muscles beginning to stiffen slightly, but that would pass. Reuben had made good on his promise and texted Oscar's address, so that meant he'd managed to retrieve the burner cell from the garbage can, which was good news. They knew they'd have to ditch the stolen car soon. The likelihood was cameras would have caught the shooting at Battery Park and the car in which they escaped. But first they had to speak to Oscar de Blasio.

"Remind me why we're here," said Falcone as he stared through the windshield at the people beyond. They were parked outside Oscar the doorman's apartment building, waiting for him to return from his shift. All around them were black or Hispanic faces, and

Falcone was restless. A strong thread of racism ran through the mob, but Falcone had never shared it. He had nothing against black people, because their money was green like everyone else's. But two white faces in the Ville could be asking for trouble. Lang was unconcerned. He knew about Brownsville's reputation, he'd read all about the teenage gangs and the playground violence and the street killings, but he had spent time in the most vicious parts of the globe, had witnessed brutality and bloodletting on an epic scale, and these streets held no terrors for him.

"Whoever murdered Gina had to pass him on the way," said Lang. "Obviously he hasn't mentioned any of this to the police, so that means he was paid off. I want to know what he knows before we head to Westport."

He had never been in Brownsville as he'd never had any reason. The people he met through the agency didn't come from here, the clients didn't target the people here. It was made up of low income housing and projects, but it didn't look as bad as he expected. The streets were wide, the parked cars mostly in good condition, the buildings in the main looked reasonably well cared for, but he knew that didn't mean shit. He knew about gangs from the differing projects waging wars with one another, he'd seen news reports and read about how the poverty and deprivation had led to disaffection and even anarchy. But the people he could see were just ordinary folks—men, obviously unemployed, walking by singly or in groups, a group of youngsters at the corner, lounging, smoking, talking, horsing around. He'd watched them intently, but they didn't seem to be dealing drugs. Women carried shopping or shepherded children. They'd only been there 15 minutes, but he'd seen nothing to suggest that this was the Afghanistan of the five boroughs, as the media had it. But then, it was still daylight. Things might be different when the sun went down.

He'd seen the statuesque woman watching them as she stood in the doorway of the project building, talking to an older woman who could've been her mother. She kept looking at them, and the two were obviously discussing why two white folks were sitting in a shitty little car outside their building. Finally, she motioned the older woman to stay where she was and approached the passenger window. Lang wound it down.

She was a strikingly beautiful woman, he noticed, with almond-shaped eyes, full lips and flawless coal-black skin. Had it been two weeks ago, he'd've considered talking to her about doing some modelling work for the agency, but that was a different world. As he studied her closely he noted her gaze had a hardness to it, and there were care lines around her eyes and puckering at her mouth. Life in Brownsville was no picnic.

"You gennelmen lookin' fo' somethin'?" she asked, her voice carrying a melodic quality that was oddly soothing. It was a song of the south set to the beat of the inner city.

He gave her his best nice guy smile. "Waiting for a friend, thanks. Maybe you know him—Oscar de Blasio?"

Her eyes softened slightly. "Honey, you ain't never gonna see that boy no mo'. He got hisself shot this mornin', walkin' back from Rockaway Station. That boy dead."

He felt shock tingle at his fingertips. "Do they know who did it?"

She stared at him suspiciously, then at the car. "You ain't po-lice."

He shook his head. "No, I told you, I'm a friend of Oscar's."

She wasn't sure if she believed him, he could tell. "Uh-huh," she said and studied him closely. "You don't look like no one who'd be friends with ol' Oscar." She peered at Falcone through the window. "Neither of you."

"I'm not," said Falcone. "Never met the guy. I'm just the driver."

Lang asked. "Do they know who shot him, ma'am?" This couldn't have been random, he knew that.

Her smile lit up her entire face. "Ooh, ma'am—you got manners, I'll give you that. Okay, it don't make no never mind to him now. They say it was a boy called Shaymar, runs with the Young Guns."

"Why would he kill Oscar? Robbery?"

"These kids? They stone killers, but they don't do that shit fo' nuthin', less'n someone in the wrong place at the wrong time. Oscar been livin' here all his life, he part of us, even though he half white. That Shaymar had no call to go doin' what he done, and word is he just kilt him then went on his way. But we won't never know why 'cos he dead, too. He lyin' up an alley, shot through the head, surrounded by a whole mess of po-lice. Shaymar's momma can't get near her boy, she up there cryin'. That's why first I thought you was detectives, down here to check out Oscar's apartment."

Lang knew what had happened. Oscar could ID whoever he'd let in, therefore he had to go. They paid some street punk to take him out, then, in turn, killed the street punk. Oscar was an i to be dotted and the shooter a t to be crossed. He'd hoped Oscar would tell him something that they could use, but there was no chance of that. He briefly considered breaking into Oscar's apartment, but the woman was right, there would cops here soon. He thanked her and nodded to Falcone, who fired up the engine and pulled away.

"We need to get rid of these wheels," said Falcone. "Only a matter of time before they start circulating our photographs. That woman will recognize us."

Lang understood. Their only hope was to stay one step ahead of the law and whoever else was involved. The less anyone knew of where they'd been and where they were going, the better.

34

"You don't pull shit like that in my investigation!"

Santoro knew her voice would carry through the closed door of her office to the bullpen, but she was furious and she didn't care who knew it. She was as much in Burke's face as possible given the disparity in their height, her finger prodding the air between them. She wanted to grab him by the front of his fancy suit and throw him up against the wall but she wasn't stupid. The growing enmity between them would ensure that if there were any physical contact, he would have her on report before you could say West Coast Wuss.

Burke kept his voice low, but his own anger was evident. "When are you going to realize this is NOT just your investigation, Lieutenant?"

"We're all in this together, right?"

"Right."

"Partners?"

"Right."

She nodded took a step away. "Then *partners* don't pull that kind of shit on each other. You released photographs and information without one word of a discussion. Is that what partners do in federal service? Because that is NOT what partners do in NYPD."

He sighed and looked at McDonough, who was seated in a chair beside the door, watching the exchange with dancing eyes. Clearly, Burke expected support, but when there was none coming from that quarter, his jaw tightened and he returned his attention to Santoro.

"It's a perfectly valid tactic in situations like this," he said. "These two men are on the run. Everyone's looking for them. The NYPD. The US Marshal Service. Whoever these other gentlemen are. Now,

Falcone and Lang are not friends, far from it I'd imagine. So what we have to do is turn the screw on them, heighten the tension. They'll be pretty paranoid right about now. By releasing those photographs, we increase that paranoia, stretch their nerves. Nervous men make mistakes, they get sloppy. Now we've got a whole city on the look-out for them. Now they've got nowhere to turn."

Santoro, her anger dissipating, moved behind her desk and slumped into her chair. She treated Burke to a withering glare. "You really think these guys are going to be spooked by that? We're talking about a known Mob killer and, if I'm right, a graduate of some special force or other. This could force them so deep underground we'll need ground-penetrating radar to find them."

Burke shook his head. "No. They're on a mission. Falcone wants to find who killed his daughter. Lang is his number one suspect. Now he's not killed him yet, God knows why. Lang has obviously convinced him that he's innocent, or at least he's created sufficient reasonable doubt to keep him alive so far."

"How the hell do you know that?"

Burke looked at McDonough. This time she spoke up. "Falcone isn't some crazed psycho, Rosie..." Santoro noticed Burke's eyebrow twitching at the use of her Christian name. Now he knew McDonough and her were getting pally. Screw him, she thought.

McDonough continued, "He kills when he has to but not indiscriminately. If he knew for sure Lang murdered his girl, we'd already have the man's body in the morgue. We know they're working together, for now. But the moment Falcone is convinced your guy is responsible? He'll whack him, just as he's whacked 32 other guys that we know of."

It was Santoro's turn to raise her eyebrows. "32...?"

McDonough inclined her head slightly. "That we know of."

"And this is the guy the State's Attorney got into bed with?"

McDonough didn't flinch. "To bring down a whole bunch of guys who were worse than him. Don't forget that. There's always someone worse..."

35

Falcone and Lang took the Lincoln Tunnel to New Jersey where they abandoned the car in Hoboken and risked a cab to Jersey City. The driver was an Asian guy who chattered away on his Bluetooth throughout the journey and paid little heed to his passengers. That was good. Lang didn't know Jersey that well, so he didn't recognize the address Falcone gave the driver. As the cab pulled away, he asked, "Where we going?"

"We need wheels," said Falcone. "We'll get a new ride there."

Falcone didn't say another word for the rest of the journey. He looked out of the window, watched the buildings flash past, his arms folded. Lang sensed the man would not respond to any further questioning, so he remained silent too.

The cab turned onto a street lined with stores, and Falcone leaned forward, told the driver to let them out on the corner. They climbed out, and Lang waited for a hint as to where the vehicle was coming from. He studied the storefronts. He saw bars. He saw hair salons. He saw a hardware store and an electrical goods outlet and clothes chains.

"I don't see any car rental places," he said, eventually.

Falcone was still strangely quiet. He stepped off the sidewalk into the mouth of an alley, his eyes ranging up and down the street. Lang did the same, automatically studying parked cars, looking for people sitting inside. He saw nothing particularly suspicious, so he studied the windows above the storefronts, looking for any hint of surveillance. He saw nothing to worry him, no open windows, no one paying unusual attention to the street or any of the doorways in the street. That didn't prevent him from worrying, anyway.

He asked, "Okay, we're here, what's the plan?"

Falcone's attention was now focused on one particular frontage about 100 yards away and on the opposite side of the street. It was one of those trendy gyms catering to people with money and the time to spend on overpriced workouts. It was called Up-Town and Toned, which told Lang everything he needed to know.

"We going to work on our pecs and quads?"

Falcone ignored him.

Lang was undeterred. "Because, I've got to tell you, I haven't got my shorts with me."

Still nothing.

"And I'm allergic to body oil."

Falcone faced him then. His voice was tense. "We're here to see a guy who can get us some wheels. Clean, untraceable wheels. We can't keep boosting cars, too risky."

Lang began to worry in earnest now. "This an old associate? Because I can't even begin to tell you what a bad idea that would be."

Falcone looked away. "As bad an idea as meeting up with your lawyer buddy? That turned out real well. And calling the cops? That was a terrific notion. No risk at all there."

It was Lang's turn to be silent. He knew Falcone was right.

They waited for an hour, Falcone never taking his eyes off the door to the gym. Lang had no idea who he was watching for, so he spent most of the time checking out the lay of the land in case they had to make a swift exit. He wandered down the alleyway, looking for open doors or windows, anywhere they might hide if need be. The alley petered out at an open lot peppered with detritus. The lot was bounded by buildings and fences, so he didn't think it was a viable escape route. He wanted to walk around the perimeter, but he didn't want to go out of earshot of Falcone.

He did need some time away from the man, though. This was too risky, but they were here, and if there were surveillance teams in play they'd've been spotted by now. The feds would know just about everything in Falcone's past. The fact that no one was screaming up to arrest them—or shoot them—suggested the people after them maybe didn't know about the person they were here to see, hadn't reached him yet, or they'd decided he wasn't a viable conduit. Lang stopped short when he thought those words. Viable conduit—Jesus! He was slipping back into old ways, for that was a phrase straight out of the Janus Big Book of Report Writing. He wanted—he needed—those long dormant skills to reawaken but not that, for God's sake.

He thought about the men at Battery Park. They weren't cops, they weren't feds, and they sure as hell weren't the Mob. They had an ex-military vibe in the way they held themselves and operated. He closed his eyes, let the sound of the traffic fade as he cast his mind back to the men in the bar, the ones who had followed Gina and him out that night. They were not the same men, but they had been wearing dark suits, just like the guys in Battery Park. Maybe they were connected, maybe not. If not, that meant there was another player in this game. Just what they needed.

He heard a low whistle, which he took to be Falcone needing him back. He trotted back up the alley, saw Falcone had flattened against the wall in order to take advantage of the shadow afforded by the pale sunlight, but his eyes were intent on the roadway. Lang positioned himself behind Falcone as he flicked a finger towards the opposite sidewalk.

Falcone said, "See the guy with the jogging pants and the sneakers? Blue top?"

Lang saw him. He was directly across from the mouth of the alley, hands in the pockets of a hooded sweatshirt, his walk loose and confident, shoulders swaying like there was music only he could hear. He was maybe about 25, his hair cropped tight, his skin tanned, his body slim but tightly packed with muscle.

"So who is he?"

Falcone paused, took a deep breath. Then he said, "My son."

36

Asa sat in a comfortable chair in the corner of her office, staring through a large window onto the green sward of the University common. Students sat on benches, talking, enjoying a brief glimpse of the sun as it burned through the cloud cover. It wouldn't last, she thought. There was the feel of winter in the air.

Her hands rested on her lap, a color print-out of the *New York Post* front page held loosely in them. It was a late edition, not yet on the streets, emailed to her by a Janus operative on the newspaper staff. She stared at the face of Coleman Lang, the man she knew as Dagda. It was a face she was familiar with, although they had never met. She had studied his file when all this began, knew every one of his assignments by heart. That was her gift. The ability to memorize documents after only a few readings. She could now quote sections of his reports verbatim, if she ever had the need. Odin had chosen well, but talent spotting was his gift. He had, after all, recognized her strengths when she was a postgraduate in politics. Her sharp mind, her organizational skills, her ability to see a path through any forest of thorns had set her out from her peers and an ideal candidate for the world of covert operations. The dangerous world of the field, where Dagda thrived, was not for her. Odin had recruited her to toil in the trenches of government, clearing a way for Janus to operate largely unencumbered by oversight committees and congressional interference. Odin had already established the organization's untouchable status, and it was Asa's responsibility to both maintain and to extend it where she could. As the poet almost said, she also serves who only plots and plans.

It was Odin who gave her the codename Asa. She was African-American, but she knew nothing of her heritage then. She learned that Asa was "father" of the Kenyan Akamba people. Asa was a merciful god, a creator and provider, a god who stepped in when the humans were ineffective. Being called "father" may have upset a less secure woman, but not her. She recognized the inherent sexism of the legends and myths of the world but did not let that interfere with her work. She knew that by giving her the codename, Odin has chosen his successor, and when he decided that he had laboured too long in service of his country, that was what happened.

The cell phone on her desk buzzed. It was her Janus phone. She checked the door to her large office was securely closed before she answered.

"Asa," she said.

"You've seen the press?" She recognized the voice. Hera, Dagda's supervisor in New York. As far as Dagda knew, he had been totally off the grid, but that didn't mean he wasn't being watched. Hera in Greek mythology was protectress of marriage, childbirth and the home. Asa had read her file, too. In her day, she had been fearsome in the protection of her country. In semi-retirement, she became the unseen mother to Janus agents who had left the fold. They were off the grid but not forgotten. Never forgotten. Mostly she kept an eye on them from afar, but Dagda's special gifts meant that she had to be closer to him, so Odin had seen to it that he was placed in employment with the firm Janus had set up for her. Cole Lang knew her as Katherine. Dagda's quick and nimble mind had been useful in his service, and his creativity found a fresh outlet in advertising. Odin helped by ensuring that a steady flow of business came their way at first. After that, their own talent helped them to thrive.

"I'm looking at it now," Asa said.

"We should bring him in." Hera's voice was fat with concern.

"No."

The outright refusal caught Hera by surprise. There was a pause before she continued. "Leaving him in the cold could prove dangerous. What if he's caught?"

"Dagda will not implicate Janus."

"It'll bring unnecessary attention. There is risk…"

"There is always risk, Hera. We let him follow this through."

"And if he finds who killed his lover? And in turn kills them?"

Asa smiled. "That, my dear Hera, is what I'm banking on."

37

When Falcone told him that the young man walking ahead of them was his son, Lang was stunned. Gina had never mentioned a brother. But then, she'd told him her father was dead, and there he was standing alongside him. Before he could say anything, Falcone was moving. To be honest, Lang didn't know what he would've said anyway.

Instinct told him what was required of him, so he crossed the street while Falcone kept himself out of sight as much as he could on the opposite sidewalk. Lang kept his eyes on the man's back, but his mind was turning over a number of possibilities. From what he could see, the young man up ahead didn't resemble his father. He'd seen traces of Gina in Falcone's face, in the look he gave him when he didn't believe him. He'd seen Gina give people that look. Never him, though. Never him. He'd never lied to her, not once. Except by omission.

The young man's gait was relaxed, his shoulders straight, and he nodded occasionally to a familiar face. He didn't look around, didn't look back. But then, he had no reason to do so. Unlike Lang, he wasn't on the run from anything.

He veered into an alleyway so suddenly that Lang almost missed it. One minute he was striding along the sidewalk, the next he had ducked out of sight. Lang quickened his pace to reach the opening, paused at the corner. He peered round, saw the man sauntering past a line of dumpsters towards a doorway at the far end. He stopped, rifled through his pockets, found a set of keys, unlocked the door, stepped inside without looking back. Lang scanned the sidewalk opposite him, saw Falcone watching, and signalled to him he was going to follow. Falcone nodded and waited for a break in the traffic.

The door had no sign, no number, nothing to advertise what lay beyond. There were no windows on ground level, but there were a few blacked out on the second and third floors. It was unlikely to be an apartment, but it could be a storeroom. It could be a brothel, for all Lang knew. He sighed. There was only one way to find out. He turned the handle.

The door was snatched out of his hand, and he found himself staring into the business end of a Ruger Blackhawk .357 revolver. It was a small gun and only fired five shots, but at that range the guy wouldn't need more than one. The grim face behind it was that of Falcone's son. With a weapon in his hand, Lang now saw the resemblance. He also had the feeling that he'd seen this young man somewhere before.

"Okay, creep," the man said, "why the hell you following me?"

Lang backed up a couple of steps. "Take it easy…"

"I'll take it easy when I know who you are and why you're on my ass."

"I'm a friend of your father's," said Lang. He was overstating the relationship, but this was no time to be a stickler for accuracy.

The man's face contorted. "That shitbag didn't have no friends, so try again."

Okay, Lang thought, maybe playing the Falcone card was the wrong approach, but the hand had been dealt and he had to follow through. "I'm telling the truth, he's right behind me…"

The man raised his head from the pistol's sights to peer down the alley. "I don't see him."

Lang twisted to look but couldn't see Falcone. Where the hell was he? The traffic wasn't so bad that he would still be on the other side of the road. He turned his attention back to Falcone Jr, who was still aiming the weapon two-handed right at his face. He thought about taking it off him—he was rusty, but he was confident he could do it. He just had to time the moves correctly.

Lang said, "You've heard about your sister?"

A blink. "I don't have a sister."

Lang was stunned. He had learned that with the Falcone family nothing was ever simple, but he really didn't expect that. "Gina," he said. "Scolari... Falcone..."

Two more blinks. Lang was less stunned. The man was lying. He knew the name, but he carried on regardless. "What the hell you talking about, man? I don't know no Gina Scolari, or Falcone, or whatever name you decide to come up with."

Lang played along, kept his voice smooth and even. "So, what you're saying is, you're not Tony Falcone's son?"

"I'm saying you better get out my face or I'll blow yours off."

Lang saw the young man was ready to snap, and whatever action he was going to take he'd have to take it now. The guy was nervous, the barrel of the weapon wavered like laundry in the breeze. He didn't know what kind of set-up Falcone had dropped him into here, but he couldn't get to the bottom of it now. He threw another look over his shoulder, knew the young man would follow his gaze, then whipped both hands up, one grabbing his wrists, the other taking hold of the weapon, while at the same time he stepped to his right, and twisted the gun free. Whoever this young guy was, he was no gunman. Falcone Jnr made a lunge, but Lang expected it, so he sidestepped again and kicked his feet from under him while a hand placed firmly on his back helped put him on the ground. Lang stood over him, the weapon in his hand unwavering and aimed at his head. He had no intention whatsoever of using it, but the young man on the ground had to believe he would. Now that there wasn't a gun between them, or at least now that the gun was pointing in a direction Lang found more comfortable, he was certain this was not the first time he'd set eyes on this guy.

"I've told you once to take it easy," said Lang. "I won't tell you again. And for future reference, single-action revolvers only fire if you have the hammer cocked, like this."

The man's eyes were wide with fear, and he kicked his feet at the ground as he tried to scramble away, but Lang allowed the muzzle to follow him. "You can try running, but you can't outrun a bullet."

He stopped, found something of his prior defiance. "Did Declan send you? 'Cos, I told him, I ain't selling the gym, no way."

"Declan who?" Falcone's voice. Lang looked up, saw him walking past the dumpsters and realized he must've been hiding behind them.

"Were you there all the time?" he asked.

Falcone nodded, kept his eyes on his son. "Who is this Declan, Pietro?"

Pietro seemed to have forgotten about Lang and the gun, for he glared at Falcone. "You son-of-a-bitch, I'd heard you were dead. I hoped it was true."

"Yeah, son, you and the rest of the world. Now, who is this Declan and why has he got you so scared you're carrying a gun? Your momma not raise you right?"

"She raised me right, for all you care."

Lang was not surprised by this lack of familial warmth. With the gun still aimed at Pietro's head, he said, "So you do know him?"

Pietro sneered. "I know him, but I wish I didn't."

"And he is your father?"

Pietro hawked up some phlegm, spat it at Falcone's feet. "I may have his blood in me, but he's no father."

Lang sighed, eased the hammer of the Ruger back in place and let the pistol hang loose at his side. He leaned down, proffered Pietro his free hand. The younger man looked at it, and for a moment it looked like he was going to spit on it too, but he allowed Lang to help him to his feet.

"You want to explain all of this?" Lang said to Falcone. "For instance, why you hid behind a dumpster while your son put a gun in my face?"

Pietro yelled, "I'm not his son!"

They both ignored him. Falcone said, "I didn't know what kind of reception I'd get, so I thought I'd send you first. I didn't think he'd have a weapon, though."

"And if he'd been so scared that he shot me, what then?"

Falcone shrugged. "Then I'd've known he really didn't want to talk to me."

Pietro's voice broke in, "I don't want to talk to you, you piece of shit!"

Lang and Falcone each looked at the young man, whose face had turned bright red with his anger. Lang said, "We better move this family reunion inside."

He gripped Pietro by the arm and propelled him through the door. Falcone followed.

38

It looked like the stockroom of a busy electrical store. Pietro flicked on an overhead light to reveal a large space packed with unopened cartons, all bearing top brand names. In one corner there were about twenty larger boxes for TVs of varying types and sizes, plasma, LED, 3D. In another there were Blu-ray players, home cinema kits, TiVo devices. One wall was given over to kitchen appliances—microwaves, blenders, bread makers—another to an array of power tools. Pietro himself stood beside a stack comprised of top-of-the-range vacuum and steam cleaners.

Falcone looked around and then fixed his son with a glare. "What is this, Pietro?"

The young man stared back at him with defiance. "The name's not Pietro, it's Petey. And what the hell's it matter to you?"

Falcone didn't answer that. "What you into?"

"None of your goddamn business! You never cared what I did till now, what makes today any different?"

Falcone took a step closer to his son. "You been jacking electrical gear? You a thief, Pietro, that the way your momma raised you?"

Pietro's face contorted with rage. "Don't you talk about her, just don't you mention her name. I don't wanna hear it from your lips!"

Falcone stepped back again as if he had been slapped. Pietro looked away, one hand brushing his cheeks because his anger was overflowing from his words into his eyes. It had to go somewhere. His back to Falcone, his voice slightly strangled, he said, "It's a buddy's place. He sells this stuff. We're partners. It's all legit."

"You sure?"

Pietro whirled again, the tears gone now but the fury still there.

"You wanna see receipts?"

Falcone backed off again, gave Lang a look that suggested he'd rather be alone, but Lang didn't move. The guy had left him hanging out there with a gun in his face and he wasn't about to cut him any slack. He made a point of leaning against a stack of boxes as if he was making himself comfortable.

Falcone's face was frozen when he spoke again to Pietro. "Look, son…"

"I'm no son of yours," Pietro said, his lip curling.

"Pietro…"

"And I told you already, it's Petey. I don't go by Pietro no more. It's Petey."

Falcone gave a slight sigh. "I know you don't understand why I stayed away…"

"Oh, I understand. I get it, I really do. I was an inconvenience. You had—what? A fling? With my mom? And then I come along, and I don't fit in your world, so I see you how many times in my life? Maybe ten? Twelve?"

"It was best I stay away. It was the way your mom wanted it. I… well, I wasn't a good man to have as a father."

"No shit."

"But I always kept in touch with your mother. I sent money…"

"Oh, yeah? Money? Well, good for you. Where were you when she died?"

Falcone looked away. Lang could tell he'd known the woman was dead, but there was shame there.

"So where were you, Mr-I-Really-Gave-a-Shit, when she was in the hospital and the cancer was eating at her? Huh? You sent money, big deal, because what I really needed was a father, and what she really needed was a man who could be with her and comfort her."

The young man's words ended abruptly, as if his bitterness had closed his throat. He turned his face away from them, swiftly wiped the tears away. Falcone took a step forward as if he were going to touch his shoulder, then thought better of it. He stepped back again and waited. When Petey looked back again, more tears flooded his eyes, but Lang couldn't tell if it was rage or heartache.

"And now Gina's dead," he said, his voice lower. So he did know about Gina, Lang thought. "And I'd lay odds it's because of you."

Falcone shot Lang a look. "We don't know. Yet."

"Yeah, but I know, in here…" He tapped his chest and his lip curled in disdain once more as he spoke. "You're to blame, for what you did back then. Oh, sure—Mom told me all about you, Mr Big Hotshot Mafia Man. She told me who you were, told me never to tell anyone you were my father. Then I saw you on TV, when you turned rat. If ever I wanted to tell the world you were my father, it ended then."

"What I did, I did for everyone's benefit. I did it to protect Gina. And your mom. And you."

"Yeah? Why do I find that so hard to believe?" Petey made a show of thinking. "Wait a minute, I got it—it's because you're a self-serving son-of-a-bitch who don't care for nobody but himself."

Falcone winced. "You know all this, you know why I couldn't get in touch."

Petey thought about this, his teeth working at the side of his mouth. "Didn't make it any easier."

There was a silence then, and Lang decided he should finally leave them alone. He'd hung around to punish Falcone but felt now he was intruding on private business. He pushed himself off the boxes. "I'll wait outside," he said.

"What about my gun?" Petey asked.

Lang wasn't sure he should hand it back, but a nod from Falcone made up his mind. He tipped the bullets out before he passed it over, grip first. "Always check the safety, kid," he said and walked away.

39

Word had obviously got out, because right away, when he reported for duty, Barney's LT called him into his office, told him to take the day. In fact, he told him to take the rest of the week. Barney objected, but the lieutenant pointed to the welts on his face and said he wasn't in any fit state to work. Barney couldn't help but agree, it was only his own cussedness that had got him into the precinct that day. But he knew what this was about. They had nothing on him to merit a formal suspension, not yet anyway, but this they could do.

As he left the squad room, he was aware of the looks darted in his direction by the other detectives. In the hallway he bumped into his partner, a little pissant fresh out of the bag named Jaeson Tolliver—what the hell that extra "e" was doing in his Christian name was anybody's guess—and even he gave him the fish-eye. That did it. Barney snapped in an explosion of expletives, demanding to know what the hell his problem was. The kid stammered an apology and retreated into the squad room. Barney steamed out of the station house but right away felt guilty over his outburst. It wasn't Tolliver's fault. There was a stain on Barney's name now which might never be washed away. The Rat Squad—the Internal Affairs Bureau—would be on the case, he could make book on that. He was confident they couldn't prove anything, and he knew if Tony was caught he'd back up the story, but the doubt would follow Barney like a bad smell. To hell with them. He could ride it out till retirement, and then they could all kiss his rosy red Irish ass.

Still, he knew they might have a team on him, and he wasn't about to make life easy for them. He decided he didn't want to go back to his apartment, so he had some lunch, went to the movies—some superhero piece of shit with more special effects than storyline, but it was ideal for his mood. He bought tickets for three other shows, leaving each theatre by a back exit and then going into the next. When he made his way home he took the subway, saw no one watching him. He got off a few stops away, caught a cab the rest of the way, looking through the back window all the way. He saw no one. Maybe they hadn't mobilized yet. Maybe he was being paranoid.

He got home after dark. He'd checked his cell, but it had finally given up on him. The tiny screen was blank, and no matter what he did it didn't come to life. It was done for. He wondered if Tony had been trying to contact him but then realized it was unlikely. He'd know for sure they'd be monitoring his home and cell phone. Good luck with that, he thought, all they'd get is static, or whatever they got on a digital line.

He saw no suspicious vehicles in the street, no strange vans, but that didn't mean they weren't there. Climbing the stairway of his building was harder than ever, Lang sure had put his shoulder into cocking him, and he was never so glad to see the inside of his apartment, shithole that it was. He was weary to his bones. He hadn't slept much, he'd been pistol-whipped, seen his star fall in the department, and all he wanted to do was climb into bed and fall asleep with something mindless on the tube.

He found the note shoved under his door. The writing was careful, almost copperplate, and it was just one line: an address in Red Hook and the words "Come now". It was signed Tony. He held the slip of paper in his hands, turned it over, read it again. He couldn't remember Tony's writing. He didn't know if it was legit. But if it was, there was an urgency here, despite the impeccable script.

Shit.

He closed the door again and set off back down the stairs.

40

Lang waited in the alley for 30 minutes. He didn't mind, for he enjoyed the solitude and the sense of security afforded by the darkness. He even appreciated the chill in the air. He'd been more active in the past 24 hours than he had been in years and it, and the stress that continually gnawed at his belly, was taking its toll. He couldn't recall feeling like that when he was working for Janus, although it must've been there, the constant feeling of being on edge, of walking a tightrope, but he was a different person back then. He held out both hands, watching them tremble, and willed them to still. They didn't listen. He leaned against the wall and kneaded the corners of his eyes with one hand, saw Gina's image projected on his eyelids. He missed her so much. He needed her so much. But she was gone, and he had to accept that. Accept it but keep going. He owed her that.

The door opened and Falcone reappeared, Pietro at his back, his eyes red and wet. There had been more tears, then. The relationship between fathers and sons can be tricky. Lang's own father had been a university professor, a kind man, a caring man, a liberal who had campaigned for the human rights of others. He'd tried to teach his son basic decency and compassion, and sometimes he wondered what the old man would have thought had he ever learned of his work for Janus. But he died, when Lang was in his teens, along with his mother and sister. An automobile accident. A Mack truck ploughed into them when the driver fell asleep at the wheel. He came out without a scratch. Lang wanted to kill that driver, and the pain and loss he'd felt after the loss of his family found some release in minor civil disobedience, a smashed window here, a fight there, some drunk and disorderly conduct but that rage grew. His father's brother, an ex-Marine, took him in and put him through college, but the fury was still there and he was constantly in some kind of trouble. Arguing with tutors. Fighting in bars. Even the constant succession of women going through his dorm room. His uncle thought the Corps would help what was roiling and boiling inside him, but it took Janus to bring focus.

"Give him the envelope, Pietro," Falcone said, his voice softer than Lang had ever heard it before. The young man didn't correct him this time. Whatever had been said in there, this father and son had reached some kind of understanding, although Lang could still sense a tension between them. Pietro stepped forward, holding out a white envelope that had been folded twice and crumpled as if it had been thrust into a pocket.

"She wanted you to have this," he said.

Lang stared at the blank envelope. "Who?"

"Gina," said Pietro. "She gave me this two, three weeks ago. Said that if I ever heard anything had happened to her, I was to give it to you. You're Cole Lang, right? She said you needed to see this."

Lang looked from the envelope to the young man, then at Falcone. "You know what's in here?"

Falcone shook his head. "It's for you. She wanted you to open it."

Lang held his gaze for a moment. Something was changing between them. Lang looked back at the envelope in his hand. Gina had left this for him, with a brother she'd never told him she had. He had questions about how Pietro, or Petey, came to have it, but first he had to know what was in it. He ripped open the seal, slid a single sheet of paper out. It bore a single line in Gina's handwriting.

When the light fades at first meet, ask for Julio.

Lang held the paper out to Falcone, "This make sense to you?"

Falcone read the line, a warm smile beginning to grow. "When she was a kid, Gina used to set up these treasure hunts. She'd leave clues for me, riddles, you know? I had to follow the trail she'd created to find the prize."

Lang considered this, thought about the puzzle books she loved. Gina left this with her half-brother mere weeks before she died. Did this mean she knew something was going to happen to her? "Petey, what did she say when she gave you this?"

The young man shuffled his feet. "Just that if I hear of anything happening to her that I was to take this to Coleman Lang, and she gave me your address in SoHo. She said I could trust you, and that I had to give it to you and nobody else. I didn't know you was him until Falcone told me in there." Falcone. Not dad, pop, the old man or even Tony. Falcone. That rift hadn't healed, although Gina's words to Petey had clearly made Falcone amend his stance with regards to Lang.

Lang asked, "She explain what it was about?"

"She wouldn't say nothing more. Just get it to you. When I read about her in the papers, I tried to bring it to you, but when I got there last night the street was filled with cops, and I couldn't get into your building. They said there'd been a shooting."

That was where Lang had seen him. He'd been outside the apartment house when they came off the fire escape, talking to a patrolman. "How did you get in touch with Gina in the first place?"

Pietro looked at Falcone. "When I read about him in the papers, it said he had a daughter, a law student. One story showed her picture. I tracked her down."

"That wouldn't've been easy, she was using a different name," Lang said, impressed.

The young man looked embarrassed. "It wasn't easy, took me almost a year, but I did it."

"I'll bet the news she had a brother wasn't welcomed."

A slight smile. "She sure wasn't jumping for joy. But she got that I disliked him as much she did, and after that we kept in touch, met up now and again, had dinner, stuff like that. She came to see my mom in hospital…" The words were aimed directly at Falcone, who had the decency to look shamed again. "She even came to the funeral. She was my sister, she was my family. I loved her."

Falcone coughed, decided to move the conversation onto firmer ground, at least for him. He waved the sheet of paper. "This mean anything to you?"

Lang thought for a moment, then said, "Could be. I met Gina in the Il Tramonto bar on 55th Street."

"Tramonto's Italian for sunset," said Pietro.

Falcone's mouth was set in a firm line. "So she left something with this Julio in this bar. I know her, she's sending us on a trek before we get to what she wants us to find."

"Why would she do that? Why not just leave whatever she wants me to have with Petey here?"

"Because she didn't want to risk leaving it with him in case someone found out about him. This way, they'd have to work hard to find it, even if they could crack her riddles."

Made sense, thought Lang, but he was beginning to understand how little he really knew about Gina. Nonetheless, he felt pride warm the cold that had been aggravating his guts. "We need a car, Petey," he said.

Pietro stared at him, then reached a decision. "This is for Gina, not him." He didn't need to say who he meant. Lang caught the keys when they were thrown to him and spotted Falcone's hurt look being forced down. Whatever had been said inside, no bridges had been built. Maybe he didn't deserve them. He watched the man walk away from his son without a further word, his shoulders set straight, as if he was holding something in. Anger, maybe. Pain, probably.

Pietro said, "Blue Taurus, Jersey plates, Jets sticker on the back window, parked in a lot the other side of the gym, right up against the wall."

"Thanks," Lang said, but Pietro batted it away.

"There was something wrong with Gina. She wouldn't tell me when I asked, but I knew there was something bothering her."

"Something to do with me?"

"No. She cared for you, a lot. I could tell. Whatever it was, it wasn't you. But this past few months? It's like she was haunted, does that make sense?"

Lang thought about Gina's silences and the way she would drift off when they were together, then her attempts to cover it up. "Yes, it makes sense."

Pietro jutted his chin at his father's back, by now at the end of the alley. "You want my advice? Don't trust him. He's no good. When it comes to it, he'll turn on you or let you down."

"How can you be so sure?"

He gave his father's back a long stare, watched him turn out of the alley. "Because it's what he does."

Lang thanked the young man again and sprinted after Falcone. He drew level with him in the street. "Want to talk about it?"

"What are you? Oprah?" snapped Falcone. "I told you before, we ain't buddies, so don't get to thinking we are."

"Okay," said Lang and fell silent for a moment. Then, "We've got wheels now. We can head back to Manhattan, hit that bar."

Falcone had taken another few steps before he spoke again. "But first, we got a stop to make."

41

Barney was on edge looking out for the Rat Squad, so he really should've been more careful.

The Red Hook address was a crumbling old wood and brick warehouse right on the waterfront, surrounded by other similar buildings, all empty, or at least they appeared to be. The cabbie gave him a look that cast doubt on his sanity as he drove away. Barney understood that look. He was questioning the wisdom of this trip himself. He should've got right back in the cab and gone home. He should've called this in. But then he might've been betraying Tony, and he couldn't bring himself to do that. It was the third cab he'd hopped that night, as well as two subway trips. It was exhausting, but he felt he had to be careful. Now, though, he was certain there was no one on his tail.

A large pair of wooden doors faced him, a smaller one set into the right-hand wing. It was ajar. He pushed it open, drew his Sig and stepped over the lip.

It was dark in the warehouse, so he took a small flashlight from his pocket and swung it around. The place was a real mess. Beams had collapsed from the roof, tiles and wood lay everywhere. Empty beer cans, vodka bottles and chip bags were scattered here and there. There was other, less appetizing, garbage. If he looked hard, he knew he'd find used hypos, so he reminded himself to watch where he put his feet. Last thing he needed was a goddamn needle through his shoe and a trip to the emergency room. He could hear water dripping somewhere, and there was a pervading smell of damp exuding from the walls, the floor, the river. He thought he heard something scurrying through the debris that littered the floor. He vowed he'd blow away the first one of the beady-eyed little bastards he came across.

He moved through the building, wrists crossed, flashlight in his left hand, weapon in his right. He called out for Tony, his voice echoing round the empty rooms. No answer. He didn't like that. What the hell was he doing here? He must need his head examined, coming to a place like this alone.

Then he heard what he thought was a groan. He stopped. Held his breath. Listened.

"Tony?" he shouted.

He cocked his head, straining to hear. Something with little claw-like feet scraped away to his right and he swung the beam round but saw nothing. Listened again. The water of the Upper Bay lapped softly against the wharf outside. Somewhere, there was a distant siren. The dripping in the dark sounded like it was marking the seconds. He exhaled softly, inhaled again, held it. Listened.

The groan came again. It seemed to be coming from above him.

He jerked the flashlight around, found a stairway against a far wall. It didn't occur to him then that it was pretty new, the wood still fresh. He thought about that later, though, when he rued his stupidity. When the pain came.

He moved up the stairs carefully, calling out Tony's name again, his Sig tracking the flashlight as it bounced ahead. He reached the top and found himself on a section of decking that had been completely cleared of debris. The door to a large loading bay lay open, and through it Barney could see the lights of Jersey twinkling far across the bay. A wooden chair was positioned in the center of the cleared area, a table beside it. His nerves tingled a warning, so Barney paused, crouched, swept the perimeter, but saw no one.

He didn't hear the man step up behind him.

The first he knew he was there was the sensation of cold steel on the back of his neck.

"Drop the gun, detective," said Nicky the Juke, pressing the muzzle of his own weapon deep into Barney's flesh. Barney hesitated, and Nicky leaned in closer to his ear. "Don't make me kill you. We haven't even had a chance to chat."

Barney let the Sig slip from his fingers to clatter on the wooden floor. Nicky placed his free hand on his back and gave him a powerful shove further into the room. Barney stumbled forward a few steps then whirled in time to see Nicky had stooped to retrieve his gun and was slipping it into the pocket of the long coat he wore. He had never met the Juke, but he knew him. The scumbag was notorious in the department for sliding free of any beef, and there wasn't an honest cop who didn't want to get something on him.

Nicky's smile broadened. "Detective Mayo, nice to meet you. I'm Nicoletto Bruno."

Barney didn't return the smile but did try for nonchalance, even though he could hear his blood pounding in his ears. "I know who you are, and I thought you were a smart guy. I'm an NYPD detective and you broke into my home, lured me here on false pretences and now you're threatening me with a gun. Not too clever."

"A disgraced NYPD detective, is what I hear. And your home didn't take much breaking into, let me tell you. That lock? Don't even deserve the name."

Barney thought about Tony breaking in. "Yeah, tell me about it. But you know about my problems with the department, you know IAB might be all over me. You took a risk delivering that note."

"I like risk. It tells me I'm alive."

Barney would bet this son-of-a-bitch did enjoy taking chances. He took another step back, checked out his surrounding, his eyes falling on the scarred wooden chair to his left and wondered how many other souls had sat in that chair while the Juke held a weapon on them. "So, to what do I owe the pleasure of this little trip to the riverside?"

"Oh, I think you know."

Barney gave him a thin smile. "I don't know where Tony is."

Nicky grinned as he took a silencer from his pocket and screwed it in. He did it slowly, almost lovingly. If that wasn't bad enough, he was singing softly. Barney recognized the song. It was "The Games People Play". Joe South sang it back in the late 60s. He'd not heard it for years and didn't much like hearing it now.

"What you gonna do, Nicky? Kill a cop?"

"Wouldn't be poppin' my cherry in that department, my friend. But no, I'm not gonna kill you." He leveled the gun, fired once, blew out Barney's knee. Barney screamed, pitched to the floor, but Nicky was on him instantly, grabbing him by the collar of his coat and dragging him towards the chair.

Barney groaned as the agony seared through his body from its source. His voice was hoarse with pain as he rasped, "You son-of-a-bitch bastard…"

"Leave my momma out of this, she was a saint." Barney winced as he was dragged along the floor and dropped beside the wooden chair. "The bastard part is true, though. I never did know my poppa. You know they say he was the local Don? Not the Cosa Nostra, a real honest-to-God Don. I got nobility in my veins."

"You got shit in your veins," Barney said, his voice still strangled by white hot fire coursing through his body. "You better just kill me. I won't tell you nothing."

Nicky came to a halt and sighed, sadly. "You'll talk, my friend. Everyone talks. As for killing you? Not gonna happen." He stepped away, the gun centered on Barney's forehead. He wiggled the barrel towards the chair. "Now, do me a favor, detective—get in the chair."

Barney had both hands clasped to his wound and blood streamed through his fingers. "Are you shittin' me? You just took out my knee!"

"You still got one good one. Get in the chair."

The agony was intense, and Barney thought he'd pass out, but he managed to struggle into the chair. He slumped, feeling a wave of nausea flood upwards, but he dammed it up, forced it back. He wouldn't throw up, not in front of this son-of-a-bitch. He wouldn't give him the satisfaction.

Nicky stepped behind him, wrapped some zip ties round his wrists, fastened him securely to the chair. It hurt, but Barney didn't flinch. At least, he didn't think he did. All the while the nutjob was singing that damn song.

"You're wasting your time, you sick bastard," said Barney, feeling good with his defiance despite the intense discomfort of both his leg and the zip ties. "I know you want to know where Tony is, but here's a newsflash—I don't know."

Nicky stopped singing. He put the gun away, rifled in his coat pocket for something else. "You do know something, *mi amico*, and we'll get to it, sooner or later. So—we can do this the easy way…" He took a pair of pliers and a screwdriver from the pocket of his coat and laid them on the table. "…or I can have some fun."

Barney stared at the tools and felt a very real terror mix with his nausea, but he was damned if he would show it. "Screw you, Bruno. And we ain't no *amicos*."

Nicky laughed. "That's it, my Mick friend. Be brave. Be the all-American hero. But you will talk. And then I will kill you. And believe me, you *will* beg me to do it…"

42

The Ford Taurus was new, clean and comfortable. Falcone's estranged son was doing well for himself. Even though it was now dark, Falcone had obviously not forgotten his way round Jersey City, for he manoeuvred through the streets with ease. For about ten minutes they drove in silence, even though Lang was desperate to know where they were headed. Falcone stared straight ahead, both hands clasped so tightly round the steering wheel his knuckles shone white. What had happened in that storeroom had affected him deeply, but Lang wasn't going to ask him about it again.

He didn't have to.

"I met his mother when I was over here doing some work for old man Marino." Falcone just started talking, and once he'd begun it was as if he was desperate to get it out, to tell someone, even a guy he didn't fully trust. "He'd made a deal with the Irish mob here over some slot machines, and he needed a guy to work with them. That guy was me, so I was here for a coupla months, on and off, setting things up, overseeing delivery, making sure Guido didn't get ripped off. Pietro's momma was a waitress in this bar we used to go to. She was beautiful, I mean Hollywood beautiful, you know?"

Lang knew what he meant. Gina had been Hollywood beautiful. At least as far as he was concerned. He'd seen photographs of her mother and she was stunning, too. Falcone was no George Clooney so he must have charms Lang was yet to find.

"Anyway, one thing led to another, we began dating. She didn't know I was married with a kid already. She was a good Catholic girl, you know? She finds out I'm already hitched, she's gonna drop me like I was a hot rock. So I'm over here two, three times a week during this period, and we're gettin' hot and heavy—she wasn't *that* good a Catholic girl—and the inevitable happens and she's knocked up." He sighed. "But she won't get rid of the kid, no matter what I say, even though I tell her that I'm married. That was a conversation I never want to have again…" Falcone stopped talking, and Lang wondered if he was recalling the scene from all those years ago or the one in the storeroom. "So what could I do? I liked her, I liked her a lot, you understand? But I also liked my wife, and Gina was just a little kid. There wasn't no way that I could leave them. So I promised I'd always be there for her and the kid, made sure she never needed nothing, got over to see her as much as I could. In the early days, anyway. But then…"

Lang waited, but Falcone had clammed up again. "But then?"

Falcone sighed. "Life, you know? Gets in the way. Shit happens. Guido always had something for me to do, and I had some deals of my own to attend to. After a while I didn't come over so much. I still sent money, I always sent money. Then me and Gina's mom, we started fighting. I mean, we always fought, but these were heavy." Falcone actually looked shamefaced. "There were other women. I'd never been what you would call a good husband, and I guess she just had enough. Even when I separated from her I didn't come over here too much. It woulda been the decent thing, right? Come over here, get my divorce, marry Pietro's momma, give the boy a real father?" He gave out a little laugh, but there wasn't much humor in it. "Guess what—I ain't been one for the decent thing. So I stayed away, did my own thing, took care of number one."

Lang cleared his throat, said softly, "Pietro seems to have done well for himself."

"Yeah, the kid's done okay. He's got a wife, too, and two kids. I'm a grandfather and I didn't even know it. He's got his gym, which is doing good. Maybe too good. It's attracted the wrong kind of attention."

"This Declan guy he mentioned?"

"Piece of shit called Declan King. He's a crime lord wannabe—does some loansharking, pushes some dope, runs a few girls. Seems he needs a few more legit businesses to clean up his take, and Pietro's gym fits the bill. He's been piling pressure on the kid, trying to get him to sell up, but the kid's been pushing back. He's been expecting it to turn nasty."

"Hence the gun."

"Hence the gun. I ain't been much of a father, but I don't like my kid being strong-armed out of something he's built himself. And I don't want him getting himself into trouble with the law when he tries to defend himself."

Now Lang understood. "I guess we're paying Mr King a visit?"

"You catch on real quick."

Lang fought the urge to remind Falcone that they didn't have time for this. It wouldn't do any good.

43

King operated out of the back room of a bar called Cuchulainn's in Greenville. Lang recognized the name, that of an Irish hero of the first century, and it made him think of Janus. His own code name, Dagda, was also from Irish mythology and meant the Good God. He hadn't heard it before he was recruited, but he'd thought it fitting because back then he thought he'd been doing good, defending his country from foreign enemies.

Falcone parked the Taurus in a side street two blocks away and said, "You can come in or stay, your choice. But you come in, you follow my lead. Understand?"

Lang nodded, climbed out of the car. He knew he was doing the wrong thing, knew that whatever Falcone was going to do in that bar was not something he wanted to be part of, but he thought perhaps his presence would at least tone it down. After all, he was the Good God.

There was a noticeable bite to the air as they walked along the street towards the bar. The double doors were thick, heavy and decorated with stained glass depictions of a huge figure in a chariot decorated with human heads. Lang assumed it to be Cuchulainn. It was an upmarket Celtic-themed bar that was doing well enough to make Lang wonder why King needed to diversify into crime. But then, greed knows no limits. Inside there were more stained-glass panels around the walls depicting scenes from Irish folklore, interspersed with pennants bearing the Irish tricolor and neon lights in the shape of harps. The bar was long and curved and made of heavy polished wood. The Thin Lizzy track "The Boys Are Back in Town" was just coming to end and was followed by something traditional by The Chieftains.

A young barman saw them approach and waited for an order. The smell of hot food made Lang's stomach growl, and he realized he hadn't eaten anything for hours. When their business here was done, he had to make sure they got something to eat. An engine doesn't run without fuel, an army marches on its stomach, all that jazz.

Falcone raised his voice over the music and smiled his best smile. "We're looking for Mr King."

The barman nodded, obviously used to people asking for his boss. "And who can I say you are?" Irish accent, that was a good touch, thought Lang, and wondered if it was real or just part of the show.

Falcone was still smiling. "Let's just say he really wants to see me."

The barman returned the grin. "Ah, now—there's many a man comes in here saying that, turns out Mr King really doesn't want to see them."

"I'll bet. The name's Tony Falcone, and I've got a business proposition for him."

"And will that be all that I'm saying?"

"That'll be all you need to say."

The young man nodded, moved down the bar and disappeared through a door midway along the gantry. Lang sidled closer to Falcone and whispered, "You sure that was a smart thing to do, giving your name?"

"Honesty is always the best policy, didn't your mom and dad tell you that? Anyway, nobody here's paying any attention to us."

Lang looked around. Falcone was correct. The crowded bar was filled with people not paying any attention to them. "What if this King guy hasn't heard of you? You've been out of the picture for ten years."

"King knows me, don't worry about that." Falcone fixed his eyes on the doorway the barman had gone through. "I killed his father."

Falcone moved abruptly away, heading along the front of

the bar, still watching the door. Lang followed, the shock of the admission still tingling. He leaned closer, spoke as quietly as he could against the music. "Are you crazy? We've got more important things to deal with right now..."

"There's nothing more important than family," Falcone had found where the bartop was hinged to allow access. "Everything we're doing is about family, don't you understand that?"

Falcone raised the cutaway and stepped through. Lang looked around, saw two or three faces looking in their direction but dismissed them as a threat. They were merely looking, not noting. Mostly people were simply getting on with having a good time. He exhaled heavily through his nose and followed Falcone.

The door in the gantry led to a narrow stairway heading to a basement level. Falcone had pulled his gun and was halfway down the steps when Lang caught up with him. Voices drifted their way and he recognized the young barman. At the bottom of the stairs the floor turned right and leveled out into a cramped corridor. No fancy Irish decoration here, just unpainted plaster walls, wooden floors and one light fitting with a bare bulb. At the far end he saw a fire exit, to the right a doorway opened to a dark area he presumed to be the bar's cellar and stockroom, further along to the left he could see the barman's back in another doorway.

Falcone didn't miss a step as he closed in and shoved the young man further into the room, his gun level as he followed him in. Lang moved swiftly behind him, finding a small room made even smaller by the amount of men crammed inside—in addition to Falcone and the barman, there was an Incredible Hulk lookalike standing against the far wall like a pillar of stone, a thin man with the androgynous features of a 70s rock star sitting in a wooden chair to the right reading the *New York Post*, and the man he presumed to be King behind a desk. He was soft-featured, with flabby jowls and pouting lips, his hair thinning but long. He wasn't pretty. Behind him was a bank of three small TV screens, each showing the interior of the bar upstairs. Each screen was linked to a single laptop computer which sat on a wooden shelf below them. Lang assumed none of them had been paying attention to the monitors, otherwise he and Falcone might not have reached this far.

The rock star moved first, started to rise, his hand darting under his brown leather jacket but Falcone swung his weapon in his direction, shook his head in warning. The man saw sense, his hand fell to his side and he sat back down.

"Let's have all your weapons on the floor, right now," ordered Falcone.

Rock star and the Hulk each looked to King, who nodded, and two guns were thrown onto the worn rug in front of the desk. Falcone hardly gave them a look. "And the back-up pieces."

No one moved.

"I wouldn't advise pissing me off, guys. I've had a long day, and I'm not a patient man at the best of times. You know that, don't you, Declan?"

King stared at Falcone with no emotion at all, then jerked his head to his men and another two weapons were thrown to the floor.

"Okay," said Falcone, waved his weapon quickly towards the barman. "You—Liam Neeson—sit on the floor, hands under your ass." The young man did as he was told. He looked terrified. "The rest of you, one of you as much as twitches, things get ugly, you understand?" They looked as if they understood. Falcone stared at Declan, who hadn't moved a muscle since they entered. "So, Declan, how you been?"

"I thought you were dead, Falcone."

"Yeah, I get that a lot, but as you can see, I'm still alive and kicking."

King smiled, but it was little more than a sneer. "Not for long, is what I hear."

"We're none of us long for this world, Declan, that's the way of things. Your father learned that the hard way."

"That what this is about? You think I want payback for you

taking the old man out after, what? 20 years?"

"It's 21, but who's counting?"

Declan finally moved, waved a dismissive hand. "Let me tell you something, I don't bear no grudge over that. Sure, I was sore when it happened, what ten-year-old kid wouldn't be? But see, now I understand. I'm a businessman, and I understand about hostile takeovers. Shit—I've done a few myself. You and old Guido? You wanted what my father had, and you took it. He got in the way, and you dealt with him. Looking back, you did me a favor. He wasn't no prize, my old man. He used to beat me, abused my sister." His mouth fell open when he saw the surprise on Falcone's face. "Ah, you didn't know he was a piece of shit pervert? So, now you see, you did the world a favor, you did my family a favor. Why you think I never came after you before?"

"Frankly, Declan, you never even crossed my mind."

If King was hurt by that he didn't show it. He didn't show much. Lang couldn't read whether what he was saying was true. "There's no bad blood between us, is what I'm saying, Falcone. You don't need the armory."

"You don't mind, I'll keep it out. It feels more natural."

King raised his hands. "Suit yourself. So—what brings you to Jersey after all these years?"

"I got my eye on some real estate here, thought I'd get back into business. I've been away for a few years."

"Yeah, saw you on the news all those years ago. You really did a number on old Guido, huh?"

"It seemed like the thing to do."

"Not a good idea to come back, I'd say. Vinnie is still pissed, is what I hear. And then there's Nicky the Juke to consider. He ain't the type to kiss and make up."

"They're my problem, Declan. I'm yours."

"Hey, you not been listening? We got no beef, you and me."

"Good to hear, Declan. That means you'll back away from the up-town and toned gym."

211

King paused then, a frown creasing his forehead, his lips puckering as he took this in. "What's your interest in that place?"

"Had my eye on it for a time. Seems like it might be a good place to sink some cash into. I hear you got the same notion, and I need you to back away."

King's lips parted into a grin, showing some amazingly white and even teeth. "Hey, you want it, you got it. It ain't no skin off my nose, I got plenty of other interests. But that guy who runs it? That Pietro Ventimiglia? He don't want no partners."

"You leave that to me. All you need to know is that from this moment on, the gym and Ventimiglia are mine. Do we have a deal?"

"I'm a reasonable man, Tony—can I call you Tony?" Falcone shrugged his consent. "You want me out of the picture, then I'm gone. Just like that. That kid, he gets left alone, no problem. I'll give you my hand on it."

King stood up slowly, his right hand extended. He was being reasonable. He didn't hold a grudge over the death of his father. He was happy to leave Pietro alone. He was oozing goodwill. Lang sensed something wrong about the whole thing, but Falcone moved forward slightly, ready to shake the proferred hand of friendship.

And then King's left hand came up from his side and he had a gun there, maybe it had been taped to the side of his chair. He fired off a shot, but he'd moved too fast and it went wild. Lang ducked, even though the bullet buried itself harmlessly into the wall two feet away, and instinctively reached for his own weapon under his woollen coat, but Falcone had already fired, hitting King on the shoulder, a puff of red, jerking him to the side. Falcone's second slug slammed into the man's torso, and he flew back into the monitors. Now the Hulk was moving, coming round the desk, heading for the guns on the floor, but Falcone fired again, catching him on the chest. He didn't stop moving, so Falcone put another one in him before swiveling towards the rock star who had remained frozen in his chair at first but now lunged to reach a weapon. Two bullets in the back put him face down, but the Hulk wasn't done—he was on the floor and reaching for the nearest gun when Falcone stood over him and calmly fired into the base of his skull.

It was impossibly quiet in the little room after the gunfire. Lang had his gun in his hand, but he hadn't fired a shot. Falcone loomed over the big man's body, his gun still trained on his head, as if he expected him to move again.

A whimper from the corner made him whirl round, the Glock snapping up, then he checked himself. The barman was curled into a ball on the floor, weeping like a child, his hands over his ears. Falcone moved to his side and stood over him. The barman opened his eyes, saw the weapon pointed directly at his head, closed his eyes again and screamed.

"He's no threat, leave him," said Lang, but Falcone ignored him and kept the gun aimed at the young man. "Tony, I said leave him." Something in his voice made Falcone look back. Lang had the Beretta on him, but it didn't worry him one bit. His eyes were dead, the same way they had been in his apartment the night before, as if drained of all humanity. The look was flat, there was no depth, like the windows of an empty building. Lang wondered if that was how his own eyes were after he'd killed for Janus. He hoped not. Falcone stared at the weapon aimed in his direction but didn't seem to care. He turned back to the young man cowering on the floor.

"What's your name?" he asked. The young man didn't answer. "Tell me your name."

Finally, the young man said, "Patrick."

Falcone nodded. "What did you see, Patrick?"

The young man shook his head. Falcone leaned in, pressed the barrel into the side of his head. The young man groaned and tried to press himself further into the floor. Lang took a step forward, but Falcone waved him away. "What did you see?" he asked again.

"Nothing," the barman whispered.

"No, you saw something," corrected Falcone. "You saw three men come in here and gun your boss down. Three men. And they looked nothing like us, you understand?"

Patrick nodded his understanding.

"Say it," ordered Falcone.

"Three men." Patrick was thinking fast. The Irish accent was gone now, and he was pure New Jersey. "One was tall and skinny, another kinda fat. The third was black."

"Okay," Falcone breathed. "You stick to that, Patrick, and you'll live a long and happy life." He checked the TV screens, ensuring that no one upstairs had heard the shots. They'd sounded loud in the room, but the ceiling was old and thick, and the music up there was turned up pretty high. "That computer the only place the camera images are stored, Patrick?"

Patrick nodded without raising his head. Falcone gave Lang a wave to get the computer, then positioned himself at the door to monitor the hallway. Lang stepped over the bodies to jerk out the cables leading to the laptop before thrusting it under his arm. Falcone kept his Glock ready as he backed down the corridor towards the emergency exit.

Lang's eyes settled again on Patrick, who was still curled into a ball and crying. He might live a long time, but he might not be happy. Some things can haunt a person.

Falcone had pushed open the fire exit and was in an alley striding towards the street when Lang caught up with him. "Was that necessary?"

Falcone stopped, turned to face him. "Did you see the front page of the newspaper in there?" Lang shook his head. He hadn't paid any attention. "We were on it, you and me. And King knew that. He was going to turn us over to Nicky and Vinnie."

Lang took this in, annoyed that he hadn't noticed it. Time was he wouldn't have missed a detail like that. "How can you know?"

"Because I know these guys. Because I am one of these guys, don't forget that, Lang."

"But did you have to kill them all?"

Falcone took a deep breath. The life had returned to his eyes, and Lang thought he saw something fresh there. Pain, maybe, as if he wasn't proud of what he'd done, but he'd done it. "Those guys? They just *threatened* my blood. Think what I'll do to you if I find out you killed my Gina."

"Jesus—you still think I had something to do with it? After all this? After Gina's note?"

"All I know is Gina must've felt she was in some sort of danger. She may not've known where it was from. It could've been you, but she might've not seen it. I'm a careful guy, Lang, that's why I've lived this long. We see where this leads, see how it plays out. Then we'll know."

Then he turned, leaving Lang standing alone in the dark alley.

44

Vinnie Marino didn't like speaking to cops. He especially didn't like speaking to them in his own home, when his wife was in bed upstairs naked and he was wrapped only in a dressing gown. They'd been having maritals when Tommy Lorenzo buzzed through on the intercom. Tommy was stationed out front of the house all night along with his cousin, Alphonse Carpozi. The Marino family might not be top of the heap no more, but there were still people out there who did not wish them long lives. Tommy told him there was a cop and two feds here to speak with him. Vinnie's wife sighed, slid off him, wrapped her luscious body in the bedsheet and told him not be too long, otherwise the mood would wear off. Vinnie promised her he'd have them gone before the sweat on her back dried.

He told Tommy to show them into his study, where he sat behind his father's old desk and glared at them. He didn't offer them any refreshment. This wasn't a social call.

"What you want to come calling this time of night?" he asked. "You disturbing my beauty sleep."

"Yeah, sorry about that, Vinnie," said the small Latina, who'd ID'd herself as Lieutenant Santini, or some such, from Manhattan. Vinnie hadn't been paying much attention because his mind was still on his wife's curves and the way she felt under his hand. He forgave the cop for being familiar, calling him by his first name. He was easy-going that way. He knew it was a cop's way of showing dominance. They know your first name, they call you by it, but you don't get to know theirs. It was all a game.

He waved the apology away. It wasn't sincere anyway. "So, what's so important that it couldn't wait till business hours?"

"Anthony Falcone." It was the handsome black guy who spoke. Vinnie hadn't caught his name either. He just knew he was with the US Marshals, as was the good-looking redhead. Where did they recruit, the pages of *Vogue* magazine? "Did you know he was back in the city?"

Vinnie saw no reason to lie. "Yeah, I heard something 'bout that."

"You any idea where he might be?" The cop again.

Vinnie snorted. "He ain't likely to be filling me in on his itinerary."

"You think maybe Nicky the Juke knows where he is?"

"Who can say what Nicky knows?"

"You know where Nicky is, Vinnie?"

He laughed. "Nicky? He comes, he goes. He's like a goddamn will o' the wisp."

The cop smiled. Vinnie wondered if she knew what a will o' the wisp was. Truth was, he wasn't too sure himself. He'd heard it in a movie, thought it sounded cool.

"Is he out looking for Falcone, Vinnie?"

"How the hell should I know?"

"He's your man."

"Nicky's his own man."

"You're his Don."

Vinnie laughed again. "His Don? Jeez, lady, you been watching too many movies. I'm no Don. I'm just a businessman, pure and simple."

"You may be simple, Vinnie, but you sure ain't pure."

Vinnie frowned, getting the feeling he'd just been insulted. "Hey! No need for that. I invite you into my home in the middle of the night..."

"It's 9.30, Vinnie."

"So? I'm an early-to-bedder. Makes a man healthy, wealthy and..."

"A wise guy," the cop said as she leaned over his desk. "Here's a word to that wise guy, Vinnie. I've got a morgue full of bodies. I've got two dead cops. I've got a homicide suspect and a high-profile government witness on the loose and the top brass breathing down my neck. If your attack dog is out there making things worse and I find out, then I will make it my personal mission to screw with you and your business. And these US Marshals here will pull every string they can to bring down federal heat. Now, here's what you have to decide, Vinnie—is all that grief worth it to protect a will o' the wisp? So, my advice? You get word to Nicky and you pull in his leash."

Vinnie extended his hands, palm up. "Hey, Lieutenant, there's no need for animosity here. I'm a law-abiding citizen. I pay my taxes. I want the good guys to win. You got two guys on the run? Of course I want them apprehended and tucked away safe in a prison cell. And, naturally, I'll help in every way I can. I got lots of friends out there. I'll put the word out."

"And Nicky the Juke?"

"Nicky, too. Sure thing."

When they left, Vinnie sat at his desk for a few minutes, thinking the conversation over. He was not overly concerned with the cop's threat. The law and the feds were always on his ass, one way or the other. He wanted Falcone whacked, but maybe Nicky was proving too reckless. He knew he wouldn't be able to rein him in, as the cop said, for he had the bit between his teeth now. The only thing that would stop him was a bullet.

Maybe it was time.

He hadn't heard from Nicky since he'd watched him get patched up, but he knew he'd be in contact as soon as he had something tangible. Whatever Nicky was, he was dependable that way. Vinnie would find out where he was, then see to business. He'd go himself, he owed that much to the guy for his service to the family. And Nicky would never expect him to get his hands dirty.

Vinnie returned to the bedroom, unfastening his robe as he walked in the door. The anticipation of the pleasures ahead were showing in the bulge underneath. Or maybe the thought of finally ridding himself of the one man who scared the living daylights out of him was proving to be an aphrodisiac. He could hear a TV on, but that didn't matter. Nothing would distract him from the delights of his wife's body.

He stood in the open doorway, the robe hanging loose, his erection peeking out like it was Groundhog Day. His wife was on her back, mouth open, snoring. He thought about waking her up but decided against it. She was always cranky when she just woke up. He fastened the robe, flipped the TV to a movie channel and settled down beside her. There would be other nights, he told himself. Anyway, he had to think about Nicky. This had to be done right.

45

It took some driving around before Lang and Falcone found a parking space in the city. They had to walk a few blocks to reach Il Tramonto, and Lang could feel his nerves fray with every step. It was dark, thankfully, but when a cop car cruised by, he had to resist the urge to turn his head away from it. That would be fatal. Falcone simply walked on, for he knew that to do anything unusual like duck down or dive into a doorway would merely attract their attention, but Lang saw him watching the car as it proceeded along 55th Street. The only time his step faltered was when they saw two cops standing at a corner, their cruiser parked nearby, questioning a young guy with the zombie look of a terminal junkie. One of the cops was snapping on a pair of rubber gloves and asking the guy if he had anything in his pockets that could stick him. The addict shook his head, but the cop asked again, warning him if he got stuck the shit would hit the fan.

A cruiser driving past was one thing, walking within two feet of two of New York's finest when their faces were all over the press and probably TV was another—even if Lang had altered his appearance slightly. It was a chilly night so they each huddled down into their jackets as they walked, partly obscuring their faces, reasoning the cops wouldn't think that unusual.

"So she says to me, 'Where the hell you been?'" Falcone said, suddenly, taking him by surprise. He hadn't said a single word on the journey from New Jersey, and Lang had left him to his anger. He didn't say anything for a moment, but Falcone expected a response because carrying on a normal conversation was part of hiding in plain sight.

"So what'd you say?" He tried to give his voice a Bronx twang, wasn't sure he'd quite managed it and resolved to keep his end of the conversation as short as possible.

"Told her I'd been at a ball game. She says, 'There ain't no ball game on tonight.' I mean, jeez, right? First time she ever takes an interest in sports and it's to bust my balls…"

Lang risked a glance at the cops. They were carrying on their own conversation with the addict, not paying any attention to the two guys walking by.

"So how'd you square it with her?" he asked.

"I didn't, we ain't talked since. She said she was gonna go home to her mother. Let me tell you, her mother's welcome to her. All they need is that bitch sister of hers to come, too, and you'd have the opening scene in *Macbeth*…"

They were safely beyond the officers by now, and Falcone stopped talking again. Lang sighed inwardly. Of all the Mob hitmen he had to partner up with, it was one with issues.

Il Tramonto hadn't changed since that night the year before. No reason why it should, he supposed. The customers were uniformly in their 30s and 40s because it wasn't the kind of place to attract the younger crowd. They stood or, if they were lucky, were seated in groups or pairs, the occasional single male roamed around or stationed himself at the bar, watchful eyes stroking the women. They were the predators, the hunters, and the females were their prey. And then there were the women who had the same look in their eyes, the pursuit of sex no longer recognising gender barriers. To an anthropologist it might be fascinating—the mating rituals of the 30 something—but it held no allure for Lang. He had dreaded going back to that life when he separated from Sophia, and it was only his good fortune that he'd met Gina.

Falcone moved straight to the bar, made a space his own and motioned the bartender over. He leaned in, said something Lang couldn't hear over the sound of David Bowie blasting from the hidden speakers. His final album, he noticed. He recalled the outpouring of grief over the singer's death from people who'd never known the man personally, had only heard his music. He thought it was only another way that everything had to be a drama in the 21st century. The thing was, Bowie wasn't dead, not really. He lived on in his music.

The barman pointed to a tall, skinny, astonishingly handsome black man working at the other end of the bar. He was leaning over the counter talking to two 30-something women who appeared to be hanging on his every word. Lang would lay odds he got lucky with many of the women who came into the bar looking for a casual hook-up.

Falcone interrupted the flirting by sliding in beside the two women and saying, "Excuse me, ladies, I need a word with this guy." The women looked as if they were going to take issue, but Falcone gave them a look that told them it might be hazardous to their health and they drifted away. Falcone said, "You Julio?"

If the barman was annoyed over losing his conquests he didn't look it. To him, plenty more fish in the sea was an understatement. He smiled. "That's the name, man, don't wear it out."

"Gina Scolari sent us."

The smile faltered, froze and melted. Julio's gaze flicked from Falcone to Lang and back again, his eyes narrowing. He thought for a moment, then nodded and motioned that they should stay where they are. He stepped back, strained to see over the heads of the customers, finally saw what he wanted and crooked his finger. A lanky blonde carrying a tray pushed her way towards them. She was young and she was beautiful, and she knew that some of the predator males were watching her, but she didn't seem to care. Used to it, Lang guessed.

"Janine, spell me for a while, huh?" said Julio. "Gotta talk to these gentlemen."

"Sure, Julio, glad to," she said. "Be great to get out from the press of humanity." Her voice was cultured, and Lang pegged her as a student earning some cash.

Julio jerked his head for them to follow him and he moved out from behind the bar to a doorway. They found themselves in a small windowless room with one wall taken up by lockers, another wall with a sink, some kitchen cupboards, a microwave and a coffee maker. A square table carrying dirty coffee cups and plates sat in the center with four chairs arranged around it.

"Sorry about the mess," said Julio, the sound of the islands in his voice. Another student, Lang would bet his life on it. Julio sat down, pushed a cup away from him, motioned to the other chairs. "Please."

They sat. It would've been churlish not to when he was so mannerly.

"So," Julio said, leaning forward, his hands clasped in front of him, "Gina sent you?"

"She's dead," said Falcone in his usual manner. Julio jerked like he'd been slapped, and Lang saw tears well up, tears that wouldn't dampen the pain that burned in his eyes.

"I'm sorry," said Lang, "but we haven't much time. You didn't know?"

Julio shook his head, the movement dislodging a fat blob of moisture from the inner corner of his right eye. He reached up to wipe it away. "What happened?"

"She was murdered," Falcone again, and Lang shot him a look that told him to dial it back. Falcone ignored him. "Did she give you something before she died? Something for Coleman Lang?"

Julio's eyes were still filled with shock and pain as he looked at Falcone. Lang wondered what this good-looking young barman from the islands was to Gina. He felt shame as jealousy stabbed through him, and he forced it down.

Falcone jerked his thumb. "This is Coleman Lang."

Julio's gaze turned to him. "She told me that if anything happened to her you'd come."

Falcone edged forward. "Look, kid, we don't got a lot of time here. Did Gina leave something with you or not?"

Julio nodded, wiped more moisture away from his cheek, and stood. He opened one of the lockers, reached in and withdrew a white envelope similar to the one Pietro had given them. He handed it to Lang. "She gave me this a couple of weeks ago, asked me to keep it, not to give it to anyone else but you. She said that chances were it'd gather dust and never be opened."

"She tell you why she was giving you this?" Lang held the envelope for a few seconds, knowing Gina had touched this, wishing he could feel her touch him. Just once more.

"She told me it was important, that's all." His voice began to tremble, and Lang feared the young man was going to lose it entirely. "She was a wonderful person. She helped me. She used to come in here, with her friends. Always had a smile. When she found out I was having landlord problems, she helped me out, pro bono. Got it all worked out. She was a lovely lady."

Yes, she was, Lang thought, as he ripped the envelope open. Inside was a sheet of paper with another line of her handwriting.

China doorstop on the fifth

Another clue. Another riddle. He knew what it meant immediately.

"You said Gina was murdered," Julio said. "Who did it?"

"He did," said Falcone, nodding to Lang. Julio's eyebrows jerked, and he took a step back. "That's what the cops think anyway."

Julio had recovered from the surprise and he moved back to the table, stood directly over Lang. He studied him hard, then shook his head. "You didn't do it. No way."

"How do you know?"

"I trust Gina, man. The way her face lit up when she spoke of you, the things she told me about you. She cared, man." He shook his head again. "You're not the type to kill."

Lang stared into the young man's eyes and saw he meant every word. He was grateful for the affirmation, but he knew both Gina and Julio had him all wrong. He *was* the type who could kill. He just didn't kill Gina.

He nodded his thanks and stood up. Falcone did the same, and Lang saw he had his Glock at his side. Julio saw it, too, and his eyes widened again.

Falcone's voice was level. "Julio, the cops would be very interested to know we were here."

The barman waved his hands in front of him. "Hey, man, it's all cool. I'm not going to tell them a thing, you have my word."

Falcone nodded. "Over the next day or two you're going to hear a lot of bad shit about us. I mean, really bad shit. You might feel that Gina was wrong and that Cole here—and me—are the type to kill." He raised the weapon, rested the muzzle on the table top. "And you know what? You may not be wrong."

"Falcone, for Christ's sake," said Lang.

Falcone ignored him. "Well, let me tell you something, if the law catches up with us and we think for one second that you put them on our trail, so help me God, I'll come back here and make you very, very dead."

"Falcone, this isn't necessary," said Lang. "Gina trusted him, that's good enough for me. Should be good enough for you."

"I won't say a word, man," said Julio, fear pulsating through every word. Lang felt shame. This young man had been a friend of Gina's, he'd helped them, and now he was in fear for his life because Falcone was a goddamn psychotic.

Falcone's eyes didn't leave Julio's face, his expression unchanged, he stood very still, the gun pointed down at the table as if he was going to shoot it. And there was that deadness in the eyes again.

"Put the weapon away, Tony," said Lang.

Falcone didn't move.

"Tony!" Lang's voice was sharp, reaching across the table like a raised fist. Falcone's eyes shifted to him. "Julio's okay, we can trust him."

Falcone remained like a statue. Then, slowly, he relaxed, and the gun was removed from sight. He turned and walked out. Julio's breathing was short and sharp, and Lang feared he might hyperventilate. "Easy, Julio," he said, his voice soft. "It's fine. He's got trust issues."

"I really thought he was going to use that gun."

"I wouldn't have let him." Lang raised his own hand to let Julio see the Beretta he'd carefully drawn as the tension mounted. Julio stared at it, but Lang knew he felt no fear now. "But he was right, you will hear some things soon, about me, about what's happened in the past few hours. But I did not kill Gina, that you have to believe."

Julio swallowed. "But you're trying to find out who did."

"Yes. I think Gina was involved in something, that's what this is about." He raised the sheet of paper. "Whatever it was, it scared her enough to leave me a trail to follow. This is the next step on that trail. Now, did she tell you anything when she left this?"

"Just that you would come if something happened to her. That I was to give it you. That you'd understand what it meant and do what had to be done."

"She didn't give you any kind of hint what it was all about?"

"She was worried, man, that's all I know. She was the same Gina but there was a shadow, you know what I mean? Like a cloud had passed over her sun."

Lang thought about the darkening of her moods, of her frequent lapses in concentration. Something had been on her mind, and she hadn't told him about it. Why? He felt more shame lance through him. He should've talked to her, forced her to tell him what was wrong.

Whatever it was, though, he'd get to the bottom of it now. He wouldn't let the law or the mob or even Janus stop him. He'd solve Gina's puzzle.

46

Falcone was halfway down the block heading back to the car when Lang drew level, gripped him by the arm, whirled him round.

"Get your hands off me," Falcone spat, his own hand already reaching for his weapon.

Lang gave him a small laugh. "That's your answer to everything, eh, Falcone? Draw your gun, start blasting, start killing."

The hand dropped away once more. "That's why I'm still around."

"Yeah—and that's why you lost your family, too."

That one hit home. Lang could see it in Falcone's eyes just before his gaze dropped to the ground. "You don't know me, Lang. You don't know nothing."

A young couple walked by arm in arm, and Lang waited until they were out of earshot before he spoke again. "I know you're hurting. I know you're grieving. But killing anything that moves isn't going to change anything. You put the fear of death into that kid over in Jersey. Julio in there? He was trying to help, and you threatened to kill him."

"They both needed to know what would happen if they talked…"

"You're just making it worse for us."

"Jesus, Lang—how much worse can it get? Huh? We got the NYPD and the US Marshals on our asses. We got Nicky the Juke out there hunting us down. We got bodies piling up all around us…"

"Most of them thanks to you."

"Your hands ain't so goddamn clean, buster, don't you kid yourself. And while we're having this open and frank conversation, what about you? Huh? I see the way you handle that piece. You know about all this evasion shit. You boost cars like a pro. What's your deal? And don't say you're complicated because that much I got."

Lang kept his eyes level with Falcone's. He'd known this would come, but he still wasn't prepared. He couldn't tell the man about Janus, for the need for secrecy dies hard. Part of the truth would have to suffice. "When I was a kid I was a handful, okay? Even at college I was always getting myself into trouble. I was brought up by my dad's brother, he'd been a jarhead, and he wanted me to shape up, so after graduation he talked me into enlisting in the Corps, okay? They taught me what end of a weapon is up, and some things you never forget."

Falcone thought this over, then shook his head. "No dice, kid. I think there's more. See, what it comes down to is this—I don't think there's much difference between you and me. I'm a killer. I've known it since I was a teenager. I admit it, before God and the world, mea culpa, mea maxima culpa. You think it's easy for me, but you're way off. It's not easy. I do it because I have to. I do it because if I don't then the other guy will. But those kids, that Patrick and Julio in there? I wouldn't've shot them, but they had to believe I would."

"You were very convincing." Lang couldn't keep the sarcasm from his words.

Falcone looked him up and down. "You're very superior, with your expensive shirts and your sharp suits and your fancy SoHo apartment. You think you're so much better than me, don't you? But let me tell you, underneath all that you're the same as me. Oh, you hide it, you hide it good, but I see it, I see the killer in your eyes. As they say, it takes one to know one."

Falcone let this sink in for a moment then started walking again, leaving Lang to consider his words. Was it true? Was he just the same as Falcone? When it came down to it, did he kill with just as much ease? He thought back to his apartment. The gun he'd snatched up had felt so snug in his hand, and he'd killed with little thought. And in Battery Park he'd placed his shots square on the man's chest. He was sure he'd felt the body armor under his shirt when he pushed him, but just how certain had he been? And he could've missed, his bullets could've found the head or the throat. Kill shots. Was he really so different from Falcone? Ten years before, he'd been Janus's top man. He had been good, so very good. Yes, he'd begun to question, but he still carried out each assignment to the letter. The questions always came after the job was done.

He stared at Falcone's back and wondered if they were different after all.

And before they were finished, would that be the one thing that got them through?

47

When they returned to the car, Falcone's only question was where they were going, and when Lang told him, he received the now customary blank look in return. He couldn't read how the man felt. Falcone asked the address and set off. For the entire journey the only words spoken between them were when Lang gave him directions.

When they reached the Brooklyn Heights street, Lang told Falcone to drive around the block a couple of times, not too fast, not too slow, so he could ensure there were no surveillance details. He saw nothing that rang any alarms, but that didn't mean they weren't there. They had to risk it, though. They had to get to whatever Gina had left for them. He'd feared there would be a police guard on the door of Gina's apartment, but thankfully fate cut them a break. He had a key, something he knew Falcone noted but didn't comment on, and they slipped inside without anyone seeing them. This time of night it was unlikely anyone would be up and around, but they moved stealthily anyway.

Lang paused just inside the doorway, peering through the darkness. The last time he'd been here he was happy. They'd been on the couch, Gina's head nestling on his chest as they watched some show on TV. He breathed in, was certain he could still smell her perfume in the air. He listened, thought he heard her laughter in the dark, soft and musical. He felt his own grief stab at his chest and burn his eyes, but he fought it down. This was the place for it but not the time. He had a job to do.

The cops had clearly been through the apartment. They'd been fairly sensitive about it, but there were still items out of place, book spines poking from a shelf, a drawer half open, clothing hanging out.

Falcone whispered, "How long she live here?"

"Two, three years, I think."

Falcone moved around the room as if fearful to touch anything. The bare brick wall between Gina's two bookcases was covered in framed photographs, her mother and her second husband, a couple of Gina and her friends. There had been four of her with Lang, too, but one was missing. That was what the cops had issued to the press, cutting her out, of course. Falcone studied the pictures, and Lang wondered if he was looking for one showing his own face. If so, he'd be disappointed.

Falcone didn't turn when he said, "She looked happy."

"She was."

Falcone leaned in closer to one of Gina and Lang. It had been taken on Long Beach that summer. They were on the long strip of silver sand, beachfront properties behind them, and he recalled fumbling with the camera's self-timer in order to get a shot of them together. It had taken three attempts before he got it right, and again her laughter echoed down through the months to fade in the darkness and silence of the apartment.

Without turning, Falcone said, "Did you love her?"

The question caught Lang unawares, and he didn't know what to say. The question was that of a father to a suitor, not a killer to the man he thought could be responsible for his daughter's death. When he didn't get a response, Falcone turned to face him. "I know you said you loved her, but did you really love her? Was she all you thought of for days? When you were away from her did you feel the need of her? Was she the first thing you thought of when you woke up and the last thing before you went to sleep?"

The words were surprising, coming from a man like Falcone, who could kill without a qualm. But Lang could see he meant every word. Gina's father was a killer, but he wasn't stone cold. He was a womanizer, but he knew what feelings were. "All of those things," said Lang, quietly. "And more."

Falcone nodded, perhaps satisfied. He stared at him, his head slightly to one side, as if seeing him for the first time. "Okay, Lang, maybe you didn't kill my girl. Maybe you're in the clear, far as I'm concerned."

"What made you decide?"

Falcone shrugged. "Everything. Nothing. Maybe I've never been fully convinced, not since we was back in your apartment."

"I'm glad to hear it."

Falcone took a deep breath. "So, you gonna tell me about yourself now? You know all about me. How about giving something back."

Lang hesitated. "What do you want to know?"

"You know what I want to know. And don't give me no more of that juvie delinquent bullshit. That may well be true, but it isn't all, is it?"

Lang couldn't blame the man for wanting to know more about him. He had conceded that he wasn't to blame for Gina's death. He had accepted that he had loved her. Now he needed to know more. Lang was unsure what he could tell him, what he should tell him, but after all they had been through, the father of the woman he loved deserved more.

Falcone saw the hesitation and said, "Jesus Christ, Lang, the chances are we won't live much longer. What the hell you hiding?"

Lang took a deep breath. "Everything I told you before was true, but you're right, there's more. I was recruited out of the Marine Corps for a black ops section called Janus. My Marine postings were my cover."

"Cover for what?"

"Missions to eliminate our country's enemies."

Falcone smiled. "You tellin' me you were a hitman for Uncle Sam?" When Lang said nothing, Falcone laughed. Lang thought at first the man hadn't believed him, but then he saw him shake his head and wave a hand. "Christ, I was right—we ain't so different after all."

Lang couldn't argue with that. "I gave it up ten years ago."

"Why?"

"I was a burnout. I was done."

"Why? You were taking out our country's enemies, weren't you? You were a soldier. You were killing the bad guys. You were doing good."

Lang considered this. He took out his Beretta, jerked a single round from the chamber into his hand. He laid it upright on the coffee table, stared at it for a moment before he said, "A bullet doesn't know good from evil, right from wrong. A bullet only knows how to kill. I was a bullet, and I didn't care who I killed. My bosses just pointed me and pulled the trigger."

Falcone stared at the bullet on the table, picked it up, weighed it in his hand. "But you began to care."

"Yes."

Falcone threw the bullet up, caught it again. Then he tossed it to Lang. "That was your first mistake. As I said, you and me? We ain't so different, except in one thing. I'll do what has to be done, no questions asked. I may think on it after. I may need a drink or two to burn out the memories, but when it comes down to it, next time? I still get the job done."

Lang stared at the slug in his hand as Falcone moved around the room again. "So, what does this latest clue mean?"

Lang replaced the round in the magazine, slammed it home again then walked to the bookcase, took down a heavy hardback book. "She bought this years ago, she told me." He held it up for Falcone to see. It was *Noble House* by James Clavell. "She told me she tried four times to read it. It wasn't that it was bad, it was just so damn big, over 1,000 pages long. Sometimes, in the summer, she used it as a doorstop to get a through draft on hot days. She finally cracked it on the fifth try. It's set in Hong Kong."

Falcone understood. "*China doorstop on the fifth.*"

"Yeah." Lang riffled the pages, but nothing fell out. He held the book by its hardback covers, shook it, but nothing. He frowned. Was he wrong? Did she mean something else? He stared at it. It had to be this. This was her China doorstop. So where was the clue?

Falcone took the book from him, rippled the pages. "Some kind of code, maybe? She underline anything?"

"I don't think it would be that complicated. She's set up this trail to put other people off track, not me."

Falcone closed the book, stared at it, his brow furrowed. He turned it over in his hands, front cover, to back, studied it. Then his face brightened as something clicked, and he opened it wide, stared into the space created at the spine, and a thin smile cracked. He pushed his finger inside and hooked out a rolled-up piece of paper. He handed it to Lang. "She did that to me once, years ago."

Lang smoothed out the paper and read the single line on it.

"I think this'll be the end of the line," he said and handed it to Falcone, who read it then closed his eyes, as if he was in pain.

"Oh, shit," he said, like a prayer.

48

Angelina Ferraro was far from pleased to see them. She spoke quietly, leaving them standing in the doorway to her home in Queens, but there was venom dripping from every Italian word she spat at them like bullets. Lang couldn't tell whether her fury was because she'd been told that he'd killed her daughter or because of who his traveling companion was. If she was devout, he knew she'd be confessing some of those words in the morning. Lang glanced at the gardens and doors on the street around them, checking no one was paying attention.

"Mrs Ferraro," he said, trying hard to interrupt the torrent of abuse which he chose to believe was directed at Falcone. Ferraro was her married name. Gina had abandoned Falcone and used her mother's maiden name. "Please…"

She ignored him, and the invective continued unabated. He saw the daughter's face in the mother's, but he'd never seen it contorted with such hatred. Falcone stood in the doorway and took it, as if he knew he deserved it.

She paused for breath, and Lang seized his chance. He kept his voice low. "Mrs Ferraro, you know why I'm here. Gina left something for me."

The dark eyes darted in his direction and she switched to English. "And you! The police tell me you killed my Gina!"

"It's not true, Mrs Ferraro, I give you my word."

The eyes narrowed. "You give me your word. You give me your word. And I should believe the word of this man I have never met, despite him being with my daughter for a year? Why should I believe the word of this man?"

"Because Gina told you that you could trust me." She'd told

Pietro. She'd told Julio. There was every chance she told her mother, too.

The woman fell silent. "And yet you are with this *stugots?*"

Lang didn't know what that meant, but he knew it wasn't good. "He came back to find Gina's killer. We both are. We think whatever she left with you will help."

Mrs Ferraro considered this then shook her head. "No, she left nothing with me." She began to close the door. "You go now. I will call the police and they will come and arrest you. Both of you."

Falcone brushed past Lang and held the door open. "Angie…"

Her face twisted again. "Don't you call me that, you *stronz'*."

"Please," said Falcone in a pleading tone Lang hadn't heard from him before. "Don't let your hatred of me blind you to this. Our daughter was murdered…"

"*Si*—and it was probably something to do with you! That *animale*, Nicky the Juke, he was here. He hurt my husband…"

Falcone leaned into the doorway, the tension evident in his body. "What did he want?"

She carried on as if he hadn't spoken. "I thought when you left I was out of that, that our family—*nostra famiglia*—would finally be free of it all. But no, my Gina, she is dead, and my husband lies upstairs with a bullet hole in his leg. And you! You come here and… and…"

Words finally failed her, and she turned away, plucking a paper tissue from the pocket of the robe she was wearing. Falcone moved closer, raised his hands as if he was going to embrace her, then thought better of it. Lang had seen him do the same with Pietro. She walked down the short hallway into the house, leaving the door open. Falcone stepped over the threshold, jerking his head to Lang, telling him to follow. Lang closed the front door behind him.

They found her standing in a spacious, comfortably furnished living room. Hanging on the wall above the fake fireplace was a framed photograph of Gina on graduation day. It was rimmed with black lace.

"Angie, the Juke, what did he want?"

She dabbed at her eyes, and for the first time Lang saw something like guilt in her face. "He wanted to know who you would talk to in the city."

They waited, but she was unwilling to say more. Whatever she'd told him, she was ashamed.

"What did you tell him, Angie?" Falcone's voice was soft, but there was a hoarseness there, as if he knew what she was going to say.

She couldn't look at him. "I told him about your cop buddy."

Falcone wasted no time in pulling out his cell, but Lang laid his hand on his arm. Falcone jerked it away, prepared to select Barney's number.

"Tony," said Lang, "don't do it. They could be monitoring Barney's phone."

"I have to know he's okay."

"If he's not okay there's nothing we can do for him." Lang could barely believe he was saying this. Dagda was beginning to take over. "Drawing the law to us won't help him."

"I got him into this."

"He's a big boy. He got himself into this when he agreed to help. He knew the risks. He helped us anyway." Falcone began to thumb in a number. Lang knew there was nothing more he could say, so he merely stood by and watched. Falcone completed the sequence and his thumb hovered over the button to connect. Conflicting emotions fought for control of his face. He looked up at Lang, then to his ex-wife.

Lang said, "We'll get to the Juke. We'll find Barney. But first, we have to finish here."

Falcone looked back at him, and Lang saw the agony in his eyes, but he cancelled the number, put the cell phone away. Lang gave him a nod of thanks, turned to the woman.

"Mrs Ferraro," said Lang. "You have to help us. Did Gina leave something with you? Did she tell you that if anything ever happened to her that I would come and ask for it?"

She didn't answer. She was crying now, all her anger diluted by her ongoing grief. Lang looked to Falcone for help.

"Angie," he said, moving closer. "Gina left a treasure trail for us to follow. Remember? Like when she was a kid? She used to do that for me? Leave me clues that I had to solve to find the prize? She did it that birthday for me, when she gave me this lighter—remember?" He produced the gold lighter from his pocket, held it out to her.

The woman looked at the lighter, then back at Falcone. When she spoke, her voice was softer. "You still have that?"

"I'll have it with me always. I'll have it with me the day I die."

She gave a little laugh. "Let's hope that day comes soon."

Falcone sighed, tried to ignore her. "Angie, what did Gina leave for this man? We need it, whatever it was."

She took the lighter from his hand, held it in her palm, stared at it. Then she looked back at the photograph on the wall, shook her head as if her daughter could see her, then handed the lighter back. "I hate you. I hate you both."

Lang thought she had decided against helping them, but she turned away and walked to a heavy wooden bureau standing against the far wall underneath a window. She opened a drawer, took out a small, black thumb drive. She moved back to stand in front of Lang, the narrow tech clasped tightly in her fist.

"My Gina, she told me that she loved you."

"And I loved her," he said.

She nodded. "Maybe so. But you did not protect her. In the end you were not there for her." She glanced at Falcone. "She had enough of that in her life, men who were not there for her. I do not know you, but I know this—you did not deserve her."

Lang knew that was true. For both him and Falcone.

Mrs Ferraro handed him the thumb drive. "Take it. Do what you must. You will not bring her back."

He thanked her and stared at the tiny wedge of plastic now resting on his palm. "Mrs Ferraro, I have one more favor."

She sighed, waited.

"I need to know what is on this. Do you have a computer?"

She stared at him. "No," she said. "No more. I want you out of my home. I want *that*…" She jerked a thumb at the flash drive. "… out of my home."

Falcone stepped forward again. "Angie, listen to me. Whatever is on this thing is the reason why Gina was killed. We need to know what it is. We need to know now."

She looked from Falcone and back to Lang, her face set in stone but her eyes still burning. Then, muttering something dark and Sicilian, she left the room.

Falcone watched her go. "Did Gina inherit her mother's temper?"

Lang thought of the few times they had argued, usually over silly, inconsequential things. "She had a temper. But when she swore, she did it in American."

"Don't make it any easier," said Falcone. Lang had to agree.

Mrs Ferraro returned with a laptop PC. She'd already powered it up and put in her password. She laid it on the coffee table without a word then stepped away to the fireplace to stand in front of Gina's photograph. Two pairs of eyes watched Lang as he inserted the thumb drive into the USB port and clicked the files open.

Some of the documents were scans of hard copies. There were accounts and memos and reports. There were copies of emails. Lang couldn't really make much sense out of the maze of figures and corporate speech patterns, it all seemed too intricate for him. He was concentrating so intently that he barely noticed Falcone leaning in at his side to see the screen. "So, what we got?"

Lang flicked another page and shrugged. "Beats me. Best I can say is that Gina has been collecting this data for months and they all relate to a company called Enconomy."

"Never heard of it."

"Nor me, but they seem to be pretty big, far as I can make out. Their head office is in Manhattan, but they've got offices everywhere—London, Paris, Saudi Arabia, Hong Kong."

Falcone craned over to study what looked like a balance sheet. "There must be something there. Gina didn't do all this for a bunch of figures that don't add up to shit."

"They'll add up to something, I'm just not the guy to make sense of them."

"So who is?"

Lang ejected the thumb drive and turned back to Gina's mother. "Mrs Ferraro, we need one more favor…"

He saw the flames kindle in her eyes.

49

Lang walked down the pathway, giving Falcone some measure of privacy with his ex-wife, although he could still hear their conversation. She stood with her hand on the door, ready to close it. She wanted them gone. She wanted them out of her life. But Falcone had one last thing to say. "Angie, I'm sorry, so very sorry for all that I have done."

There was a pause, and when she spoke there was no anger, no bitterness, no rancor in her voice. There was just a mother's sadness. "Sorry is just a word, Tony. It does not make it right. It does not make it better. It is too late for sorry."

Lang heard nothing further. He climbed back into the car before he punched in the only number saved on the next burner phone. He heard Reuben's voice and said, "It's me."

"Jesus, Cole, thank God you called." Reuben sounded agitated, and Lang felt a stab of concern. "I've been calling for what seems like hours."

Lang glanced at the phone's read-out, saw he had three missed calls. "Been kinda busy, Reuben."

A slight laugh. "I won't ask what. Listen—do you know a gentleman called Nicky?"

"Nicky the Juke?"

A pause on the line and Falcone climbed back into the car. Reuben said, "The fact that he has the word 'the' in his name doesn't make me warm to him."

"What about him?"

"He called me."

How the hell did the Juke know about Reuben? Lang leaned forward. "He called you? What'd he say?"

"He's at Westport, Cole. He says if you don't meet him there, there'll be more bodies."

Lang closed his eyes. Sophia and Silvio. They may be the Psycho Twins, and he may have suspected they were involved in this at one time, but that was long ago and far away. At least, it seemed like that. It had only been that morning he'd still harbored suspicions. If he was at Westport then they must've told him about Reuben. But what led him to them in the first place? Even as the question rose in his mind, he knew the answer.

"Barney must've told him," he said, and Falcone's eyes narrowed at the mention of his friend's name. He raised his chin, silently asking what was going on, but Lang held his hand up to tell him to wait.

"Who's Barney?" Reuben asked. "And who the hell is this Nicky character?"

"Someone you don't want to know about, Reuben."

"Maybe I should contact the police."

"No." Lang was firm. "I'll meet him."

Reuben's voice was thick with worry. "Cole…"

"It'll be fine, Reuben. We'll get it all cleared up." Lang recalled why he'd phoned his friend. "Reuben, how are you at reading accounts and deciphering corporate speak?"

"I'm a lawyer, Cole, I live for that kind of stuff."

So did Gina, thought Lang. And it got her killed. "Listen, someone will come see you first thing in the morning. Gina's mother. She's got something you need to study. I need you to make sense of it all."

"Can't you email it?"

"Don't want to risk it, Reuben. Emails can be intercepted."

"Dear God, Cole, what the hell is going on here? What are you into?" Reuben sounded both concerned and exasperated. "What is this you're sending me?"

"It's what got Gina killed…"

50

Nicky's cell rang, and he checked the number before answering. The read-out said Unknown. He frowned. He didn't expect it to be Falcone or Lang, and the lawyer didn't have his return number. He answered it anyway.

"Nicky," he heard Vinnie's voice say.

"Yeah."

"Vinnie."

"Shit, Vinnie, you don't think I know your voice?"

"Where you at?"

"Why you care?"

"I need to see you."

"What about?"

"Jeez, Nicky, you want me to say on the phone? We got business. Important business."

"So do I."

"It's about your business that I wanna talk. I'll come to you, where are you?"

Nicky thought about this. If Falcone was with Lang, then Vinnie had a right to see him put down. After all, it was his father he'd betrayed. He gave the address, heard Vinnie whistle.

"That's pretty high-toned," he said.

Nicky looked around him, ignored the woman sobbing to look at the expensive furnishings, the exotic rugs, the original artworks on the walls. Yeah, it was high-toned alright.

"See you when you get here," he said. "But Vinnie—you better be quick."

Vinnie cut the line and looked over his desk at Tommy and his cousin, Al. "He's in Westport," he said.

Tommy nodded. Al didn't react. They had little love for Nicky, which was why Vinnie had chosen them as his personal body-guards. It also made them perfect for this hit. They weren't as cre-ative as the Juke, but they got the job done. And Vinnie trusted them as much as he trusted any man. Which was never fully. His old man had taught him well.

"Let's go," he said.

They left White Plains in Vinnie's SUV, a one-of-a-kind number with armor plating that could stop anything short of a tomahawk missile. It ate up the gas, but that was a small price to pay for security. Vinnie was very careful. He picked his personal protec-tion carefully, he made sure his transportation was secure, he said nothing on the phone that could bite him in the ass. His home was swept regularly for bugs because he knew the cops and the feds could be tricky sons-of-bitches.

The thing was, he hadn't swept it since Santoro and the US Marshals came calling a few hours before.

And two streets away, in the back of a surveillance vehicle, they heard him say he was heading for Westport.

"What's in Westport?" Burke asked.

Santoro knew.

51

Lang and Falcone took the Van Wyck out of Queens to link up to the I-95 that took them to Connecticut. They managed the journey in less than an hour, thanks to Falcone's determination to get to Nicky the Juke and the roads being quiet. The sun was beginning to rise above Compo Beach, streaking the striated clouds blood red as they cruised into Westport, and Lang hoped it wasn't a sign of what was to come. But Nicky the Juke was here, the answer to what he had done with Barney was here, and that meant there would be death, sure as taxes. He thought about the beach. He had walked there with Sophia in happier days, bare feet in the sand, the white clapboard houses facing water that sparkled in the sun. They had kept secrets from each other then. His was his past, hers a streak of lunacy.

Lang relayed directions to reach the Manucci house, set well back from the road in grounds peppered with mature trees and guarded by high walls. The lawns were always immaculate, as if the grass had been genetically modified never to grow over a certain height. The place was worth $3.25 million, as Sophia never ceased reminding him. The Manuccis always knew to the last penny what they were worth, and Sophia was a Manucci to the very core. She'd never missed an opportunity to remind him that her family could buy and sell him. Guilt washed over him once again. Sophia and her brother were crazy, but they didn't deserve to be sucked into this madness. He wondered if Nicky had hurt them. He wondered if he'd be able to stop him if he planned on hurting them.

Large wrought iron gates normally blocked the gravel driveway that led to the large house, but they were open. Lang knew they'd been left open for them.

He saw the deep lines etched on Falcone's face. They were both tired, they'd been on the go for almost 24 hours straight and hadn't had much sleep prior to that. Now Falcone was worried about his old friend, Barney. Exhaustion and worry were a lethal combination in this situation. They were going to face a man who wouldn't hesitate to kill them, a man who had perhaps had the chance to rest. He had the edge, and that was bad news. They had to create one of their own.

"You ready for this?" Lang asked.

Falcone raised his Glock, rammed a new mag into the chamber. He nodded.

"Okay," said Lang then pointed through the windshield towards a lane half hidden by bushes. "That runs all the way up the wall to the rear of the property. There's a small pond up there and a gate, which is probably locked, but you'll be able to climb over. You'll find a back door tucked away behind a small outhouse. It'll be locked—can you open it without being heard?"

Falcone gave him a look that told him not ask stupid questions.

Lang half smiled. "Okay, good. Hopefully I'll be inside by then, and I'll keep him talking as long as I can."

"How you going to do that? Nicky isn't known for his conversational skills."

Lang opened the car door. "I'll think of something…"

52

The light grew stronger as Lang trudged up the driveway, feet rasping on the gravel, conscious that he presented an easy target. However, he was confident Nicky the Juke wouldn't gun him down on his approach. He'd want to be within spitting distance of his target. Perhaps confident wasn't the right word. Hopeful would be closer to the truth.

He studied the windows as he neared the white building but saw no one watching him. He knew eyes were upon him, though.

It was an impressive house. He had caught a few glimpses of Paul Newman's old home in Coleytown, just down the road, but the Manucci house was nothing like that. The actor's home was understated, tasteful, but the Manucci family didn't do anything in an understated fashion. It wasn't that it was garish—no gold lamp standards or anything so obvious—but it screamed money and power. The brilliantly white masonry and the colonnaded, antebellum-style porch always seemed out of place in its New England setting. The lone driveway, the manicured lawns, with their carefully cropped shrubbery and trees, and the marble fountain outside the front door were all designed to instil shock and awe in the visitor. Lang was neither shocked nor awed by the house and what it represented. He just hated the place.

The front door was ajar, and he pushed it open to see into the spacious reception hallway and the wide staircase that led to the nine bedrooms and a further two public rooms on the upper floors. A body lay face up, a halo of blood congealing on the Italian floor tiles. Lang recognized it as Stefan, Senator Manucci's secretary. He would have opened the door, and Nicky killed him instantly. If Stefan was acting as butler, that meant the Senator was home. Lang stepped into the hallway, gun at the ready, and listened for any sound but heard nothing. It was as if the house was empty, even though he knew it wasn't. The tension in the air spoke to him, alerted his senses, made his blood tingle, and every muscle was primed and ready. He hadn't felt that level of preparedness in a very long time, and he welcomed it now. He needed to be ready.

Then he heard the voice drifting towards him. A song he recognized, one his grandmother used to play. "Welcome to my World", originally sung by Jim Reeves, an old country and western singer from way back when. It wasn't him singing now, though. It was Nicky. Then the singing stopped, and Nicky shouted, "Hey, Coleman Lang—why don't you join us, huh? We're havin' us a party."

The voice came from the family room on the right. The door swung open as Lang neared it and he was faced by a bulky man with a heavily jowled face and a broken nose. A deep scar ran down his cheek, he wore a thick padded jacket and his thinning black hair was obviously dyed. If Central Casting were ever looking for a New York gangster, this was their guy. Somehow, this was not how Lang had pictured Nicky.

"Lose the gun out there, pal," the man said, waving his own weapon. His voice was high and nasal, not Nicky after all, and it completely ruined the image created by his appearance. The way he held and waved his weapon was the real thing, however. Lang complied, and the man gestured for him to move closer. "Don't try nothin' stupid," he warned and gave him a professional pat down. Finding no further weapons, he stepped back to let him pass.

It was a big room, with heavily cushioned sofas arranged before a brick fireplace, dark and unlit, set deep into the wall. The walls were heavy with landscapes, a large bookcase made of thick dark wood was crammed with leather-bound volumes that Lang would lay odds hadn't been read for a long time. Maybe Sophia's grandfather, Supreme Court Justice Manucci, had leafed through them once or twice but not his son and not his grandchildren. Now, they were there only for show.

Sophia and Silvio sat on one sofa, holding hands. Naturally. Even now, with the atmosphere replete with threat, Lang felt something jolt at his stomach when he saw them together like that. The Senator was in a heavy armchair near the fireplace, his handsome face as immobile as a Roman bust. He had always claimed he could trace his lineage back to the days of the Empire. He would've been a senator back then, too, sending people off to be eaten by lions. Now, though, he had to be content with sending young men off to war and doing what he could to cut welfare. They all looked tired, which was to be expected. They wouldn't have slept much with all the armory around them.

The man who had frisked Lang stepped behind the sofa, his pistol held loosely at his side. Another gunman stood behind the Senator's chair. He might've been the first man's brother, they looked so alike. A third thug holding a semi-automatic AR pistol was sitting at the large oak table by the French windows, beyond which lay a paved terrace. Sophia and he used to play cards on that table. They sipped cocktails on that terrace and watched the shadows of the trees lengthen. Back when he thought they had a future.

Sophia looked up at him as he entered. Her dark eyes were bright and fluid, as if she was on the verge of hysterics, but the skin beneath them was puffy and shadowed. Beside her, Silvio was pale, and his eyes revealed his terror. His fleshy features had sagged, as if weighed down by his fear. All his cockiness, all his big talk, was gone now. Now he was playing big boy games, and he was out of his depth. Despite his dislike of the man, despite the feeling of revulsion he felt as he saw those stubby fingers tighten around Sophia's hand, Lang felt sorry for him.

"Cole, he said he was a police officer," Sophia said, her voice quivering. "He had a badge."

"I know, Sophia," said Lang. Of course Nicky would use Barney's badge. "Where is he?"

Nicky appeared in the doorway that led from the family room to a small kitchen, a large sandwich in his hand. Lang felt his muscles tense further—that was where the back door was. The door he expected Falcone to come through soon. Unless he encountered a problem even he couldn't handle out back. Nicky stretched out his good arm, exuding *bon homie* as well as some tomato, cheese and slivers of ham onto the Chinese rug under his feet. Nicky didn't notice. He didn't care. "Hey—Cole! How you been?"

"I'm okay," said Lang, feeling Sophia's terrified eyes silently pleading with him to do something. For the first time in a long time he felt something like tenderness towards her. All the jealousy, all the fighting, all the crap she'd put him through—none of it deserved this.

"Good to see you, *paisan*," said Nicky.

Lang said, "Why don't you come here and give me a hug, Nicky?"

Nicky laughed and came to a halt in front of the fireplace, where he took a bite of his sandwich. "You'd like that, I'll bet," he said, his mouth full. He chewed some more. "But you know? I don't do much hugging no more, not since someone left a bullet in me here." He raised his wounded arm slightly.

"Shame his aim was off," said Lang.

"Yeah," said Nicky, "he'll pay for it, though." He made a show of looking around the room, as if searching for something. "So, where's my old buddy, Tony?"

Lang paused. He was ready for this question, and he hoped his answer would be sufficient to buy them all some time. "He's dead."

Nicky was surprised by that. He stopped chewing. "That so? What happened? You take him out?"

Lang shook his head. "Some cop or other, this morning. On our way here. He spotted us, followed us, Falcone started blasting and caught one. I was lucky to get away."

Nicky moved closer to study Lang's eyes. The two men stared at each other, the Sicilian searching for signs of a lie but finding none. He smiled, stepped away again, transferred his sandwich to his injured arm, fished a cell phone from his pocket. He hit a number on speed dial.

"It's me," he said. "Don't give me that now, I'm too busy. What I need to know is this—Falcone, did one of your guys take him down this morning?" Nicky watched Lang's face as he listened to whoever was at the other end of the line. One of your guys, he'd said. He was talking to a cop. Was that where he got his SoHo address in the first place? And Reuben's name?

Nicky ended the call without saying anything further. He gave Lang a rueful shake of the head. "Cole, you think I'm some sort of *idiota*? You think you can come in here and tell me lies?"

He nodded at the goon standing behind Sophia and Silvio. A second later there was an explosion and Silvio's head erupted. His body slumped forward, slid off the leather couch and crumpled to the expensive rug. Sophia sucked in her breath sharply, opened her mouth but nothing came out. Her entire body wanted to scream, but it couldn't. She shrank away from her brother's corpse, legs kicking at the front of the couch and she half rose against the arm, but the goon grabbed her by the hair and yanked her back to her seat. She stared at what had once been Silvio, then looked down at her clothes and hands, saw the splatter. She held her shaking hands up to her face, turned them round, stared at the blood and other matter dripping off them. Her mouth gaped, but she made no sound, the scream that was gathering within escaping only through her wide and terrified eyes.

Lang was so shocked by the suddenness of the murder that he was momentarily stunned. Only the Senator made to stand, but Nicky glared at him and he remained half out of the chair.

"You son-of-a-bitch," said the Senator, his eyes dripping hatred. "You had no reason to do that!"

Nicky laughed and took another bite of his sandwich, started to hum something Cole couldn't quite identify. He stared straight at him when he said, "Just needed to focus everyone's attention, is all."

Sophia couldn't help herself now. She squeezed herself into the corner of the couch and screamed.

Nicky said, "Shut the bitch up."

The goon behind her backhanded her across the mouth. It didn't help. She barely felt it. Nicky tutted and stepped over to her, pointed his sandwich at her like a gun. "Lady," he said, "you don't shut the fuck up, you'll be joining this guy on the floor, *capisce*?"

She stopped screaming, but the need didn't die. Lang could see it still bubbling away, like a living being trembling in her throat.

The Senator's gaze fell on Lang, and the hatred was still there. "You," he said, a slight curl to his upper lip. "You brought this to my house. You brought this…" He looked for a word to describe Nicky, jerking his head towards him. Nicky watched and smiled, humming to himself. Finally, the Senator couldn't think of a harsh enough term for him and he gave up, aimed his venom back at Lang. "I never cared for you, never wished you to be part of my family. I always knew there was something… off… about you. But Sophia loved you, and so I agreed to the marriage. But now look at us." He gestured towards his son lying dead on the floor. "Now look at us…"

Lang looked at the body of his former brother-in-law then at Sophia, who was staring at it as if she'd been frozen. She didn't appear to be breathing. She merely sat stock still, gawking at her dead brother.

"Sophia," said Lang, but she didn't move. He raised his voice, sharpened his tone. "Sophia!" Slowly, very slowly, her head moved, and her eyes swiveled towards him. "Don't look at him, Sophia."

"*Si*, Sophia," said Nicky, "Don't look at him. He's dead, Sophia. His brains, they all over the upholstery. Need a professional to get those stains out."

Lang gave Nicky a long hard stare. "That wasn't necessary."

Nicky considered this. "No, you're right. It wasn't." He smiled, threw the remainder of his sandwich into the fire and wandered towards the terrace doors. "It was fun, though, just for the look on your face." He had his back to Lang as he looked out at the terrace and beyond to the driveway. "So, I'll ask you again, and now you know what'll happen if you lie to me again, so I know you'll answer true, where's my old pal Tony?"

Lang was asking himself that question. It shouldn't've taken him this long to reach the back door.

"What do you care now? It wasn't him who put that bullet in you."

There was silence as Nicky continued to stare at the outside world. He absently massaged his wounded shoulder. "This is true, we still got unfinished business." He turned. "Don't we?"

"This doesn't concern Sophia and her father."

Nicky pointed to Silvio's body. "It didn't concern this guy, but there he lies."

"This has nothing to do with them, Nicky."

"No, but it has everything to do with you. And when you heard I was here, you came running. What's that about, Mr Coleman Lang? You divorce this woman, yet you still come when she's in peril?"

Lang felt Sophia's eyes on him, but he didn't meet them. "I want no further bloodshed, Nicky. You've done enough. You wanted me here. I'm here. Let them go."

"I want that rat Falcone, too."

"We split up. We heard you'd snatched his cop pal. He went to find him. I came here."

Nicky considered this. Lang hoped he was buying it and cursed himself for not saying that in the first place. But then, he didn't think Nicky would have been able to check his story out so quickly.

"Now, why didn't you just say that before? That I would've believed. Then." He flicked a finger to the man who had shot Silvio, pointed to the door leading to the kitchen and the rear of the house. The man left to check it out. "But see, I know he's here, somewhere. I can smell him."

"Let them go, Nicky," Lang said, trying to appear unconcerned.

"That would be the reasonable thing to do, wouldn't it?"

"Yes."

"But here's the thing—I'M NOT A REASONABLE MAN!" he yelled, making Sophia jump. It seemed to break something inside her, and she began to cry. Nicky ignored her, strode across the room towards Lang, stopping just out of reach. "You put a bullet in me and for that you must pay. No one puts a bullet in Nicoletto Bruno and lives, not while I have breath. Your buddy, that rat Falcone, he became a secondary target for me the minute you fired that gun the other night. These people? They mean nothing to me. They're rich, sure, but that don't mean shit to me. They're bugs, like all the rich people, like all the *pezzonovante*. And what do you do with bugs? You bring in the exterminator." He looked at the gunman standing next to the Senator's chair and nodded. The man took a step closer, raised his pistol, aimed it at the Senator's head.

Lang took a step forward, cried out, "No!"

"Nicky," said the man at the table. He was standing now, looking at the driveway. Nicky held up a hand to halt the Senator's execution, moved back to the window. A large SUV had come to a halt in the courtyard beside the fountain. Vinnie Marino and his two bodyguards climbed out and entered the house.

"Looks like Vinnie won't have a wasted trip, after all." He smiled. "Hey, we got a real Sons of Italy thing going on here. Apart from you, Lang, of course." Then he began to sing "That's Amore".

* * *

Santoro brought the police-issue vehicle to a halt just short of the gates leading to the Manucci home. They hadn't followed Marino in the surveillance van because it was too conspicuous. This was what they once called an unmarked police sedan, and it looked

254

like a piece of crap, but the engine ran like a dream. Burke was in the back, McDonough riding shotgun, but without a shotgun, of course. They'd kept a decent distance behind Vinnie's SUV even though Santoro had already guessed where he was headed. It had been McDonough's idea to bug Vinnie's office, see where it led. While Santoro and Burke talked, she had slid the microphone in between two books. She doubted Vinnie ever read them. They knew he had Nicky out looking for Falcone and, absent news of the Juke's whereabouts, keeping tabs on him seemed like the best bet. It wasn't legal but it had paid off. The fact that Nicky had involved Lang's former in-laws meant they were close to him, too.

Santoro stared at the Taurus parked a few yards beyond the gate. She wondered whose it was. She committed the tag to memory, just in case.

McDonough opened the passenger door. "You got any vests in the trunk, Lieutenant?"

She stared at her. "We are not going in there without back-up, TP."

"We don't have time to waste. We know Bruno and Marino are in there, and they're not making a social call. We have civilians at risk here, and I for one am not waiting."

Burke said, "You're not armed, TP."

She held a hand out over the seat towards him. "Then arm me."

He shook his head. "I'm not authorized…"

"You know what? Screw not being authorized. Do what's right for once, Hank, not just what's right for you. Now, give me a weapon and let's go in there and end this."

The two Marshals stared at each other for a few moments, then finally Burke sighed, reached down to his ankle and pulled a Ruger SR22 3600 from a holster. "It's only a .22," he said, almost apologetically.

McDonough checked it was fully loaded. "It'll do."

Santoro watched them with mounting apprehension. "Are you two crazy? We don't know how many guns are in there waiting for us, and you want to go in like gangbusters?"

"You don't need to come," said McDonough then climbed out. Santoro hear the click of Burke checking his own weapon.

"You, too, Burke?"

He shrugged. "Like she said. There are innocent people in there."

She stared at him, trying to see what was in it for him. He wasn't a glory hunter, and it was a risk, but if he could help save a Senator and his family, he could do himself some good. He climbed out and stood beside McDonough in the sidewalk. Santoro sat in the car alone for a few seconds, silently cursing the pair of them for goddamn fools. Then she laid her head on the steering wheel.

Shit.

They were right. She couldn't sit there while known killers were in that house, and she didn't know how long back-up would take to arrive out here in the goddamn sticks.

"What the hell am I doing?" she said aloud. Then she climbed out of the car, walked to the rear of the vehicle and popped the trunk to reveal four Kevlar vests and a pump action shotgun.

53

Vinnie surveyed the living room, looked first at the Senator, then the woman who was sobbing on the couch and finally the dead man. He didn't know who they were, didn't much care, but he knew this was not a good situation. The good-looking guy in the middle of the room he took to be Coleman Lang. He knew the two men with Nicky. They were loyal Marino soldiers. He thought he could rely on them to do the right thing when push came to shoot.

And then there was Nicky.

"So, where's Tony, Nicky?" he asked.

"He's around," Nicky said. "I've got a guy out back, looking for him."

Vinnie scanned the room again, then went to the window to look down the driveway. He saw nothing there. Falcone on the prowl was not good. He turned his back to the window and looked towards the door opposite him. "Where does that lead?"

"Kitchen," said Nicky.

Vinnie jerked his head at Tommy, and he went through the door to check it out.

"My guy is on it," said Nicky.

Vinnie waved his objection away, as if it was of no consequence. "This is a situation, Nicky."

"Yeah, but I'm just about to resolve it."

"How?"

Nicky snapped the fingers of his good arm and the gunman behind the Senator raised his weapon again. Sophia screamed, Lang took a step forward. "Don't do it, Nicky!"

"Then tell me where Falcone is. You got three seconds to tell me or this *pezzonovante* here will be the guest of honor at a memorial service pretty soon."

Lang wanted to know where Falcone was himself. He should've been here by now, unless he was too old and weary to climb that fence out back. Or maybe the guy Nicky sent to look for him was better than he looked. Nicky watched him. Vinnie watched him. Sophia watched him. The Senator watched him. The assorted goons watched him.

"For God's sake, Cole," Sophia pleaded, "tell them what they want to know."

"You heard the lady," Nicky said. "And guess what—time's up."

He turned to his man, nodded, and Lang saw the pistol tense in the gunman's hand. "Okay," he said, "I'll tell you."

He paused again.

Nicky's patience snapped. "Jesus Christ, where the fuck is he?"

"Right here, Nicky!"

All eyes swiveled to where Vinnie's man Tommy filled the kitchen doorway, and just behind him was Falcone, a gun to his head. The gunman behind the Senator adjusted his aim and fired, hitting Tommy in the gut. Falcone held him erect and fired round him, taking the gunman squarely on the chest. That was the signal for all hell to break loose.

Lang yelled at the Senator to hit the floor, but he could've saved his breath for he was already moving. Sophia seemed frozen again as bullets whipped around her, but when he called her name, she snapped out of it and dropped to the floor, just as Nicky's man behind her spun away, his weapon flying from his grasp, blood spraying from his chest. Falcone tossed Tommy's bullet-riddled body to one side, where it wedged the door open, and ducked back into the kitchen. Vinnie lay on the floor, his head covered by his hands as if that would ward off bullets. Alphonse Carpozi knelt beside him, his finger jerking at his automatic, his bullets thudding into the brickwork around the kitchen door. Then he remembered why he was there, and he looked for Nicky the Juke.

But Lang got there before him. Nicky had been momentarily surprised by Falcone's appearance, but his good hand was reaching for the gun in his belt as Lang lunged and slammed into him, throwing him to the floor. The gunman by the window had also been slow to react but now he was on his feet, the semi-automatic in his hands, and was about to spray the room, but Falcone threw himself from the kitchen in a crouching run and fired a couple of rounds in his direction, compelling him to duck below the table. Alphonse had hauled his boss to his feet and was attempting to drag him from the room, but he was also forced down when Falcone loosed a couple of rounds in his direction. Lang rammed the heel of his hand hard into Nicky's wounded shoulder, ignoring the man's scream as he fed his need to inflict real pain on him, and then plucked the weapon from his hand and rolled away. The goon with the machine pistol had bobbed up again and was spraying bullets wild but he couldn't control the recoil and the weapon bucked in his hands. Falcone dropped behind the arm of the sofa as bullets ripped into the wall behind him, while Lang rolled and rolled. The shooting stopped, and the guy began to replace the empty magazine, but he was nervous and he was shaking and he was slow.

Lang knew he was going to have to put this man down, he didn't want to, but he had to because if he didn't, indiscriminate as his shooting was, this guy was going to hit something sooner rather than later, so he came to a halt, prone on the floor, the gun held in his right, his left keeping him aim steady, and he was about to squeeze a round off when he heard Santoro yell, "Police! Stop firing—and I mean right now!"

She and Burke had come in the front door and were standing over Alphonse and Vinnie, both flat on the floor. She had a shotgun, and Burke had a Magnum .44 held on the two Sicilians, but Lang didn't see McDonough—where the hell was McDonough? And then he realized the guy with the semi-automatic had finally rammed the fresh magazine home and his blood was up and he was not about to stop firing. He raised the weapon and renewed his aim. Lang took a deep breath because he'd seen the hesitation in Santoro's eyes and was unsure if she would take the shot.

The man jerked back as the bullet hit him on the left shoulder, but it didn't come from Lang's gun, it came from behind him, where McDonough stood in the kitchen doorway, a .22 in her hand. But the guy wasn't ready to go down, and at that range he wouldn't, not with a .22 unless she went for a kill shot, which would take quite a sharpshooter. The thug steadied himself and raised the automatic weapon again and Lang began to squeeze the trigger but Santoro beat him to it, letting go with the shotgun, blowing the man's chest wide open and sending him hurtling backwards to crash through the terrace doors, his body coming to rest halfway into the patio outside.

Burke wasn't paying attention to the men on the floor and Al was bringing his weapon level. McDonough saw him and didn't waste time with a warning. His head snapped back with a little dark hole in the forehead, and his arm flew to the side, the gun sailing off into the corner of the room. She was a sharpshooter, after all.

It seemed as if the shots echoed on and on, but in reality there was no sound as Falcone and Lang let their breath out slowly, thankfully. Santoro looked pale, Burke shocked, Vinnie still cowered under his tented hands, but McDonough seemed unperturbed. Nicky began to draw himself upright.

And then, suddenly, Falcone was moving again. He darted forward, grabbed Sophia and pulled her to her feet none too gently. He held her in front of him, his gun under her chin, as he backed away towards where Lang lay.

McDonough leveled the .22. "Jesus, Falcone, don't you know when to give up?"

Santoro got over her shock and raised the shotgun. Burke kept his on Vinnie.

"I'll give up when the job's done, honey." He looked down at

Lang and jerked his head towards Nicky. Lang rose quickly and placed the barrel of the gun against Nicky's temple. "Now," said Falcone, "here's how this works. We're all leaving. You're all staying. I'll be watching. I see as much as an eyebrow and the woman dies. You know who I am, you know what I am. You know I'll do it."

"Lang," said Santoro, "you can't want this."

Lang glanced at Sophia's face, saw the fear etched in her beautiful features, then he looked at the Senator, still lying on the floor, wise enough to remain quiet throughout, but his eyes pleading for his daughter's safety.

"I don't," he agreed. "Like the man said, the job's not done. I didn't kill Gina, Lieutenant, but I'm getting close to who did." He backed up to the patio doors, pulling the Juke with him. "Nicky, take it easy. Slow now. You move too fast and you won't move again."

Nicky did as he was told, still favoring his wounded shoulder, which had begun to bleed following the pummelling Lang had given it. He was smiling, some song humming under his breath. Lang realized it was "Que Sera, Sera". Christ, this guy really was a few bars short of a full symphony.

Falcone exhaled volubly, then his attention snapped towards McDonough, who had been edging forward, the .22 leveled. "Far enough, honey," he said, pulling Sophia tighter to him. "I know you're good with that thing, but are you good enough to miss her and hit me? I don't think so."

McDonough came to a halt and lowered the gun, but not by much. Lang pulled Nicky through the doors, and Falcone backed out, still with Sophia as a shield. He stopped on the patio. "Hey, Vinnie," he shouted, "tell your old man I said hello. Hey—maybe they'll let you share a cell. Wouldn't that be cosy?"

Vinnie Marino twisted his head from the rug to glare at the shattered doors.

54

They backed slowly down the driveway, but no one followed. Lang imagined an argument raging in the house, Burke and McDonough on one side, backed up by the Senator, all calling for action, and Santoro telling them to be calm. They reached the street where Falcone let Sophia go, but she stood beside them as if in a dream. He raised his gun to Nicky's face. "What did you do to Barney, Nicky?"

Nicky smiled. "Hurt him a little bit maybe. But he's still alive. For now..."

"Where is he?"

Nicky shook his head. "Uh-uh. I'll take you to him, but then you let me go, that's the deal. Otherwise, just go ahead, shoot me. Let him die."

Lang had a thought, so he reached inside Nicky's coat, found his cell phone. He handed it to Sophia.

"Go back, Sophia," said Cole. "Your father needs you." She stared at him, bewildered. "Sophia, I'm sorry. I'm sorry for everything. I'm sorry you were drawn into this. I'm sorry about Silvio. I never wanted any harm to come to you, you have to believe that."

"Let's move, Lang," said Falcone as he opened the car door.

Lang took her hands, pressed Nicky's phone into them. "Take this," he said, "give it to Lieutenant Santoro. Tell her this is Nicky the Juke's phone. Tell her to check the call log. I think she'll find something interesting in his last call."

He glanced back at Nicky and saw him tense. Then Falcone thrust him into the back seat, giving his shoulder a squeeze. Nicky cried out. Falcone didn't apologize.

Lang didn't know whether Sophia heard him or understood

what he said. She wandered back towards the gate as if in a daze.

"Keep an eye on him," said Falcone as he walked back to what Lang presumed was Santoro's car and shot out the front two tires. "That'll slow them."

He climbed behind the wheel, Lang dived into the passenger seat, and the car rocketed away from the curb as the sound of approaching sirens built in the air.

They passed the convoy of law enforcement vehicles as they neared the turnpike. Falcone drove slowly so as not to draw attention, but he kept them in view of his rearview for as long as possible. None of the vehicles peeled off to pursue them. Falcone visibly relaxed.

When Nicky spoke, his voice was thinned with pain. "So I take it we got a deal? I give you your buddy, you let me walk?" Falcone didn't reply. "I gotta hear it from your lips, Tony. We got a deal?"

"Why you got to hear me say it? It don't mean nothing. I could still kill you as soon as we get to Barney."

"Nah," said Nicky. "You're many things, Tony Falcone, but one thing is certain—you keep your word. You say it, it's done. So, I don't hear the words, you just do me now. Get it over with."

Falcone sighed. "You take us to Barney, he's still alive, you walk. Okay?"

"Good enough," said Nicky.

55

"We should've gone after them."

Burke was fuming as he paced back and forth in front of the live Vinnie and dead Al. The Senator had moved to the patio doors and was looking down the long driveway towards the gate. He couldn't face his dead son on the rug. McDonough leaned against the doorframe, the .22 still held loosely in her hand. Santoro had taken a seat, the shotgun cradled across her lap.

"Couldn't take the risk," said Santoro. She was tired. She'd been on the go for too long. And now she'd killed a man. The thought of it drained her. The thought of the paperwork depressed her. IAB would want to talk to her. She hated talking to IAB. They always made her feel guilty when she had nothing to feel guilty about.

"He was bluffing," said Burke.

"Can't be certain of that."

"We had him," Burke said, as if he couldn't believe it. "We had him, and we let him go." He shot a look at Santoro. "You let him go."

Santoro sighed. She was wondering if it was time to put in her papers. She couldn't do this anymore. She'd done more than her twenty. The kids were out of the house. They'd get by. She sighed again. Yeah, like that would happen. She took out her cell, punched the precinct number, got through to the squad room.

She said. "Take a note of this plate…" She rhymed off the vehicle registration she'd memorized in the street. "Get a BOLO out, let me know when ALPR picks it up." ALPR, Automatic License Plate Recognition. If any surveillance cameras caught the car Lang and Falcone were in, they'd track it.

Then she heard the Senator call out his daughter's name and

dash outside. Santoro hung up, hauled herself from the chair and moved to see what had happened. She saw the Senator heading across the terrace, half carrying his daughter. She looked washed out. Santoro knew how she felt.

Sophia held out the cell phone in both hands, they were trembling. Santoro took it. "Cole gave this to me," Sophia said, her voice very small. "He said it's that man's phone. He said to check the call log." Then her eyes found her brother's corpse, and she began to cry. Her father pulled her away, comforting her, as Santoro looked down at the cell phone. Nicky's phone. Well, well.

56

Nicky stared out the window, singing to himself as they hurtled towards the city on a bright November day. He'd told Falcone to head for Red Hook and then settled in, singing a medley of songs that ranged from soft rock to show tunes. Lang kept an eye on the wing mirror, making sure no one followed. They were coming to the end of the road, he felt it. Reuben would decipher the figures Gina had uncovered, and they'd find out why she was murdered.

He realized the singing had stopped, and he twisted round to see that Nicky was staring at the back of Falcone's head.

"Why you do it, Tony?" Nicky asked.

Falcone's eyes flicked to the rearview. "Do what?"

"Turn against your own."

"Way I see it, they turned against me first."

"You were skimming, Tony."

"Nickels and dimes, more or less. Not enough to whack a guy for."

"Nickels and dimes build up to dollars. But it wasn't about the money, you know that. It was all about respect."

Falcone snorted. "Respect, my ass. That's just another way of saying 'gimme the dough.'"

"You wrong, Tony. We don't have respect, we don't have shit in this world. Money comes and goes, women come and go, but if a man don't have the respect of his neighbor, he got nothing. You showed none when you ripped off the old man. What did you expect him to do? What would you have done if one of your crew had been holding out on you?"

"I wouldn't've had him whacked."

Lang saw Nicky smile. "Sure, Tony, you keep telling yourself that. But I know you. I know there ain't much difference between you and me, when you get down to it."

Falcone glared into the rearview. "Nicky, I'm nothing like you. I've killed, sure, I've killed too much. But only when I had to. You? You enjoy it."

"And you don't?"

"No."

"So what you do with Joe Torturro?"

"Who the hell is Joe Torturro?"

"The guy back there, the one I sent out back to find you. And Vic Tommasino, who I'd told to keep watch out there?"

Falcone didn't reply. He stared straight at the road. Lang knew neither of those men would be getting up again. So did Nicky, and he started to laugh.

Nicky looked out the window again. "Sure, Tony, we're different, you and me. Just keep tellin' yourself that, too."

57

Barney was still tied to the chair in the middle of the warehouse floor, his head slumped on his chest. Neither Lang nor Falcone could see any movement. "You son-of-a-bitch," breathed Falcone.

"He's alive, don't worry," said Nicky, his breezy confidence annoying Lang.

They stood at the top of the stairway, and Falcone stepped closer, but Lang grabbed his arm, shook his head. As soon as they had entered the building, he'd proceeded with caution. They had stood at the main door below while he scanned the expanse of the empty building, the Beretta at the ready, looking for anything out of place, listening for anything alien to the surroundings. He wanted to familiarize himself with the layout before they took another step. He did the same again now they were on the upper level.

Nicky watched him. "Just what the hell are you?"

"I'm in advertising," said Lang, still checking the place out.

"Must be a helluva tough business," said Nicky. Lang's eyes ranged over the sagging ceiling, watched for shadows in the sky-lights. He saw nothing.

"It's all clean," said Nicky. "Jeez! How many guys you think I got? You already killed most of my crew."

"We good now?" Falcone asked, and when Lang nodded, he loped to his friend's side. Lang nudged Nicky with his hand, motioned him to follow.

"I don't get you," said Nicky as they walked.

"You don't need to get me."

"I mean," Nicky continued, ignoring him, "you handle that gun like a goddamn pro. You've kept yourself at arm's length from the law. You ain't no office worker, not deep down."

Lang said nothing. Even when Nicky said his next words.

"You're just like us, Tony and me. Believe me, we all know our own kind. You're just like us."

Falcone had already hinted at that. Lang had already suspected it himself. But to hear it from Nicky was like a thunderclap.

Falcone had reached Barney, who gingerly raised his head to look into his face. Congealed blood crusted around his mouth and chin, and his face was puffy and bruised. "He's alive," said Falcone with relief.

"Told you he would be," said Nicky as they reached his side.

Lang stared at the blood and the wounds. "What did you do to him?"

Nicky smiled. "He needed a little dental work done."

Lang saw the pliers and the screwdriver lying on the floor. He'd pulled teeth with one, and God knows what he'd done with the other. Probably jammed it into the socket after the tooth was gone. The pain would've been excruciating, and it was little wonder Barney had told him where to find him. Nicky had said he was just like him, but he wasn't capable of this. At least, he didn't think so.

"So," said Nicky, "here's your buddy and he's alive, although I hope the Department has a good dental plan. I've lived up to my end of the bargain. Time for me to go."

Falcone was untying Barney, who was beginning to come round. Without looking up, he nodded. Nicky smiled and turned to leave, but Lang blocked his way.

"Are you kidding me here?" he said to Falcone. "You're just going to let him go?"

Nicky said, "You wanna tell him Tony, or shall I?"

Falcone straightened, his face grim. "I gave my word I'd let him walk."

Lang was incredulous. "You gave your word? Your *word*? Look at Barney. Look at what he did back at Westport. And you let him

269

go because you gave your word? Seriously?"

Falcone sounded weary when he said, "In my world, you give your word, you keep it, no matter what. If you don't have your word, you don't have nothing."

Lang looked from Falcone to the grinning Nicky. "Your world? You guys would double cross your own mothers if there was a profit in it. Don't talk to me about your word."

Falcone sighed. "Don't make this no harder than it is, Lang…"

Lang thought about Silvio lying in a pool of his own blood and brains. He thought about the young cop in the alley. He looked at the wreckage of Barney's face. He shook his head and raised his gun, the barrel aimed steadily between Nicky's eyes. "No," he said, his voice harder, younger. Dagda's voice. "No. He doesn't walk."

"Cole," said Falcone, his voice soft. "Do this for me. Do it for Gina."

Lang stared at Nicky's face, hating the man, hating the smile, hating the knowledge that shone in his eyes that he'd walk out of this dirty, stinking, rotting warehouse.

"Put the piece down," said Falcone. "It's okay."

Lang kept the gun level. It would be so easy, pull the trigger, see the man's brains spray out. So easy. Dagda could do it. Dagda wanted to do it.

But Cole Lang couldn't. He wanted to, but he couldn't.

He lowered the Beretta, stepped aside.

Nicky laughed. "See? I told you, I know Tony Falcone. He's a man of his word. Been good doing business with you, boys," he said as he stepped around Lang and headed for the stairway. He began to sing "We are the Champions" then stopped, turned back. "Tony, this ain't over between us, you know it." He looked to Lang. "You, too, tough guy. You won this round, but the bell ain't been rung yet. You and me…"

The bullets ripped into his chest, sending blood splashing in the air and his body jerking. He was still on his feet when the final one took off the edge of his skull and he slid to the side.

Lang turned back to see Falcone, his face was blank, his eyes cold. "I said I'd let him walk," he said, lowering his weapon. "I didn't say how far."

58

Lang ended his call to Reuben by telling him to destroy the cell and smash the SIM card. The lawyer tried to argue, but Lang told him this was the last time they'd talk, then hung up. He felt bad about being so abrupt, but he had to cut ties with his old friend and he couldn't debate it. It was for the best. Reuben had done everything he could, but it was time there was distance between them for his own good. He'd explained what the figures meant, and now they were reaching the end—and the lawyer couldn't be anywhere near it. Lang was keenly aware that Reuben should never have been involved as much as he had been.

He and Falcone were walking away from the entrance to the emergency room where they'd deposited Barney Mayo. They'd also left Pietro's car in the car park. They knew it had been made and was now a liability.

As they walked, Falcone asked, "So what did he say?"

Lang told him.

* * *

Joshua Kinberg was small and stocky and balding, but even at 63 years of age he carried himself well. He walked with his back straight because his mother used to rap him on the shoulders with an old cane stick she kept around the house whenever she saw him slouching. He dressed impeccably, not simply because he was a senior partner in an uptown law firm but also because his mother had told him that if a man dressed well, he'd do well. It had proved to be correct, although he would debate whether it was because he had always insisted on bespoke tailoring rather than off-the-rail. He believed he had reached his position in life through his own hard work and intelligence and not down to him having a shine on his shoes and a crease in his pants.

He could have retired years ago but had continued to work. It wasn't because he had nothing else in his life. He had friends, he had a wife whom he loved and who loved him, he had four children who had all turned out to be decent human beings, he was on the board of many charitable trusts, and he supported organizations that brought aid to the poor and the homeless. He saw himself as a good man, and had he retired he could have devoted more time to those worthwhile causes. However, he had continued to work for one simple reason—he loved it. He loved the cut and thrust of mercantile law, he loved the thrill of a take-over, he loved knowing that his efforts enriched not only him but others, for he sincerely believed he helped sustain employment for thousands, maybe millions, across the globe. Yes, there were those who suffered, but that was a necessary evil. And didn't he do everything he could to help those who were less fortunate then himself? He assured himself it all evened out in the end.

He had his routines. He was in a position to keep regular hours—late nights and early mornings were left to associates—so he liked to leave the office by 6pm and have his driver get him to his Manhattan apartment by 6.30pm, traffic willing. There his wife would have a martini waiting, dinner would be served by 7pm, they would sit down to watch something on TV, perhaps a Blu-ray, for Joshua loved his movies, and then to bed. His world was comfortable, ordered, even structured.

He felt that world fall apart in the elevator that took him from his office to the basement parking level when the man sharing the car with him turned round and Joshua saw the gun in his hand.

He shot a look at the camera in the top corner of the elevator. The man saw him, held up a laser pen, and Joshua understood. He'd burned out the lens. No one would see. The man's eyes carried a look of grim determination, and Joshua wondered if this was the last thing he would see on this earth. He thought of his wife, of his children. He thought of his mother, long dead but still very much part of his life. He thought of how hard he had worked throughout that life, to build a business, to build a home, to build a family, and that it could all be torn down in a fraction of a second, just as long as it took to pull a trigger.

"Take it easy," said the man, "and everything will be all right. We just want to talk."

The words were reassuring, but the cold look in his eyes were not. Joshua tried to gather his composure, the same steadfast superiority he adopted when in a tricky negotiation. It always helped to look and sound like the only man in the room who knew exactly what he was doing, that his position was the only one that was right and proper. But the most lethal thing in those rooms was usually a carefully worded contract, whereas this person was aiming a gun. Even so, Joshua was determined to remain composed. As much as possible.

"If that's the case, then why not make an appointment and see me in office hours," he said, proud that his voice sounded steady and calm, even though he could feel a tremor building in his legs. He hoped he'd keep control of his bladder. It had been proving most undependable for the past few months, and his wife had suggested he get his prostate checked. He thought that a far from pleasant prospect—firstly the image of his doctor's fingers up his ass and secondly the notion that there might be something wrong. Now here he was with a gun in his face and wishing he was in his doctor's office listening to the snap of the latex gloves.

"What we got to talk about isn't something for office hours," said the man just as the doors opened, and he waved the gun to tell Joshua to get out. He did as he was told.

He asked, "Where are we going?"

"Just go to your car as normal. We'll talk in there."

Joshua's personalized parking space was a short distance from the elevator, and he could see another man, younger than the one with the gun, leaning against the hood. Like the man behind him, he looked familiar. He straightened as they approached and said very politely, "Mr Kinberg, I'm very sorry to inconvenience you like this…"

"No inconvenience, I'm often accosted in elevators by armed men and forced at gunpoint to my car."

The younger man nodded. "Perhaps I'd better introduce myself. My name is Coleman Lang, and my friend here is Anthony Falcone."

That was when it hit Joshua. Of course, he'd seen their faces in the newspaper and on the TV. Lang was suspected of the murder of Gina Scolari. Suddenly, all his composure left him. If they were here, they knew something.

"Let's talk in the car," said Lang as he opened the rear door. Joshua ducked in, recoiled when he saw his driver sitting upright in the seat, his eyes closed. "It's okay," said Lang, "he's not dead. Just unconscious. Now, get in."

Joshua did as he was told, and Lang climbed in after him, took a seat opposite. Falcone took the wheel but kept the limousine's partition between them open. He began to drive.

"You know who we are?" Lang asked, and Joshua nodded. He studied his driver's face. Lang had said he wasn't dead, but he looked dead to him. "Then you know why we're here."

"I had nothing to do with Gina's death. I was very fond of her."

"We don't believe you were directly involved. But you know who was, and we want a name."

Joshua had a name, but he didn't want to part with it. That way lay certain death. These men scared him, but the thought of sharing that name scared him even more. "I've no idea what you're talking about. The papers say you are responsible."

"The papers get things wrong." This was from Falcone.

Lang leaned closer to him. "Tell us about Enconomy."

Joshua felt panic begin to bubble up. They knew about Enconomy. Of course they knew about it. That wasn't good. "It's a multinational energy company. A subsidiary of the Excelsis Corporation."

"Tell us about the deal it made with certain groups in the Middle East."

He forced a shrug. "They deal with all kinds of companies in the Middle East and beyond."

"Not companies, groups. Come on, Mr Kinberg, we know you know what we're talking about. Gina left us documentation…"

Damnit! She copied documents! They had suspected as much, but he was assured her apartment had been thoroughly searched and nothing was found.

"She stumbled onto something," Lang went on. "She didn't want to believe it at first, after all, Enconomy is a big company, but the more she looked the more she saw. Took her a while before she pieced it all together, it had been hidden and fudged so much. It took her months, but she got there in the end. And she was killed because of it."

"No!" said Joshua. "You killed her and now you're trying to shift the blame. Companies don't kill people because they stumble on some accounting deficiency." He had convinced himself that it was true. He couldn't believe that his employee had been murdered by one of his own clients. But there was always that little voice, nagging away, at the back of his mind. Logan Fitch could have it done. Logan Fitch would have it done.

"This was no accounting deficiency, Mr Kinberg, this was a deliberate attempt to cover up something. A secret, Mr Kinberg, the kind of secret that could never be made public. After all, providing a terrorist organization with material support isn't something that would go down well with shareholders, is it? Or the government."

"Enconomy didn't provide material support to any terrorist group…"

"But they did. They bought petroleum from certain terror groups. The money they gave them was converted into weapons and bombs, funded terror attacks in the mid-East and in Europe. It pays for cells here in the United States. It pays for murder, Mr Kinberg."

"The trades were made through an intermediary!"

"But Enconomy didn't probe too deep to find out where the oil was coming from, did they? They saw a way to make a killing and they took it. And the people they were buying it from made a killing in other ways. Enconomy helped them slaughter innocent people. Enconomy helped them kill. And all to save a penny or two on gas."

Joshua fell silent.

"It's all there in the figures. I had a friend go over them. Gina knew exactly what documents to copy. But she made one mistake. She should've gone straight to the authorities, but she didn't. She came to you, didn't she? She came to her boss, the man she admired and trusted. And you told her to leave it with you, didn't you? And then you told Enconomy."

Joshua closed his eyes. It was true. She had come to him with the original documents, showed him what she had found. He hadn't known about the trading, not then, but he knew the kind of billing Enconomy generated for the firm. He had an obligation to discuss it with them, which he had, with Logan Fitch. And then Gina had been murdered. He'd told himself that her boyfriend was responsible, just as the press had inferred, the very man staring at him intently in the limousine now, but deep down he'd known that wasn't true. It was all too coincidental. She had come to him with her suspicion, he had told the client. A few weeks later she was dead. And he had remained silent. He had tried to justify it, at least to himself, to rationalize his behavior. The deals with the intermediary had been shut down long before Gina happened on the figures, he told himself. There would be no good in exposing it all now. It was water under the bridge.

But first and foremost, Enconomy were clients, and his first duty was always to his clients.

Now, sitting in the back of his own limo, his driver unconscious beside him, a stranger driving him God knew where, he wanted to say all that to the man staring at him, to make him understand that his hands were tied by client confidentiality, but he didn't. Whatever he said would sound weak and self-serving. Now, as the car headed towards the river, he knew with sudden clarity that he had been wrong. So he sat there, his eyes closed, and said, "What do you want from me?"

"Who did you talk to at Enconomy? Who did you tell?"

59

Logan Fitch stood at the window offering a panoramic view of Central Park across to the Upper East Side. He sipped coffee from a china cup. He watched the gray November clouds roll across the city. There would be rain before the day was out. He checked his gold Patek Phillipe watch, saw it was almost time and nodded to Miles Jefferson in the doorway. The big South African left Fitch's home office and walked down the long hallway to step into the apartment's wide vestibule and spoke to the three men waiting beside the elevator. They were all armed, all ex-special forces, all loyal to Jefferson, himself a former of the 451 Parachute Battalion, part of the South African Special Forces known as the Recces. Fitch had flown back from meetings in Washington that morning and had no meeting scheduled with Joshua Kinberg, but when his secretary called him to say that the lawyer had to see him urgently, he agreed. After all, the last time Joshua had said it was urgent it had proved to be near disaster for Enconomy. He instructed his secretary to have Kinberg come to his Manhattan apartment in an hour. He had a gut feeling that whatever Joshua had to say would sooner or later involve Miles, whose expertise had proved so useful over the years.

Nevertheless, he had been troubled.

Fitch's gut instincts had served him well. They had led him—and Enconomy—down some highly lucrative avenues as well as away from more problematic ones. He had learned to listen to his gut. The Middle Eastern gas trade five years before had been one where it had failed him. He should have known that if it sounded too good to be true, then it probably was. To buy such a supply of oil at such a rate made good financial sense, but when he discovered that the agent involved had obscured the source, it had proved to be very disadvantageous. Had the truth leaked—as it almost had, thanks to that silly young woman—it would've proved disastrous for Enconomy. Thankfully, Joshua had alerted him to the threat, and he'd turned to Miles for advice. Miles advised an outside contractor in order to maintain degrees of separation and had brought in Mr Jinks. Although troubled by the speed of the operation, he had done well, which was as expected given his fee. For his part, Joshua had ensured that the paper trail the young lawyer had stumbled upon was destroyed, the accounts suitably amended, and there was little chance of anyone else putting those figures together. No one would ever know of Enconomy's little blunder. Not the federal authorities, not the shareholders and, more importantly, not the parent company. Had they discovered it, then the repercussions for Fitch would have been quite severe.

Now Joshua was calling unannounced. They had no business scheduled. It was most peculiar. Perhaps even suspicious. Hence the cadre of men waiting in the lobby. By rights, Mr Jinks should have been there also, but he had proved unreachable.

Miles entered the room again. "They're at the front desk."

"And was I correct in my assumption?"

Miles nodded. "Lang and the girl's father are with him."

Fitch almost smiled. He loved being proved correct. "Then have them sent up. Your men know what to do?"

Miles smiled. It was a thin smile. "They know, Mr Fitch. Lang and Falcone won't leave this building alive."

* * *

As they rose in the elevator to the top floor of the building, Lang studied Falcone. At first, he couldn't catch the man's eye, but when he did he saw the look. Falcone felt it too. This was far too easy. Kinberg watched them, his eyes wide with terror, as they each produced their weapons and checked the load.

"We're here to talk," he said.

"Don't think it'll be much of a conversation," said Falcone.

"Hasn't there been enough killing? You can't honestly believe that Logan Fitch can mean you harm in his own home!"

Falcone's face tightened into what might've been a grin, but Lang knew better. "Mr Kinberg," said Lang, "this man has been directly responsible for three murders that I know of. The chances are he's given the nod to more. Now, if you want to come out of this alive, you'll keep behind us, you'll keep your head down, and you'll keep quiet."

Kinberg looked as if he wanted to say more, then thought better of it. He stepped to the rear of the elevator car, pressed himself against the wall and slid down.

Lang studied the control panel, then punched the button for the floor below Fitch's.

"They'll know the elevator stopped there," said Falcone.

"That's the idea," said Lang.

* * *

Miles Jefferson and his men were in the wide entrance hallway, monitoring the elevator's progress on the panel above the door. It was a big building, and the elevator was not an express, so it was a slow process. He glanced at the three men who stood in the circular space, their weapons at the ready. The idea was to take no chances, they would kill the men in the car out as soon as the doors slid open. What the three guns for hire did not know is that none of them would survive the encounter—Miles himself would shoot them as soon as Lang and the others were dead. Using Lang and Falcone's weapons, of course. Miles had long ago learned that witnesses, no matter how well paid or how much you trust them, are liabilities.

He looked back at the panel just as the elevator stopped at the floor below. He frowned. He'd ordered that no one else be sent in that car.

"They're getting out!" he said, pointing at the two men nearest the stairway. "Get down there. Check it."

The men nodded and hurried through the door to the stairway. As it swung shut behind them, Miles heard the double cough of a silenced pistol then the sound of two bodies crumpling to the stone floor. He glanced at the display above the elevator doors, saw it was still at the floor below. Lang and Falcone wouldn't have had time to reach this floor. So who the hell was in that stairwell?

He didn't have time to dwell on that before the door was thrown wide open and Mr Jinks stepped into the vestibule. He took down the third man, who hadn't even had time to register what had happened. Miles was also stunned but he moved quickly, throwing himself to the side. Mr Jinks was unperturbed. He fired once, and Miles felt something burn in his leg. He landed badly on the polished floor tiles, tried to raise his weapon, but a bullet ploughed into his eye before his finger could even tighten on the trigger.

Mr Jinks glanced at the illuminated numbers and saw the elevator car was rising again.

60

Lang and Falcone burst out of the elevator, fast and low, then came to a sudden stop when they saw the two dead men sprawled in the vestibule. Lang spun, the Beretta at shoulder height, and surveyed the room. He saw a door that he presumed led to the emergency stairs and shouldered it open, peered round it, then held two fingers up to Falcone before clenching his fist. Two down. He moved back to the bodies in the vestibule, studied them, then gave Falcone a quizzical glance.

Falcone shrugged. "Don't look at me, I was with you."

Lang moved back to the elevator, motioning at Kinberg to follow. The man did as he was told, doing his best not to look at the carnage around him. Lang didn't know who was responsible for the slaughter in the vestibule, but he was certain of one thing, he was no guardian angel. There were wheels turning within wheels here, he'd felt it all along, and he was nothing more than a cog. However, he'd throw a wrench in that particular engine if he could.

The door to Fitch's apartment was open, but Falcone kicked it in anyway. They had no way of knowing if whoever had taken these men out was waiting within, so Lang might've preferred to be more covert, but Falcone clearly wanted to make an entrance.

It was a large apartment, but spartan. The Senator's home in Westport had been a monument to his wealth. This one made the word minimalist seem expansive. The walls were uniformly white and unadorned, the highly polished hardwood floors devoid of rugs. The wide hallway in which they stood had no furnishings. There were six doors leading off it, all closed apart from one at the far end. Lang cocked his head at Kinberg and the lawyer pointed to the open door as the one they wanted. They moved quickly towards it, opening each door as they did so and quickly scanning the rooms beyond for further gunmen. They found none.

Fitch was seated at his desk looking out over the city. The room was as sparsely furnished as the other rooms they'd looked into. Just the desk, a big, glass-topped affair, the comfortable leather chair, a large plasma TV tuned to MSNBC, an expensive leather armchair near to a low table with a row of crystal decanters and glasses. Again, the floors were bare. Lang wondered what the man spent his millions on.

Another room led off to the left. The door was closed. Lang tried the handle but it was locked.

'What's in here?' he asked.

Fitch merely smiled but there was a weary look to it. He seemed unsurprised to see them there, and Lang looked to the right to see a bank of monitors showing the other rooms in the apartment and the vestibule outside, where the dead men's blood spread across the floor. Fitch watched them, that strange little smile still on his face, his hand resting on the glass desktop beside a revolver.

Falcone saw the gun. "Touch that piece, mister, and you're a dead man."

Fitch's smiled twitched. "Mr Falcone, I'm a dead man whether I touch it or not."

Lang asked, "Who killed those men, Fitch?"

"I did." He saw their surprise and raised a hand.

Falcone straightened his aim. "Easy…"

Fitch waved him away. "Oh, I didn't pull the trigger, but ultimately, I'm responsible."

Falcone edged forward. "You had my Gina killed."

"I did."

"Because she found out about your company's deal with god-damn terrorists?"

"Yes."

Lang could tell the man had given up. There was no attempt to explain, to justify, to even evade responsibility. Whatever he'd seen on that monitor had convinced him there was no point. Lang stepped back into the hallway, looked down at the apartment door. It was closed. He tried to recall if they'd closed it when they came in. He saw them in the vestibule, he saw them coming in, he saw them pause in the hallway, Falcone just ahead of him, Kinberg just behind. He saw Kinberg automatically close the door behind him.

That didn't mean someone hadn't followed them in or been there before them.

That locked room bothered him.

He darted back into Fitch's office and was about to kick the door in when it opened and a tall man with fair hair and small rimless glasses stepped out, a silenced weapon aimed directly at Lang's face. A second silenced pistol was aimed into the room. Falcone spun, but the tall man fired, his aim low, and Falcone yelped as a chunk of his thigh was torn out by the bullet. He went down on one knee, still aiming his weapon.

"Mr Falcone," said the man, his other gun remaining steady on Lang's face, "please let your weapon fall." Falcone dropped his gun. "You, too, Mr Lang. My work here is almost complete."

His face was impassive, his body relaxed. Lang recognized him immediately. He was one of the men who had followed them out of the bar the night Gina died. Whoever this man was, he was a professional. Lang could swing the Beretta up, maybe even get off a shot, but he'd never hit anything. Chances are he'd be dead before he even squeezed the trigger. He dropped the gun.

The man pursed his lips. "Now, step back a few paces, if you please."

Lang did as he was told. "I saw you, that night. In the bar."

The man inclined his head slightly. It was an acknowledgement, not an apology.

Lang said, "Who are you?"

"It is of no consequence. However, for ease, you may call me Mr Jinks. All you need to know is, at this moment, I am your ally."

Falcone gasped. "How you figure?"

"You wish Mr Logan Fitch dead. I am here to facilitate that."

Lang glanced at Fitch, who seemed unsurprised by the news. Lang asked, "Why?"

Mr Jinks turned his cold, pale blue eyes on him. "He has become an embarrassment to my employers. They do not like being embarrassed."

"And who are your employers?"

"Ah, Mr Lang, we are both men of death. Mr Falcone here is a crude tool, but you and I are surgical implements."

"Hey," Falcone said, his voice cracked with pain, "who you calling a tool?"

The man ignored him, continued to address Lang. "Ah, yes—I know of your past. I know of your skills."

Lang saw no reason to deny it. "How can you know about that?"

He smiled. "My employers have vast resources and access to all kinds of information."

"Again, who are your employers?"

"You above all must understand the need for discretion when it comes to those who give us orders. It is sufficient only for you to know that, at this juncture, they wish you no ill."

That explained why they weren't already dead. Lang presumed his employers were Excelsis, Economy's parent company. "So, what happens now?"

"Now?" He seemed surprised by the question. "You pick up your friend and you leave."

"Simple as that?"

"Could not be any simpler." The man smiled. Like him, it was thin and bloodless.

"And Fitch?"

"No longer your concern. Neither is Mr Kinberg."

The lawyer had pressed himself against the wall, his eyes fixed on the guns. Lang felt pity for him. The blood he shed was on paper and in boardrooms. He wasn't used to the real thing.

"He comes with us," said Lang.

"No," said the man, jerking the weapon away from Lang long enough to fire once. Lang had barely registered it had moved before it snapped back to its previous position.

"Let me guess," he said, his voice a little hoarse as he looked at the lawyer's body on the floor, "another embarrassment?"

The man smiled, dipped his head again. "I would leave now. My advice, gentlemen, is that you do so quickly. I believe the police are already on their way."

"Your employers cannot possibly believe this leaves them high and dry? I'm going to tell the police everything. And I have documents to back it up."

The man shook his head. "No, Mr Lang, you do not. I relieved Mr King of the material early this morning."

Lang hid his shock, but his voice was low. "How did you know about...?" Then another thought. "You'd better not have hurt him..."

"He is unharmed, I assure you. I kill only when necessary. Or if I am paid. Mr King's death was neither necessary nor a business arrangement. But I have the documents and the thumb drive. As to how we knew of their existence, I long felt that Ms Scolari had a back up file but it was not in her office, it was not in her apartment, or yours. When you abducted the late Mr Kinberg here I suspected that you had found it. And it was no great leap to work out who you would ask to make sense of it."

"You're a clever guy, Mr Jinks."

"I am thorough, Mr Lang. I do not like guesswork but sometimes it is all we have, is it not? As for you and Mr Falcone, I was never engaged to remove you. And you may tell the authorities what you know but who will believe you? As far as the law is concerned, you are persons of interest in a number of murders across the city, including two police officers."

Lang unconsciously glanced at Fitch's bank of monitors.

"The recording devices have been disabled," said the man. "Mr Fitch could monitor events, but there is no record of them. That was the way he wished it to be, and it proved to be a mistake. Not his first, I might add. Now, time is pressing, and I have work to do here, so please help your friend to his feet and leave. Now."

Lang didn't move. He stared at the man, knowing that he was responsible for Gina's death. Fitch had ordered it, Mr Jinks had carried it out. Unfortunately, there was nothing he could do about it. The man with the guns held all the cards, and if it was true the police were already on their way, there was no way he could ever get him if he was serving life in prison. He sighed and helped Falcone to his feet. Mr Jinks kept one gun on them, the other on Fitch, who hadn't moved as much as a muscle throughout the conversation. He seemed to have resigned himself to his fate.

Lang supported Falcone as he hopped towards the door, where they stopped, looked back at Mr Jinks, who had eased over to stand behind Fitch.

Lang said, "It doesn't end here, you know that, don't you, Mr Jinks?"

"I would be most disappointed if it did, Mr Lang," said Jinks.

Lang nodded at him and gave Falcone a slight push through the door.

"Wait a goddamn minute," said Falcone. "So we just leave? And that pale-faced son-of-a-bitch gets to live?"

"Let's go, Tony" said Lang, quietly. "There's nothing more we can do here."

61

Falcone knew of a doctor who would treat his gunshot wound and not report it as long as they paid him. The doctor took a look at the bloody thigh and observed it was little more than a scratch.

"Easy for you to say," said Falcone.

The doctor smiled and got to work while Lang used one of his burners to contact Reuben. He was concerned about the hard drive.

"Jesus, Cole," said Reuben, "they came and took it."

"Who came and took it?"

"The FBI. They had a warrant, there was nothing I could do. I had to hand it over."

Lang said nothing. He knew whoever had paid Reuben a visit wasn't the FBI, or any other law enforcement organization. And the warrant was fake. And now the only proof they had was gone.

"Cole? You still there?"

"I'm here."

"I'm sorry, Cole, I tried to hold out but, well, the warrant and everything. And the FBI."

"You did the right thing, Reuben," Lang reassured him. And he had. If Reuben had held out, then his life would've been forfeit. A business deal would be struck with Mr Jinks, there would be an office break-in that went tragically wrong or an accidental death. All easily arranged. Lang had done it himself in the past.

Reuben asked, "What are you going to do?"

Lang thought about it. What could he do? They had him boxed in. His life, the one he'd lived for ten years, was over. It ended when Gina died. He was a fugitive, on the run for multiple homicides. Handing himself in was out of the question. Prison was not an option. He had only one choice left open to him. "Disappear," he said.

62

Santoro sipped at her gin and bitter lemon and McDonough her Jack Daniels as she ignored the looks from a silver fox in a sharp suit at the other end of the hotel bar. Santoro smiled to herself. There had been a time she'd've drawn that kind of attention, maybe still could if she lost a little weight and smartened herself up, but she really didn't give a shit anymore. She had her Max at home, he was enough. Pot belly and everything.

"So where's Burke?" she asked.

TP half-smiled. "Already preparing the report that exonerates him in everything from when Cain killed Abel to the present day. I don't think you'll come off well, though."

"Screw him." Santoro took another sip.

"Been there, done that," TP said, raising her glass. "You still looking for Lang?"

"Sure, but he's vanished again. We found the car they were using, it had been reported stolen from Jersey City, although God knows why they were over there." Santoro had a notion, though. She found the report of a multiple homicide in a Jersey City bar, a small-time hoodlum. She'd lay odds Falcone had something to do with that. "Barney Mayo don't know shit, he says, and this time I believe him."

"What'll happen to him?"

"There'll be an inquiry, but my guess is that nothing will stick. IAB can't prove he colluded with Falcone and Lang. He'll be urged to put his papers in, take his pension."

"What about the cell phone Lang gave you?"

"The number of a cop named Ralston was on there. He'll face some fierce shit, let me tell you. He won't get off so lightly. I hate dirty cops."

"So what about Lang? You think he's guilty?"

Santoro thought about it for a moment. "Not my call to say. I just follow the evidence, pull them in, let the courts sort it out."

"But what does your gut say?"

"It says there's something not right about the whole set-up. I mean, what the hell is this guy? A hired killer? Who spends a year with his victim then kills her in his own bed and leaves the hypo a few blocks away with his fingerprints all over it?"

McDonough said, "Prints can be lifted and transferred."

"Yes, they can. And then there's everything else. The mob. The mystery gunmen at the park. Dead cops, dead doormen, dead wise guys. More dead bodies than the morgue can handle. And your guy, Falcone. He doesn't seem to think Lang is good for killing his daughter. You ask me, the whole thing stinks."

They both considered this for a few moments before Santoro said, "So what about you?"

"What about me?"

"You being moved on?"

"Falcone's still out there. I'm still a United States Marshal. I've got a job to do."

"The Marshals always get their man, right?"

"That's the Mounties, but, yeah." TP looked at her sideways. "You okay?"

"Shouldn't I be?"

"You killed a man. I think he's your first."

"So did you."

"He wasn't my first. Won't be my last."

Santoro thought about the man as he hurtled through the glass doors. She had fired without thinking because he was a danger to them all. She had done what she had to do. She tried not to think about it too much. And, as expected, IAB put her through the wringer. The paperwork was a bitch, too.

"How do you live with it?"

TP slugged her Jack Daniels, thought about the question. "You just do, that's all. There're no pearls of wisdom. You didn't put that weapon in his hands, you didn't force him to pull that trigger. You lived, he died."

"Simple as?"

TP said, "Simple as."

The barman refilled their glasses, told TP they were on the gentleman at the end of the bar. The silver fox raised his own glass towards them.

"You got a fan," said Santoro.

"Yeah," said McDonough.

"Being beautiful is a curse, huh?"

TP raised her glass to the man, smiled. "Not if you use it right."

63

The original plan was leave the city as soon as Falcone had been patched up. There was nothing left to hang around for, and the more distance they put between them and New York the better. Lang donned another pair of glasses, pulled on a black watch cap and adopted a mid-western drawl to hire a car from the smallest rental company they could find. He used his fake ID to complete the transaction, paid in cash. It was a risk, but boosting another vehicle really wasn't an option now. They'd taken enough chances, and there were only so many old model vehicles available. If the bored clerk suspected anything, he didn't show it. He barely looked at Lang as he pushed the paperwork over to be completed. Maybe, later, he might see a photo on TV and see a resemblance, but by that time Lang and Falcone would be miles away, the rental dumped and another vehicle bought at an out-of-state dealership for cash.

But he had one stop to make before they moved on.

He stood on the bridge over the Pond and stared again at the water. He had a bouquet of flowers in his hand. Lilies. Gina had loved lilies. Falcone stood a few feet off, in the shadow of a tree, leaning on a cane and looking nervous. He was unhappy still being in the city, but he understood Lang had to say goodbye. After all, neither of them would be able to attend the funeral.

Lang leaned on the parapet, the flowers held loosely in both hands, feeling the weak sun on his face, and he thought of Gina. He thought of her smile and her laugh and the way she made him feel. He thought of how he had let her down. He should've been able to protect her. Maybe if he'd told her the truth about his past, then somehow her death could've been avoided. Maybe she would've told him about Enconomy and cheap gas and terrorist groups. Even if he'd told her that he'd loved her, it would've been something.

His breath escaped his lungs in waves, catching something in his throat. He let the flowers slip from his fingers, saw them float on the surface of the water. A duck paddled towards them, inspected them, decided they were of no interest and moved on. He saw Gina's face reflected dimly in the ripples on the water, smiling at him.

And then the image was washed away.

Goodbye, Gina, he thought. Goodbye, my love.

* * *

They were heading south on the I-95 beyond Rocky Mount, North Carolina, and Lang was reading the *New York Times* report on the death of billionaire Logan Fitch, found shot to death in his apartment along with his lawyer and security team. Reports suggested that two men seen entering and leaving the building answered the descriptions of fugitives Coleman Lang and Anthony Falcone. Mrs Fitch, who was on holiday in Switzerland, was flying home immediately…

Lang sighed. More deaths being laid at their door.

He had forgotten he had the Janus phone until it rang. Behind the wheel, Falcone gave the cell a quizzical glance when Lang fished it from his coat pocket and flipped it open.

"Dagda," he said.

The near mechanical voice said, "Designation, please?"

"Janus Alpha, service number 103."

He was aware of Falcone's sideway looks, so he treated him to a shrug.

"Authorization code, please."

"Lang, Coleman, USMC, ID tag Dagda six alpha."

"Hold, please, for Asa."

The line was filled with bleeps and crackles, and then Lang heard Asa's voice. "So, Dagda, you seem to have survived it all."

"Depends on your definition of 'survived'."

"You're alive, that's survival."

"I'm wanted for a murder I didn't commit, Asa."

"Yes, that is unfortunate."

Unfortunate, thought Lang, sure.

"But you were involved in a number of other unfortunate situations, weren't you? Murders that you did commit or were at least party to. The authorities are still hunting you, and that's something that could be turned to our advantage."

"Our advantage?"

"Yours and Janus's."

Asa fell silent, waiting for Lang to say something further. He didn't give her the satisfaction.

"The Janus brief has been expanded, Dagda. Our successes overseas have won us many supporters in high places. They wish to see us take a more active role in other areas."

"What other areas?"

"Our country has many enemies. We face many threats, both foreign and domestic. Not all of those threats are political."

Lang waited again.

"We have been tasked with liaising with law enforcement and intelligence departments at home in order to neutralize some of those threats, whether they be criminal or political."

"And what's that got to do with me?"

"It occurs to me that it may be beneficial to have an operative entrenched on the other side."

"You want me to infiltrate the underworld?"

A small laugh. "You're already part of it, Dagda. You're a wanted man, hunted by the police, the FBI, the US Marshals office. Frankly, all you need to do is kick a dog and you'll have animal welfare on your back. We can use that. That could be your new Janus cover."

Lang was aware again of Falcone beside him. "I'm not alone in this."

"We're aware of that. Mr Falcone cannot be trusted. You may have to deal with him."

"Not going to happen."

"You owe him nothing, Dagda. He is a liability."

Lang thought about the past few days. He owed Falcone his life more than once. Also, he didn't see him as a liability. They weren't friends. They weren't a team, as such. He wasn't sure what they were, but there was no way he was going to "deal with him" for Janus.

"Out of the question, Asa."

It was Asa's turn to be silent. Then, "Very well. We'll table that for now. Think about my offer, Dagda. You cannot run forever. You will need help, and Janus can provide that. Your country is asking you to serve once again. Think on it. And keep these comms with you at all times."

And then she was gone.

"What the hell was that all about?" Falcone asked.

Lang closed the phone slowly and replaced it in his pocket. "The past," he said, "catching up with me."

"Spy shit, huh?"

"A job offer," said Lang.

* * *

Asa stared at the phone for a few moments. The man opposite her waited for her to say something. When nothing was forthcoming he said, "Has he agreed?"

Asa's eyes raised to look at him across her desk. "He will."

"You're that certain of him?"

"I'm that certain."

"And Falcone? He'll deal with him?"

"We may have to rethink that."

The man nodded. "So it was as you expected."

"It's always as I expected."

The man stood up, picked up his briefcase. "I'll report to the committee right away, get the paperwork in motion." He was speaking figuratively. The paperwork involved would be minimal and untraceable. The man stopped at the door, his hand on the handle. "Do you think he suspects?"

Asa paused, replaying the phone conversation in her mind. She had sensed suspicion but not of the kind to which the White House Chief of Staff referred. "No," she said, "he suspects nothing."

The man nodded, left the room. Asa whirled her chair so she could look at the university common through her window. She was confident Dagda would come on board. He had no choice. She had known he would show some kind of loyalty to that criminal Falcone, but that could be factored into her plans. It may even turn out to be a good thing, given the job ahead of them. Falcone was known within the county's criminal underclass, even trusted to a degree. That could prove useful.

As to whether Dagda suspected that Janus had known about the plan to remove his girlfriend ahead of time, Asa doubted that very much indeed. She could've stopped it, but it had suited her plans for the murder to go ahead. It placed him where she needed him. The men who pursued him in Battery Park were Janus operatives, sent there to test him, to see if his old skills had completely deserted him. Those skills had proved to be rusty but still active. He would improve, of that she was certain.

She was also certain of one other thing.

Dagda would soon return to the fold.

Author's note and acknowledgments

This is a work of fiction. None of it happened. The businesses and bars I mentioned do not exist – and neither do some of the alleyways. I apologize to the great city of New York and the state of New Jersey but they were needed for my story! In addition, I have tinkered with the way passengers line up for the Liberty Island Ferry (Oh my—the power!).

But now, my thanks. This goes on a bit, so make yourself a coffee and grab a pastry.

My thanks go to a number of people who have guided or assisted in bringing this book onto the shelves and to e-readers.

Crime writers such as Craig Robertson, who first suggested I write something not set in Scotland. This book is not his fault but he started me on the road.

Then there are my Carry on Sleuthing cast mates and the other three crime writers in search of a plot—Caro Ramsay, Theresa Talbot, Lucy Cameron, Pat Young, Michael J. Malone, Neil Broadfoot, Gordon Brown and Mark Leggatt—who have either read the manuscript, in full or in part, passed on comments or have advised in other ways.

Thanks are also due to Alex Gray, Lin Anderson, Quintin Jardine, Denzil Meyrick, Mason Cross, Craig Russell and Iain K. Burns for their encouragement. And thank you to Jessica Stewart for the New York info. Any glaring errors are mine alone.

Shout-outs to SJI Holliday, Lisa Gray, James Oswald, Marsali Taylor and Wendy Jones.

Also, the hard-working bloggers who provide tremendous support for authors. In particular Sharon Bairden, of *Chapter in My Life*, Noelle Holton, of *CrimeBookJunkie*, and Gordon McGhie, of

Grab This Book. Thanks are also due to Alistair Braidwood of *Scots Whay Hae*.

We wouldn't be anywhere without the booksellers, so thanks to you all, but in particular Caron MacPherson, David McCormack, Kenny Bryan—all Waterstones—as well as Karen Latto of Print Point and Marjory Marshall of the Bookmark.

And there are all the libraries and librarians which are increasingly vital in this crazy, mixed up world of ours as well as the organizers of the array of incredible book festivals, particularly Bloody Scotland, Tidelines, Aye Write, West End Festival, Byres Road Festival, Edinburgh International Book Festival, Bute Noir, NL Encounters, Newcastle Noir, Glamis Noir (anything with noir in it) and the Grantown Crime Festival, who have all, at some point, invited me to take part. You know where I am if you want me back!

The usual nod of gratitude goes to Gary McLaughlin for continuing to risk his lens photographing me and Graham Turnbull for ensuring I don't make an utter mess of douglasskelton.com.

Finally, thanks to all at Contraband—Sara, Robbie, Craig and my editor Jennifer Hamrick—for all their hard work.

Douglas Skelton, shortlisted for Scottish Crime Book of the Year 2016, is a writer who specialises in the darker side of things: he's a former journalist who has published eleven true crime books. In 2011 he made the leap to writing crime fiction, beginning with the hugely successful series of Davie McCall thrillers and continuing with the Dominic Queste series: *The Dead Don't Boogie* and *Tag – You're Dead*.